FREE PUBLIC LIBRARY
DALTON, MASSACHUSETTS

First opened, May 1861   Accepted by Town, March 1885

LIBRARY RULES

1. A fine of 5¢ a day will be charged for each adult book kept overtime beyond the due date; for Juvenile and Young People's books, the fine will be 2¢ a day for each book.

2. Full value must be paid if a book is LOST; a reasonable fine if it is damaged.

3. No books or other library materials may be borrowed by persons with a record of unreturned materials and unpaid fines or losses. However, use of the reading rooms and references and advisory service are always available to everybody.

Please note that all materials may have the due date extended, either by phone or in person, unless a reserve for same is on file, or a 7 day book.

Also by Len Deighton

Goodbye, Mickey Mouse

GOODBYE, MICKEY MOUSE

Len Deighton

ALFRED A. KNOPF   NEW YORK   1982

THIS IS A BORZOI BOOK
PUBLISHED BY ALFRED A. KNOPF, INC.

Grateful acknowledgment is made to the following for permission to
reprint previously published material:
  Cromwell Music, Inc: Excerpts from "For All We Know," words
by Sam M. Lewis, music by J. Fred Coots. TRO-© copyright 1934
and renewed 1962 Cromwell Music, Inc. & Leo Feist, Inc., New York,
N.Y. Used by permission.
  Famous Music Publishing Companies: An excerpt from "That
Old Black Magic" by Johnny Mercer and Harold Arlen. Copyright ©
1942 by Famous Music Corporation. Copyright © renewed 1969 by
Famous Music Corporation.

Library of Congress Cataloging in Publication Data

Deighton, Len. [date]
Goodbye, Mickey Mouse.

1. World War, 1939–1945—Fiction. I. Title.
PR6054.E37G6 1982   823'.914   82–47813
ISBN 0–394–51259–6

And all men kill the thing they love,
By all let this be heard,
Some do it with a bitter look,
Some with a flattering word,
The coward does it with a kiss,
The brave man with a sword.

—Oscar Wilde, *The Ballad of Reading Gaol*

Mickey Mouse   *U.S. Military Slang.*
Anything that is unnecessary or un-
important. (Named for the Walt
Disney animated cartoon character,
in allusion to its childish appeal, its
simplicity, triviality, etc.)

—*The Barnhart Dictionary of New English*

Goodbye, Mickey Mouse

Prologue, 1982

Three buses moved with almost funereal slowness through the narrow winding country lanes. Overhead the sky was dark with rain clouds. The passengers stared out at the meadows and the pretty villages, defaced by advertising, TV antennas, and traffic signs, and at the orchards and streams drained of color by the long months of winter.

The buses did not stop until they reached one large ugly field disfigured by the rusting metal skeletons of old Quonset huts and brick remains. Slashed across this huge field, like some monstrous sign of plague, there was a concrete X. Here and there strenuous attempts had been made to remove this disfigurement, but only tiny pieces had been nibbled from the great cross.

Cautiously the passengers disembarked into the chilly winds that scour the flat East Anglian farmlands. Huddled against the weather, palms outstretched to detect rain in the air, zipped and buttoned to the neck, they formed into small silent groups and wandered dejectedly through the ruined buildings.

They were Americans. They wore brightly colored windbreakers and tartan hats, they carried cameras and tote bags; none of them was equipped with the heavy sweaters and thick overcoats that England's climate demands so early in the year. They were white-haired and they were balding, they were florid and they were ashen, they were fat and they were frail, but, apart from a few young relatives, they were all in that advanced stage of life that we optimistically call middle age.

The nervous clowning and the determined laughs of the men demonstrated the tense anxiety behind their movements. Wives watched knowingly as their men frantically searched in the workspace of the echoing old hangar, paced out the shape of a long-vanished barrack hut, peered into dark corners or scratched upon dirt-encrusted windows to find nothing but ancient farm machinery.

They'd waited a long time; they'd paid hard-earned money; they'd come a long way to find the man they sought. Sometimes it became necessary to consult an old photo for identification purposes, at other times they listened for half-remembered voices. But as the group grew quieter and, in deference to the cold, returned to the warm buses, it became evident that none of them had discovered the man they all so clearly remembered.

One couple separated from the others. Holding hands like young lovers, they followed a potholed tarmac road that, like a huge ring, surrounded the field, touching the extremities of the crossed runways. The man and woman talked as they took a shortcut along a farm track. They unhooked themselves from blackberry bushes, stepped over cow dung, and picked a wood violet to be pressed flat into a diary and kept as a souvenir. They spoke about the weather and the crops and the colors of the countryside. They spoke about anything except what was uppermost in their minds.

"Look at the cherry blossom," said Victoria, who had not lost her English accent despite thirty years in San Francisco. They both stopped at the orchard gate which once marked the end of Hobday's Farm and the edge of the airfield.

"Why did Jamie stay in the bus?" said the man. He rattled the farm gate. "Isn't he interested in seeing where his father flew from in the war?"

Victoria hugged him. "You're his father," she said. "You tell me."

1

Colonel
Alexander J. Bohnen

Colonel Alexander J. Bohnen's large office overlooked Grosvenor Square. The furniture was a curious collection of oddments: two lumpy armchairs from the American Embassy's storeroom smelled of mothballs, his desk and a slab-sided table, loaded with box files, bore the markings of Britain's Ministry of Works. The antique carpet and a Sheraton china cabinet were air-raid salvage that Bohnen had bought cheaply in a London salesroom. Only the folding chairs, six of them stacked tidily behind the door, were American in origin. But it was December 1943 and London was very much at war.

The clouds were dark and low over the bare trees of the Square. The soft silvery gray barrage balloon wore a crown of white and there were patches of fresh snow on the grass. But elsewhere the snowflakes died as they reached the ground and the hut that sheltered the balloon's operating crew was shiny and wet. Smoke from the stove twisted with every gust of wind, and chased the snow flurries. For once there was no sound of aircraft. Little chance of a German air raid today; nature was providing its own "barrage."

Colonel Bohnen, U.S. Army Air Force, was a tall man in his middle forties. His uniform was well cut and he'd buffered his appearance against the onset of age by a daily routine of exercise, aided by expensive dentists, hairdressers, masseurs, and tailors. Now, with the same waistline he'd had at college, and nearly as much wavy hair that was only slightly graying, he could have been mistaken for a professional athlete.

His visitor was an elderly American civilian, a sober-suited white-haired man with rimless spectacles. He was older than Bohnen, a friend and business associate. Twenty years before, he had been part owner of a small airline and Bohnen a trained engineer with contacts in the banking world. It was a relationship that permitted him to treat Bohnen with the same sardonic amusement with which he'd greeted the over-confident youngster who'd pushed past his secretary two decades earlier. "I'm surprised you settled for colonel's rank, Alex. I thought you'd hold out for a star when they asked you to put on your uniform."

Bohnen knew it was a joke but he answered earnestly, "It was a question of what I could *contribute*. The rank means nothing at all. I would have been content with sergeant's stripes."

"So all that business about your expecting a general's star at any moment is just moonshine, huh?"

Bohnen swung around sharply. His visitor held his stare a moment before winking conspiratorially. "You'd be surprised what you hear in the Embassy, Alex, if you wear rubber-soled shoes."

"Anyone I know there last night?"

The old man smiled. Bohnen was still the bright-eyed young genius he'd known so long ago: ambitious, passionate, witty, daring, but climbing, always climbing. "Just State Department career men, Alex. Not the kind of people you'd give dinner to."

Bohnen wondered how much the old man had heard about the excellent dinner parties he hosted here in London. The guests were carefully selected, and the hostess was a titled lady whose husband was serving with the Royal Navy. Her name must not be linked with his. "Work keeps me so busy I've scarcely got time for a social life," said Bohnen.

The man smiled and said, "Don't take the Army too seriously, Alex. Don't start reading up on the campaigns of Napoleon or translating Thucydides. Or practicing rifle drill in your office, the way you used to practice golf to humiliate me."

"We've got too many businessmen walking around in khaki just because it's a fashionable color," said Bohnen. "We're fighting a war. Any man who joins the service should be prepared to give everything he's got to it. I mean that seriously."

"I believe you do." There was a steel lining to Bohnen's charm, and he pitied any of Bohnen's military subordinates who hesitated about giving up "everything." "Well, I'm sure your Jamie will be green with envy when he hears you got to Europe ahead of him. Or is he here too?"

"Jamie's in California. Flying instructors do a vitally important job. Maybe he doesn't like it, but that's what I mean about the Army—we all have to do things we don't like."

"His mother thinks you arranged that instructor's job."

Bohnen turned to glance out of the window again. The old man knew him well enough to recognize that he was avoiding the question. "I don't have that kind of authority," said Bohnen vaguely.

"Don't get me wrong—Mollie blesses you for it. They both do, Mollie and Bill. Bill Farebrother treats your boy as if he was his own, do you know that, Alex? He loves your boy."

"They would have liked a son, I guess," said Bohnen.

"Yes, well, don't be mulish, Alex. They don't have a son, and they both dote on your Jamie. You should be pleased that it worked out that way."

Bohnen nodded. There was virtually no one else who would have dared to speak so frankly about Bohnen's former wife and the man she'd married, but they'd been good friends through thick and thin. And there was no malice in the old man's frankness. "You're right. Bill Farebrother has always played straight. I guess we were all pleased that Jamie was assigned to instruction."

"I suspect you had a hand in Jamie's assignment," said the man. "And I suspect that Jamie is every bit as clever as his father when it comes to getting his own way. Don't imagine he won't find a way to get into the war."

"Has Jamie written to you?" Bohnen was alert now and ready to be jealous of this man's friendship with his son. "This is important to me. If the boy is being assigned to combat duty, I have a right to know about it."

"I only know that he visited his mother on leave. He sold his car and cleared out his room. She was worried that he might have been sent overseas."

The old man watched Bohnen bite his lower lip and then move his mouth in exactly the same way he'd seen young Jamie do when calculating a sum or learning to take the controls of a tri-motor plane. Bohnen looked at his wristwatch while he considered what he could do to check up on his son's movements. "I'll get on to that," he said, and pursed his lips in frustration.

"You can't keep him in cotton wool for the rest of his life, Alex. Jamie's a grown man."

Bohnen got to his feet and sighed. "You don't understand me, you only think you do. I don't give myself any easy breaks, and if you were under my command, I'd make sure no one ever accused me of going soft on old buddies. If Jamie's looking to his old man for any kind of special treatment, he can think again. Sure, I put in a word that helped assign him to Advanced Flying training. I know Jamie; he needed more time before flying combat. But that's a while back, he's ready now. If he comes here, he'll take his chances along with any other young officer."

Bohnen's visitor stood up and took his coat from the hook on the door. "It's not a sin for a man to favor his son, Alex."

"But it is a court-martial offense," said Bohnen. "And I don't quarrel with that."

"You've fallen in love with the military, Alex, the same way you've fallen in love with every project you've ever taken on."

"It's the way I am," admitted Bohnen, helping the old man into his overcoat. "It's why I'm able to get things rolling."

"But in wartime the Army has a million lovers; it becomes a whore. I don't want to see you betrayed, Alex."

Bohnen smiled. "What was it Shelley said: 'War is the statesman's game, the priest's delight, the lawyer's jest, the hired assassin's trade.' Is that what you have in mind?"

The visitor reached for his roll-brim hat. "I envy you your memory even more than your knowledge of the classics, Alex. But I was thinking of something Oscar Wilde said about the fascination of war being due to people thinking it wicked. He said war would only cease being popular when we realized how vulgar it was."

"Oscar Wilde?" said Bohnen. "And when was he a reliable authority on the subject of war?"

"I'll tell you next week, Alex."

"The Savoy, lunch Friday. I'll look forward to it."

2

Captain
James A. Farebrother

"You're the luckiest guy in the world, I've always told you that, haven't I?"

"So what happened to the man who was going to be the richest airline pilot in America?" replied Captain James Farebrother, made uncomfortable by the note of envy in his friend's voice.

Captain Charles Stigg pulled back the canvas flap to see out of the truck. London's streets were dark and wet with rain, but even in the small hours there were people about. There were soldiers and sailors in fancy foreign uniforms. There was a jeep with British military police wearing red-topped caps, and some civil defense personnel wearing steel helmets. There must have been another air-raid warning.

"Nearly there now," said Farebrother, more to himself than to his friend. Separation from Charlie would be a bad wrench. They'd been together since they were aviation cadets learning to fly on old Stearmans, and it was easy to understand why they'd become such good friends. Both were calm, confident young men with easy smiles and quiet voices. More than one member of a selection board had said they were not aggressive enough for the ritual slaughter now taking place daily in the thin blue skies above Germany. "Why didn't I bring my long underwear?" said Charlie Stigg, letting the flap close against the chilly air.

"It's nearly Christmas," said Farebrother.

"I guess almost anything will be better than teaching Cadet Jenkins to land an AT-6."

"Almost anything will be *safer*," said Farebrother. "Even Norwich on a Saturday night."

"You know why I stopped going to the Saturday-night dances?" said Charlie Stigg. "I couldn't face another of those girls telling me I looked too young to be an instructor."

"They didn't mean anything by that."

"They thought we were ducking out of the war—they figured we *volunteered* to be flying instructors."

"The kind of girl I met at the dances didn't even know there was a war on," said Farebrother.

"Nor-rich," said Stigg. "So that's how you pronounce it; I guess I've been saying it wrong. Yeah, good. Come over there and see me, Jamie, it sure will cheer me up." The truck stopped and they heard the driver hammering on his door to signal that this was Stigg's destination, the Red Cross Club.

"Good luck, Charlie."

"Look after yourself, Jamie," said Charlie Stigg. He threw his bag out onto the ground and climbed down. "And a merry Christmas."

It wasn't fair. Charlie Stigg had been hard-working and conscientious enough to master the complications of flying multi-engined aircraft, so when they finally let him go to war they turned down his application for fighters and sent him to a Bomb Group. Farebrother deliberately flunked his conversion to twins and got the assignment that Charlie so desperately wanted. It wasn't fair, war wasn't fair, life wasn't fair.

He suffered a pang of guilt as he watched Charlie staggering up the steps of the Club under the weight of his pack, and then, with the heartlessness of youth, dismissed the feeling from his mind. Farebrother was going to be a fighter pilot; he was the luckiest guy in the world.

"Is this the truck for Steeple Thaxted?" a voice called from the darkness.

"That's the way I heard it," said Farebrother.

An officer in a waterproof mac followed by half a dozen enlisted men climbed into the truck. Realizing that Farebrother was an outsider, they drew away from him as if he were the carrier of some contagious disease. The truck started and the officer lit a cigarette and then offered one to Farebrother, who declined and then asked, "What's it like at Steeple Thaxted?"

"Ever been in the Okefenokee Swamp when the heating was off?"

"That bad?"

"Picture an endless panorama of shit with tents stuck in it and you've got it. Whenever I meet a new dame at a dance the first thing I ask her is if she's got a bathroom with hot water." He drew on his cigarette, well aware of his audience of EMs. "Of course, this being England, she usually hasn't got a bathroom." One of the men chuckled.

"You're living in tents in this weather?" said Farebrother.

The officer prodded Farebrother's bag with the toe of his shoe and pushed at it until he revealed the stenciled lettering on the side. "A fly-boy, are you?" He tilted his head to read the name.

"I'm a pilot," said Farebrother.

"Captain J. A. Farebrother," the officer read it aloud. "A captain, eh? This a second tour, or have you been in the Pacific?"

"I've been an instructor back home," said Farebrother apologetically.

The officer sniffed and wiped his nose with a dainty handkerchief obviously borrowed from a lady friend. "I've got a cold," he said as he put it away. "My name's Madigan, Vincent Madigan. I'm a captain—Group Public Relations Officer. I guess you're assigned to Colonel Badger's 220th Fighter Group?"

"Right."

"If you're a flyer, you'll be all right. That son of a bitch Badger has no time for anyone who isn't a flyer." There was a soft growl of agreement from one of the other men.

"Is that right?" Farebrother looked around at the huddled figures. There was the odor of warm bodies in wet overcoats and the pungent smell of sweet American tobacco. The men were obviously coming back from pass and would go straight to their duties in the morning. They were waiting for Madigan to stop talking so they could catch up on their sleep.

"Mud, shit, and tents," reaffirmed Madigan. "And the local Limeys hate us more than they hate the Krauts."

"Hold it there," said Farebrother. "My mother was English. The way I see it, we're in the war together; no sense in partners feuding."

Madigan nodded and puffed at his cigarette. "They gave you the lecture, then." A sergeant sitting next to Madigan rested his head back against the canvas side of the truck. There was a cigarette in his mouth, and as he inhaled, the light from it illuminated a face with a large blunt mustache, a soft flight cap tipped down to his half-closed eyes, and the collar of his overcoat wrapped around his ears. He pulled the collar tighter to close out Madigan's voice, but Madigan didn't notice. "You'll find out," he promised. "You're still on the crusade. Most of us started out that way. But you get Colonel Badger chewing your ass out. You get the Limeys screwing your last dollar out of you and then spitting in your eye. You get memos telling you how the top brass are figuring new ways to get us all killed . . . Suddenly maybe you'll start thinking the Krauts aren't so bad."

The truck jolted as it went over some bomb-damaged road surface. Through the open canvas at the back they saw a British soldier with a flashlight waving the traffic past. Behind him there was a large red sign: "Danger. Unexploded Bomb."

"Watch out, mate," the soldier called. "The red alert is still on." The driver grunted his thanks.

"Even if things are as rotten as you say, what can we do about it?" said Farebrother.

Madigan threw his half-smoked cigarette into the darkness,

where it made a sudden pattern of red sparks. He leaned forward and Farebrother smelled the whiskey on his breath. "There are ways, Farebrother, my boy," he said flippantly. "There are Swedish air-fields packed wing tip to wing tip with Flying Fortresses and B-24s. There must be room there for a factory-fresh Mustang fighter plane." He leaned back in his seat, watching Farebrother to catch the effect of his words. "Some flyers out there over the sea get a sudden hankering to make a separate peace. They steer north to the big blond girls, farm butter, and central heating. You'll be tempted, Farebrother, old buddy."

Nervously Farebrother reached for his own cigarettes and lit one. He took a long time doing it. He didn't want to talk any more with this drunken officer.

But when the cigarette was lit, Madigan said, "You've got a nice lighter there, Captain. Mind if I take a closer look?" When it was passed to him Madigan silently read the engraved "To Jamie from Dad" and then clasped it tight in his hands.

"Women are all the same," said Madigan. He was speaking more quietly now and with a fervor his earlier conversation had lacked. "I was in love this time. Ever been in love, Farebrother?" It was not a real question and he didn't wait for an answer. "I offered to marry her. Last night I dropped in unexpectedly and I find her in the sack with some goddamned infantry lieutenant." He tossed the lighter into the air. "She's probably been two-timing me all along. And I was in love with the little whore."

Farebrother murmured sympathetically and Madigan tossed the lighter to him.

"You'll be all right," said Madigan. "Your reflexes are okay for three o'clock in the morning. And any guy who goes to war carrying a solid-gold lighter is well motivated for survival. From Dad, eh?"

Farebrother smiled and wondered what Captain Madigan would say if he knew that Dad was one of the top brass who were figuring new ways to get them all killed.

Lieutenant Colonel Druce "Duke" Scroll was the Group Executive Officer. He was a fussy thirty-nine-year-old who made sure everyone knew he'd graduated from West Point long before most of the other officers were out of high school. The Exec dressed like an illustration from *The Officer's Handbook*. His wavy hair was always neatly trimmed and his rimless spectacles polished so that they shone.

"What time did you arrive, Captain Farebrother?" His eyes moved quickly to look out of the window. Two aircraft were parked on the muddy grass, their green paint shiny with the never-ending rain. Some men were huddled against the control tower, the outer walls of which were patchy from a half-finished paint job. Behind it the airfield was empty, its grass darkened by the sunless weeks of wintry weather.

"A little after eight o'clock this morning, sir."

"Transport okay? And you got breakfast, I trust." The Exec was bent over his desk, his hands flat on its top, reading from an open file. There was no solicitude apparent in the questions. He seemed more interested in double-checking the motor pool and the mess staff than in Farebrother's welfare. He looked up without straightening his body.

"Yes, thank you, sir."

The Exec banged a hand down on the bell on his desk, like an impatient hotel guest. His sergeant clerk appeared immediately at the door.

"You tell Sergeant Boyer that if I see him and the rest of those lead swingers goofing off just once more, he'll be a buckass private in time for lunch. And you tell him I'm looking for men to do guard duty over Christmas."

"Yes, sir," said the sergeant clerk doubtfully. He looked out of the window to discover what the Exec could see from here. "I guess the rain is pretty heavy."

"The rain was heavy yesterday," said the Exec, "and the day before that. Chances are it will be heavy tomorrow. Colonel Badger wants the tower painted by tonight and it's going to be done by tonight. The Krauts don't close down the war every time it rains, Sergeant. Not even the Limeys do that."

"I'll tell Sergeant Boyer, sir."

"And make it snappy, Sergeant. We've got work to do."

The Exec looked at Farebrother and then at the rain and then at the papers on his desk. "When my sergeant returns he'll give you a map of the base and tell you about your accommodations and so on. And don't kick up a fuss if you're sleeping on the far side of the village in a Quonset hut. This place was built as an RAF satellite field, it wasn't designed to hold over sixteen hundred Americans who want to bathe every day in hot water. The Limeys seem to manage with a dry polish—they think bathing weakens you." He sighed. "I've got over three hundred officers here. I've got captains and majors sleeping under canvas, shaving in tin huts with mud floors and cycling three miles to get breakfast. So . . ." He left the sentence unfinished.

"I understand, sir."

Having finished his well-rehearsed litany, Colonel Scroll looked at Farebrother as if seeing him for the first time. "The commanding officer, Colonel Badger, will see you at eleven hundred hours, Captain Farebrother. You've just got time enough to shave, shower, and change into a clean class A uniform." He nodded a dismissal.

It seemed a bad moment for Farebrother to tell him that he had already showered in the precious hot water, shaved, and was wearing his newest and cleanest uniform. Farebrother saluted punctiliously, and then performed the sort of about-face that was said to be de rigueur at West Point. The effect was not all he'd hoped for; he lost balance performing what the Basic Field Manual describes as " . . . place the toe of your right foot a half foot length in rear and slightly to the left of your left heel. Do not move your left heel." Farebrother moved his left heel.

Everything good or bad about the base at Steeple Thaxted during those days was largely due to the Group Exec. It was Duke Scroll who—like all executive officers throughout the Air Force—made life a pleasure or a pain, not only for the flyers but also for the sheet-metal workers, the parachute packers, and the clerks, cooks, and crew chiefs who made up the three Fighter Group squadrons, and the Air Service Group, which supplied, maintained, policed, and supported them.

The Exec stood behind Colonel Daniel A. Badger, station commander and leader of the Fighter Group. They were a curious pair—the prim, impeccable Duke and the restless, red-faced, squat Colonel Dan, whose short blond hair would never stay the way he combed it and whose large bulbous nose and pugnacious chin never did adapt easily to the strict confines of the molded-rubber oxygen masks the Air Force used.

Colonel Dan rubbed the hairy arms visible below the shortened sleeves of his khaki shirt. It was a quick nervous gesture, like the few fast strokes a butcher makes on a sharpening steel while deciding how to dissect a carcass. In spite of the climate he never wore long sleeves and only put on his jacket when it was really needed. His shirt collar was open, ready for his white flying scarf—"ten minutes in the ocean and a GI necktie will shrink enough to strangle you." Colonel Dan was always ready to fly.

"Captain Farebrother!" The Exec announced him as if he were a guest at a royal ball.

"Yeah," said Colonel Dan. He went on looking at the sheet of paper that the Exec held before him, as if hoping that some more names would miraculously appear there. "Just one of you, eh?"

"Yes, sir," said Farebrother, restraining an impulse to turn around and see.

Colonel Dan ran a hand across his forehead in a movement that was intended to both mop his brow and push back into position his short disarranged hair. "Do you know what I've had to do to get this Group equipped with those P-51s out there?" He didn't wait to hear the answer. "No officer on this base has tasted whiskey in weeks! Why? Because I've used their booze rations to bribe the people who shuffle the paperwork at Wing, Fighter Command, and right up to Air Force HQ. In London a black-market bottle of scotch can cost you four English pounds. You can figure the money, I suppose, so you can figure what it's cost to get those ships."

"Yes, sir," said Farebrother. He'd understood the British currency ever since parting with two pounds to get his travel-creased uniform sponged and pressed in time to wear it at this interview.

"I was hanging around Wing so much," went on Colonel Dan, "that the General thought I was dating his WAC secretary." He chortled to show how unlikely this would be. "I bought lunches for the Chief of Staff, and had my workshops make an airplane model for the Deputy's desk. When I finally discovered that the guy who really makes the decision was only a major, I spent over a month's pay taking him to a nightclub and fixing him up with a girl." He grinned. It was difficult to decide how much of all this was intended seriously, and how much was an act he put on for newly arrived officers.

"So I get my airplanes, and what happens? I lose six jockeys in a row. Look at this roster. One of them's got an impacted wisdom tooth, one's hurt his ankle playing softball, and one's got measles. Can you beat that? The Flight Surgeon tells me . . ." He tapped the papers on the table as if to prove it. "He tells me this officer's got measles and can't fly." He looked at Farebrother. "So just when I get three squadrons of Mustangs here ready to fly, I'm short of men. And what do they send me? Not the eleven lieutenants the T/O says I'm supposed to have from the replacement depot, but one lousy flying instructor . . ." He raised his hand. "No offense to you, Captain, believe me. But goddammit!" He banged on his desk in anger. "What do you think they want me to do, Duke?" The CO twisted around in his swivel chair to look up at his Exec. "Do they want me to set up Captain Farebrother in a dispersal hut on the far side of the field and have him train a dozen pilots for me? Could that be the idea, Duke?"

Colonel Dan scowled at Farebrother and tried without success to stare him down. Finally it was the CO who looked down at his paperwork again. "Fifteen hundred flying hours and an unspecified amount of pre-service flying," he read aloud. "I suppose you think that's really something, eh, Captain?"

"No, sir."

"We're not flying Stearman trainers in neat little patterns over the desert, following the train tracks home when we get lost, and closing down for a long weekend whenever a cloud appears in the sky." He stabbed a finger at the window. "See that pale gray shit up there? It's two thousand feet above the field and it's ten thousand feet thick. And you're going to be flying an airplane up through that stuff . . . an airplane you never dreamed existed even in your worst nightmare. These P-51 Mustangs are unforgiving SOBs, Captain. No dual controls on these babies . . . just a mighty big engine with wings attached. For the first few rides they'll scare you half to death."

Colonel Dan banged the file shut. "We're stood down right now, as you can see. Plenty of airplanes for you to try your hand on. Most of my pilots are on pass—flat on their faces drunk in some Piccadilly gutter, or trying to buy their pants back from some Cambridge whore. Am I right, Colonel Scroll?"

"Most probably, sir," said the matronly Exec, moving one lot of papers away before placing a new pile in front of the CO. His face was expressionless, as if he were playing the role of butler to a play-boy he didn't like.

"Get yourself a helmet and a flight suit, Captain," said Colonel Dan. "And take my advice about logging some hours on a P-51 before the Group's assigned to its next mission." He scratched his arm again. "One of my Flight Commanders is still waiting for his captain's bars, and that boy has five confirmed kills. How do you think he's going to feel when he sees you practicing wing-overs with those shiny railroad tracks on your collar? Having you turn up means he'll wait even longer for promotion. You know that, don't you?"

"Yes, sir."

The Colonel touched the edges of the papers the Exec had placed in front of him. Then, as he looked up, his eyes focused upon Farebrother and dilated with amazement. "Captain Farebrother," he said in a voice that suggested that all the foregoing had been part of some other conversation. "May I ask what, in God's name, you are wearing? Is that a pink jacket?" His voice croaked with indignation.

"At my previous assignment it was customary for instructors to have jackets made up in tan gabardine, like the regulation pants."

"I swear to you, Farebrother," said the Colonel with almost incoherent vehemence, "that if I ever see you wearing that pansy outfit again . . ." He rubbed his mouth as if to still his own anger.

"You make sure you wear the regulation pattern uniform, Captain," said the Exec. "The enlisted men have been getting tailor shops to make up all kinds of cockamamie 'Ike blouses' and the Colonel will not tolerate it."

"One of my top sergeants had a uniform custom-made in Savile Row," added Colonel Dan. His voice was not entirely without a note of pride.

"We stamped on it all pretty hard," said the Exec. He picked up the cardboard folder and nodded, to show that the interview was coming to an end.

"Good luck, Captain Farebrother," said Colonel Dan. "Get yourself somewhere to sack out and make sure you report to the orderly room of the 199th Squadron sometime this afternoon. The Squadron Commander is Major Tucker—he'll be back tomorrow."

Captain Farebrother saluted but this time did his own, modified version of the about-face.

It was still raining when a sergeant—his name, Tex Gill, stenciled on his fleece-lined jacket—helped Farebrother strap into one of the P-51s parked on the apron. The aircraft smelled new with its mixture of leather, paint, and high-octane fuel. On its nose a brightly painted Mickey Mouse danced, and stenciled in yellow, under the cockpit, was the name of its regular pilot: Lt. M. Morse.

"Parking brake on, sir?"

"On," said Farebrother. He plugged in the oxygen mask and microphone and checked the fuel and the switches.

"Did I see you on the truck from London last night, sir?" His voice was low and leisurely with the unmistakable tones of Texas in it.

"That's right, Sergeant Gill."

"Take it real easy, sir. These airplanes are a handful, even for someone who's had a full night's sleep."

"Is she a good one?"

"She's not my regular ship, sir. But she's a dandy plane, and I've got to say it." Gill smiled. He was a big muscular man with a black square-ended mustache that drooped enough to make him look mournful. "Mixture off, pitch control forward," he prompted.

"It's okay, Sergeant Gill," said Farebrother. "I have a few Mustang flights in my log."

"You don't want to listen to what people tell you," he said. "This place is no better and no worse than any other unit I've been with."

Farebrother nodded. The rain continued to drizzle down from the gray stratus. Its droplets made a thousand pearls on the Plexiglas canopy. He almost changed his mind about flying up into such an overcast, but it was too late now. He grinned at Sergeant Gill, who seemed reassured by this but remained on the wing watching the whole cockpit check.

When Farebrother set the throttle a fraction forward and switched on the magnetos and battery, the instruments sprang to life. Gill used his handkerchief to wipe the rain from the windshield, and then he raised the side of the canopy and thumped it home with the heel of his hand. It was a gesture of farewell. He jumped down. Farebrother looked around to be sure Gill was clear and then hit the fuel booster and starter.

There was a salvo of bangs from the engine, and the four-bladed propeller turned stiffly and halted. To the south sunlight lit the cloud. The rain was lighter now but still coming into the cockpit. He closed the side panel.

Sergeant Gill's jacket collar was up high around his neck, but his knitted hat and fatigue trousers were dark with rain. He put his fist in the air and swung it around. Farebrother tried again. The big Merlin engine fired, stuttered, almost stopped, and then after some faltering picked up and kept going. At first not all the cylinders were firing, but one after the other they warmed up until all twelve combined to produce the ragged but unmistakable sound of a Merlin engine.

Farebrother checked the magnetos one by one before running the power up. He left it there for a moment. Sergeant Gill gave a thumbs-up and Farebrother throttled back to fifteen hundred revs and looked at his instruments once more. She seemed okay, but Merlins were notoriously susceptible to water vapor and he let her warm up until she was very smooth.

The rain stopped and a beam of sunlight spiked through the overcast. By now there was someone on the balcony of the control tower and the men painting it had paused in their work to watch the Mustang taxi out to the runway. The engine cowling obscured his view and Farebrother steered a zigzag course along the perimeter track to make sure he didn't let the wheels go into the muddy patches on each side. At the runway he stopped. The figure on the balcony waved an arm and Farebrother ran the engine against the brakes before letting the plane slip forward and gather speed.

She lifted easily off the ground and he brought the wheels up quickly. The cloud was lower than he'd thought; even before he was turning into a gentle circuit there were tiny streaks of gray cloud rippling across his wings.

A man has to be very young, very stupid, or very angry to do what Farebrother did that December afternoon in 1943. Perhaps he was a little of all three. First he went up to find out how low the overcast was, and then he took her on a circuit to test the controls and look over the local terrain. He treated her gently, just as he had treated the ones at Dallas every time Charlie Stigg had been able to persuade his test pilot brother that two hard-working Air Force instructors needed the taste of real flying once in a while.

Farebrother decided that, by luck or judgment, the unknown Lieutenant Morse had chosen a fine machine. *Mickey Mouse II* responded to every touch of the controls and had that extra agility the Mustang has when its main tank is more than half empty.

He pulled back the stick and eased up into the overcast. A few wisps of dirty cotton slid over the wings, then suddenly the cockpit was dark. The wet rain cloud swirled off the wing tips in curly vortices but the Merlin gave no cough or hesitation. It drank the wet cloud without complaint. Contented, Farebrother dropped out of the lower side of the stratus in time to see the crossed runways of

Steeple Thaxted just ahead of him. He leveled off and slow-rolled to
a flipper turn that gave turning force to the elevators. Then he went
high, banked steeply, and came back. This time he dived upon the
field to gain speed enough for a loop. As she came up to the top of
the loop, belly touching the underside of the stratus, he rolled her
out and snaked away, tearing little pieces from the underside of the
cloud base.

He had their attention now. Men had come out of the big black
hangars, and others stood in groups on the parade ground. There was
a crowd outside the mess tents and Farebrother saw their mess kits
glint in the dull light as he made a low run across the field. There
were people in the village streets too, and some cars had pulled off
the road so the drivers could watch. Farebrother wondered whether
Colonel Dan and the Exec were among the men standing in the
rain outside the Operations Building.

By now he had enough confidence in the plane to move lower.
He made another pass—this time so low that he had to ease her up to
clear the control tower, and only just made it. The men working
there threw themselves onto the wet ground, and on his next run he
saw pools of spilled white paint that made big spiders on the black
tarmac. He went between the hangars that time, and did a perfect
eight-point roll across the field. For a finale he half-rolled to buzz
the runway, holding her inverted until the engine screamed for fuel,
and then split-essed in for a landing that put her down as soft as a
caress.

If Farebrother was expecting a round of applause as he got out of
the plane, he was disappointed. Apart from the amiable Sergeant
Gill, who helped him unstrap, there was no one in sight. "Everything
okay, sir?" said Gill, deadpan.

"You'd better change the plugs, Sergeant," said Farebrother. He
noticed that Gill had put on a waterproof coat, but his face and
trousers were wet with rain.

"She's due for a change. But I figured she'd be okay for a familiarization flight," Gill said in his Texas drawl.

"You were quite right, Sergeant Gill."

"You can leave the chute there. I'll get one of the boys to take it
back."

Gill walked back to the dispersal hut with Farebrother. There
was a primitive kitchen there and some coffee was ready in the percolator. Without asking, Gill poured coffee for the pilot.

"She's a good ship, and well looked after."

"She's not mine," said Gill. "I'm crew chief for *Kibitzer* just across the other side of the hardstand. That one belongs to a crew chief named Kruger."

"But he allows Lieutenant Morse to fly it once in a while?"

"That's about the way it is," said Gill without smiling.

"Well, I hope Kruger and Lieutenant Morse won't mind me borrowing their ship."

"Lieutenant Morse won't mind—Mickey Mouse they call him— and he's mighty rough with airplanes. He says planes are like women, they've got to be beaten regularly, he says." Gill still didn't smile.

Farebrother offered his cigarettes, but Gill shook his head. "Kruger, he won't mind too much," said Gill. "It don't do an airplane any good to be standing around in this kind of weather unused." He took off his hat and looked at it carefully. "Colonel Dan now, that's something else again. Last pilot who flew across the field . . . I mean a couple of hundred feet clear of the roofs, not your kind of daisy-cutting . . . Colonel Dan roasted him. He was up before the commanding general—got an official reprimand and was fined three hundred bucks. Then the Colonel sent him back to the U.S. of A."

"Thanks for telling me, Sergeant."

"If Colonel Dan gets mad, he gets mad real quick, and you'll find out real quick too." He wiped the rain from his face. "If you ain't heard from him by the time you're unpacked, you ain't going to hear."

Farebrother nodded and drank his coffee.

Sergeant Gill looked Farebrother up and down before deciding to give him his opinion. "I don't reckon you'll hear a thing, sir. See, we're real short of pilots right now, and I don't think Colonel Dan's gonna be sending any pilot anywhere else. Especially an officer who's got such a good feel for a ship that needs a change of spark plugs." He looked at Farebrother and gave a small grin.

"I sure hope you're right, Sergeant Gill," said Farebrother. And in fact he was.

3

Staff Sergeant
Harold E. Boyer

Captain Farebrother's flying demonstration that day passed into legend. Some said that the men on duty at Steeple Thaxted exaggerated their descriptions of the flight in order to score over those who were on pass, but such attempts to belittle Farebrother's aerobatics could only be made by those who hadn't been present. And Farebrother's critics were confuted by the fact that Staff Sergeant Harry Boyer said it was the greatest display of flying he'd ever seen. "Jesus! No plane ever made me hit the dirt before that. Not even out in the Islands before the war when some of the officers were cutting up in front of their girls."

Harry Boyer was, by common consent, the most experienced airman on the base. He'd strapped into their rickety biplanes nervous young lieutenants who were now wearing stars in the Pentagon. And no matter what aircraft type was mentioned, Harry Boyer had painted it, sewn its fabric, and probably hitched a ride in it.

Harry Boyer not only told of "Farebrother's buzz job," as it became known, he gave a realistic impression of it that required both hands and considerable sound effects. The end of the show came when Boyer gave his fruity impression of Tex Gill drawling, "Everything okay, sir?" and then, in Farebrother's prim New England accent, "You'd better change the plugs, Sergeant."

So popular was Boyer's re-enactment of the flight that when he performed his party piece at the 1969 reunion of the 220th Fighter Group Association, a dozen men crowding around him missed the exotic dancer.

Staff Sergeant Boyer's reputation as a mimic was, however, nothing compared to his renown as the organizer of crap games. Men came from the Bomb Group at Narrowbridge to gamble on Boyer's dice, and on several occasions officers turned up from the 91st BG at Bassingbourn. It was his crap game that got Boyer into trouble with the Exec.

Although Boyer and the Exec had carried on a long, bitter, and Byzantine struggle, the sergeant's activities had never been seriously curtailed. But whenever it leaked out that some really big all-night game with four-figure stakes had taken place, Boyer subsequently found himself mysteriously assigned to extra duties. So it was that Staff Sergeant Boyer had found himself in charge of the detail painting the control tower that day.

At the end of Farebrother's hair-raising beat-up, Boyer looked over to the Operations Building, expecting the Exec and Colonel Dan to come rushing out of the building breathing fire. But they did not come. Nothing happened at all except that Tex Gill finally rode over to the tower on his bicycle, carefully laying it on the ground rather than against the newly painted wall of the tower. "And how did you like that, Tex?" asked Boyer. "On those slow rolls he was touching the grass with one wing tip while the other was in the overcast. Did you see it?"

"He's clipped the radio wires off the top of the tower," said Tex Gill.

Determined not to rise to one of Tex Gill's gags, Boyer pretended not to have heard properly. "He's what?"

"He clipped the radio wire on that low pass." Tex Gill was a deadpan poker player who'd frequently taken money from the otherwise indomitable Boyer, so, still suspecting a joke, the staff sergeant would not look up at the antenna.

Tex Gill held out his fist and opened his hand to reveal a ceramic insulator and a short piece of wire attached to it. "Just got it off his tail."

"Does Colonel Dan know?"

"Even the guy who just flew those fancy doodads don't know. I figured that you and me could rig a new antenna right now, while your boys are finishing up the paint job."

"That's strictly against regs, Tex. There'd have to be paperwork and so on."

"That captain just arrived," said Tex Gill. "I was with him on the truck from London last night. We don't want to get him in bad with the Colonel even before he's unpacked."

Staff Sergeant Boyer rubbed his chin. Tex Gill could be a devious devil. Maybe he figured there was a good chance that the new pilot would take *Kibitzer*, in which case Tex would be his crew chief. "Well, I'm not sure, Tex."

"If someone reports that broken antenna, the Exec is going to come over here, Harry. And he'll see your paintwork is only finished on the side that faces his office, and he'll see that some clumsy lummox has spilled two four-gallon cans of white on the apron . . ."

Boyer looked at the flecks of spilled paint on his boots and at the insulator that Tex Gill was holding. "You got any white paint over there at your dispersal?"

"I'd be able to fix you up, Harry." Tex Gill threw the insulator to Boyer, who caught it and winked his agreement. By the end of work that day the tower was painted and the antenna was back in position. Captain Farebrother never found out about it and neither did the Exec or Colonel Dan.

4

Lieutenant Z. M. Morse

Lieutenant Morse returned from four days in London with a thick head and a thin wallet. He desperately wanted to sleep, but he had to endure two young pilots sitting on his bed, drinking coffee and eating his candy ration and telling him all about the fantastic new flyer who'd been assigned to the squadron. "What the fuck do I care what he can do with a P-51?" asked Morse. "I was happy enough with my P-47, and if I'd been Colonel Dan I wouldn't have been so damned keen to re-equip us with these babies. Jesus! They stall without warning, and now they tell us the guns jam if you fire them in a tight turn." Morse was sprawled on his bed, his shirt rumpled and tie loose. He grabbed his pillow and punched it hard before shoving it behind his head. A large black mongrel dog asleep in the wicker armchair opened its eyes and yawned.

Morse, who'd grown so used to being called Mickey Mouse, or MM, that he'd painted the cartoon on his plane, was a small untidy twenty-four-year-old from Arizona. His dark complexion made him seem permanently suntanned even in an English winter, and his longish shiny hair, long sideburns, and thin, carefully trimmed mustache caused him to be mistaken sometimes for a South American. MM was always delighted to act the role and would occasionally try his own unsteady version of the rumba on a Saturday night, given a few extra drinks and a suitable partner.

"They say it was terrific," said Rube Wein, MM's wingman. "They say it was the greatest show they ever saw."

"In your ship," added Earl Koenige, who usually flew as MM's number three. "I sure would have liked to see it."

"How old are you jerks?" said MM. "Come on, level with me. Did you ever get out of high school?"

"I'm ninety-one going on ninety-two," said Rube Wein, Princeton University graduate in mathematics. There was only a few months' difference in age between the three of them but it was a well-established vanity of MM's that he looked more mature than the others. This concern had led MM to grow his mustache—which still had a long way to go before looking properly bushy.

"I see you guys sitting there, Hershey bars stuck in your mouths, and I can't help thinking maybe you should be riding kiddie cars, not flying fighter planes to a place where angry grown-up Krauts are trying to put lead into your tails."

"So who gave the new kid the keys to your car, Pop?" said Rube Wein. This broody scholar knew how to kid MM and was prepared to taunt him in a way that Earl Koenige wouldn't dare to.

"Right!" said MM angrily. "Why didn't he take *Cinderella* or *Bebop*? Or even better, *Kibitzer*, which is always making trouble? Why does he have to go popping rivets in my ship? Isn't my goddamned crew chief paid to look after that machine? He should never have let this new guy fly her."

"Why didn't he use Tucker's plane?" said Rube Wein, who strongly disliked his Squadron Commander. "Why didn't he take that fancy painted-up *Jouster* and maybe wreck it?"

"Colonel Dan's orders," explained Earl Koenige, a blond-haired farmer's son who'd studied agriculture at Fort Valley, Georgia. "Colonel Dan told this guy to go out and fly a familiarization hop. Of course, it's only scuttlebutt, but they say Farebrother asked was it okay to fly it inverted." Meeting the blank-eyed disbelieving stares of the others, he added, "Maybe it's not true but that's what they say. The Group Exec is furious—he wanted Farebrother court-martialed."

"There should be a regulation about taking other people's airplanes," said MM. "And inverted flying is strictly for screwballs."

Earl Koenige tossed back his fair hair and said, "Colonel Dan said the new pilot hadn't been on base long enough to make himself familiar with local regulations and conditions. And the Colonel said that the especially bad weather that day created a situation in which low flying in the vicinity of the base was a necessary measure for any pilot new to the field about to attempt a landing in poor visibility." Earl laughed. "Or to put it another way, Colonel Dan needs every pilot he can get his hands on." Having related this story, Koenige looked at MM. He always looked to his Flight Commander for approval of everything he did.

MM nodded his blessing and put another stick of gum into his mouth. It was his habit of chewing gum and smoking at the same time that made him so easy to impersonate, for he'd roll the cigarette from one side of his mouth to the other with a swing of the jaw. Anyone who wanted an easy laugh at the bar had only to do the same thing while flicking an imaginary comb back through his hair to create a recognizable caricature of MM. "Sure! Great!" MM shouted, clapping his hands as if summoning hens out of the grain store. "And beautifully told. Now cut and print. Get out of here, will you! I'm not feeling so hot."

Rube Wein leaned over MM where he was sprawled out on the bed and said, "It's chow time, MM. How would you like me to bring you back some of those greasy sausages and those real soggy french fries that only the Limeys can make?"

"Scram!" shouted MM, but the effort made his head ache.

"Rumor is that this new guy is going to get *Kibitzer*, and that means he'll be flying as your number four, MM," said Rube Wein.

MM threw a shoe at him, but he was out of the door.

Winston, MM's dog, looked up to see if the thrown shoe was intended for him to bring back, decided it wasn't, growled unconvincingly, and closed his eyes again.

Not long afterward there was a polite tap at the door, and without waiting for a response, a tall thin captain put his head into the room. "Lieutenant Morse?"

"Come in, don't just stand in the draft," said Morse, stubbing out his cigarette in the lid of a hair-cream bottle.

"My name's Farebrother, Lieutenant. I'm assigned to your flight."

"Kick Winston off that chair and sit down." MM's first impression of the newcomer was of a shy stooped figure in an expensive non-regulation leather jacket, wearing a gold Rolex watch and with a fountain pen that was leaking through the breast pocket of his shirt to make a small blue mark over his heart. His captain's bars had been worn long enough to become tarnished. It was a nice conceit and MM noted it with admiration.

"I'm going to be flying *Kibitzer,* I understand."

MM recognized the slight eastern accent.

"So you're the bastard who popped rivets in my ship."

"You've got a beautiful bird there, Lieutenant. She ticks like a Swiss watch," said Jamie diplomatically. MM purred like a cat with a saucer of cream. "But I didn't pull enough G to pop any rivets."

"Where are you from, Captain?" said MM. "New York? Boston? Philly?" These rich eastern kids were all alike; they treated the rest of the nation as if they were just off a farm in Indiana.

"I live in California, Lieutenant. But I went to school in the East."

"You want a drink, Captain? I've got scotch."

Farebrother held up a thin hand to indicate that he wouldn't. MM settled back in the pillows and looked at him—a poor little rich boy. Junior figured that single-seat fighters might be a way he could fight the war without rubbing shoulders with the riffraff.

Farebrother said, "Are we going to fight the entire war with me calling you Lieutenant and you calling me Captain?"

MM grinned and held out a hand that Farebrother shook. "Call me Mickey Mouse like everyone else does."

"My friends call me Jamie."

"Take the weight off your legs, Jamie, and throw me a pack of butts from that carton on my footlocker." Morse opened a book of matches to make sure it wasn't empty. "Are you fixed up with a room?"

"I'm sleeping downstairs—sharing with Lieutenant Hart."

"Then you're on your own. Hart got some kind of ulcer. He won't be back. If you take my advice, you'll leave his name on the door and try to keep the room all to yourself, like I have this one. No sense in sharing if you can avoid it."

"Why are we living in these little houses?"

"The RAF built them to house officers and their families. That narrow storeroom downstairs, where they fix sandwiches and fry stuff, used to be the family kitchen." Farebrother looked around the smoke-filled room. Lieutenant Morse had left no space for anyone else to move in with him. The second bed had been upended and a motorcycle engine occupied its floor space. Parts of the engine were strewn around the room; some were wrapped up in stained cloths and some were in a shallow pan of oil on the floor. In the corner there were Coca-Cola bottles piled up high on a milk crate and on the walls were pinup photos from *Yank* and a colored movie poster advertising *Dawn Patrol*. Above the bed MM had hung a belt with a holstered Colt automatic clipped to it, and above that there was a beautiful gray Stetson.

"And that old civilian sweeping the hall?" said Farebrother.

"We have British civilian servants, batmen they call them. They'll fix up your laundry and bring you tea in the morning . . . well, you can make a face, but it's better than British coffee, believe me. If you want coffee, fix it yourself."

"I hear you're the ranking ace here."

MM lit his cigarette carefully and then extinguished the match by waving it in the air. "You don't have to be any Baron von Richthofen to be best around here. Most of these kids should still be in Primary Flight School learning how to do gentle turns in a bi-plane."

"Does that go for the pilots in your flight too?"

MM inhaled on his cigarette, closing his eyes as if in deep thought. "Rube Wein is my wingman—sad-eyed kid with jug ears, rooms downstairs. He's no better, no worse than most as a flyer. He's a brainy little bastard whose idea of a good time is to sit through an evening of Shakespeare, but he's got eyes like an Indian scout and reaction times as good as any I've seen. And don't let all that book learning fool you, he's a tough little shit. When he's on my wing I feel good." MM fiddled with his cigarette and tapped some ash into the tin lid. "You'll probably fly wing for Earl Koenige—better pilot than Rube, he's got that natural feeling for it, but he's a shy kid and he just won't get in close enough to get kills. Earl likes airplanes, that's his trouble. He's always frightened of bending something or damaging his engine by using full power. He flies these goddamned Mustangs like he was paying the maintenance out of his own pocket."

Winston sighed and slid gracelessly off the wicker chair, which creaked loudly. Farebrother, who had been standing, sat down on the dog's cushion and put his feet up on a hard chair. It gave MM a chance to admire Farebrother's hand-tooled high boots.

"When do you think we'll go again?" Farebrother asked.

"After that Gelsenkirchen foul-up I thought we'd never go again. I had a hunch we'd all be transferred to the infantry."

"What happened?"

MM shook his head sadly. "Track in to Colonel Dan leading us to the rendezvous with the Bomb Groups at Emmerich, near the Dutch frontier. We're tasked to give them close support all the way to the target, and then back as far as Holland again. We're all tucked in nice and tight behind Colonel Dan. It was like an air show except that the stratus is under us and no one could see anything."

"Not even the bombers?"

"What bombers?" MM waved an arm to indicate that he could see nothing. "I never saw any bombers."

"So what happened?"

"I'll tell you what happened—nothing happened, that's what happened. The bombers never found the target. The little magic black boxes that are supposed to see through cloud went on the blink, and the B-17s went miles north of our route. Cut to Colonel Dan, who's taking us round and round Gelsenkirchen—at least he insists it's Gelsenkirchen—but all we see is cloud. Then we fly back to England in a nice tight formation, do some low passes over the field to show what split-ass aces we are, and there's plenty of time for drinks before dinner. Jesus, what a fuck-up!"

"The mission didn't bomb?"

"Oh, they bombed. They bombed 'targets of opportunity,' which is a cute name the Air Force dreamed up for shutting your eyes, toggling the bombload, gaining height, and getting the hell out."

"I heard the Bomb Groups were having a tough time," said Farebrother. "I saw replacements by the truckload heading for the bombers."

"Slow dissolve to the Bremen mission one week later," said MM. "Seems like the target-selection guys at High Wycombe have some kind of private feud with the inhabitants of Bremen."

Farebrother nodded politely. "It's accessible; it's near the ocean," he said. He reached into his shirt pocket for a pack of Camels and flicked a cigarette up with his fingernail. MM watched him light it. His hands were as steady as a rock. These rich kids are all the same—maybe it's the schools they go to on the east coast. Keep it cool, never laugh, never fart, never shout, never cry. MM admired it. "So what happened?" said Farebrother.

MM realized he'd been daydreaming. He was tired and hung over—he should have told Farebrother to go away and leave him alone, but he didn't. He told him about Bremen. He told him about the one that got torn in half.

"We found the rearmost task force miles behind their briefed timings," MM said, and stopped. He'd never told the others about that midair collision, not even Rube, his closest buddy. So why tell this guy? Maybe because it was easier to tell a stranger. "Thank God we weren't escorting those B-24s. They call them banana boats; they say they were flying boats that leaked so bad they put wheels on them and christened them bombers."

Farebrother smiled, but he'd heard the joke before. He could tell that MM was stalling.

"Those ships need a lot of babying. By the time they were above the cloud cover they were skidding all over the sky. The pilots couldn't hold formation."

"It's that Davis wing," said Farebrother. "It wasn't designed for high loading at that altitude."

"Sure, something like that," said MM. "It was a bad start, flying past those banana boats, and they've taken so many casualties over the weeks that by now the pilots are mostly replacements who've never flown a tough one before." He flicked ash into the lid that was still resting on his chest. "You say Bremen's easy because it's on the coast, what you don't know is that the Kraut radar chain goes right along that coast. Anything coming in over the sea comes up clear on their screens. So the fighters were waiting—hundreds of them. Did we have the shit beat out of us!" MM found his hands were sweating and he knew his face was flushed. "I drank too much last night," he explained.

"You engaged the enemy fighters?"

"Hey, Jamie! Where'd you pick up that kind of talk? You training to be a general or a reporter or something? Sure, we engaged the enemy—we engaged him good and proper. Another engagement like that and our parents are going to insist we get married." He puffed his cigarette vigorously in silence for a moment. "Colonel Dan is leading Red—Red are always nominated as the troubleshooters, so Colonel Dan likes to take Red—and I'm leading the second element. We've passed the B-24s and found our Forts and we're keeping real close to them just like it says in the book. But while we're watching that we don't get so close the trigger-happy gunners shoot us down, the Messerschmitt 110s come up on the horizon and suddenly they're loosing off rockets."

"No one goes after them?"

"By the time anyone guessed they were going to fire long-range rockets it was too late, the Krauts were away and heading for their beer ration. Then the Messerschmitt 109s come roaring through the formation—and all this time we're still over the sea, we're nowhere near the target—they dive down through the bombers and lift their noses for a second go at their undersides. Colonel Dan goes for them and a few of us get some shots in before they're diving away. It's while we're wrestling with these babies that the withdrawal support group arrives. They're Thunderbolts, and those guys think anything with square wings is a Messerschmitt. So who should be surprised when the T-bolts come out of the sun and clobber two of our boys in the first pass? We lost two good pilots that day and we didn't get one confirmed kill. Then just as we're getting ready to form up and go home I see some lunatic Kraut come sneaking back toward the bombers. I did a wing-over and chased him, but he was going fast, really fast. I got a couple of squirts at him, but he just flies straight on, no evasive action. For a minute I think maybe the pilot is dead or out of action, then I realize what this crazy bastard is going to do. He's picked himself one of the Forts in the low box and he just drives straight into its side."

Farebrother said nothing.

MM dashed his hands together and held them locked. "I was right behind him. I saw everything. He ripped the whole side out of that bomber. I could see the guys flying her. I could see the seats and the equipment, the wiring and the bright aluminum interior. I was so close I could have touched those guys. I saw their faces as the whole thing broke up. Shit! It wasn't a million laughs." MM stubbed his cigarette hard into the tin lid and forced a smile. "Pour yourself a drink if you want one. Loosen up."

"I'm loose enough already," said Farebrother. The chair creaked as he shifted uncomfortably. "Do you know what the flying schedule is likely to be over Christmas?"

"Hell Jamie, you ain't been here five minutes. Are you looking for a pass already?"

"I have a close friend stationed near Norwich. We said we'd try to get together over Christmas."

"You're not thinking of visiting a Bomb Group, are you?"

"Why not?"

"Oh, sure. You'll have a good time. The bomber guys love us, Little Friends they call us on the radio, right? They'll buy you beers and sing songs around the piano. And headquarters encourages all that bullshit."

"What's wrong with it?"

"Sure, it's swell. Me and Rube and Earl used to go across to Narrowbridge. B-17s, easy to recognize them, red diamond on the tail plane, white letter A inside it. I met this guy who knew my brother. His family has a restaurant near Phoenix, and I'm from Arizona myself. It was great talking to him about places and people we knew. He's got his navigator there and we're talking about home and showing each other photos of girls and mothers and kids, all that family shit, you know."

"I know," said Farebrother. He could see the rest of it in MM's eyes. "And he was in the ship . . ."

"I could *see* him. The side of that ship opened like a sardine can. He was sitting at the controls, but there was only half of him left, Farebrother." MM was flicking at his stubbed-out cigarette just to keep from discovering if his hands were trembling. "Slow dissolve. No partying at Narrowbridge, right?"

"It would upset anyone, MM."

"Sure it would, I don't need you to tell me that. Screw the bomber Joes. I didn't tell them to join the lousy Air Force. It's not my fault that Colonel Dan wants us to keep tight cover. I can't help it if Göring tells his fighter jocks to go after the heavies and avoid us . . ."

"Is that the time?" said Farebrother. "I'd better get out of here and let you get some sleep." He got to his feet and the wicker armchair creaked. Winston looked out from under the bed.

"You go to hell, Captain goddamned Farebrother! You don't have to look down your thin white nose at me. You're heading there too, Captain, and that eastern schooling won't mean a thing when the Krauts are putting lead into your ass."

Farebrother nodded politely and went out, closing the door quietly. Farebrother knew how to be rude in a really high-class way.

"And keep your lily white hands off my goddamned ship!" MM yelled at the closed door.

5

Captain
Charles B. Stigg

Officers' Club
280th Bombardment Sq. (H)
Cowdry Green
Norfolk, England

Dear Jamie,

You get your five bucks! I've never been happier in my life. These guys are friendly and the Group Commander ("Call me Porky the way the rest of them do") plays the trumpet in the dance band. He also slams his B-24 down onto the runway with the kind of bang that reminds me of Cadet Jenkins, but it's just his style, I guess.

This Group has taken a beating, and there are plenty of hair-raising stories told when the beer flows. But they're good boys—I feel so old! We've got kids here who only shave once a week, but good guys. No backbiting and none of that gossip that the staff of you-know-where enjoyed so much. And I got a great crew—instead of duds from the replacement pool I took over a ready-crewed ship when they lost their pilot. He got VD (in Norwich, the Flight Surgeon says, and we got a tub-thumping lecture complete with color slides that made two or three of the guys go outside for air!).

Good ship too. Nearly new and the crew all like her, which is a plus. *Top Banana* she's called, so look out for us over Hun-land.

It looked like we were going today, but while we were all trundling around the perimeter track it was scrubbed. Can't think why it took them so long to decide. I could hardly see the red flare from where the *Banana* was sitting—five hundred yards away. What an anticlimax! And two ships damaged when wing tips touched on the taxiway. Porky put up a notice saying, "Goosing big birds on the apron is a privilege restricted to officers of field grade." Of course all the guys love him.

Tomorrow I take my crew for ditching practice in the unheated water of the municipal swimming pool. In December? War is hell. So today I've spent the unexpected leisure improving my bridge game at a cost of four and a half pounds and putting a little scotch into my bloodstream as protection against tomorrow's swim. And writing drunken letters (like this) home. I sure wish you were with us, Jamie, it would make everything perfect. What's happening at Christmas? Looks like I won't be OD or get any duties. How are you fixed?

Your pal,

Charlie

Captain
James A. Farebrother

Jamie Farebrother read Charlie's letter for the fifth time. Then he folded it, together with the five-dollar bill that was inside the envelope, and placed it in his billfold like an amulet that would protect him, not from evil, but from misery.

What could he write in reply? How could he describe this tent city in the monsoon season, and the red-nosed, rheumy-eyed bums clad in ragged oddments of GI uniforms? What was there to say about the overworked comedian who was in command, or the unfriendly Exec, or MM, the Flight Commander, who seemed to be twitching himself into a nervous breakdown? Perhaps it would all come right when the sun came out, and these mud-spattered planes began operations, but it wasn't easy to visualize.

Flying the well-worn Mustang *Kibitzer* provided Jamie's only happy moments and there weren't many of them. The weather did not improve. The big black hangar doors were shut and clanking mournfully in the wind. Flyers sat for hours in the Club and got in each other's hair, bickering like children kept in after school. There were only a few brief breaks in the monotonous gray days. Apart from some local flights MM had arranged to make sure that his new flyer was able to take off in pairs, keep formation, and get down in one piece, there had been only one scheduled flight in seven days. The group went in formation across country to Yorkshire but encountered unpredicted thunderstorms that couldn't be penetrated. The Mustangs came back to the base from all points of the compass. There were no casualties, but two pilots landed at other airfields.

Kibitzer had engine trouble on the return. Farebrother nursed her home carefully, and MM, Rube, and Earl stayed with him, but when Tex Gill ran her up that night she purred sweetly for him.

"She's a whore!" Tex said of *Kibitzer*. "A heart of gold, but you can't depend on the old bitch."

Colonel Dan was not pleased with the Group's cross-country flight. He assembled the pilots in the Briefing Room that afternoon and chewed them out for nearly an hour. The Exec sat on the rostrum with his arms folded and head up, his eyes focused on some far corner of the ceiling. It was a pose meant to be both heroic and contemplative.

Colonel Dan was never still; he went striding up and down, hugging himself and flailing his arms, shouting, whispering, threatening and promising, and stabbing his finger angrily at his resentful audience.

MM sat behind Farebrother at the back of the room, with Rube and Earl on either side of him. "More training," said MM in disgust. "I can smell it coming."

"That's only Yorkshire," said Rube. "With long-range tanks we'll be trying to find our way back from Austria. Imagine the chaos!"

"We've got to get Farebrother a new ship," said MM. He put a flying boot against the back of Jamie's seat and nudged it hard to make sure he was listening. "One jalopy like that in the flight could get us all written out of the script."

There was a Betty Grable movie being shown on the base that evening and the house was packed. There wasn't much drinking at the Officers' Club bar. Highly colored accounts of the chewing out Colonel Dan had given his pilots soon reached the senior NCOs, and in the Rocker Club the sergeants argued bitterly about the merits of their charges. There was a fistfight outside the Aero Club and a jeep was stolen. The Exec sighed; these were all signs of lowering morale. Colonel Dan agreed.

"I came over here to fight a war," sang a pilot named "Boogie" Bozzelli, playing piano at the Club that evening. He improvised a tune to carry his words. "All I've done since getting here is duck the weather. Can I have a rain check, Colonel, and come back next summer?" Colonel Dan was not amused. He picked up his drink and moved away from the piano.

The feelings of frustration were not relieved when, in the small hours of the next morning, the sound of aircraft engines—synchronized Merlins—circled the base ceaselessly until the Duty Officer switched on the runway lights. The noise woke everyone up. Farebrother opened the blackout shutters of his bedroom and saw Rube and MM fully dressed outside. The eastern sky was streaked with the pink light of dawn. The night air blew in like a gale. Farebrother closed the window and went back to sleep.

Next morning there was an RAF Lancaster parked on the apron. It was a big matt-black four-engine bomber. A noisy crowd of GIs were gawking at it and taking photos. Its crew—seven sergeants— were treated like visitors from Mars. Thaxted's only air-crew mess being in the Officers' Club, the RAF men were eating breakfast there when Farebrother arrived. MM waved to him and he took a seat at MM's table, chosen to provide a close look at the British flyers.

Perhaps the sergeants were uncomfortable at being cast adrift on an ocean of officers, for they were shy and uncommunicative. They'd been to Berlin that night and lost a section of tail plane and a chunk of wing over the target. The pilot was a gray-faced boy of about twenty, and the rest of them looked like undernourished schoolboys. These flyers who fought by night were pallid and withdrawn by comparison with the noisy suntanned extroverts which U.S. Army selection boards seemed to prefer as crews.

Mickey Morse was a good example of that. He was wiry, and swarthy enough to make some suggest that his antecedents had swum across the Rio Grande. He never stopped fidgeting with the salt and pepper and tapping his fork against the tablecloth. "Look at those guys," he said, indicating the bomber crew with his fork. "The British have been fighting too long. They're tired and low."

"Maybe you'd be tired and low after a night over Big B without fighter escort and half your tail missing," said Farebrother.

MM gave him a sly grin. "We'll be finding out soon," he said. "With these new external gas tanks we'll be able to fly our ships to Cairo if the brass dream up a reason for it." He used the tip of his tongue to search out a piece of ham stuck between his teeth. "Paper gas tanks. Sounds like they're carrying the metal-saving campaign too far, right?"

"Will they come off the shackles when I jettison?" said Farebrother.

"You've got something there, pal." MM turned in his seat for a better view of the RAF men. "One of the topkicks asked the Limeys to stick around. There's some kind of celebration in the Rocker Club tonight."

"And?"

"They want to grab some gas and get back to their squadron. Look at those kids, will you? Are we going to look like that by the time we're home again?"

"Did you hear the radio this morning? The RAF lost thirty heavy bombers over Germany last night. Thirty crews! Sure they want to get back, to see if their buddies made it."

Lieutenant Morse got to his feet and said, "I'm going into Cambridge on my motorcycle, want to come?" Morse's black mongrel, Winston, crawled out from under the table and shook itself.

"I've got some letters to write."

"So can you lend me five pounds?" MM drained his coffee cup while standing up. Farebrother passed him the money and MM nodded his thanks. "So they went to Berlin last night," he said enviously. "You get headlines going to Berlin. No one wants to know about the flak at Hannover or the fighter defenses at Kassel. But go to Berlin and you're a headline."

"And you want to be a headline?"

"You bet your ass I do. A kid at school with me was on a sub that sank a Jap ship. The town gave him a parade. A parade! He was a hashslinger on a pigboat. He never even finished high school."

The Officers' Club bar was a gloomy place, most of the blackout shutters permanently fixed over the windows. Farebrother found a corner of the lounge, and despite the noise of the men fixing up the Christmas tree in the hallway, he began writing a letter to his mother.

"Can I get you a drink, sir?" It was one of the British waiters, a completely bald, wizened man, bent like a stick and flushed with that shiny red skin that makes even the most dyspeptic of men look jolly.

"I don't think so," said Farebrother.

"You won't be flying today, sir," he coaxed. "The rain is turning to sleet." Farebrother looked up to see wet snow sliding down the window glass fast enough to obscure the view across the balding lawns to the tennis courts. Over the loudspeakers came a big-band version of "Jingle Bells" on a damaged record that clicked.

"It's too early for booze, Curly. The Captain wants a cup of coffee." It was Captain Madigan—Farebrother recognized him from the night journey on the truck from London. "None of that powdered crap, real coffee, and a slice of that fruitcake you sons of bitches all keep for yourselves back there."

The bald waiter smiled. "Anything for you, Captain Madigan. Two real coffees and two slices of special fruitcake, coming right up."

Madigan didn't sit down immediately. He threw his cap onto the window ledge and went across to warm himself at the open fire. When he turned around he kept his hands behind him in a stance he'd learned from the British. "My God, but this must be the most uncomfortable place in the world."

"Have you tried the Aleutians or the South Pacific?"

"Don't deny a man his right to grouse, Farebrother, or I'll start thinking you're some kind of Pollyanna." He bent over to remove the cycle clips from his wet trousers. "I suppose you're sleeping in a steam-heated room here in the Club?"

"I'm in one of the houses across the road."

"Well, buddy, I'm in one of the tents that blew down last night. There's clothing and stuff scattered over three fields. The mud's ankle deep in places."

"There's a spare bed in my room."

"Whose?"

"Lieutenant Hart's."

"The one who was shot down over Holland?"

"Lieutenant Morse told me Hart has an ulcer."

Madigan looked at him for a moment before replying. "Then let's keep it an ulcer."

"I don't get it."

"Lieutenant Morse isn't really a fighter pilot," said Madigan. "He's a movie star, playing the role of fighter pilot in this billion-dollar movie Eisenhower is producing."

"You mean he doesn't like talking about casualties?"

Before Madigan could reply the loudspeaker was putting out a call for the Duty Officer.

Farebrother said, "It's room three in house number eleven. Dump your things in there and wait till you're kicked out. That's what I would do."

Madigan slapped Farebrother on the shoulder. "Farebrother, you are not only the greatest pilot since Daedalus, you're a prince!" Madigan repeated this to the waiter when he arrived with the coffee and cake.

"I'm sure you're right, Captain Madigan," said the waiter. "And thanks for the toy planes."

"Aircraft-recognition models," Madigan explained when the old man had gone. "What do I need them for in the PR office? He's giving a party for the village children next week."

"You're a regular Robin Hood," said Farebrother. He gave up the attempt to write to his mother and began to drink his coffee.

Madigan remained standing, searching his pockets anxiously as if he was looking for something to give Farebrother. "Look," he said as he relinquished the search, "I can't find my notebook right now, but you haven't made any plans for Christmas, have you?"

"I figured we might be flying."

"Even the sparrows will be walking, Farebrother. Look at that stuff out there. You don't need to have majored in science to know that the Eighth Air Force birdmen are going to be having a drunken Christmas."

"And what about the Public Relations Officers? What kind of Christmas are they going to be having?"

"London is a dump," said Madigan, sitting down on the sofa and giving Farebrother enough time to consider this judgment. "And over Christmas, London will be packed with big spenders. Not much tail there for a captain without flying pay." Self-consciously, he touched the top of his large bony head. There wasn't much hair left there and he pushed it about to make the most of it. "I've got the use of a beautiful house in Cambridge over the holidays. See, Farebrother, I was determined to get out of this hellhole." He smiled. It was an engaging smile that revealed large perfect white teeth and emphasized his square jaw. "You stick with me, pal. I'll fix us up with the most beautiful girls in England."

"What about your engagement?" said Farebrother, more to be provocative than because he wanted to know.

"The other night . . . what I said on the truck, you mean?" He leaned forward and smiled at his mud-caked shoes. "Hell, that was never really serious. And like I say, London is too far to go for it." He drank some coffee and patted his lips dry with a paper towel—a delicate gesture inappropriate to a two-hundred-pound man built like a prizefighter. "I fall in love with these broads, I'm sentimental, that's always been my trouble."

"I'm glad you told me," said Farebrother. "I would never have figured that out."

Madigan grinned and drank more coffee. "Two of the most beautiful broads you ever saw . . ." He paused before adding, "And fuck it, Farebrother, you can pick the one you want." He looked up as if expecting Farebrother to be overcome by this selfless offer. "One thing I'll say, buddy, you'll never be sorry you fixed me up with a decent place to sleep."

Farebrother nodded, although he was already having doubts.

It took Captain Vincent Madigan the rest of the day to move into 3/11. He had water-soaked possessions stored all over the base as well as an electric record player and a small collection of opera recordings that he brought from his office. The musical equipment was placed on the floor to make room for a chest of drawers Madigan had obtained in exchange for cigarettes. The top of the chest was reserved for Madigan's photographs. Apart from a picture of his mother, they were all of young women, framed in wood, leather, and even silver, and all inscribed with affirmations of unquenchable passion.

Farebrother re-examined Vince Madigan. He was a burly, amiable-looking man with thin hair whose nose was blunt and wide like his mouth. Although seldom seen wearing them, he needed eyeglasses to read the print on his record labels. Was this really the man who had won declarations of love from such beautiful young women? And yet who could doubt it, for Vince Madigan did not treat the photos like trophies. He never boasted of his exploits. On the contrary, it was his style to tell the world how badly the opposite sex treated his altruistic offers of love. By Vince's account he had always been unlucky in love.

"I'm just not any good with women," he told Farebrother that evening while turning over a record, and totally disregarding the pounding noises coming from the unmusical occupants of the next room. "I tell them not to get serious . . ." He shrugged at the perversity of human nature. "But they always get serious. Why not just be friendly, I say, but they want to get married. So I say okay, I want to get married, and wham—they change their mind and just want to be friends." He used a cloth to clean the record. "Sometimes I think I'll never understand women. Sometimes I think these goddamned homos have got something, buddy."

"Is that right," said Farebrother, who hadn't been listening. He'd been reading and rereading the same passage of the P-51 handling notes. Under it there was tucked a thick wad of regulations, technical amendments, orders, and local restrictions. Reading it all through and committing it to memory would be a daunting task. "I'm not sure I'll be through learning all this stuff by Christmas, Vince."

"You're too darn conscientious, buddy. Who else in this Group, except maybe Colonel Dan, has waded through all that junk?"

"I'm a new boy, Vince. They'll be expecting me to screw it up." He riffed through the pages. "And to think I quit law school to get away from this kind of reading!"

"Man can't escape his fate, Farebrother."

"How's that?" said Farebrother, puzzled by the tone of Madigan's voice.

"Man can't escape his fate," said Madigan. He was smiling, but in his eyes there was a look that told Farebrother that this was the kind of joke that isn't a joke. "Isn't that what Mozart is saying in *Don Giovanni?* Every one of us is trying to be some other kind of person—your pal Morse, for instance—in fact, half the guys who joined the Army just wanted to escape from themselves."

"What have you got against MM?"

"Aw, he's just a pain in the ass, Jamie." He put the record on the turntable but didn't start the music. "Each new officer who checks in, I give him a questionnaire so I get parents' names and addresses and details of any relatives who work in newspapers or radio. It also has spaces marked 'Education,' 'Hobbies,' and 'Civilian occupation.' You know—you filled one out. It's only so I can use it for publicity. Morse fills his out to say he's got a degree in engineering from Arizona State. You've only got to talk to the guy to know he never finished college . . ."

"He knows a lot about engines."

"Sure. His folks have a filling station."

"Okay, but . . ."

"I don't give a damn about where he went to college. I'm no kind of snob, Farebrother. A girl helped to pay my way through college . . . a woman she was, really, married and all. Ten years older than me. We ran away to New York and lived in a tenement on Tenth Street on her alimony while I got my degree in English at NYU." He rubbed his face. "I paid her the money back eventually, but I guess she thought we were going to get married and live happily ever after."

"So you suspect MM didn't finish college, so what?"

"So why the hell can't he say so? And if he tells lies about that, why does he get mad when the Intelligence Officers question his claims?"

"Now wait a minute, Vince. The board decides claims on the basis of the film he brings back."

Madigan put up both hands in a placatory gesture and changed the nature of his complaints. "I take a cockpit photo of every new pilot, right? I send a glossy to his hometown paper and a release to anyone who might be remotely interested. I did that with you last week—my sergeant already sent a pile of junk off. In a few weeks' time one of your friends or neighbors, or your folks, will send you some cuttings. You'll show them around, and before you've got them back in the envelope MM will be in my office asking why you're getting the publicity and he isn't. Can't you see how that pisses me off?"

"Take it easy, Vince."

Madigan gave the record a flick of his cloth and checked the needle for dust. "Morse is a Mozartian character," he said while bending down to look along the surface of the record. "Running away from himself, searching for something he can't even describe."

"Let's hear more of *The Abduction*, Vince."

For the first time Madigan heard a note of annoyance in his roommate's voice. He should have known better than talk about Morse; these pilots always stuck together against the rest of the officers. He smiled and read the label again. "Listen to the way Constanze's recitative builds up to the word *Traurigkeit* and Mozart goes into a minor key to change the mood. To me, this is one of the most moving arias in opera. It's wonderful!"

"How did you learn so much about opera, Vince?"

Madigan folded his arms and looked up at the ceiling as he thought about it. "My first newspaper job after leaving college, they sent me to interview this girl who'd won a scholarship to Juilliard. She was a wonderful girl, Jamie." Madigan turned on the music and sat down to listen, eyes closed.

Farebrother went back to reading his papers and for almost another hour Madigan played his records, sorted through his newly assembled possessions, and said hardly anything. Farebrother decided he was deeply offended, but eventually Madigan's spirits revived enough for him to say, "I've just had a thought, old buddy. How's about this one for you?" He was wearing his glasses and holding up a photo for Farebrother to look at. "A tall brunette with big tits, gets drunk on lemonade."

"You don't owe me anything, Vince."

"Very loving, Jamie. Very passionate." He looked at the photo to help him remember her. "Unattached; no husband or boyfriends to worry about."

Farebrother turned the page in the P-51 handbook to find that "Ditching Procedure" was headed with the warning that the aircraft could be expected to sink in "approximately two seconds," and shook his head.

"What about her for your pal, the banana-boat captain?"

"Charlie would like her, yes."

"I invited the PX officer too. Is that okay with you? See, we'll need the liquor and candy and cigarettes."

"It's not my party, Vince."

"Our party, sure. You don't have to do a thing except be there." He put the record away in its paper sleeve. "I invited Colonel Dan too, just out of politeness, but I don't imagine he'll turn up."

"How many people are you expecting?"

"I should have kept a list."

"Maybe I'll volunteer for OD."

"Don't be like that," said Madigan. "This is going to be the greatest party of all time." He slid the record into the carrying case in which he stored his recordings. "Victoria Cooper!" he said suddenly, and snapped his fingers in the air. "Intellectual, Jamie. Very English, very upper-class. Dark hair and a beautiful face. Exactly your type—tall and a wonderful figure. Victoria! You'll be crazy about her."

"Is she another one of your sentimental indiscretions?"

"I've hardly said a word to her, she's a friend of Vera's. I told you about Vera, didn't I?"

"Take it easy, Vince," said Farebrother nervously.

"You could be the first person there, Jamie. Victoria Cooper—I'm sure Vera could swing a double date for us."

"Knock it off, Vince, will you? I go along with the opera and all that, but stay out of my private life, huh?"

"You said there were no women in your life . . . What do you mean, you 'go along' with the opera? You're not telling me you don't like Mozart?"

"I can take him or leave him, Vince. I've always been a Dorsey fan myself."

"That's dance music." Madigan's mouth dropped open and he seemed truly shaken. "Christ, I thought at last I'd found a real pal in this dump, a guy I could talk to."

"Only kidding, Vince."

Madigan recovered from his state of shock. "Jesus, I thought you were serious for a minute." He smiled to show his perfect teeth. "You wait until you see this girl Victoria Cooper . . . and she'll go for you too. She lives with her parents, that's why I'm not interested." He took off his glasses and put them into a leather case. "My dad practically threw me out of the house because of my girlfriends. Mom never seemed to mind. It's funny that women never seem to mind their sons tomcatting around. It's almost like they get some kind of kick out of it.'

Victoria Cooper

Victoria was the private secretary to a newspaper owner. The newspaper was a local one, appeared only once a week, and since newsprint was scarce and rationed, consisted of only eight pages, but she enjoyed this job that gave her access to the teleprinter news and the excitement of meeting men who'd come from far-distant battlefronts. She was updating the wall map when Vera came in. "American forces, supported by Australian warships, have secured a firm beach-head on the south coast of New Britain." She found an appropriate stretch of coastline and inserted a pin.

"I've brought your tea, Miss Cooper."

"That's kind of you, Vera." Her visitor was a trim vivacious woman with short curly hair dyed blond. She was no longer a girl and yet her freckles and snub nose gave her a youthful tom-boy look that appealed to men, if the reaction of the office staff was anything to judge by.

"I had to come upstairs anyway." Vera brandished a handful of press photos before dropping them into the tray on the desk, re-arranging some papers there to make a reason for delay. "A friend of mine has been lent a wonderful house for Christmas. It's in Jesus Lane. You should see it—central heating, carpets, and little table lights everywhere. It's the sort of place you see in films . . . romantic, you know."

"Lucky you, Vera."

"He's an American, a captain. Drink your tea, Miss Cooper. Captain Vincent Madigan, Vince I call him. He's tall and strong and very handsome. He looks like Pat O'Brien, the film star . . . and talks like him too."

"It sounds as if you're smitten."

"Nothing like that," said Vera hastily. "Just friends. I feel sorry for those American boys, so far away from their homes and families." She picked up some photos and pretended to look at them. "I said I'd take a few friends along to their party at Christmas. You told me your parents will be away, so I wondered . . ."

"I don't think so, Vera." She'd been introduced to the American friend once, picking Vera up at the office, and wondered whether Vera had forgotten that or if she just enjoyed describing him again.

"It's Christmas, Miss Cooper," Vera coaxed. "I'm calling in to see them on my way home. Since it's only round the corner I thought you might come with me—I'd rather not go on my own. They have wonderful coffee, and gorgeous chocolate . . . candy, they call it."

"Yes, so I've heard," said Victoria. It was a patronizing remark and Vera recognized it for what it was. Hurriedly, she gathered up some pay slips she was delivering to the cashier and turned to go.

And since Victoria didn't want to be rude to this genial woman, who would think it was because of her accent, or because she hadn't been to university, she said, "I'll go with you, Vera—I'd enjoy a break. But I mustn't be too late home. I have to wash my hair."

Vera gave a little shriek of delight, a sound borrowed no doubt from some Hollywood starlet. "Oh, I'm so pleased, Miss Cooper. It will be nice—he'll have a friend with him . . . to help with the decorations and that," she added too quickly.

"Am I what they call a 'blind date,' Vera?"

Vera smiled guiltily but didn't admit as much. "They're ever so nice . . . real gentlemen, Miss Cooper."

"I hope you won't go on calling me Miss Cooper all evening."

"See you at six o'clock, Victoria."

Victoria could see why Vera was so impressed with the house the Americans were using. It was both elegant and comfortable, furnished with good, but neglected, antique furniture, well-worn Persian carpets, and some nineteenth-century Dutch watercolors. The bookcases were empty except for the odd piece of porcelain. She guessed the place belonged to some tutor or fellow of the University now gone off to war. The current tenancy of the Americans was unmistakable, however. There were pieces of sports equipment—golf clubs, tennis rackets, even a baseball glove—in various corners of the room and brightly colored boxes of groceries, tinned food, and cartons of cigarettes on the hall table.

She had arrived at Jesus Lane with some misgivings, half expecting to meet the predatory primitives her mother believed most American servicemen to be. She wouldn't have been greatly surprised to find half a dozen hairy-chested men sitting around a card table in their underwear, smoking cheap cigars and playing poker for money. The reality couldn't have been more different.

Captain Madigan and his younger friend were wearing their well-cut uniforms, sitting in the drawing room listening to Mozart. Both men were sprawled in the relaxed way only Americans seemed to adopt—legs stretched straight before them and heads sunk so low in the cushions that they had difficulty getting to their feet to greet their visitors.

Vincent Madigan acknowledged that they'd met before, remembering the time and place with such ease that she had little doubt that the invitation had originated with him. "I'm glad you dropped by," said Madigan, keeping to the pretense that Victoria was there only by chance. He stopped the music. "Let me introduce Captain James Farebrother." They nodded to each other. Madigan said, "Let me fix you ladies a drink. Martini, Vera? What about you, Miss Cooper?" He leaned over to read the bottle labels. "Scotch, gin, port, something called oloroso—looks like it's been around some time—or a martini with Vera?" His voice was unexpectedly low, contrived almost, and his accent strong enough for her to have some difficulty understanding him.

"A martini. Thank you."

James Farebrother offered them cigarettes and then asked permission to smoke. It was all so formal that Victoria almost started giggling. She caught Farebrother's eye and made it an opportunity to smile. He grinned back.

Farebrother was a little taller than his friend but not so broad. His hair was cut very short in a style she'd seen only in Hollywood films. She guessed him to be about her own age—twenty-five. Both men were muscular and athletic, but Madigan's strength was that of the boxing ring or football field, while Farebrother had the springy grace of a runner.

"You must be the Mozart lover?" she said.

"No. Vince is the opera buff. I just beat time."

His uniform was obviously made to order and she noticed that, unlike Vince Madigan's, his tie was of silk. Was it a gift from girlfriend or mother, or a revelation of some secret vanity?

"We'll eat at a little Italian spot down the street," Madigan announced as he served the drinks. "They do a great veal scaloppine . . . as good as any I've had back home in Minneapolis."

It was a bizarre recommendation and the temptation to laugh was almost uncontrollable. Madigan mistook Victoria's amusement for indignation. Self-consciously he ran a hand over his bony skull to arrange his hair and backed away, almost spilling his drink as he blundered into the sofa. "Okay," he said. "Okay. I know what you British think about Mussolini and all that, and you're right, Victoria."

"It's not that," said Victoria. She glanced at Vera, who was rummaging through the sports equipment. It was all right for her, she had short curly hair that always looked right, but Victoria was appalled at the thought of going to a smart restaurant wearing the dowdy sweater set she often wore at the office, and with her hair in a tangle.

"Look at all this equipment," said Vera, waving a baseball-gloved hand. "Have you boys come over to fight a war, or just for the summer Olympics?"

"We'll go to the Blue Boar," said Madigan. "That would be much better."

"No . . . please," said Victoria. "Keep to your original plan, I'm sure it will be wonderful, but I really do have to get home."

"Please don't go, Victoria," said Farebrother. "There's plenty of food right here in the house. Why don't we all just have some ham and eggs?" His accent was softer and less pronounced than Madigan's.

"Oh, Victoria!" said Vera. "You don't really hate Italians, do you?"

"Of course not," said Victoria. She watched her friend silently acting out tennis strokes with one of the new rackets she'd taken out of its cover. There was no mistaking the disappointment in her eyes—Vera loved restaurants; she'd often said so. "You and Vince go—don't let me spoil your evening."

"We won't be long," Vera promised softly. She became a different person in the company of men, not just in that way all women do, but animated and amusing. Victoria looked at her with new interest. She was older than Victoria, thirty or more, but there was no denying that she was the more attractive to most men. Her critics at the office, and there was no shortage of them, said Vera fed the egos of men, that she was doting and compliant, but Victoria knew that wasn't so; Vera was challenging and contentious, ready to mock the priorities and values of a masculine world. And certainly the war provided her with ample opportunities to do so.

Now she looked in a mirror to pat her curly yellow hair and pout long enough to apply lipstick. "We won't be long," she repeated, still looking in the mirror. It was an appeal as much as a declaration—she wanted Vince Madigan all to herself across that restaurant table. She turned to exchange glances with Victoria and saw that the idea of an hour with James Farebrother was not unattractive to her; the alternative was going home to her parents' chilly mansion in Royston Road.

"I'll cook something here," said Victoria. The promise was to Vera as well as to James Farebrother.

"That's great," he said. "Let me freshen that drink and I'll show you the kitchen."

The other two left with almost unseemly haste, and Victoria

began to unpack the groceries the officers had brought from the Commissary. It was a breathtaking sight for anyone who had spent four long years in wartime Britain. There were tins of ham and butter, tins of fruit and juice, biscuits, cigarettes, and cream. There were even a dozen fresh eggs that Madigan had obtained from Hobday's Farm near the airfield. "I've never seen so much wonderful food," said Victoria.

"You sound like my sister opening her presents on Christmas morning," said Farebrother. He started the music again but lowered the volume.

"The ration is down to one egg a week. And that tin of butter would be about four months' ration." He smiled at her and she said, "I'm afraid we've all become obsessed with food. When the war's over, perhaps we'll regain a sense of proportion."

"But meanwhile we'll feast on . . ." He picked up some tins. "Ham and eggs and sweet corn and spaghetti in Bolognese sauce. Unless, of course, your embargo on things Italian is all-embracing, in which case we'll ceremonially break Captain Madigan's *Rigoletto* recordings."

"I don't hate Italians . . ."

He put his hand on her arm and said, "Strictly between you and me, Victoria, the Italian cuisine in Minneapolis is terrible."

She smiled. "I really don't have any . . ."

"I know. You simply don't have a thing to wear and you think your hair is a mess."

She put up a hand to her hair.

"I'm sorry," he said. "I was only kidding, your hair looks great."

"How did you guess why I didn't want to go?"

"Vicky, I've heard every possible excuse for being stood up."

"I find that difficult to believe." No one had ever called her Vicky before, but coming from this handsome American it sounded right. "Can you find a tin opener and cut up some ham?"

While she warmed the frying pan and sliced bread, she watched him opening tins. He hurt his finger; clumsiness was a surprising shortcoming in such a man. "You're a flyer?"

"P-51s, Mustang fighter planes." He reached across her to get a knife from the drawer, and when his hand touched her bare arm, she shivered.

"Escorting the bombers?"

"You seem well informed." He used the knife to loosen the ham from the tin.

"I work in a newspaper office."

"I didn't know the British newspapers ever mentioned the American air forces." He looked up. "I'm sorry. I didn't mean it to sound that way."

"Our papers do give most attention to the RAF—it's only natural when so many readers have relatives who . . ." She stopped.

"Sure," he said. He shook the tin of ham violently until the meat slid out onto the plate.

"How many raids have you been on?"

"None," he said. "I just arrived. I guess I was a little premature in feeling neglected."

"The weather's been bad. How many eggs may I use?"

"Vince gets them by the truckload. Use them all if you like."

"Two each then." She cracked the eggs into the hot fat.

"We need clear skies for daylight bombing. The RAF have magic gadgets that help them see in the dark, but we only fly by day." He arranged the sliced ham on the plates.

"But in daylight, with clear skies . . . doesn't it make it easy for the Germans to shoot you down?" She pretended to be fully involved spooning fat over the frying eggs, but she knew he was looking at her.

"That's why they have us fighters."

"What about the antiaircraft guns?"

"I guess they're still working on that problem," he said, and grinned. Abruptly the music from the next room came to an end. He reached out to her. "Victoria, you're the only . . ." He gently took her shoulders to embrace her. She gave him a quick kiss on the nose and ducked away.

"I'll turn Mozart over," she said. "You bring the plates to the table."

They sat in the cramped kitchen to eat their meal. He poured two glasses of American beer and was amused to encourage Victoria to spread butter thickly on her bread. He hardly touched his food. Victoria told him about her job and about her silver-tongued cousin who had recently become personal assistant to a Member of Parliament. He told her about his wonderful sister who was married to an alcoholic bar owner. She told him about the caraway-seed cakes with which her mother won annual prizes at the Women's Institute competition. He told her about Amelia Earhart arriving at the Oakland airport in January 1935, solo from Honolulu, and how it made him determined to fly. At the age of fourteen he'd been permitted to take over the control wheel of a huge Ford tri-motor, owned in part by a close friend of his father.

There's so much to say when you're falling in love, and so much to listen to. They wanted to tell each other everything they had ever said, thought, or done. Their worlds were in collision. Victoria was overwhelmed by the magic of a bewildering people who dressed their humblest officers like generals, ate corn while leaving eggs and ham untouched, invented nylon stockings, and allowed their children to fly airliners.

"Vince says every one of us has two faces; he keeps trying to prove that everything Mozart wrote is based on that idea."

What had he been about to say? she wondered. Victoria, you are the only one for me. Victoria, you are the only girl I could ever marry. Victoria, you are the only girl in England who can't fry four fresh eggs without breaking the yolks of two of them. She coveted the ones abandoned on his plate and wished she'd kept the unbroken ones for herself.

"Not just the dressing up they do in the operas, but the music that comments on each character."

"Are you both opera fans?"

"If anyone could turn me off, it would be Vince."

She smiled. "He's intense—Vera told me that. Does everyone in Minneapolis have that sort of accent? At times it's hard for me to understand just what he's saying."

"Vince has moved around—New York, Memphis, New Orleans. He says that women like men with low, slow-spoken voices."

She looked at the clock. Time had passed so quickly. "I must go. My parents are away and there is so much I have to do before Christmas."

"Vince and Vera will have gone dancing."

She stood up; she knew she had to leave before . . . and suppose Vera came back and found her here?

"Don't go, please," he said.

"Yes, or it will spoil."

"What will spoil?"

"This. Us."

In the hallway she resisted his embrace until he pointed to the huge bunch of mistletoe tied to the overhead light. Then she kissed him and hung on as if he was the only life belt in a stormy sea. She was desperate that he wouldn't ask when he might see her again, but just as she was on the point of humiliating herself with that question, he said, "I've got to see you again, Vicky. Soon."

"At the party."

"It's not soon enough, but I guess it'll have to do!"

Such mad infatuations don't last forever. The greater the madness, the shorter its duration—or so she told herself the following morning. Was she already a little more level-headed, and was this a measure of the limited enchantment of the handsome young American who had come into her life?

"It's all right for you," said Vera trenchantly, when Victoria made a harmless joke about the lateness of her return. "You're young." She smoothed her dress over hips that a stodgy wartime diet had already made heavy. "I'm twenty-nine."

Victoria said nothing. Vera pouted and said, "Thirty-two, if I'm to be perfectly honest with you." She fingered the gold chain she always wore around her neck and twisted it onto her finger. "My hubby is much older than me." She always referred to her absent husband as her "hubby." It was as if she found the word "husband" too formal and too binding. "Who knows when I'll see him again, Victoria." She ignored the possibility that her husband might be killed. "It will be ages before they're back from Burma. Do you know where Burma is, Victoria? It's on the other side of the world. I looked it up on a map. What am I supposed to do? I might be forty by the time Reg gets back. I'll be too old to have any fun."

Victoria wondered how long she'd keep pretending that Vince Madigan was no more than a good friend. She sympathized. How could she tell poor wretched Vera to cloister herself for a husband who might never return? Yet she could never encourage her to betray him either. "I really can't advise you, Vera," she said.

"It's *unbearable* being on my own all the time," Vera said, almost apologetically. "That's why I married my Reg in the first place —I was lonely." She gave a croaky little laugh. "That's a good one, isn't it?" She twisted the gold chain until it was biting into her throat. "Little did I know I was going to be left all on my own within two years of getting hitched. I was 'in service' when I was fifteen. With the Countess of Invessnade. I started as a kitchen help and ended as a lady's maid. You should have seen the shoes she had,

Victoria. Dozens of pairs . . . and handbags from Paris. I was happy there."

"Then why did you leave?"

"The government said domestics had to be in war jobs. Not that I know what I'm doing to win the war here, helping the cashier with the wages and getting tea for all those lazy reporters."

"Don't be sad," Victoria said. "It's Christmas Eve."

Vera nodded and smiled, but didn't look any happier. "You're coming with me tonight, aren't you?"

"I have to go home to change first." She tried to keep her voice level—she didn't want to reveal how eager she was to see Jamie again —but Vera's shrewd eyes saw through her.

"What are you wearing?" Vera asked briskly. "A long dress?"

"My mother's yellow silk, I had it altered. The sister of that girl in the personnel office did it. She shortened it, made big floppy sleeves from what she'd taken off the bottom, and put a tie-belt on it."

"Vince must be sick of seeing me in that green dress," Vera said. "But I've got nothing else. He's offered to buy me something, but I've got no ration coupons."

"You look wonderful in the green dress, Vera." It was true, she did.

"Vince is trying to wangle me a parachute. A whole parachute! Vince says they're pure silk, but even if they're nylon it would be something!" She picked up the outgoing mail from the tray as if suddenly remembering her work. "Victoria," she asked in a low voice as if the answer was really important to her. "Do you hate parties?"

"I'm sure it will be lovely, Vera," she answered evasively, for the truth of it was that she did hate parties.

"They'll all be strangers. Vince has invited lots of men from the base and they'll have girls with them. There's no telling who might see me there . . . and start tongues wagging."

"Cross that bridge when you come to it," Victoria advised. So Vera didn't realize that her extramarital associations were already a subject for endless discussion in the typist pool downstairs. Vera wears the new utility underpants, Victoria had overheard a girl say; one Yank and they're off. The others had laughed.

Vera stood in the doorway looking at her friend quizzically. "You never cry, do you? I can't imagine you crying."

"I'm not the crying type," Victoria said. "I swear instead."

Vera nodded. "All you girls who've been to university swear," she said, and smiled. "I won't wait for you tonight, I'll go on ahead. I know what Vince is like. If I'm not there and he sees some other girl he fancies, he'll grab her."

Victoria could think of no reassuring answer.

The noise could be heard from as far away as the river. There were taxis outside the door as well as an RAF officer holding a fur coat and handbag for some absent girl.

Victoria didn't have to knock at the door. She'd raised her hand to the brass knocker when the caretaker swung the door open, spilling some of his whiskey as he swept back the curtain. "Quickly, miss, careful of the blackout." He said it carefully, but his smile and unfocused eyes betrayed his drunkenness.

The house was obviously packed with people. Some of the table lights had been broken, others shielded with colored paper, but there was enough light to see that the drawing room had become a dance floor. Couples were crowded together too tightly to do anything but hug rhythmically in the semi-darkness.

Among the American uniforms she could see a few RAF officers and some Polish pilots. Men without girls were seated on the stairs, drinking from bottles and arguing about the coming invasion and what was happening "back home." There were low wolf whistles and appreciative growls as Victoria climbed the stairs, picking her way between the men. More than one fondled her legs under the pretense of steadying her.

She found Jamie and Vince Madigan on the next landing, trying to revive a female guest who'd lost consciousness after drinking too much of a mixture that had cherries and dried mint floating in it. Described as fruit punch, it smelled like medicinal alcohol sweetened with honey. Victoria decided not to drink any of it.

"She needs air," Vera said, appearing from another room. "Take her downstairs and out into the street." Vera seemed to be in command. Although she was always saying how much she hated crowds and parties, she thrived on them.

"She's Boogie's girlfriend," explained Jamie. "He's a pilot . . . the one playing the piano downstairs." Victoria took his arm, but he seemed too busy to notice. Vera smiled to indicate how much she liked Victoria's very pale yellow dress, and both women watched dispassionately as two officers in brown leather flying jackets carried the limp girl downstairs with more enthusiasm than tenderness. The men on the stairs hummed the Funeral March as the unfortunate casualty was bundled away.

"Did you invite all these people?" Victoria asked.

Jamie shook his head. "They're mostly friends of Vince, as well as a few who wandered in off the street. What are you drinking?"

"Not the fruit punch." Was it too much to expect that he would notice her hair, swept back into a chignon, and the high-neckline dress with its standing collar and the tiny black bow?

"Whiskey okay?" He was pouring it before she could answer, and then he stuck the bottle back into the side pocket of his uniform jacket. His eyes were bright and restless as he kept looking around to see who else was there. He wasn't drunk, but she guessed he'd started drinking early that day. "How's that?" He held up the half-filled glass of whiskey.

Victoria had never drunk undiluted whiskey before, but she didn't want to give him any reason for leaving her. Even while they stood there, she was continually being patted and stroked by men who passed, looking for food or drink or the bathroom. "It's lovely," she said, and brought the whiskey to her lips without drinking any. It had a curious smell.

He noticed her sniffing at it. "Bourbon," he explained. "It's made from corn."

He was watching her; she tasted her drink and thought it smelled remarkably like damp cardboard. "Delicious," she said.

"I can see that you go for it," Jamie mocked.

Victoria smiled. He still hadn't kissed her, but at least there was no sign of any other girl with him. He pulled her closer to make way for an American naval officer who was elbowing his way to the bathroom. Finding it locked, he hammered on the door and yelled, "Hurry up in there! This is an emergency!" Someone laughed, and a man sitting on the next staircase said, "He's got a girl in there with him. I'd try the one upstairs if you're in a hurry, Mac." The sailor cursed and hurried upstairs past him.

Victoria looked at Jamie, trying to enjoy the party. "Are most of them from your squadron?"

"That's Colonel Dan over there. He's the Group Commander, the big cheese himself."

Victoria looked around to see a short cheerful man with a large nose and messy fair hair talking earnestly to a tall dark girl with a floral-patterned turban hat and a black velvet cocktail dress.

"Is that his wife?"

"She's one of the chorus from the Windmill Theatre. They gave a show on base last month . . . before I got here."

"Was it an American general who said war is hell?"

"And that's Major Tucker." The major was standing near the stairs drinking from his own silver hip flask and scowling disapproval. Victoria felt a common bond with him but did not say so.

Jamie tightened his hold on her shoulder, but only in order to pull her aside to make way for a middle-aged sergeant who was carrying a case of gin upstairs and into a room that was being converted into a bar. "Thanks for the invite, Captain," said the sergeant, out of breath.

"Good to see you here, Sergeant Boyer," said Jamie.

Harry Boyer's arrival with the gin was greeted by loud cheers. Downstairs, Boogie and the musicians he'd collected for tonight began to play "Bless 'Em All," to which the dancers jumped up and down in unison.

"You hate it, Vicky. I can tell by your face."

"No," she yelled, "it's really fun." By now the whole house was shaking with the vibration of the dancers downstairs. "But is there anywhere to sit down?" Her yellow shoes had never been particularly comfortable, and she'd slipped them from her heels for a moment.

"Let's try downstairs," Jamie said, and plunged into the crowd. She tried to follow, but with drink in one hand and shoes loosened she couldn't keep up with him. One shoe came off, and only with some difficulty could she get everyone to stand back far enough for her to find it again. When she did, there was the black mark of a boot across the yellow silk, and one strap torn loose. They were the last pair of pre-war shoes in her wardrobe. She told herself to laugh, or at least keep her sense of proportion, but she wanted to scream.

"If you hate it, say so," said Jamie sharply as she reached him at the bottom of the stairs.

She wondered what would happen if she did tell him how unhappy she was, and decided not to take the chance. "Why don't we dance?" she said. At least she'd feel his arms around her.

If she was trying to find the limit to James Farebrother's skills and talents, inviting him to dance provided it. Even in that crush, with the tireless Boogie playing his own dreamy version of "Moonlight Becomes You," Jamie trod on her toes—especially painful as she'd decided to dance in stockinged feet rather than risk the final destruction of her shoes.

"I'm no great shakes at dancing," he said finally. "Maybe we should call it quits."

He found a place on the sofa, but they'd only been sitting there a few minutes when a lieutenant arrived with a message asking Jamie to go upstairs to help Vince. Jamie offered her his apologies, but she feared he was secretly pleased to get away from her. She regretted her flash of bad temper, but she'd so wanted the evening to be perfect.

"Promise you won't move?" Jamie squeezed her arm. She nodded and he planted a kiss on her forehead as though she were a docile infant.

The newly arrived lieutenant dropped heavily into the place Jamie had vacated beside her. "Known Jamie long?"

She looked at him. He was a handsome boy trying to grow a mustache. He had a suntanned sort of complexion, with jet-black wavy hair and long sideburns that completed the Latin effect for which he obviously strove. "Yes, I've known Jamie a long time," she said.

He smiled to reveal flashing white teeth. His battered cap was still on his head, but he pushed it well back as if to see her better. He was chewing gum and smoking at the same time. He took the cigarette from his mouth and flicked it toward the fireplace without bothering to look where it went. "Jamie only just arrived in Europe," he said. "My name's Morse, people call me Mickey Mouse."

Victoria smiled and said nothing.

"So you're a liar. Slow dissolve."

"And you are no gentleman."

He slapped his thigh and laughed. "Are you ever right, lady."

They were crushed tight together, and although she tried to make more room between them, it wasn't possible.

"Gum?"

"No, thanks."

"Where did Jamie meet a classy broad like you?" he asked. "You're not the kind of lady who hangs around the Red Cross Club on Trumpington Street."

"Really?"

"*Rilly*! Yes, *rilly*."

"I'm surprised you've never noticed me there," said Victoria.

MM grinned and tore the corner from a pack of Camels before offering them to her. She never smoked, but on impulse took one. He lit it for her. "You Jamie's girl?"

"Yes." It seemed the simplest way of avoiding further advances. "What's happened to Captain Madigan?"

"Nothing's happened to Captain Madigan, lady, and nothing is going to happen to him. Vince is smart—he's a paddlefoot. He stays on the ground and waltzes the ladies, we're the dummies who get our tails shot off."

"I mean, what's happened now?" said Victoria. "What does he want Jamie for?" She inhaled on the cigarette and it made her cough.

"Madigan needs close escort," said MM vaguely.

Victoria got to her feet and looked for the door.

"Lights! Action! Camera!" said MM, holding thumbs and forefingers as if to frame a camera shot. "Where are you going, lady?"

"I'm going," said Victoria, "to what you Americans so delicately call the powder room."

"I'll save the place here for you."

"Please don't bother," said Victoria. MM chuckled.

She made her way past the musicians and started up the stairs. A lot of drinking had taken place since the last time she'd struggled up through the people sitting on the staircase. They were mostly couples now, locked in tight embraces and oblivious to her pushing past them.

On the upper landing there were two officers sprawled full-length and snoring loudly. A girl was going through the pockets of one of them. She straightened up when she saw Victoria. "I'm just trying to find enough for my taxi fare home, love," she announced in the broad accent of south London.

Victoria stepped past without replying. The middle-aged man whom Jamie had called Sergeant Boyer was leaning against the wall inside the first room. He was in his shirt sleeves and wore no tie. He was watching Colonel Dan about to throw a pair of dice against the wall. There was a huge pile of pound notes on the floor and as her eyes became accustomed to the gloom Victoria could see that there were other men there too, all holding wads of money.

"Come on, baby," Colonel Dan yelled into the confines of his clenched fist before throwing the dice. "Snake eyes!" he screamed as they came to rest. There was pandemonium all around, and Victoria was almost knocked off her feet as the Colonel stooped to pick up the dice and lost his balance to fall against her. "Ooops, sorry, ma'am."

She found Jamie on the next floor. He was holding tightly to the bare upper arms of a brassy-looking girl in a shiny gray dress that was cut too low in the front and too tight across the bottom. "You've got to be sensible," Jamie was telling her. "There's no sense in making a scene. These things happen, it's the war."

The girl's eye makeup had smudged with her tears and there were streaks of black down her cheeks. "For Christ's sake, spare me that," she said bitterly. "You bloody Yanks don't have to tell *me* about the war. We were bombed out of my mum's house years before Pearl bloody Harbor."

Vince Madigan was there wearing a short Ike jacket complete with a row of medals and silver wings. He too was trying to reason with the tearful girl. "Let me walk you to Market Hill . . . we'll find a cab and get you home."

The girl ignored him. To Jamie she said, "You think I'm drunk, don't you?"

From downstairs there came some spirited rebel yells, and the piano struck up the resounding chords of "Dixie." Suddenly Jamie noticed Victoria watching them. "Oh, Victoria!" he said.

"Oh, Victoria," parroted the girl. "Whatever have you done with poor Prince Albert?" She gave a short bitter laugh.

Jamie let go of the girl and turned to Victoria, smiling as if in apology. "It's one of Vince's friends," he explained quietly. "She's threatening to tear Vera to pieces." From downstairs came a chorus of joyful voices: "In Dixie land, I'll take my stand, to live and dieeee in Dixie . . ."

Vince Madigan moved closer to the girl in the gray dress and began talking to her softly, in the manner prescribed for an excited horse. Now that the light was on her she looked no more than eighteen, younger perhaps. The desperate stare had gone now; she was just a sad child. She raised a large red hand to stifle a belch.

"Or was it you who invited one girl too many?" said Victoria coldly.

"She's not my type," said Jamie amiably.

Over Jamie's shoulder Victoria saw Madigan take the girl in a tight embrace and caress her hungrily. Victoria turned to avoid Jamie's kiss. "Not now," she said, "not here."

"I think I need a drink," Jamie said, standing back from her. "I've had about as much as I can take for one day."

"*You* have!" said Victoria angrily.

"I didn't mean enough of you."

"Would you take me home?"

"Wait just a few minutes more," said Jamie. "My buddy Charlie Stigg still might get here. I told you I'd invited him."

"Then I'll go home alone," she said. Jamie took her arm. "You'd better help Captain Madigan," she said, pulling herself free. "I think his lady friend is about to vomit."

The girl was holding on to the balustrade and bending forward to retch at the stair carpet.

Victoria pushed her way downstairs and found her coat where it had fallen to the floor under a mountain of khaki overcoats. She glimpsed Vera standing with MM's arm around her, watching the men who had climbed on top of the piano. One of them, Earl Koenige, was waving the Confederate flag. "Look awaay, look awaay, look awaay, Dixie laand!" She tried to catch Vera's eye to tell her she was leaving, but Vera had eyes for no one but her newfound lieutenant. She was cuddling him tightly. That was the trouble with Vera; for her, men were just men, interchangeable commodities like silk stockings, pet canaries, or books from a library. Any man who would give her a good time was Mr. Right for Vera. She wasn't looking for a husband, she had one already.

Victoria had no trouble finding a taxi—they were arriving at the house in Jesus Lane every few minutes, bringing more and more people to the party.

She got back home just as the rain began. It was an old Victorian mansion, elaborate with neo-Gothic towers and stained-glass windows. Its dark shape behind the wind-tossed trees did little to raise her spirits as she hurried down the gravel path in the quickening rain. The house was cold and empty, but she closed the carved oak door behind her with a thankful sigh. Sometimes she almost envied Vera those histrionic sobs, lace handkerchief delicately applied to her face without smudging her makeup. Vera always seemed so completely revived afterward—a release which tonight Victoria needed as she'd never needed one before. But still she didn't cry.

She walked through the hall and up the grandiose staircase. She would go to the place where she always had to be when unhappy, her sanctum at the very top of the house. She passed the door of her parents' bedroom and the storeroom that had once been her nursery. On the next floor, she passed the maid's room, empty now that they no longer had live-in servants. She passed the locked door of her brother's room and the doors of the toy cupboard, their pasted-on flower pictures now faded and falling.

From the top corridor window she looked down at the dark garden and the tennis court, covered for winter. She couldn't get used to the emptiness of the house and found herself listening for her mother's voice or her father's clumsy cello playing.

Thankfully she went into her bedroom and closed the door behind her. Here at least she could be herself. A pretty row of dolls eyed her from the chest of drawers where they sat among her hairbrushes, but the balding teddy bear had fallen, and was sprawled, limbs asunder, on the floor. She picked him up before running a bath and undressing with the same studied care she gave to everything. She put her dress on its hanger and fitted trees in the battered yellow shoes before placing them in the rack.

"A museum" her mother called it derisively, but Victoria refused to let any of it go. She would keep it all—the butterfly collection in its frame on the wall, the dollhouse, and her box of seabirds' eggs. She ran her finger along the children's books, as well as her huge scrapbooks. She was determined to keep it all forever, no matter how they teased her.

She switched on the electric fire, took off the rest of her clothes, and wiped off her makeup before getting into the hot bath. Sitting in the warm, scented water, the taste of bourbon on her tongue and too much cold cream on her face, she tried to remember everything he'd said to her, searching for implications of love or rejection. The wireless was playing sweet music, but suddenly it ended and the unmistakably accented voice of the American Forces Network announcer wished all listeners a happy Christmas and victorious New Year. "Go to hell," Victoria told him, and he played more Duke Ellington.

She was drying herself when the doorbell rang. Carol singers? Party-goers looking for another address? It rang again. She put on a dressing gown and ran downstairs. Immediately she noticed the envelope that had been pushed into the letter-box. Caught by its corner, the envelope was addressed to a military box number and had been opened and emptied. She turned it over and found scribbled on the back, "I'm sorry, darling. Jamie."

She pulled the robe around her shoulders and opened the door. It was dark in the garden and the rain was coming down heavily, so that the trees were loud with its sounds. "Jamie?" She thought she saw a man sheltering under the holly trees. "Is it you, Jamie?"

"It all went wrong tonight, darling. My fault."

"You'd better come inside."

"I couldn't get a cab. I was going to borrow MM's motorcycle, but he went off somewhere with Vera."

"You're soaking wet. Hurry, the blackout."

"I always forget about the blackout," he said. The water was running off the leather visor of his cap and down his face. She could feel the rain from his coat dripping onto her bare feet. "I waited in Market Hill, but once the rain started everyone wanted cabs."

"You walked? You fool!" She laughed with joy and embraced him, cold and wet as he was.

"I think I love you, Vicky."

"A note of doubt?" she teased. "Have you learned nothing from Vince?"

He laughed. "I love you."

"I love you, Jamie. Let's never quarrel again."

"Not ever. I promise."

They were childish promises, but only childlike pledges are proper to the simple truth of love. She loved him with a desperation she'd never known before, but she took him to her bed for the same prosaic reason that has motivated so many other women—she could not bear to dispel the image of herself in love.

Afterward he said nothing for what seemed an age. She knew he was staring at the ceiling, his body so still that she could hear his heartbeats. "Are you awake?" she said.

He stretched out his arm to hold her closer. "Yes, I'm awake."

"It's Christmas Day."

He leaned over and greeted her with a gentle but perfunctory kiss.

"Are you married?" she asked, making it as casual as possible.

He laughed. "Lousy timing, Victoria," he said. Then, aware of her anxiety, he held up hands bare except for a class ring. "Not married, nor engaged, not even dating regularly."

"You're making fun of me."

"Of course I am."

"That girl . . ."

"She was very sick. It was the fruit punch, it put a lot of people out of action. Vince threw everything he could find into it."

"Who was she?"

"Vince met her last week. She works in the laundry. He made me promise not to tell you she was there, he knew you'd feel bound to tell Vera." He turned over to look into her eyes. "You must guess what Vince is like by now. He's everything a girl's mother warns her about."

"He's not a flyer, is he?"

"No. He's the PRO, the Public Relations Officer. He buys drinks for reporters and takes them around the base and sends them press handouts."

"He told Vera he'd flown twenty missions over Germany."

"He keeps that blouse with the wings and stuff in his suitcase. He tells his girls they have to be nice to him, he might never come back from the next one." He laughed.

Victoria laughed too, but it was unconvincing laughter. She held Jamie very tight and wondered what it would be like enduring the strain of knowing that Jamie might not come back. Why wasn't Jamie a PRO, or someone else who didn't have to risk his life?

"Did you see Earl Koenige?" asked Jamie. "Straw-haired kid with a you-all accent and big incredulous eyes?"

"The one you're going to be flying with? He looks no more than sixteen."

"He can handle his ship pretty well," said Jamie. It was not the sort of compliment he gave freely. "But he fell off the piano just after you left. He was trying to tap-dance and wave the Stars and Bars at the same time."

"Did he hurt himself? He looked drunk."

"I don't think Earl's ever tasted whiskey before. His folks are teetotal, church-going farmers. No, he bounced up okay and said he hoped he hadn't hurt the piano."

"And did your friend Charlie arrive?"

"He sent a message. His navigator had to stay on base, so the whole crew stayed with him. Say, do you have an aspirin?"

"On the table under the light."

He tore open the packet and swallowed two tablets without water. "I thought he'd cracked his skull at first, but Earl's always falling off his bicycle or spilling hot coffee down himself. He writes to his folks every day and I guess without his accidents he'd have nothing to tell them."

"Well, he should have no lack of material for his next letter," said Victoria. "Was that really your commanding officer! He was playing dice with a sergeant, and calling him Harry, and passing a bottle of whiskey back and forth. There were wads of five-pound notes changing hands on one roll of the dice."

Jamie frowned. "The Colonel's not an easy man to understand," he said. "Vince nearly ran afoul of him tonight."

"Vince?"

"He was wearing that damned jacket when Colonel Dan got there. I thought we were heading for a real showdown. 'What uniform are you wearing, Captain Madigan?' the old man said. Vince saluted smartly and said, 'The one with the Christmas decorations, sir.' The Colonel smiled and took the drink Vince offered him. 'If the Provost Marshal comes in here tonight, Madigan,' said Colonel Dan, 'they'll throw us both in the cooler.' Vince grinned and said, 'That's just the way I figured it, Colonel . . .' That Vince can talk his way out of anything. He told me he ran off with some married woman when he was still a kid in high school."

"Poor Vera."

"Poor Vera nothing! She was sitting on the stairs petting with MM after Vince took off."

"Is it the war that's made us like this?"

"Don't be so female," said Jamie. "People grab a little happiness while there's a chance. All I'm saying is, don't let's worry about Vera or Vince. Let them work out their own lives. Who knows when MM will buy the farm, who knows when I will."

"Buy the farm?"

"Collect our government insurance."

"Don't say things like that, I can't bear the thought of anything happening to you!" She buried her head under the bedclothes.

"Come out of there, you crazy girl." He pulled the blanket down and admired her bare body. "Are you sure your parents won't come back?"

Her head was under the pillow; she grunted a negative.

"How can you be so sure?"

She threw off the pillow and turned over to laugh at his nervousness. "Because they're with my grandparents in Scotland. They phoned this morning. You can relax."

"You didn't want to go?"

"We were working. My father said I shouldn't ask for extra time off—the war comes first."

"Your father's right," he said, caressing her. "Fathers are always right." She watched him. He hadn't looked so tanned before, but now, compared with her own skin and the white sheets, he seemed like a bronze statue.

"Was your father always right too?" she asked.

"I don't know anything about my father," he replied.

"I'm sorry."

"He's not dead. My parents were divorced when I was only a kid. I stayed with my mother, and she got married again, to a man named Farebrother. I guess a bridegroom gets a little tired of checking into a hotel and explaining why his kid has a different name."

"What's your father's name?"

"Bohnen. Alexander Bohnen. His family came from Norway originally, they were boat builders."

"Was your father one too?"

"Not enough money in that, I guess." He was still staring at the ceiling. "Give me a cigarette, will you, sweetheart?"

"You sound like Vince when you say 'sweetheart.' " She gave him the pack of cigarettes he'd put on the bedside table and the gold lighter that was balanced on top of it.

"My father is an investment consultant in Washington, D.C. Or rather he was. Now he's become a full colonel—a chicken colonel they call them—in the Army Air Force. He went from civilian to colonel overnight, and naturally he's a staff officer, the difference between a staff officer and an investment consultant being largely sartorial."

"Naturally? I don't know what an investment consultant does."

"I don't either," Jamie admitted. "But I guess he tells people who need a million dollars where to get them cheaply."

Victoria laughed. It was just another glimpse of this crazy American world. "He sounds like a man who works miracles."

"You took those words right out of my father's mouth."

"You don't like him."

"He's tough and practical and successful. My father works twenty-four hours a day, drinking with the right people and dining with the right people. My mother had to play hostess in a town where entertaining is a highly competitive sport, and my father's a harsh critic. He never married again—he didn't need a wife, he needed a professional housekeeper."

"And your mother's happy?"

"She's always been quiet and easygoing. My stepfather isn't a genius, but he makes enough dough for them to sit in the sun a lot and take it easy. Santa Barbara is a great place for taking it easy." Jamie lit his cigarette. "My father should have been a politician. He's Mr. Fixit. I guess he figured Uncle Sam would lose the war unless he got into uniform and told the Army what to do."

"Don't you ever write to him?"

"I get a monthly bulletin—mimeographed, but with my name inserted in his own handwriting—the same chatty little newsletter that he sends to all his important business contacts. That's how I know he's with the Air Force here in England."

"You never write back?"

He drew on his cigarette. "No, I never write back. You're not going to start chewing me out already, are you?"

"It is Christmas, Jamie. He's your father, you could phone him."

"My father will not have noticed it's Christmas." He'd only taken a couple of puffs at the cigarette, but now he decided he didn't want it anymore and stubbed it out on the back of Victoria's powder compact, tossing the stub into a flower vase. She was appalled but decided not to "chew him out." Instead, she leaned across and switched the light off again. When she'd snuggled down into the bedclothes he put his arm around her. "Okay," he said. "I'll phone him in the morning."

She cuddled closer to him and pretended to be asleep.

Colonel Alexander J. Bohnen

Even the Savoy Hotel's youngest waiter could tell at a glance which men were Americans. They toyed with their food, holding forks in their right hands, and they distanced themselves from the table, turning their chairs sideways, and sometimes pulling back so they could sit with crossed legs. Only the British guests kept their knees under the table and addressed themselves wholeheartedly to the food.

Colonel Bohnen knew most of the men lunching in the private room that day, and even those he'd never met weren't strangers, for he'd spent all his life with men like these—businessmen and civil servants and diplomats, even though so many of them now wore military or naval uniform. His white-haired companion was one of his closest frends. "If I live to be one hundred years old," Bohnen was telling him, "I'll never equal the bang I got out of hearing my son's voice on the phone."

"I'm glad he called, Alex."

"P-51s! He's a captain assigned to the 220th Fighter Group. He'll be flying fighter escort missions over Germany." Colonel Bohnen put his fork down and abandoned his meal.

"You've arranged everything for him, no doubt," said the older man, with just a trace of mockery in his voice.

"It's my only son!" said Bohnen defensively. "Certainly I had one of my assistants phone his commanding officer and mention that headquarters had a special interest in this newly assigned captain." Bohnen scratched at his face. "He got a rather insubordinate response. To tell you the truth, I'm beginning to have misgivings about Jamie's CO." His voice trailed away.

"Don't leave me in suspense, Alex."

"His colonel's efficiency rating is 'excellent'; that's the Army's way of saying he stinks. His efficiency reports are larded with words such as 'unorthodox' and 'over-confident' and 'reckless'; fine and dandy for a young lieutenant who's going places but not the kind of language I want applied to a colonel leading a Fighter Group."

"With your son in it, you mean. Is he an Academy man?"

Bohnen shook his head. "A West Pointer I could swallow, but this guy is a down-at-the-heels pilot who joined the Air Corps when barnstorming got too tough for him."

"Is this young Jamie's opinion?"

Bohnen was alarmed. "My God, don't let Jamie ever find out I've been checking up on his commander! You know how prim and proper Jamie always is."

"I'd never even recognize the boy after all this time. I haven't seen Mollie for nearly three years."

Bohnen frowned at the sound of his former wife's name and tapped cigar ash. "Jamie was a gentle child, careful with his toys, considerate to his friends, and trusting his parents—too trusting, maybe. Mollie poisoned the boy's mind against me. But as terrible as that sounds, I've never allowed myself to become bitter about it."

"Mollie's father was a tough man to do business with. She gets it from him."

"He inherited a going concern," said Bohnen. "What did old Tom have to be so tough about? He inherited a fortune and poured it down the drain. He died nearly penniless, I've heard. His grandfather must be turning in his grave. Look at any picture book of America's history and you'll find a Washbrook harvesting machine or tractor. When old Tom Washbrook gave me permission to marry his daughter, I was walking on air. I loved Mollie dearly and I was sure I could make her father see what had to be done to save the factories, but he would never listen to me—I was too young to give him advice. Sometimes I think he deliberately did the opposite of anything I suggested. And Mollie gave me no support, she always sided with Tom. He has a right to make his own mistakes, she liked to tell me."

"Mollie loved her father, Alex. You know that. She doted on him."

"She watched him run that giant corporation right into the ground. What kind of love is that?"

"So you never hear from Mollie?"

"Mollie is a one-man woman, always was and always will be, I guess. Once she'd turned her back on me she didn't want to even think about me again. A clean break she said she wanted, and I went along with that, even when it meant losing my son. I knew someday he'd find his way back to me and I thank the good Lord that he chose this Christmas to do His will."

Bohnen's companion looked at his watch. "I wish I could hang on here and see the boy again, Alex."

"He tells me he's met a wonderful girl," said Bohnen, "and he's giving me the chance to meet her."

"The British trains are all to hell, Alex. Does he have to come far?"

"I sent a car," said Bohnen.

The other man smiled. "I'm glad to see you're not letting the war cramp your style, Alex. Do you think I should get myself a khaki suit?"

"Running an air force is no different from running a corporation," Bohnen told him solemnly. "The fact is, running an air force in wartime is easier than running a corporation. As I told my boss, the opportunity to threaten a few vice-presidents with a firing squad would have done wonders for Boeing and Lockheed when they were having their troubles."

"You can say that again, Alex!"

"And what about that damned airline you sank so much good money into? A few executions in *that* boardroom would have worked wonders."

"Military life obviously suits you."

"It's fascinating," said Bohnen. "And it's a big job. There are now more U.S. soldiers in these islands than British ones! And our planes outnumber the RAF by about four thousand!"

"What's the next step, Alex, Buckingham Palace?"

"Think big," Bohnen said, and laughed.

"Must go." The older man looked around the room and then back at Bohnen. "Who is hosting this feast?"

"Brett Vance. You know Brett—made a fortune out of cocoa futures just before the war . . . the big gorilla with glasses, over there in the corner, tearing blooms out of the flower arrangement. No need to overdo the grateful thanks. He just persuaded the Army to put his candy bars on sale at every PX in the European Theater."

"Nice work, Brett Vance!" said the old man sardonically.

"Can you imagine how many candy bars those soldiers will consume? Countless divisions of fit young men, hiking and digging and so on, night and day in all kinds of weather."

"Does that mean you're buying stock in candy bars?"

Bohnen looked shocked. "You know me better than that. Let others play the market if they want, but while I'm in the Army there's no way I could be a party to that kind of thing." He saw his companion smiling and wondered if he was being tested.

"You're becoming a kind of paragon, Alex. I think maybe I prefer that wheeler-dealer I used to know back home."

"I missed the first war. I feel I owe something to Uncle Sam, and I'm going to give this job all I've got."

The older man could think of no response to Bohnen's passionate declaration. From the other end of the room there was laughter as guests took their leave. "Give my love to Jamie. I look forward to hearing your opinion of his girl."

"Jamie's too young to marry," said Bohnen.

"And how about his CO—are you going to let *him* get married?"

"Very funny," said Bohnen. "I suppose you think I interfere too much."

"Let the boy live his own life, Alex."

"See you next week," said Bohnen. "You could take a couple of messages for people in Washington."

"Go easy on the boy, Alex. Jamie doesn't have that hard cutting edge that we grew back in 1929."

"He'll get no preferred treatment. He's a soldier, and this is war."

"It's serious, Dad. We're in love." He found it difficult to talk to his father after so many years apart.

"And when exactly do I get a chance to meet the young lady?" Colonel Bohnen consulted his watch.

"Three-fifteen. She thought we'd like to have some time together. She's downstairs right now, having lunch with her aunt."

"That's most considerate of her," Bohnen said, and wondered whether it was intended as an opportunity for Jamie to get his blessings for an intended marriage.

"You'll like her, Dad. It was her idea that I phone you."

How like Mollie the boy looked, the same mouth and the same wide-open earnest eyes and the same nervous manner, as if he expected Alex Bohnen to bite his head off. What did the boy expect—a paternal chat about the unhappiness that can follow from a hasty marriage? Or the senior officer lecture about the socio-medical consequences of casual relationships? He would get neither. "Sure I'm going to like her," said Bohnen, pouring more of the Château Margaux. "Eat the lamb chops before your meal gets cold." Jamie had let his father choose the food and wine, knowing how much pleasure that would give him. He was right; Bohnen had been through the room-service menu with meticulous care and questioned the waiter at length about the temperature of the wine and the locality in which the lamb had been reared.

"It's a fine meal," said Jamie.

"It's better to have it served up here in my suite. I would have eaten with you but I had an official lunch."

"It's a fine claret too." Bohnen noted his son's Britishism and wondered if he'd been tutored by old Tom Washbrook, who kept a legendary table, or by his no-good brother-in-law who was drinking away the profits of the bar and grill he owned in Perth Amboy.

"The Savoy cellars go on forever. This is the finest hotel in the world, Jamie. And the management know me from way back before the war."

"Nineteen thirty-four," said Jamie, turning the bottle to examine the label. "So you're still very busy?"

"We're in the middle of the biggest expansion program in history, and now Doolittle has arrived to take over from General Eaker."

"What's the story behind that one?"

"Go back to last October and read about the Schweinfurt raid, the way I've been doing to prepare a confidential report. It was a long ride through clear skies, our bombers punished all the way there and all the long way back again. No escorting fighters, and the Germans had plenty of time to land and refuel before slaughtering more of our boys. Twenty-eight bombers were lost on the outward leg, and by the time the formations reached the target, thirty-four had turned back with battle damage or mechanical failure. The return trip was even worse!"

"I'm listening, Dad."

Bohnen looked at his son. He didn't want to frighten him, but he knew that a son of his would not be readily frightened. "If the truth of it ever gets out, Congress will tear the high command to pieces. Any chance of America getting a separate air force will have gone for good. Even now we're not publishing the whole truth. We don't tell anyone about our ships that crash into the ocean on the way back, or the ones that land with dead and injured crew. We don't say that for every three men wounded in battle there are four crewmen hospitalized with frostbite. And we don't tell anyone how many bombers are junked because they're beyond economical repair. We don't talk about the men who would rather face a court-martial than go back into combat, or about the psychiatric cases we dope up and send home. We don't let reporters go to the bases where we're having trouble with morale, or admit to the decisions we've had to make about not sending unescorted formations back to those tough targets again."

"It sounds bad."

"We never released the true Schweinfurt story, and my guess is we never will."

"With the Mustangs we'll escort them all the way." Jamie had forgotten how intense his father always became about his work. He wished he could see him relax, but he never did.

"I spent last month pleading for long-range gas tanks. We're using British compressed-paper ones, but we can't get enough. Then on Friday I got a long report from Washington telling me it's impossible to make drop tanks from paper. That's what we are up against, Jamie, the bureaucratic mind."

"The Mustang is the most beautiful ship I ever flew."

"And everyone knew it last year except the 'experts' at Materiel Division who seemed to resent the fact that she needed a British-designed engine to make her into a real winner. The Air Force lost months due to those arguments, and all the time the bomber crews paid in blood."

"Will things be better under Doolittle?"

"New machines, new ideas, new commander. I sure hope he'll get tough with the British. That's the most urgent thing at present."

"The British?"

"Churchill wants us to fly at night on account of the casualties we're suffering."

"Doesn't night bombing just mean area bombing—just tossing bombs into the centers of big towns? There's no industrial plant in town centers, so how could his policy ever end the war?"

"Night raiding would mean taking more advice and equipment from the RAF. First we take advice from them, then lessons, and eventually we'll be taking orders."

"But Eisenhower's been appointed Supreme Commander of the Anglo-American invasion forces."

"It sounds pally," said Bohnen. "It sounds like the British are resigned to taking orders from us. But wait until they announce the name of Ike's deputy and he'll be a Britisher. It's one more step in the British plan to absorb us into RAF Bomber Command. Churchill is using the slogan 'round-the-clock bombing' and is suggesting that we coordinate it under one commander. Get the picture? Only one commander for the Army, so only one commander for the Allied bombing force. And who's the most experienced man for that job? Arthur Harris. If we squawk, the British are going to remind us that Eisenhower's got the top job. And that's the way it's going—the British will get all the powerful executive jobs while reminding us that they're serving under Eisenhower."

Jamie was sorting through his vegetables to set aside tiny pieces of onion that he wouldn't eat. Bohnen remembered him doing the same thing when he was a tiny child; they'd often had words about it. Fastidiously Jamie wiped his mouth on his napkin and took another sip of wine. "The British are good at politicking, are they?"

"They excel at it. Montgomery can pick up his phone and talk with Churchill whenever he feels like it. Bert Harris—chief of RAF Bomber Command—has Churchill over for dinner and shows him picture books of what the RAF have done to Germany. Can you imagine Eaker, Doolittle, or even General Arnold having the chance to chat personally with the President? The way it stands now, Montgomery, via Churchill, has more influence with Roosevelt than our own chiefs of staff have." Bohnen drank a little of the Château Margaux and paused long enough to relish the aftertaste. "Nineteen twenty-eight was the great one, but this thirty-four Margaux is a close contender. One day I'll retire and devote the rest of my life to comparing the twenty-eights and twenty-nines."

"I guess we've got to keep hitting strategic targets," said Jamie quietly. He hadn't wanted to get into this high-level argument that his father so obviously relished.

Bohnen shook his head. "We're going after the Luftwaffe, Jamie. There's no alternative. There's not much time before we invade the mainland—we have to have undisputed air superiority over those beaches. General Arnold's New Year orders will make it public record: destroy German planes in the air, on the ground, and while they're still on the production lines. It's going to be tough, damned tough."

"Don't worry about me, Dad."

"I won't worry," said Bohnen. His son looked so vulnerable he wanted to grab him and hug him as he used to when he was small. He almost reached across the table to take his hand, but fathers don't do that to their grown-up fighter pilot sons. In some ways mothers are lucky.

Victoria arrived on time, and Bohnen was surprised by the tall, dark, confident girl who greeted him. She was obviously well bred, with all those old-fashioned virtues he'd seen in Jamie's mother so long ago.

"You have a suite on the river, Colonel. You're obviously a man of influence."

"How I wish I were, Miss Cooper."

"Charm, then, Colonel Bohnen."

"I'm not even a real colonel, just a dressed-up civilian. I'm a phony, Miss Cooper. Not one of your gilt or electroplated ones either. I'm a phony all the way through."

She laughed softly. Bohnen had always said that a woman, even more than a man, will reveal everything you need to know about her by her laugh—not just by the things she'll laugh at, or the time chosen for it, but by the sound. Victoria Cooper laughed beautifully, a gracious but genuine sound that came from the heart rather than from the belly.

"You look too young to be Jamie's father," she said.

"Who could argue against a compliment like that?" said Bohnen.

She went across to the table where Jamie was finishing his meal, and they kissed decorously.

"Can I order some tea or coffee for you, Miss Cooper?"

"Please call me Victoria. No, I'll steal some of Jamie's wine." Jamie watched the two of them; already they seemed to know each other well enough to spar in a way Jamie had never done.

Bohnen brought another wineglass from his liquor cabinet. "Jamie tells me his mother is English," said Victoria.

"Mollie likes to say that. The truth is, she arrived a little earlier than the doctor anticipated and her parents were in England. Tom was setting up a tractor plant near Bradford. Mollie was born in a grand house in Wharfdale, Yorkshire, delivered by the village midwife, so the story goes, with old Tom boiling up kettles of water and only an oil lamp to light the room."

"How romantic." She looked at Jamie, who smiled.

"Do you know that part of the world, Victoria?"

"I've passed through it on the train to Scotland."

"What a crime," said Bohnen. "I've ridden to hounds there more times than I can count. Marvelous countryside. Do you like horses?"

"Not awfully," she admitted.

"Well, I knew you had to have one major flaw, Victoria." He smiled. "Luckily it's one my son will happily put up with. I remember the first time I put Jamie on a horse. He was very small, and he yelled enough to shake the stables down. The master of foxhounds came running out to see if I was beating the child to death." He turned to Jamie. "Remember that time at your uncle John's farm in Virginia?"

"Airplanes for me," said Jamie with some embarrassment.

"He knows how to avoid questions he doesn't like," said Bohnen. "He learned that from his mother."

Jamie poured a little wine and said nothing.

"My son has a mind of his own, Victoria. Perhaps you've already discovered how stubborn he can be." It was said in fun, but there was no mistaking the admonition behind it.

Victoria put a hand out to touch Jamie. His head was lowered but he raised his eyes to her and smiled.

"Wouldn't go to Harvard. Instead he went to Stanford."

"They let me start a year early," Jamie said.

"And a lot of good that did," said Bohnen, smiling to show that he was no longer annoyed by it. He turned to Victoria. "He graduated a year early and started his law studies a year early . . . then he throws it all away to join the Air Force. You could have been practicing law by now, Jamie. I could have placed you in the office of some of the smartest lawyers in Washington or New York."

"I wanted to join the Air Force."

"You would have been a colonel in the Judge Advocate's Corps." Getting no response to this, he added, "But I suppose that wouldn't be much substitute for flying P-51s over Germany."

"No, sir, it would not be."

"I have to admire him, Victoria. But he'll never take my good advice." Bohnen laughed as if at his own failings.

"And how much advice did you take from your father?" asked Victoria. She had endured the same sort of criticism from her mother, always cloaked in geniality. And so often it was done like this, through a third party.

Her point was not lost on Bohnen. "I hope we Americans aren't too brash for you, Victoria."

"My fortune-teller told me I'd meet two dark handsome forceful men."

"You don't believe in fortune-tellers, Victoria? A sensible modern young woman like you?"

"I believe in what I want to believe in," she said with a smile. "Surely you understand that?"

"Exactly the way my analysts treat the strike photos. I understand that all right." Jamie was fidgeting with his wineglass, obviously getting ready to leave. "Finish the wine, Jamie. Don't go before you finish the Margaux."

Victoria heard a note of anxiety in Bohnen's voice and felt sorry for him now. She could see how desperately he wanted his son to stay.

Jamie drank his wine slowly and got to his feet. "I'm taking Vicky to a show tonight. Then I have to go back to the base."

Bohnen did not ask him which show, in case it was just a polite fiction. His son wanted his girl to himself, and why not? "Have a good time, Jamie."

"Good to see you again, Dad."

"Take care of yourself, Jamie. And you, Victoria." She gave him a kiss on the cheek. The girl understood, thought Bohnen. Children stop being children, but parents never stop being parents, doting parents. That's the tragedy of it.

Bohnen picked up a heavy briefcase and opened it. "I've got a whole lot of reading to do in the next two hours," he told them. "It's just as well you have to leave. The car is at your disposal— he'll take you wherever you want to go. The driver's used to late nights."

"Take care of yourself," Jamie said.

Bohnen pretended to be fully occupied with the contents of his briefcase. "Don't get into trouble out there at Steeple Thaxted," he said without looking up from his papers. "Or my general will take it out of my hide."

He still hadn't looked up when they went out. Jamie closed the door gently so as not to disturb him.

Captain
James A. Farebrother

One of the disadvantages of sharing a room with Vince Madigan was the way in which he spread his possessions about him. Farebrother seldom saw his bed under the array of magazines, opera records, sports gear, lotions, unguents, hair restorers, half-completed love letters, and beribboned little packages of nylons or canned fruit that were a fundamental part of Vince Madigan's love affairs.

It was Mickey Morse who woke them the first morning after the 1943 Christmas stand-down. He was looking for a cigarette. "What's been going on in here?" said MM, looking at the stuff that Vince had

strewn around the room. "Looks like you just took a hit from a
105." Winston came in and sniffed at Madigan's foot locker.

"Don't look at me," said Farebrother. "I went to London yesterday. I didn't get back here until five this morning."

"I went to Cambridge," said MM. "My motorcycle's out of action. I missed the liberty truck and it cost me seven pounds for a
taxi."

"Jesus," said Vince, climbing out of bed. "Seven pounds! A cab
driver will take you to London and find you a piece of tail for a
carton of Luckies."

MM said, "That's just the kind of dumb remark you can expect
from a PRO." He grimaced. "I didn't have a carton of Luckies,
dummy!"

Madigan yawned and pushed Winston away from his secret
hoard of candy bars. "Where did you get to after the party, Jamie? I
saw you picking Earl Koenige off the floor and then you and Vicky
had disappeared."

"Hey," said MM. "That Vicky! She's some dish!" He described
an hourglass with his outstretched hands.

"You sure left me in a jam," Madigan complained. He had one
of his socks on but couldn't find the other one. "The little dark girl
came back after you'd left. Vera went crazy. If MM hadn't been there
she would have hospitalized me. Right, MM?"

"Vera's okay," said MM quietly.

"Vera's not just okay," said Vince Madigan indignantly. "She's
the goods. I told you she's a sure thing, MM."

MM didn't want to hear that Vera was a sure thing. "Colonel
Dan was looking for you yesterday, Jamie," he said to change the
subject.

"In person?" said Farebrother.

MM nodded. "Well, that's fame," said Vince Madigan.

"I guess he figured you'd gone over the hill," said MM. He
found Winston quietly gnawing a sock and tossed it back onto the
bed without Madigan noticing.

"My pass didn't expire until roll call this morning," said Farebrother.

"He said to be sure you knew you were on the board," said
MM.

Farebrother nodded. It was no surprise to find that he was
scheduled to fly. The shortage of pilots was such that Colonel Dan

and the rest of the Group HQ officers were flying each and every mission that came along. "Operational?"

"We're not practicing for a fly-by," said MM. "Who's coming to eat?"

Farebrother ate with MM—they left Vince Madigan still searching for his sock—and after breakfast they played cards. He said something about Vera, but MM didn't encourage further questions. He didn't want anybody thinking that he had to make do with Vince Madigan's cast-off girlfriends. There were too many jokes told about Madigan's women lining up at the main gate, red-eyed and fat-bellied and asking to see the Chaplain.

The pilots spent all morning waiting. The bombers were attacking the naval base at Kiel. It was a heavily defended target, but the 220th Fighter Group was assigned to the role of withdrawal support force and wouldn't be needed until the bombers were on their way home.

The relaxed postures of the flyers were deceiving. Like amateur actors in a bad play, they held books and magazines without reading them, smoked without inhaling, and spoke without listening. Colonel Dan, wearing the short-sleeve khaki shirt he favored, was standing in the corner, nervously scratching his upper arms, his fingernails leaving red weals. Major Kevin Phelan, Group Operations Officer, was with him. They were having a conversation they'd had many times before.

"Last year Notre Dame had the greatest football team it's ever had . . . begging your pardon, Kevin."

Major Phelan fingered the nose he'd broken playing for the Fighting Irish, grinned, and said, "Second greatest."

"But I'm not talking talent, I'm talking tactics. I'm talking about Clark Shaughnessy, and what he did for those University of Chicago kids, back in the thirties." The Colonel took a quick look at his watch before going on. "You're too young to remember them winding up in the Rose Bowl, having won every last game on the schedule."

Major Phelan, who was by no means too young to remember it, said, "That was 1940, the same year the Chicago Bears whipped the Redskins seventy-three to nothing. I was there, Colonel! I saw that game."

"And every coach in the land switched to the T formation," said Colonel Dan. "Did you see the Aggies play the year before that, when they won the national championship?" He looked at his watch again. They both knew their conversation was only something to keep themselves occupied while they waited.

"Lots of time yet," said Major Phelan.

"We should be escorting the mission over the target," said Colonel Dan. "Do those people at Wing think we're not good enough to go all the way?"

Phelan didn't answer.

Through the window Colonel Dan saw Boogie Bozzelli pitching a ball to his inseparable buddy, Costello, who caught it and with one easy motion sent it back again. "Are those guys crazy? Playing ball out there in the rain?"

Diplomatically, Major Phelan did not point out to the Colonel that it was no longer raining. "They're from Florida, Colonel."

Colonel Dan grinned. Phelan and the Colonel had long since agreed that all Southerners were slightly crazy. "We'll be over the sea most of the way," he said disgustedly. "Another lousy milk run."

"We can't be sure of that, Colonel. That whole northern coastline is lousy with fighter bases. Remember Bremen—the Krauts came up like wasps at a picnic the moment we reached the coast." Phelan looked around the room. "A few kills could really raise morale around here."

MM was stretched out with his feet on the table, pretending to be asleep. Earl Koenige was looking through an aircraft-recognition booklet. Rube Wein was sitting at a table with a pocket chess set and a copy of *Great Chess Games of the Great Masters* and working through the moves piece by piece. Rube Wein had said very little to Farebrother since his arrival. He said very little to anyone. Even his successes at college sports had been in events like vaulting and swimming, in which a man is left to himself. He was a muscular figure with black hair brushed straight back so that it looked like a shiny helmet. No one sat at the table with him. Some said that Rube Wein spent long hours alone because he was studying for the Ph.D. he was determined to get as soon as possible after the war. Others said he was just moody and unsociable. Either way, he did little to encourage conversation beyond what was necessary. Only MM seemed to get along with Rube Wein—they even laughed and joked together—but MM was feigning sleep. Wein looked up and his eyes met Farebrother's, but he gave no sign of recognition before going back to his chess problem.

It was noon by the time they were briefed, and then came the truck ride to the squadron huts on the muddy side of the airfield. Their hardstands were near the firing butts, a bitterly cold place where the rain puddles and mud never disappeared until summer.

The squadron pilots filed into the Equipment Room. There were open racks along one side of it, and each pilot was assigned a stall and an old metal locker. In the racks each had his parachute, dinghy, helmet, goggles, oxygen mask, Mae West, and flight suit. The personal equipment sergeant was waiting for Farebrother with a set of long underwear. The long johns were torn and grubby, but he said Farebrother would be glad of them up where they were going, and Jamie took his advice.

The sergeant lived in a tiny room at the end of the Equipment Hut. He looked like a pneumonia case, his eyes red and rheumy and his nose clogged enough to impair his speech.

Major Tucker said, "Careful where you sneeze, Sergeant, I don't want you spreading those germs through the squadron." At the other end of the room, Rube Wein laughed, but the Squadron Commander was not making a joke. "Who was it laughed?" he said angrily, but went on speaking, as if not expecting the guilty party to confess. "We're losing a thousand man-hours a day through these infections."

"Shit!" said MM in mock consternation. "I always said those goddamned germs were Nazis."

Tucker looked at him, sniffed, and turned back to Farebrother. He was a tense thirty-year-old West Pointer. Older than almost all the other pilots, he was something of a dandy with his light brown wavy hair and thin mustache. They called Major Tucker "the wine waiter." His cold pedantic manner and air of condescension contributed to his unpopularity. Rumor said that he was with the Group only until he went into a staff job at Air Division.

"Clear your pockets of all personal effects, Captain Farebrother, you know the regulations." Jamie put his billfold, photos of his sister and mother, some letters, and loose change onto the shelf of his locker. Its door was bent and dented. The Squadron Commander watched him.

"Is there a key for this locker?" Farebrother asked him.

Nervously, Tucker fingered his mustache. "It belonged to a pilot from B Flight," said Tucker. "He went down in the Channel, with the key in his pocket. We had to open it with a tire iron to send his personal effects home. . . . Better to leave it open. The personal equipment sergeant will be here all the time."

Tucker moved away, and Farebrother took a box of aspirin, some dollar bills, and a paperback edition of *The Last Time I Saw Paris* by Elliot Paul and stuffed them into his pocket.

MM was watching. "The trouble is," he said, "things that keep you warm are too damn conspicuous to escape in."

"So I'm wearing everything," Farebrother said. He felt ridiculous and could hardly move.

"As long as your circulation isn't constricted," said MM, "you might be glad of the extra duds. Some of these cockpit heaters don't work. Mustangs were designed for the RAF, and those British just don't feel the cold."

The sergeant handed Farebrother an escape kit containing foreign paper money, colored escape maps printed on silk squares, some candy bars, and one rather ancient cube of compressed dates, reputed to be nourishing for airmen on the run. Most of the other pilots were wearing their Colt pistols in shoulder holsters, but Farebrother left his in the locker together with the extra clip of bullets that was part of the escape kit. He tightened the straps of his Mae West life jacket.

"Not taking your gun?" said the sergeant.

"It's heavy and I can't shoot worth a damn." The sergeant helped him into the harness of his parachute. "I'd better take care of that gun for you. There are guys around here who'd sell their own mother to get one of those Colt automatics." Farebrother bent forward so the tightened straps would be right for his seated position in the cockpit.

Earl Koenige, ready long before, was lounging against the lockers, watching his new wingman get dressed with the keen eye of a debutante at a fashion show. "I hear you know about the law and stuff, Cap," he said.

Farebrother looked up and wondered where he'd got that information. Earl Koenige was a blond open-faced boy with large feet and that sort of awkwardness that so often marks those who grow up on a farm. He'd spent the years of college that the Army required of pilot candidates studying agriculture. "I need advice, Cap." He'd been sitting near Farebrother at breakfast, but hadn't said anything.

"What do you need to know?" said Farebrother unenthusiastically.

"A year and a half ago, I loaned my brother-in-law two thousand dollars. He wanted to buy a piece of land to extend his chicken farm . . . Athens, Georgia, not too far from where I grew up. He reckoned he was going to get contracts to supply the army installation they got there. He said I'd be a kind of partner."

"What kind of partner?" said Farebrother, unsnapping the parachute release so that he could straighten up. "Thank you, Sergeant."

"I get no answer to my letters. I don't like to bother my folks about it, and my sister don't answer letters either. You think I need a lawyer?"

"You got anything in writing, Earl?"

"I paid by check. I got his signature on the back of that, I guess." Outside, the crew chiefs were beginning to warm up the Merlins. The hut shook as the prop wash of some nearby plane hit the tin exterior and the sound echoed inside. "Man your planes," Major Tucker shouted from the doorway, and Mickey Morse slapped Earl on the back and said, "Let's get going, guys."

Jeeps were waiting to take the pilots the short distance to their aircraft. There was some horseplay as the men climbed into the cramped seats.

"It's all my savings," said Earl to Farebrother. "I figured it would be something for me after the war."

"It could be just the mail," said Farebrother. He went to get into the seat beside the driver.

Earl Koenige said, "I always sit in front."

Farebrother climbed out and squeezed into the back seat alongside Mickey Morse and Rube Wein. Earl twisted in his seat to continue the conversation. "For a year and a half?"

"You've been moving," Farebrother said. "Reception Center, Primary, Basic, Single-engine Advanced, and then to your Group and on to Europe. There could be sacks of mail chasing you."

Earl nodded but looked unconvinced. The driver gunned the motor and the equipment sergeant nodded to Farebrother and said, "Good luck, sir," in recognition of the fact that it was Farebrother's first operational trip. Farebrother waved as the jeeps roared away, their tires hissing on the rain-wet tarmac of the perimeter. There was a smell of cut grass and high-octane fuel. It was a heady mixture.

"Mickey says I could serve an order on him," Earl went on, leaning right back in his seat. "He said I should write to my brother-in-law's bank."

"I'd save that for a last resort," said Farebrother. He was looking around him like a tourist. This was his first taste of war and he didn't want to miss a moment of it; he certainly didn't want to be discussing chicken-farm shares.

"Maybe it's not much money for a guy like you," said Earl huffily, "but it's all my savings, plus what my aunty left me."

"It's a lot of dough," said Farebrother in an effort to placate him, but Earl pretended to be studying his route map and didn't look back again.

The jeeps turned in to the hardstands and stopped between Earl's plane and *Kibitzer*, to which Farebrother was assigned. The men dropped off, the weight of the parachute packs almost toppling them as they hit the slippery grass. Farebrother's boots squelched as he touched the muddy verge. In spite of his heavy clothing the damp wind cut into him like a blade.

Sergeant Gill was standing on the wing of *Kibitzer*, having revved her up. His head was huddled deep into the collar of his fleece-lined jacket. He opened the canopy as Farebrother arrived. The Mustang was not very old, but the bad weather had exposed metal under the dull green paint. There were black stains trailing back across the wing chords from the gun ports, and there were newly painted metal patches to cover battle damage.

"Hello, Cap." Sergeant Gill extended a hand to help Farebrother up to the cockpit. Gill's hand steadied him while he fastened the leg straps of his chute and scrambled in. He pushed the chute pack into the metal seat box and then heaved at the inflatable dinghy pack upon which he sat. There was a knack to getting the compressed-air cylinder into a position where it didn't hurt for the entire flight.

The four Mustangs that made up A Flight, commanded by MM, were parked close together on four loop-like hardstands just off the perimeter track. A wall of sandbags protected the aircraft against low-level enemy strafing attacks that had never come, and the sandbag pens were broken in places. At the closed end of the dispersal, the ground crews had used huge packing crates and sheets of corrugated iron to construct shelters for themselves. Crisscrossing this little shanty town were muddy tracks that skirted the deep puddles of rainwater. Overhead wires brought electricity to the windowless shacks, so that on this gray overcast day there was yellow light inside, revealing bad joins between wood, metal, and tarpaulin.

Earl Koenige's *Happy Daze* was nearest to Farebrother. There was a lightly clad girl and a bottle of whiskey painted on its nose. MM's *Mickey Mouse II*, now turned away from him, featured the cartoon rodent toting six-guns and a ten-gallon hat. *Kibitzer* bore a beautifully painted nude girl hiding behind playing cards. Rube Wein's plane was austere by comparison, bearing only the carefully lettered name *Daniel*. His Irish crew chief called the ship *Danny*, but Farebrother suspected that Rube Wein had chosen the name as evidence of his own soul-searching, for it was the Hebrew for "God is my judge."

Sergeant Gill found Farebrother's shoulder straps and helped to get them fastened. Gill was the sort of crew chief who never trusted any pilot to do things right. "Plug in oxygen mask, mike, and headset," he muttered, and watched to make sure Farebrother did it properly. "Mixture off, pitch control all the way. Half an inch of throttle. Are you taking off in pairs today?"

Farebrother felt a moment of panic. "I don't know."

"Keep behind Lieutenant Koenige while you're on the perimeter track," he advised. "Then do whatever Lieutenant Morse and his wingman do. You'll have plenty of time to pull up wing tip to wing tip."

"Thanks, Sergeant." It only needed one such error to delay the whole Group.

"Best pilot on base needs the best crew chief. Give me time and maybe we'll get the best ship too." He leaned over to slap the nude's rump with the flat of his hand.

"She sounds okay to me."

"Engineering Officer says some of the ships have had supercharger trouble. I can't find anything wrong with this one, Captain, but if it surges you'd better turn back."

"And if it's a long way back?"

"Cut back the manifold pressure and baby her while you look around for a big field." He slapped Farebrother's shoulder. "You won't have any trouble with her, Captain. But take it real easy while the fuselage gas tank is full; a heavy tail don't suit your kind of aerobatics."

Farebrother looked at his instruments again and checked the back of his hand to see the briefing notes he'd written on the skin in pencil. If captured, he was to lick the pencil off. He looked at his watch and wondered if it had stopped, but when he held it to his ear he could tell it was still working.

"Colonel Dan's going out on the runway now," said Gill. He could see right across the field by standing tiptoe on the wing.

Farebrother switched on the magneto and battery, then hit the starter and fuel booster in unison. The engine whined and there was a bang as the first cylinder fired and the propeller blades jerked forward and stopped. Then, just as it seemed it wasn't going to start: Primer! He worked the booster pump energetically. There was a second bang and a third. And then the sound was echoing on the metal framework like a thousand Furies as the prop moved, blurred, and then became a pale gray disk.

He moved the throttle a fraction to hear the engine's note change. The vibration of the engine was now pounding upon the soles of his feet. He glanced at Sergeant Gill, who nodded approval of the sound. Farebrother waved him away, and he jumped down to the ground. Farebrother released the brakes and waited until the prop blades bit into the cold air and slowly dragged the heavy plane forward. To the left he saw Earl's *Happy Daze* rolling out of its blast pen, and he touched the brake to bring his own plane into line behind him on the taxiway.

Today A Flight was flying in Blue position. The four planes moved along to form a line behind Tucker's flight at intervals of about one hundred and fifty yards. The flagman at the end of the runway was waving the planes off as quickly as he could. Colonel Dan's *Pilgrim* was airborne, and behind him planes were ascending the same invisible ramp in the sky. As Earl turned off the perimeter track and onto the runway, Farebrother brought his aircraft alongside. He felt the wheels go from the smooth tarmac onto the ridges of poured concrete and looked across at Earl. Now that he was away from his friends, the boy's face was drawn and tense. He looked at Farebrother but gave no sign of having seen him before closing the side panel of his canopy. Farebrother did the same and was thankful to be protected from the cold damp wind while waiting his turn. By now the sky seemed full of aircraft.

To the south, Colonel Dan, first to take off, was coming around to start forming up. By now all the lead squadron was in the air. The flag officer was signaling continually, and the planes raced away down the runway two by two, like children holding hands.

Then it was their turn. Forward view totally obstructed by the aircraft's nose, wings blocking off the chance to see the runway's edge, they raced forward in response to the frantically waved flag.

The engine roared its full power, the tires drummed on the runway, and there was ever-quickening vibration shaking the airframe. Then the noise and feel of the tires on concrete ceased suddenly and, with a slight yaw, *Kibitzer* slid into its own element, the air. Some dispersal huts, "tent city," and then the village high street passed under him. He turned with Earl, giving it no more than a slight bank to come in neatly behind the lead squadron. By the time Colonel Dan had completed his third circuit of the field, all three squadrons were in loose formation and heading east and up toward the thick gray layer of cloud that now seemed close enough to touch.

It was a measure of Colonel Dan's reservations about the Group that they made a mass penetration of the weather. More experienced Groups went up through such overcasts in pairs and did not get lost.

Every aircraft has its own individual relationship with the air about it. The lightweight training biplanes, little more than powered kites, bob uneasily in skies where big passenger planes sail like ocean liners. But fighter aircraft are a breed apart. Bred for a specific purpose, they are unnatural creatures, like sumo wrestlers or castrati. A fighter plane is a manned missile and its pilot sits astride an engine as a witch sits on a broomstick.

Farebrother nursed the temperamental *Kibitzer* up through the thick gray porridge, watching Earl's plane all the time and keeping close formation. Farebrother had flown solo before he was sixteen years old and was undaunted by bad weather, but he had no experience of this sort of stormy mess, with occluded fronts and an overcast that reached to heaven.

Still they climbed. Earl pulled away a little to open up the formation as they went up through the clouds with fifty other planes in formation. Frightened of losing him, Farebrother moved the throttle to close up again. He saw Earl turn his head and wave. He might have been telling his wingman to float out a little, but, with no other plane in view, Farebrother stuck with him. How could Earl spare a hand for waving? Farebrother had one fist tight on the stick while the other constantly moved the throttle to hold position. He looked around but could see no other planes.

They were at 25,000 feet by the time they broke out through the top. The weather briefing had been wrong by three thousand feet, but everyone was too relieved to complain of that. Farebrother squinted into the blinding light. He hadn't seen such sunshine since leaving America, and yet, even in this anonymous skyscape above the clouds, there was no mistaking its foreignness. No sky over those training airfields had ever had such wind-dragged tufty clouds, and not even in the depths of winter had he seen the noonday sun so low on the horizon.

Once above the weather it was easy to keep station on *Happy Daze*. Earl was a natural pilot who flew with such effortless skill that he carried his wingman along with him. On the port side of Earl, *Mickey Mouse II* was leading the flight, with Rube Wein beyond him, the "index finger" of this finger-four. Neither of them had Earl's graceful ease, but the formation was good compared to some of the ragged station-keeping to be seen elsewhere in the Group.

Major Tucker led this low squadron. Colonel Dan was at the front of the squadron abreast of them, and the sixteen aircraft of the high squadron were about a mile away on the down-sun side.

Farebrother pressed the buttons of his radio, but there was no sound except the crackle of static on any channel. One by one, three pilots called "Slingshot" (Colonel Dan) to say they were turning back due to mechanical malfunctions. Three of the spares dropped into the vacated slots, and the three unneeded spares turned back to go home. Now they settled down for the long flight. Farebrother watched the time, and when he had lightened his fuselage tank he switched over to the drop tanks. Only his clock could help him estimate their position, for the blanket of cloud was unbroken beneath them. The first indication that the Group was crossing the Frisian Islands was the high-pitched screech of interference in his earphones—the electronic sounds of the German radar. Two minutes later there was a cluster of black puffs ahead as German radar-directed guns began firing through the clouds. The ugly cauliflowers of smoke were almost a thousand feet below them, but Colonel Dan changed course to make the German radar plotters think it was violent avoiding action. The ruse seemed to work, for the next salvos were also well below their flight path.

Soon they passed beyond the heavily defended islands and the firing stopped. The Group reached the "rendezvous point" off the German coast four minutes ahead of time, but there was no sign of the returning bombers. Glad of the opportunity to fly farther over enemy territory, Colonel Dan continued on course.

Weather systems over the Baltic Sea had broken the clouds, so that now they glimpsed the grayish-green flat land of Schleswig-

Holstein. From this height they could see all the way to its far coast-line, and soon the radio was busy with the calls of pilots who had seen on the horizon finely hatched white contrails meticulously stippled with the black dots of flak. The mission had bombed late and the leading force was only now turning away from the target.

"Slingshot from Sparkplug Blue Two . . ." Rube Wein was calling Colonel Dan in his usual measured laconic voice. ". . . Big Friend; nine o'clock, very low."

While everyone else had been concerned with the planes on the horizon, Rube Wein had spotted a Fortress limping home far below, near the ground.

"Sparkplug Leader from Slingshot. Assign a flight to help that cripple home."

"Roger. Wilco," said Major Tucker, and then: "Sparkplug Blue Leader from Sparkplug Leader. Take your flight and escort the Big Friend home."

There was a double click on the radio as MM touched the transmit button to acknowledge the order. Then *Mickey Mouse II* did a sudden wing-over. The other three followed into a diving turn and, pleased with a chance to chase across the sky, the four pilots dived steeply so that the altimeter needles raced around the clock until they pulled out close to the ground.

A village with a tall church spire flashed past close under them, and there were garlands of bright lights looping across their path as some light flak opened up. They could see the Big Friend now; a B-17 silhouetted ahead of them against the dull pink western sky. There was more gunfire as they approached the coast, 40-mm. stuff that added red lines to the silvery white 20-mm.'s. But the tracers arched lazily into the sky and then raced over them with room enough to spare.

Suddenly the landscape changed—an ancient bus, some cyclists, a modern hotel, a strip of sand, and then the sea.

The world looked different from this low level. Shining like wet steel in the light of the setting sun, the sea stretched out to where the anvil-headed cumulonimbus marked the progress of the cold front. The badly damaged bomber was steering well away from the offshore islands that guarded the northern coastline of Germany and Holland. But this longer route would take it nearer to the bad weather. The four Mustangs began to weave alongside the damaged bomber. Their props in fine pitch, the four pilots now twisted their heads anxiously in case the Germans were up there waiting.

There was a sudden flurry of rain spots streaking over the canopy and a drop in air temperature, so that the heat inside the cockpit caused condensation to form. Farebrother used a gloved hand to wipe a clear patch and noticed Earl doing the same. The wet air caused the engine to change its note; richer mixture smoothed it out again.

"Sparkplug Blue Leader from Sparkplug Blue Two. Something in the water. Can I go look at it?"

"Sure thing," said MM. "Sparkplug Blue: punch your babies!"

The four aircraft dropped their external fuel tanks. *Daniel* banked steeply and turned away to fly close against the spumy sea. The other three continued the weaving pattern that was the only way they could match the speed of the slower bomber alongside them. They kept well out of range and gave the bomber crew plenty of time to study them and be sure they were friendly. Attempts to reach the bomber on the emergency frequency came to nothing.

The angry blur of white-capped waves flashed past them, then the gloom was lit by a line of tracer bullets out to sea. Rube Wein was shooting at something, and the something was returning his fire. It was one of the big Heinkel floatplanes, painted gray like the wintry sea. Rube circled and came back for another pass. The Heinkel was taking off and having difficulty in getting unstuck from the heaving waters. This time there were strikes—bright silver flashes—along its fuselage, and now there was no return fire.

Rube's *Daniel* turned again to fire another long burst at the slowly moving seaplane. The sea around the Heinkel was turned white by gunfire, and its fuel—housed in the floats—ignited and the floatplane exploded in a ball of flame. *Daniel* came out through the other side of the smoke and, banking almost vertically, circled the floating wreckage before returning to where the others were escorting the crippled bomber.

There was no exchange of congratulations over the radio. Rube Wein took up his position on MM's wing and joined the lazy weaving pattern. The Mustangs pulled a little closer now that the bomber's crew had grown accustomed to their presence.

The bomber—*Clarissa Mine*—had taken severe damage from flak. Jagged shapes were torn from its structure, and each hole was marked with the silver scar that red-hot metal burns into paintwork. The whole length of her, from uplifted nose to the huge tail, bore such cauterized wounds. No one manned the idly swinging waist guns and the turrets were still and empty. Only the cabin showed a sign of life when the copilot raised a weary hand in greeting.

Now that he had an escort, and the danger from German fighters had lessened, the Fortress pilot tried to win a little altitude. But the big ship was combat-weary. It groaned and shuddered with each hundred feet it gained. At little more than two thousand feet, the pilot gave up the struggle and let his injured plane level off.

The port outer engine had been losing oil for a long time, and its wing was crazed with a black pattern as it streaked in the airflow. There was smoke from the cowling too, and the pilot struggled to feather the props before the engine ran away. Nothing he did could be of much use, for the engine itself had to provide the power he needed, and the engine was dying. Even as they watched, the cowling loosened, flapped, and then was torn off by pieces of engine that came flying through the air like missiles. Soon the prop blades were thrown off the spinning shaft, whirling up into the sky like a drum majorette's batons.

The two men flying the plane now had no time for waving at the escorting fighters, they were struggling desperately to save their plane and their crew and themselves. There was a lot of water ahead and daylight was beginning to go.

Miraculously the Fort didn't totter into the sea, it held altitude and plodded on, another engine making too much smoke, one wing low, its rudder twisted cruelly as the pilots heaved at the controls to hold it on course. Yawing, wallowing, and groaning, the big Boeing kept flying for mile after mile.

They saw the clouds first—the great sheer-sided gray cumulus that sat upon England, overshadowing the land like a roof. The upper layers of the cloud were getting all the sunshine; the turbulent clouds were painted with all the bright colors of the dying sun. Too well-defined for Turner, not as vulgar as Rubens, perhaps Tintoretto or Veronese saw a sky like that, thought Farebrother, but by then they were close enough to see that it was really a huge ice-cream sundae topped with honey, cherry syrup, and orange.

When the land itself came in sight, Farebrother began to believe they had a chance. There were emergency airfields near the coast, places where big birds could slump down onto patches of runway as wide as the average airfield. Places where a plane with rudder jammed could land from almost any point of the compass.

But *Clarissa Mine* was not going to get as far as the emergency fields. No one aboard had the time, the energy, or the inclination to start looking for such a place. The pilot was beginning his let-down even before they crossed the English coast. MM was flying ahead of the Fort, hoping to find a suitable landing place, but *Clarissa* dropped her nose while still over the water. There was no undercarriage to be lowered; the hydraulics had been shot away.

Lower and lower she came. Impatiently *Clarissa Mine* brushed aside the upper branches of large trees. In the gathering twilight, the grass looked gray and the trees and bushes were standing on shadows that were far too big for them. She was still lower now, the four Mustangs fussing around her like bridesmaids at a wedding. Lower still—her shadow reaching up from the ground as if to embrace her bleeding mutilated body.

Then she hit. Smashing her way through bushes and hedgerow, tracks, fences, and small trees. Chopped vegetation rose around her like a swarm of locusts, then an engine broke loose and tore a long furrow in the ground. A wing tip was snipped off neatly by a brick barn, which in turn collapsed.

The big Fort came to rest with its nose in a hedgerow and its tail blocking a farm track. People came running across the fields and others were cycling up the road. But from the battered fuselage there was no movement except for the settling dust and, far away, the thin column of smoke from a severed engine.

"Let's go," MM said, and led the flight back home.

"Shit!" said MM. "What in hell you do that for, Rube?" The argument had been festering since they landed; the men had conversed only in grunts and the brief words necessary for ground crews and the Intelligence Officer. When MM was angry no one could miss it.

"Do what?" said Rube Wein. Nervously, he used his hand to push back a lock of dark straight hair, but his face was composed; his eyes showed only amused contempt.

"That was a rescue plane," said Earl Koenige.

"Tough shit," said Wein. He lounged back and assumed an attitude of weary boredom, but the pre-flight Benzedrine tablets made him tense and restless, so that he kept fidgeting with the zipper of his jacket and endlessly wringing his hands in a gesture that could have been mistaken for contrition.

"Picking up guys in the water," said Earl.

"And that bothers you?"

"Yea-is." There was a warning of slow southern anger in Earl's voice. "Yea-is, it does."

"Maybe you figure it was a relative, Earl. You got many uncles or cousins in the Luftwaffe, Earl?"

"Cut it out, Rube," said MM.

"Uncle Sam pays me three hundred bucks a month to shoot Germans. What do you want me to do?"

"Those floatplanes wear Red Cross markings," said MM. "Could be that Kraut was hauling some of our own guys out of the ocean."

Rube got a pack of cigarettes from his pocket and lit one without hurry. Earl Koenige said, "You might have been clobbering our own."

Rube Wein turned on Earl. "Don't give me that crap, you sanctimonious little Kraut. If you guys had seen that plane first, you would have clobbered it just the way I did. Don't give me all this hearts and flowers just because you came back without even firing your guns today."

"I'm Flight Commander, Rube," said MM quietly. "You slipped off to hit that Hun because you knew if you told me about it I would have let it go."

"Bullshit!" said Rube Wein. "You'd blast your own mother out of the sky to get another victory mark painted on your ship." He went closer to MM and tried to stare him down. "Those goddamned Nazi bastards are killing my people by the thousands. You guys don't know what's going on over there. This is just a fancy rod and gun club for you, but I came here to kill Nazis, so don't give me a lot of fancy crap about backing off into a neutral corner when the other guy hits the canvas. The RAF's been shooting down Red Cross rescue planes since 1940."

"I'm the Flight Commander," said MM with no lessening of anger. The indiscipline troubled him as much as the proprieties. "You bounce Huns when I tell you to and not before."

"Or you'll report me to Major Tucker?" Rube Wein mocked him.

"Scram!" said MM. "I want to talk to Jamie."

Earl Koenige picked up his gloves and said, "Yeah, well, I've got to get going too."

MM put a hand on his arm to halt him until Rube Wein was gone. "Earl," said MM, "are you an anti-Semite?"

Earl looked at MM for a moment before answering. "You mean like hating Jews and all that kind of stuff?"

"Right."

Earl shuffled his feet nervously as he so often did when faced with a direct question. Earl didn't want to tell anyone an untruth—his father had made him promise to tell the truth always and Earl had taken this promise very seriously. "See, MM," he said apologetically, "ahm not sure."

"Bullshit!" said MM irritably.

"Before Rube, I-ah never met any . . . except my chemistry prof at college. And I liked him fi-ahn."

"Okay, Earl," said MM. "I just wondered, that's all. It's best we keep this business to ourselves for the time being. Seeing as how Rube didn't file a combat report or a claim for that kill."

"She wasn't even flying," said Earl. "You can't shoot down a ship that's down."

MM closed the door behind Earl and gave a theatrical sigh of relief. "He'll get himself *moidered*," said MM, as if the prospect was not too unbearable.

"Earl will?" said Jamie.

"Nah, Rube is just getting it out of his system. Have you noticed the way he's hitting into the Benzies? Rube's already as upset as he's going to get. It's Earl who is going to get fighting mad when it finally gets through his thick dome that Rube thinks he's a Nazi."

"I guess you're right," said Farebrother. "Is that what you want to talk about?"

"I'm sick of playing referee for those two," said MM. "Rube is getting real morbid lately. There's a big glass mountain in the sky and he's going to fly into it. It started as a gag, but now he's kinda brooding on it. He says the Germans put Jewish POWs into concentration camps . . . always takes that shooting iron with him when he flies . . . says he'll take a few with him; all that kind of shitty talk. I've tried to reason with him, but he won't listen."

"You think that's what's on his mind when he's riding Earl about being a Nazi?"

MM nodded. "The trouble is, Rube's the best damned wingman you could have, and I've got no time to waste breaking in another one."

"You want to talk to me about Rube?"

He shook his head, walked across the room, and looked out of the window for a long time. Finally he said, "I'm shacking up with Vera. She's got a little house in town."

"That's dandy," said Farebrother to encourage him over the pause.

"Vera's not my first time in the sack, not by a long way."

"Sure," said Farebrother.

MM rolled his cigarette across his mouth by twisting his jaw. "I think Vera would go back home with me after the war," he said proudly.

"You've asked her to marry you?"

"She's not like any of the kids I knew at college; she's all woman. And she's beautiful, isn't she, Jamie?"

"A dish," said Farebrother, playing for time as he thought about Vera married to MM.

"The guys at the party were all looking at me the other night. It sure makes me feel good to have a doll like that on my arm."

"Didn't you tell me that marriage had gone out of style? Aren't you going to London next weekend with those two girls Vince met at the dance?"

"Vera could have the pick of any guy on the base," said MM with a mixture of pride and insecurity. He looked up suddenly. "No. I told Vince I changed my mind about that double date of his."

"How did all this going-home-to-America talk start, MM? Did Vera bring it up?"

"We couldn't move into my dad's house. My married brother's there already and they have two kids. And that gas station don't bring in enough dough to support us all."

"Vera wants to go to America?"

"No. She likes England. I'd have to have something really good going for me if I was to get Vera to go home with me."

"We've got a lot of war to fight before we go home, MM."

MM waved away Farebrother's reminder. "You think a pilot who beat Rickenbacker's score would be famous, really famous? Famous enough to get a top job in some aviation outfit?" MM took the cigarette from his mouth and blew on it to be sure it was still alight. "The bomber pilots will get the pick of the airline jobs—they'll be counting four-engine hours in hundreds. No airline will want us fighter jocks."

"I never thought about it," said Farebrother. "I guess you're right. But a friend of my father's has stock in an airline. I could write to him . . . take the temperature, you know."

"That would be swell, Jamie."

"Is working for an airline another of Vera's ideas?"

MM's face changed. "Now don't go getting the wrong idea about Vera. She's not some kind of gold digger, if that's what you're thinking. Vera told me to be careful flying. She's worried about me all the time."

"You're a natural born pilot, MM. You don't have to worry about getting a job."

MM stubbed out his cigarette. "You're the only guy I can talk to around here. You're the only one who gives me a straight answer. And with you and Vicky . . . you understand these things."

"Anytime, Mickey Mouse."

"Do you want a ride into Cambridge on the back of my motorcycle?"

"I'm taking Vicky and her folks to dinner at Ptomaine Tommy's."

"Big deal!" He patted his pockets as if searching for loose change. "Say, could you lend me another five?"

"And my buddy from the banana boats is coming too." Farebrother passed five one-pound notes to him. MM smiled and nodded. He never said thank you in so many words.

"With your best girl!" MM shook his head. "You live dangerously. I'm keeping Vera away from all these pussy-chasers."

Jamie Farebrother could never remember Charlie Stigg in better spirits. He caught Victoria's eye across the dinner table, and she smiled to affirm that Charlie was the wonderful companion that Jamie had promised, and more besides! Charlie had already completed six missions over Germany and four of them had been very tough. And yet to hear Charlie tell it, the missions had been uproarious fiascos to which he'd contributed only bewildered incompetence.

Farebrother remembered his father telling him that real raconteurs always kept a straight face when saying funny things, but Charlie Stigg made his own rules. He roared with laughter at his own jokes, and never stopped smiling as he told them "the real story of the Eighth in action." Antiaircraft gunfire and attacks by German fighters were no more than diversionary interludes in the story of a bombardier who couldn't see through his bombsight, a navigator who couldn't remember which side was starboard until he tied a piece of string around his right arm, and an overweight gunner who had to be extricated from his tiny turret by Charlie and a crew chief.

Jamie laughed until tears came to his eyes, and Charlie's young copilot—Second Lieutenant Madjicka—despite knowing the stories by heart, was able to laugh like a man hearing them for the first time. "Call him 'Fix,'" insisted Charlie Stigg. "He's another goddamned lawyer."

Jamie Farebrother had explained a hundred times to Charlie that he'd only had one year of law, but it was no use. He saw the same despairing look in the eyes of Lieutenant Madjicka, and they exchanged knowing looks. "Hi, Fix," said Jamie.

Madjicka was a shy boy with quick blue eyes that missed nothing. His contributions to Charlie's accounts of their flights together were pertinent but circumspect, as might be expected of a law student. His humor added a dry skepticism to Charlie's outrageous romping narrative. He drank abstemiously and didn't smoke. He had none of the nervous habits so many of the flyers had—he didn't fidget or crack his finger joints or laugh when there was nothing to laugh at. He was tough. All in all, Farebrother decided, Fix Madjicka would be a good man to have at your side in a tight spot.

Ptomaine Tommy's was a name the Americans had given to the Ladbrooke Restaurant and Grill, a popular eating place on the Newmarket Road. There was always steak and lobster and wine and whiskey at Tommy's. Despite astronomical prices that ignored the regulations, and despite the "welcome to our wonderful American allies" charge that ensured that they paid double what British servicemen were charged, every table in the dining room, the grill, or any of the small upstairs dining rooms was always full and had to be booked well in advance.

It was worth all the trouble and all the expense, Farebrother decided, looking around the table while Victoria's father told one of his own anecdotes about a German bomb hitting his St. James's Street club. Charlie Stigg was attentive to Victoria's mother and applauded her father's funny story. The candlelight made all their happy faces golden, and Victoria's long straight hair shone like burnished metal. Her skin was pale and her shoulders white against a black silk dress that shone provocatively in the soft light. She looked so beautiful that Jamie wanted to reach across the table for her just to be sure she was real, and truly his.

"More coffee, Dr. Cooper?"

"I'm getting old, my boy. The wretched stuff keeps me awake at nights."

Victoria's parents were the first to leave, and Victoria felt she had to leave with them. "I'll go and get the car from the car-park," said her father. "Mother and I will wait for you downstairs."

Charlie Stigg understood what was required of him. He jumped to his feet, looked at his watch, and announced his immediate departure. But before leaving he gave Jamie a wink and a lecherous nudge. Fix Madjicka had to help his captain down the stairs. "Next week, Big B!" Charlie was shouting. "The aiming point will be the Reichs Chancellery . . . look out, Adolf!"

"One step at a time, Baron Stigg," said Madjicka in the voice of an unctuous family retainer; it was a joke between them. "Better give me your glass, my lord." Charlie giggled, and Farebrother felt a pang of regret that he no longer shared all Charlie's jokes.

When at last they were alone, Jamie turned to Victoria and embraced her with desperate want. As they stood there, silent and still, they could hear the noise of revelry all around them.

"I so hate to share you, Jamie," she said. "Is that so terrible?"

"I love you, Vicky."

"It was sweet of you to include my parents." She took one last look around the room. Maybe it was no more than a pretentious place with tasseled lampshades and cheap bentwood chairs, but she would remember it forever. "I've never dined in a private room before—it must have cost the earth. I did so enjoy it, Jamie. Thanks!"

"I owe your parents a lot of hospitality . . . and they feed me out of rations!" From somewhere downstairs there were English voices telling someone to "mind the blackout!"

"I have a present for you," said Victoria.

"A present?"

"It's a very old locket. I've put a piece of my hair in it. Is that terribly corny?"

"I'll carry it with me for ever and ever."

She covered his lips with her fingers. "You don't have to promise anything. I was frightened you'd think me silly. I've had it since I was sixteen. It was given to me by a great-aunt."

He took the locket in the palm of his hand and kissed it before putting it in his pocket. There was a discreet cough from the doorway. They turned to see Lieutenant Madjicka standing there. "Could I have a quick word with you, Captain?"

Farebrother still held her, but she said, "I must go, darling. My parents are probably pacing the hall."

Madjicka, reluctant to be the instrument of separation, answered her quizzical look with a nod.

"Transport okay?" Farebrother asked the young officer.

"It's kinda personal . . ." He frowned and, as if glad of a chance to delay, said, "Sure, transport is just fine. Our colonel's a good Joe, he gave us a car and driver."

Victoria hugged Jamie one last time and then picked up her handbag to leave.

"Where's Charlie?" said Farebrother.

"Charlie's full-length on a bench in the lobby. The doorman put a pillow under his head and Charlie's snoring."

"Snoring? So soon?"

"He's really bushed, sir. He was putting on a show tonight, but as soon as we got downstairs he practically passed out on me."

"I didn't realize," said Farebrother, giving Victoria an affectionate squeeze of the arm as she passed them and waved good night.

"We've had it tough," said Madjicka. He looked around to be sure they weren't being overheard. "You heard only half the story tonight. The gunner jammed in his turret had lost both legs; the string we tied around the navigator's arm was a tourniquet to stop arterial bleeding. . . . We've had more action in six missions than some crews take in a whole tour."

"What are you trying to tell me, Lieutenant?"

"Charlie says your father is on the staff."

"Then I wish like hell he hadn't told you."

"Charlie talks about you a lot, sir. I guess you realize that Charlie thinks you're pretty special." He noted Farebrother's discomfort and waited a moment before adding, "I'll keep it to myself, sir. You can depend on that. But meanwhile, you'd be doing your buddy a real favor if you found some way of getting him off operations." Madjicka stopped and looked at Farebrother. "I mean real quick, sir."

Farebrother said nothing. He looked Madjicka in the eyes and waited.

"Some guys just can't handle it," said Madjicka. "I'm mighty fond of Captain Stigg . . . one of the nicest guys I ever met. But when the flak starts coming up he just goes to pieces. We fly tight formation, and those B-24s aren't as stable as a Fort; it's darn tricky to hold them on course, especially when you've got a barrage to fly through, and wobbling ships on each side. Some guys can put their minds into neutral, but some . . ." Madjicka held out his clenched fist and hammered the other fist on it gently. "Charlie can't handle it. Too much imagination, I've heard people call it. He unstraps and tells me he has to go check the navigation or see the engineer. I take that ship over the target on my own. Now don't get me wrong, I'm not beefing. But the crew don't like it, sir. They figure that if I get hit, none of them stand a chance."

"The British only have one pilot in their bombers."

"I don't know about that, sir. And you know it's not relevant, anyway—we didn't join the RAF. The crew deserve four hands on the controls the way the Air Force planned it."

"You're right, Lieutenant."

"He's as brave as a lion in some respects. We ran into a squall first time out and he took us right through. Another time we got lost and he kept real cool at a time when I was plenty scared. And he got young Lange out of that turret as gently as a baby. I couldn't have done that, sir. Even the medics couldn't stomach it. Lange was blown in half. He was dead before morning." Madjicka found some virtually nonexistent spot on his knuckle and chewed at his finger joint as if wanting to cause himself pain.

"Poor Charlie," said Farebrother. His voice was a whisper.

"I'm not sure he'll fly much more, sir. I think he's had about all he can take. I think he might refuse to fly, and that would mean a court-martial for sure."

"Would it?" said Farebrother. "We've got an officer who decided he'd had enough after twenty-three missions. He's working in Group HQ as Technical Inspector. 'Spike' Larsson, nice guy . . . nothing to be ashamed of."

"Well, maybe that's the way they do it in Fighter Groups, but have you ever been on a bomber base? Ten guys to each ship—there are hundreds of crewmen. The place is so crowded that we even have separate nights for the base theater. Most crewmen are sergeants and enlisted men—gunners, guys who saw some movie back home and figured flying was going to be a glamorous way to fight the war. They see their buddies lose fingers—hands sometimes—to frostbite, watch a couple of ships go down, and they decide they made a bad mistake but it doesn't have to be fatal. You get a lot of them wanting out after a tough mission. The Colonel's got the same answer for every one of them: you fly or you go to the stockade."

"But Charlie isn't just goofing off."

"Well, you might like to explain that to some of the gunners who're behind bars right now for saying they got headaches every time they flew. The Colonel handed them an aspirin and a one-way ticket to the disciplinary barracks."

Jamie closed his eyes. It was a nightmare from which he'd soon awaken sweating. But when he opened his eyes again, Madjicka was still there, waiting for an answer.

"Maybe you think I'm . . ."

"No," said Farebrother. "Nobody would be dumb enough to concoct all that just to get himself into the left-hand seat. How soon do you think you'll be flying your next one?"

"We're short a gunner and a navigator, and we're due for crew leave next week. *Top Banana* is being patched and waiting for a new turret. She won't be flying until the end of the month . . . maybe even later."

"I don't know if I can do anything," said Farebrother.

"Charlie said he planned to see you during his leave."

"I'll probably get a weekend pass, so we can meet in London."

"Talk to him, Captain. Maybe a psychologist could help. But our Flight Surgeon won't be sympathetic, he's a real flag-waving bastard, sir, if you'll pardon me for saying so." Madjicka took a pair of leather gloves from his pocket and, gripping them in one hand, slapped them against the other in another gesture of self-punishment. "I'd better get back to Captain Stigg, sir."

"Thanks for telling me, Fix. I can imagine how tough it must be for you."

"Tougher still for Charlie," said Madjicka.

10

Colonel
Daniel A. Badger

"These guys don't need a commander," said Colonel Dan, "they need a goddamn nursemaid." He slammed his hand on the desk.

"You knew that when you agreed to come here," said the Group Executive Officer calmly. He tidied the papers that Colonel Badger had disarranged.

The Exec was right. Colonel Dan had taken command of the Group when morale was low due to poor leadership, heavy casualties, and a succession of technical troubles with the P-47 Thunderbolts they were flying at that time. That's why he was so keen to see the change to Mustangs—the Group needed a fresh start.

In fact, the top-level decision about re-equipping was made even before Colonel Dan's orders were cut. Part of his assignment was to preside over the change, but the rumor started that he was bribing the top brass with whiskey to get the new ships, and Colonel Dan encouraged the idea. He wanted them to believe that Mustangs were worth getting, and he soon learned to "sell" his pilots these slim little ships. But he didn't say too much about their long-range tanks. He didn't want anyone dwelling on what kind of deep-penetration assignments the new planes would bring with them. Anyone who could read a gas gauge would guess that the 220th would wind up doing escort missions at the extreme limit of the bombers' range; and that meant over the target.

"Six guys in the stockade," Colonel Dan said as if surprised.

"Stole a cab," explained the Exec. "And it hit a double-decker bus on Oxford Street." He was standing behind Colonel Dan and kept leaning over to put the papers in order.

"A sergeant from the mobile machine shop," said Colonel Dan, reading down the list of men sentenced. "And a crew chief! We need those people, Duke."

The Exec gave a polite cough, which was usually a sign that there was worse to come. "I'm not so worried about what happened in London," he said. "It was Christmas, and from what I hear on the grapevine, we're still ahead on averages." He folded his arms. "It's the brawling in Long Thaxted village that concerns me. It's getting too darn regular."

"When the eagle screams?"

"No, sir, not just paydays. I could handle those. It's almost *every* Friday and Saturday night. Last weekend the MPs had to assign extra men to help them. Major Tarrant says there were forty or fifty men brawling in the street outside the Crown pub. Even allowing for the Major's inclination to see any kind of high spirits as a preview of the end of the world, it still sounds like a roughhouse."

"And I won't have it, Duke! It only needs some Limey newspaper to get hold of this one and we'll be front-page news . . . and Division will roast my butt."

"We'll need more MPs," said the Exec.

"Major Tarrant is a nice guy," said Colonel Dan, although he had in fact been heard to describe the man who commanded his Military Police Company as "a narrow-eyed, barrel-chested know-it-all." "But he's only human. He wants more cops because that makes him more important."

"He needs more men," repeated the Exec stoically.

"Don't sigh at me like that, Duke. When that dumb bastard Tarrant asks for more personnel, Air Division is going to ask him why. Then he's going to tell them that his cops are quelling a riot down here every night." He banged a fist on the desk top. "And where will that put me, Duke? At the top of the Air Division shit list, that's where."

"You want Long Thaxted put off limits?"

"Why always the Crown?"

"It's a big comfortable place with an open fire in the main room and carpets on the floor. It's the sort of place a man goes with a girl. The Angel and the Lord Nelson are more primitive—sawdust on the floor and spit in the bucket, if you follow me. We don't have much trouble in that kind of place."

"What the hell are these guys fighting about?"

"British servicemen go there too, Colonel. RAF as well as soldiers from that infantry training camp at Thaxted Green. A man spills his drink, or pushes too hard to get to the bar, or expresses some opinion about the British weather . . ."

"If it's the weather they're fighting about, maybe *I'll* go over there and slug someone."

The Exec did not appreciate Colonel Dan's flippancy. He adjusted the fit of his rimless spectacles, a task that always seemed to require both hands. "Fundamentally it's money, sir. Money and sex."

"Fundamentally, Duke," said Colonel Dan with what he considered great patience, "everything in the universe is money and sex."

Ignoring his colonel's philosophical observation, the Exec said, "I have looked up the rates of pay, sir. A private soldier in the British Army is getting less than a quarter of what we give our lowest-paid GI. When you remember that the British don't get any of the cigarettes, drink, and candy that the U.S. Army virtually gives away, it adds up to quite a difference."

"You said it!"

"When some British infantryman, fresh back from fighting in Italy and being paid less than three dollars a month, walks into his local pub and finds a Yank buying scotch with five-pound notes, smoking PX cigars, and with his arm around some pretty local girl, it makes him mad. Imagine how you'd feel watching overpaid foreigners strolling through your hometown with American girls on their arms."

"This Limey pub owner ever come asking for compensation for damage?"

"No, sir. We get very little by way of civilian claims. There's the barn demolished when *Sad Sack* slid off the end of the runway last October, and some settlements with farmers about gas tanks dropped on arable land. The pilots are now reminded regularly to make sure the tanks go into the sea, or failing that, right out front on the field."

Colonel Dan swung his chair around so that he could see out of the window. "And that civilian car I dented in Cambridge last month?"

"I was able to settle that claim by means of an ex gratia payment," said the Exec, "so it doesn't go into the file."

"You swept it under the carpet, did you, Duke?"

"We have an Air Safety colonel visiting us tomorrow, sir. If you could spare him a few minutes it always makes these inspections go more smoothly."

Good old Duke, thought Colonel Dan. He reminds me of one favor and then demands repayment. "I want everyone on this base to know I'm going to make an example of the next bunch of guys who get into trouble in the village. Give Tarrant some muscle . . . airmen,

I don't want him asking for cops. And make sure the word gets around that I'm going to throw the book at anyone caught fighting down there."

"An excellent solution, Colonel. And I'll pencil in lunch for the Air Safety Inspector."

"What's the lousy weather going to do?" said Colonel Dan. He swung back to his desk and rested his feet among the colored telephones and trays of paperwork. The Exec gathered up his papers before they were scuffed, and made no attempt to answer this rhetorical question. There was only one man Colonel Dan listened to in the matter of the weather, and that wasn't any of the juju men who prepared the elaborate charts for the top brass, it was Major Phelan, the Operations Officer. Colonel Dan phoned him. "Are you sober, you no-good Irish bum?" he asked, and after listening to the consternation at the other end, blustered awkwardly, "Sure, that's okay, Lieutenant. Go get Major Phelan and tell him Colonel Dan wants to talk to him." He put a hand over the phone and pulled a face at Sergeant Kinzelberg, the Exec's clerk, who had come into the room to collect some papers the Colonel had signed. Kinzelberg guessed what had happened at the other end of the phone, but returned the Colonel's grimace with a blank stare.

Colonel Dan, still nursing the phone, said, "This is about the time they make the big decisions, Duke."

Scroll looked at the clock. It was four-thirty in the afternoon. "At High Wycombe, you mean?"

"Eighth Bomber Command, or Eighth Air Force HQ as we're now supposed to call it. See the nice new stationery? Six of the top brass, seven if you include the meteorologist, standing in that little room deep underground, looking at the pretty maps and deciding whether to hand us another milk run over the Pas de Calais."

"The Pas de Calais gives us a chance to get our planes in the air and gives the boys a little experience—without casualties so far."

"It's just a matter of time before the Luftwaffe moves some squadrons back there. One of these days that milk run's going to turn into a bloodbath. And even if it doesn't, bombing through overcast shows a faith in air navigation that I just can't share." He said into the phone, "Hello, Kevin. So is the weather going to do it?"

"It's pretty iffy," said Phelan.

"Let me put it to you another way, Kevin. Are those dummies at HQ going to *think* the weather will break?"

"The teleprinter says there's another front over the Atlantic . . . it's following darn close."

"Don't give me all that double-talk, you Polish hayseed." When Colonel Dan exhausted his jocular references to Phelan's Irishness, he resorted to a running joke that Major Phelan's name was really Phelanski. It was a joke which Phelan enjoyed: the plaque on his office door was now inscribed "Major Phelanski."

"They might want to take a chance on clear skies over Germany tomorrow morning."

"Now you're talking. Thanks, Kevin." Still nursing the phone on his knees, his feet on his desk top, Colonel Dan got through to an old friend at Air Division HQ. "How busy are you out there?"

"I'm not allowed to say how busy we are out here, especially when talking to bush-league jockeys like you."

"Can I hear the teleprinters churning out a field order or do you have a high-speed typist?"

"We're busy, Dan."

"Thanks, Mike. I'll buy you a beer sometime." Colonel Dan hung up and put the phone back on his desk. "Sounds like Division's got an order coming through, Duke."

"Maximum effort?"

"I feel it in my bones, Duke. Take an air force that hasn't been anywhere much for a long time, add a new commander plus some kind of break in the weather: you got a big one."

Colonel Dan picked up his coffee cup, found it empty, and put it down again. He could visualize the scene at Division, where they would be staring at the cryptic gobbledygook of closely teleprinted figures. It would take what was left of the afternoon to translate it all into specific orders—routes, aiming points, bombing altitudes, timings, radio procedures, and detailed instructions about the formations, forming-up procedures, and emergency measures. "I'm going to grab something to eat, Duke. And I'm going back to my quarters and get through some of this paper where no one will see me if I nod off to sleep. Call me if anything breaks. Otherwise I'll be in Ops about eleven-thirty tonight."

"You had a very late night last night, Colonel."

"And I drank too much. And I should get more exercise. And I'm overweight. And I'm too old to fly combat."

"I didn't say that."

"I'm thirty-six years old, Duke. Next time we fly a big one, each task force will have a one-star general flying in the lead bomber. That's how it goes for the heavy-bomber brass. But there's nothing like that ahead for fighter jocks. When they kick me out of this job, I'll be spending the rest of my career flying a desk. I'm not looking forward to it, Duke."

"I'll give you a call if anything comes through, sir."

It was almost midnight when the phone rang by Colonel Dan's bed. It was the Exec. "You were right, sir. The field order is coming off the teleprinters by the yard."

"On those rare occasions when I prove to be right, Duke, you are always gentleman enough to admit it. But I sure wish you could keep the note of surprise out of your voice."

"I'm in the message center, sir. Will you come down here?"

Colonel Dan rubbed his eyes and looked at the clock. There was no way he would be enticed into the windowless little room where the teletype clerks worked, the mere idea of it was enough to give him claustrophobia. "See you in Ops, Duke."

"Yes, sir."

Colonel Dan dressed quickly and went down the corridor to Major Phelan's room. The Operations Officer was snoring noisily, sleeping fully dressed on his bed. There was an empty bottle of Johnnie Walker on his footlocker. Colonel Dan kicked the locker and then kicked the bed. "Wake up, Kevin. It's on!"

The snoring stopped and Major Phelan awoke with a loud snort of surprise. He slowly swung his feet onto the floor and, still half asleep, tied his shoe laces. He yawned and got to his feet, tightening the knot of his tie. Then he reached for his soft flight cap, dumped it on his head, and pulled it forward until it almost touched his bushy eyebrows.

Kevin Phelan was a handsome man with the kind of muscular shoulders to be expected of one who'd played fullback for Notre Dame. His football days had ended with a kick in the face that had given him a broken nose and twisted jaw that made all his smiles disconcertingly sardonic. He grabbed his jacket from the hook on the door and said, "So the weather men went for it."

Colonel Dan opened the window to see the night sky. They both knew that the Air Division teleprinters did not transmit orders before Eighth Air Force meteorologists had reaffirmed their optimism.

Phelan reached for the bottle and upended it long enough to taste a final few drops of whiskey.

"You're a slob, Phelan."

"I'm afraid you're right, Colonel."

"And if you weren't the best damned Ops Officer in the whole Air Force, I'd kick your ass right off this base."

"I can see your predicament, sir," said Phelan.

"I'll drive the jeep," said Colonel Dan.

Outside the air was damp and cold, but there were a few stars to be seen through the fast-moving scud. Colonel Dan took them on a detour past number four hangar. Through the yellow slot between the doors they could see *Pilgrim*, Colonel Dan's plane.

"They did all they could, sir," said Phelan. "But there was no way she could be ready."

"It's just as well. I want to stamp out this superstition about changing ships."

"You'd better take mine," said Phelan. "You'll need a radio tuned to the bomber net."

"What about you?"

"I've got my eye on a new ship." As Ops Officer, Phelan had first choice of newly delivered planes.

"You're a goddamned schemer, Kevin."

"Us Poles gotta stick together, Colonel."

Colonel Dan smiled and deliberately drove over the bumpy track edge so that Kevin was almost jolted out through the canvas roof. He always felt good when he was with Phelan; nothing ever seemed to spoil Phelan's amiable ease.

The Operations Room was already busy by the time they got there. The senior Intelligence Officer, the Engineering Officer, the Exec, the Deputy, a couple of clerks, and a teleprinter operator were looking at the Watch Officer, who was pinning the long sheets of the order onto the bulletin board. A kid from the mess arrived carrying a tray filled with sandwiches and two vacuum flasks of coffee. The room was blue with tobacco smoke, but when the Colonel arrived the men put their cigarettes out of sight and stood awkwardly at attention.

The Watch Officer was a nervous young pilot who dropped his pack of thumbtacks when he turned around and saw Colonel Dan. "It's Brunswick, sir," he said.

Colonel Dan nodded. Phelan was already at the map. Colonel

Dan let him take his time while he read the most vital sections of a field order so long it touched the floor. "What do you think, Kevin?"

Major Phelan was something of an exhibitionist, so Colonel Dan was ready for the show he put on. Phelan's voice had already acquired that slight Irish brogue he always assumed when he got excited or angry. He reached for the plate of sandwiches. "Which are which?" he asked the Watch Officer. "I like turkey, can't stand cheese."

When he had the sandwich he wanted, he poured himself coffee and drank from one of the thick white china mugs that will always be associated with Operations Rooms in the middle of the night. "Brunswick is a nice ride." He took a bite of his sandwich, had another look at the map on the wall, and then consulted the target folder. Like so much of target intelligence, the description was no more than a translation of some pre-war gazetteer.

"Halberstadt," he read aloud. "Iron industry and meat-packing. Famous for *Halberstädter Würstchen*, it says here—Halberstadt sausage, I suppose that means." He looked up. "Gentlemen, we're going out to destroy the heart of the Fatherland's sausage-making capacity. I guess the strategists at Air Force HQ figure that's the surest way to bring the Nazis to a quick halt."

Colonel Dan was getting impatient. "It's the Junkers plant, Kevin. Seems to me I've even heard of an airplane called a Halberstadt."

"That's right, Colonel," said the young Watch Officer, who devoted a great deal of time to reading pulp fiction about World War I. "A German biplane, there were one-seaters and also some two-seat versions . . ."

"Just as I thought," said Colonel Dan, interrupting what promised to be a long explanation. "What do you make of the route, Major Phelan?"

"Straight in, straight out. It shouldn't give the Kraut plotters too much trouble planning optimum interception."

"It's all the way this time," said Colonel Dan. "Rendezvous with our assigned task force just short of the target. Stay with them until the P-38s and the T-bolts turn up as withdrawal support."

"This may be a tough one," said Kevin Phelan.

"Hit the German Air Force on the ground and in the air. That was General Arnold's New Year message and that's what we're about to do. No sense pussyfooting around with feint attacks and dogleg courses that don't seem to fool the Germans anyway. This time their fighters will have to come up and fight."

Colonel Dan sat down in the corner while they sorted out the material for the next day's briefing. Major Phelan bit into another sandwich and came to sit beside him. Quietly he said, "Colonel, who the hell could hold this Group together if you were lost? Who . . ."

Colonel Dan twisted away from him and brushed the sandwich crumbs from the sleeve of his jacket. "I'm sorry, Colonel," Phelan said, and brushed at the crumbs too.

"I'm flying this mission," said Colonel Dan. He looked over to where the Exec was engaging the other officers in earnest conversation. He wondered whether Duke Scroll had put Kevin Phelan up to this.

"Colonel, I'm serious."

"Dammit, Kevin, you think I'm some kind of gung-ho kid who's been reading 'Terry and the Pirates,' or a medal-hunter like Lieutenant Morse? I've been trying to get man-size missions for this Group ever since I got here. Well, now they've handed us a big one, and if I'm not up there with my boys, I might as well go fly a typewriter for all the respect I could look for in the future. No, Kevin, I fly tomorrow, and there's not going to be any argument about that."

The door opened suddenly and everyone stopped talking. Major Spurrier Tucker was standing in the doorway, feeling somewhat foolish at finding himself the center of so much attention, and twisting his Military Academy class ring around on his finger. Most of the men in the Operations Room looked as if they were deep into some high-stakes poker game, but Major Tucker was neat and shaved and his brown shoes were polished mirror-bright. Well, maybe that's what West Point does for a man, thought Colonel Dan. "Yes, Major Tucker?" he said.

Tucker shifted from one foot to the other, the fancy little mustache he wore along his upper lip quivering as he began to apologize for interrupting them when the red light was on outside the door. "Pardon this intrusion, Colonel," he stammered, "but I was just going to bed when . . ."

It was obvious that he'd heard about the field order. "Never mind the goddamned excuses, Tucker," said the Colonel. "By now even the girls in the Red Cross Club are discussing the aiming points."

He forced a laugh. No wonder they called him "the wine waiter." "Will I still be leading the Group tomorrow, sir?"

Colonel Dan tried to be fair, especially when dealing with subordinates whom he instinctively disliked. Tucker would never make a real pilot, but then neither would three-quarters of the flyers in the Air Force. Tucker was a West Pointer, a peacetime soldier who needed a little combat duty on his record before going on to staff duties. Well, that couldn't happen too soon for Colonel Dan. In his opinion, Tucker should never have been made a Squadron Commander, although his previous commanding officers had all given him wonderful efficiency reports.

"The arrangement was . . ."

"I know what the arrangement was, Tucker," said the Colonel. "Stand back and give me air." Squadron Commanders regularly got a chance to lead the Group, just as the Flight Commanders took a squadron sometimes. The next one had been promised to Tucker, but hell, this was a biggie, and Major Spurrier Tucker was . . . well, Tucker was Tucker. "You'll know in good time, Major," said the Colonel.

Tucker resisted the temptation to give a smart salute. Instead, he zipped up his brown leather flying jacket, shoved his hands in his pockets, and did everything he could think of to look like a fighter pilot, short of chewing a stick of gum. "The sooner I know, the better, sir," he said. "There'll be a lot of instructions and procedures that I'll need to get clear in my mind if I'm leading us tomorrow."

"You get them clear in your tiny mind anyway, Tucker. Then if I decide to leave you behind, it will still have been good practice for you."

"You wouldn't leave me behind, Colonel," he said, trying to smile but not quite making it.

"Get off my back, Major. Tomorrow is going to be a long day for all of us. By the way, how is that new captain—Farebrother—making out with you?"

Tucker knew it was best to handle that kind of query in a positive way. "Very well, Colonel. He's a very capable pilot and gets on well with the squadron personnel. Is there a special reason you're worried about him?"

"Who the hell says I'm worried about him?"

Tucker smiled nervously, as if dealing with a wealthy relative suffering from terminal senility. "You've asked me about Farebrother four times since he got here, Colonel. Is there something special about him?"

"I like to know what's going on around here," explained Colonel Dan. "Any reason I shouldn't ask how a newly assigned pilot is coming along?"

"No reason at all, sir. Of course not."

The truth of the matter was that Colonel Dan kept getting discreet telephone inquiries about Farebrother from officers up at Eighth Air Force HQ. Eighth HQ! Pinetree! Not many of those paper pushers working at Pinetree even knew what a fighter plane was, or that there was a unit called a Group from which a bunch of sad sacks flew out to fight the war. So who the hell was Farebrother that he had friends in high places? Well, it wasn't a problem that Colonel Dan intended to discuss with Tucker. "Yeah, well, we'll stick to what was agreed, Spurrier. You'll be leading the Group tomorrow."

Tucker gave him a smile and a salute all at once. Colonel Dan told himself that a promise is a promise, but his guilty conscience told him that he had a hunch "General" Tucker would be handling his personal file on the day the Air Force decided whether to renew his engagement or throw him into the street.

If Kevin Phelan had spent 1944 telling the Air Force when it would be a good day to fly deep-penetration missions—instead of the other way around—the war might have been won sooner than it was. That January raid was a case in point.

The pilots assigned to duty—which in those days meant just about every pilot on the base—assembled next morning in the Group Briefing Room. It was Major Phelan's job, as S-3, to prepare most of the briefing. He'd be flying with them, and the boys appreciated that Kevin was no paddlefoot. On the wall behind him, red ribbons stretched taut across the map from Steeple Thaxted to Brunswick nearly five hundred miles due east.

Three targets—one for each task force flying at seventy-mile intervals. The whole bombing force, from lead ship of the lead squadron to the last to bomb, would occupy some three hundred miles of airspace. To protect such a fleet was going to be a difficult job. Colonel Dan had told the Group's Intelligence Officer to lay it on the line for them, and he stood up to do just that. The German

Luftwaffe was sure to react violently to such a flagrant and provocative invasion of their airspace, he told them. The Krauts would come at them with everything they could fly.

During a few moments' delay, caused by mislaid radio codes, Mickey Morse was heard at the back of the room reading aloud from a British technical magazine. It was a fulsome account of RAF daring over "enemy territory." For this recitation MM assumed a high-pitched and exaggerated British accent. Coming at a time of tension, this reduced the pilots to delighted laughter.

Colonel Dan was pleased to keep the briefing short and sweet. He'd seen Bomb Group briefings, and the mounting tension that came from lengthy descriptions of targets, bombing points, radio procedures, and all the rest of it. For fighter pilots there was little to say but "follow me"—only today they were to follow Major Tucker. Colonel Dan was already regretting that.

After briefing, he stayed with the pilots in the ready room and played chess with Tucker. While whipping the Colonel at one game after another, Tucker expressed doubts about the high command's wisdom in sending a raid into what was obviously poor weather. This disconcerted Colonel Dan; Tucker was a man who seldom criticized someone who outranked him.

"Imagine the bombers waltzing round and round to form up in this stuff!" said Lieutenant Morse, who was standing there watching the chess game. "Soft focus!"

Colonel Dan didn't answer; he was trying to save his queen. But he was also worrying about the hundreds of bombers that would be circling over East Anglia hour after hour, as section by section, then flight by flight, then squadron by squadron, they slowly assembled into their assigned positions in the mighty bombing fleets that would set off for Germany.

"Maybe the weather is clearer over Germany," said Tucker.

"Move your bishop," Morse advised Tucker, pointing at it with his nicotine-stained finger. Tucker glared up at him and moved his castle. Morse said, "It'll be worse over Germany. With this kind of overcast the weather moves east all the time."

"Who said so?" said Colonel Dan.

"Jamie Farebrother," said Morse. "He's studied all that meteorology junk. The Colonel will track in on your castle," he warned Tucker.

"You got any more gems of wisdom for us, Captain Farebrother?" called the Colonel, looking over to where Farebrother was standing. Then he looked down at the chessboard again and decided to take Tucker's castle.

"Yes, Colonel," said Farebrother. "What Met described as 'a thin overcast' is really twenty-two thousand feet thick."

Colonel Dan tossed Tucker's castle into the box with unnecessary force. "How the hell could you possibly know that, Captain? That's just the way unfounded rumors get started and I won't have it."

"A pilot from the weather squadron is drinking coffee next door, sir. He's just landed."

"You trying to make a monkey out of me, Captain?"

"Why should I need to do that, sir?" Colonel Dan noted the implication that he was a monkey already, and Farebrother's clipped New England accent didn't lessen the Colonel's irritation. He was about to rebuke Farebrother when Kevin Phelan barged in through the door.

"The cloud build-up's getting worse," said Phelan.

"Sure," said Colonel Dan. "It's twenty-two thousand feet thick."

"That's right," said Phelan admiringly. "And do you know that some of the fighter force have turned back?"

"Turned back?"

"The P-38s found the cloud over Holland too high to get over and they're heading back."

Colonel Dan shook his head and looked down at the board, where Tucker was taking his queen, having sacrificed his castle to do so. Dammit! He should never have listened to that kid Morse. What would he know about chess? He might be a hotshot fighter pilot, but he talked too much.

"It's about time, Colonel," said Major Phelan.

"Too bad about the chess game," said Tucker. "You definitely were winning this one."

Colonel Dan looked at him and blew his nose without answering.

Tucker was too damned keen, thought the Colonel. Or too damned anxious to acquire a reputation as a leader. They were only as far as the Dutch coast when several pilots sighted aircraft.

"Slingshot. Sparkplug Green Two here. Contrails at two o'clock high. Maybe two thousand feet above us."

There were other radio calls.

"This is Slingshot. Cut out the chatter. I've got them. Topkick Yellow and Topkick Green. Punch your babies and go look at them."

"Slingshot from Topkick Yellow Leader. Roger."

"Slingshot from Topkick Green Leader. Roger Dodger."

It was futile, as Colonel Dan knew it would be. The enemy aircraft, if that's what they were, changed course, so there was no chance of the two flights of Topkick squadron getting anywhere near them. Soon the eight detached aircraft curved back and slipped into formation again.

They were scheduled to rendezvous with the leading Air Task Force just fifty miles short of the target. Colonel Dan looked at his watch; not long to go. They were over Holland, just scraping the tops of the cumulus peaks, with watery sunlight coming down through the cloud miles above. There was no break in the overcast.

Colonel Dan had heard the recall signal going out to the Second and Third Air Task Forces, but it did not affect them. The First Air Task Force was continuing on its way and they would go with it. He guessed that HQ had decided it was too late to recall them. The field order showed that pathfinder aircraft, equipped with radar, would be in the formation. They could "see" through the overcast. The rest of the formation's bombardiers would toggle when they saw bombs fall from the lead ships.

Colonel Dan, leading the 195th Squadron—Payoff—turned his head to see Major Phelan on his wing. Phelan was in a new Mustang with *Phelanski's Irish Rose* painted on its side. Yes, that was Phelan's secret joke. That's why Kevin had given Colonel Dan *The Wild Goose*. It was just one more example of Phelan's complex personality. Was the enigmatic major a jokey Phelanski, or was he one of those legendary "wild geese," an Irish exile and mercenary who, after dying on a foreign battlefield, went back to haunt the skies of his homeland? Colonel Dan looked across to where Tucker was leading the formation in his gaudily decorated *Jouster*. At least he was on course, Colonel Dan thought, and then felt ashamed of himself for thinking it. Maybe he was riding Tucker too hard. Maybe he was riding every one of them too hard. Maybe the Group just wasn't good enough. This was the Eighth's first attempt at deep penetration into Germany since the terrible bloodbaths of the October raids. Now, with two task forces recalled and most of the fighter escort defeated by the weather, it was beginning to shape up like a disaster.

Colonel Dan's reverie was cut short by "Bingo" calls from Top-kick Yellow Leader and then Green Leader too. Having jettisoned their external fuel tanks, their reserves were at a point where they had to turn back.

Everything was running late, but Tucker found the bombers not more than twenty-five miles from the map reference. He ordered the 195th Squadron—Colonel Dan leading it—into high cover position some four thousand feet above the bombers. The other two squadrons, one of them now at half strength, flew on each side of the bomber force, with two detached flights from the 199th flying cover some ten miles up-sun, or what was now a bleary white patch of backlit cloud. The fighters were weaving constantly, crisscrossing the bombers, to keep their forward speed slow enough to stay with the Big Friends.

Colonel Dan watched the planes bank and arc back, and with an easy rhythm led his flights into the next change of course. Far below him he could see the rest of the Group following the same monotonous pattern. He watched Tucker. His flying was stiff and wooden, but his other flight, Green, was good—tight and coordinated. That must be A Flight: Morse, Wein, Koenige, and Farebrother. Well, he mustn't change his mind about them now that he'd remembered who they were.

He wondered how Farebrother would enjoy his first taste of combat. He was a cool customer, with the kind of snooty insubordination that Colonel Dan found difficult to deal with. That little flying display he'd put on the day he arrived had taken place while the Group was on stand-down, but Farebrother's reputation hadn't suffered from the fact that only a relatively few men had witnessed it. On the contrary, it had given those on duty a chance to brag to their buddies coming back from pass. By now, Farebrother's aerobatics had been embroidered and elaborated into a demonstration that would have made Baron von Richthofen tremble and turn pale. Colonel Dan chided himself for allowing dislike to cloud his judgment. It had been a darn good beat-up. But standing a Mustang on its hind legs wasn't the same thing as fighting Germans. Okay, Captain, let's see where all that fancy stunting gets you today, thought the Colonel.

He banked again for the next leg of the zigzag. Down below there was only cloud and the big B-17s holding station like tin galleons on a gray, storm-tossed sea.

It was cold in the cockpit. Colonel Dan reached for the heater, but it was already fully on. He'd just decided that feeling cold was a sign of his advancing age when he saw that a sheen of frost had formed on the Plexiglas canopy. There was a fault in the heater. He reached out and scratched at the frost with his gloved finger, but could make only small patches through which to see clearly.

Over the radio came more calls. There were a dozen or so aircraft coming up to fight. Twin-engined Messerschmitts, they were well below the B-17s and climbing steeply out of the cloud on the bombers' rear quarter. Intelligence said the Luftwaffe operated with three squadrons to an airfield, just like the Americans, so there was a chance that this *Staffel* was to be bait for the fighters while the rest of them came in from some other direction to hit the bombers.

"Payoff Leader from Slingshot. Take Payoff Red and Payoff Blue to deal with those Messerschmitt 110s."

Colonel Dan hit the radio button. "Slingshot from Payoff Leader. Roger. Wilco." Two clicks on the radio button and then: "Payoff Red and Payoff Blue from Payoff Leader. Punch your babies and let's go."

Well, okay, Tucker, at least you're gentleman enough to give your colonel a crack at the Huns. Eight Mustangs should be more than enough to chase a dozen cumbersome twin-engined Messerschmitts. Colonel Dan pulled his nose back and watched the horizon of white fluffy cloud tilt and fall away, like an eiderdown sliding off a bed. Then, with the other seven tucked in tight behind him, he split-essed down, half-rolling into a power dive. The world was upside down now, the white eiderdown was a gray ceiling on which the Messerschmitts were crawling, getting bigger and bigger every second. The loss of altitude was enough to defrost some of the windshield. Colonel Dan aimed a blow at the heater in the hope of starting it working again.

Diving vertically through an enemy formation is not the kind of tactic they teach at Gunnery School, but for this Group's standards of marksmanship the plan view provided a nice big target. Sometimes the only way to get pilots to fly close enough to the enemy was to take them right through the formation. "Payoff Red and Blue. Select individual targets, over and out." He lined up the leading Messerschmitt in his sights. There was a flicker from the Germans as the rear-facing gunners opened fire.

The last half mile went past like speeded-up film. The Messerschmitts faltered and broke formation, and then the huge black shapes came up like express locomotives. He pressed the trigger. Flashes appeared on the wing of the leader as the bullets hit. The bullets reached the rockets hung under the Messerschmitt's wings, and suddenly one exploded. There was a huge orange and red flash that embraced Colonel Dan's entire vision. The force of the explosion slammed his Mustang across the sky and he could hear pieces of Messerschmitt chopping tiny chunks of aluminum out of his airframe. He lost control. Shit! What a way to go, he thought. But he pulled on the stick until it was tight against his belly, and he prayed. Slowly she righted. He could smell the burned fuel and rubber plastered onto his own plane. He glanced in the mirror and saw only a smear of black smoke.

Poor bastard. Those twin-engined Bf 110s were clumsy buggers. Burdened by the weight of the big rockets suspended under their wings, they stood little chance against a determined attacker.

Another Messerschmitt flashed past close enough for him to see the faces of the men inside its big multi-paned cockpit. There was another one ahead and time for a quick burst of fire before it tilted away from Colonel Dan's stern-quarter attack. He saw no strikes and banked steeply. Phelan was still close to him—Kevin, salt of the earth.

Colonel Dan held the tight turn until he saw another Messerschmitt. This one was still going; the only one to stay on its attack course. Beyond him there were the bombers—the lead combat wing, three boxes of them stacked up through two thousand feet of sky.

The Hun was after the lead box, but Colonel Dan lined him up and gave him a burst of fire from long range in the hope of distracting him. There was a burst of flame from under the Messerschmitt's wings. At first Colonel Dan hoped he'd got in a lucky shot, but then the rockets pulled slowly away from the smoke and the German began a turn while the heavy missiles set their menacing course toward the bombers.

There was a lot of confusion on the radio now, and Colonel Dan knew that his other squadrons were in combat. He dived after the Messerschmitt, but another Mustang came in too, so he let him take it and slow-rolled away, turning all the time to see around him. Kevin was still with him, but the rest of Payoff Red and Blue had chased their quarry into the cloud top, about a thousand feet below.

"Payoff Red and Blue from Payoff Leader. Re-form on me above cloud."

He saw black smears of smoke as the German rockets exploded

near the bombers, and he kept turning steeply enough to see below. The clouds were thin enough here to provide glimpses of the landscape. Mountains—the Harz, the snow-capped Brocken where on Walpurgis Night the witches brought terror from these same skies.

He set his nose toward the bombers. Behind him two Mustangs were climbing steeply from the clouds. Three more—no, four; no casualties, good.

He climbed to get back over the bombers. Only the other half of Payoff was providing protection now. Tucker had taken Sparkplug off to chase more Germans. He should have stayed close. It was a stupid order maybe, but it was an order: stay close where the bombers can see you're giving them support. The bomber boys don't need newspaper pictures of fighter jocks painting kills on their ships; they want protection. Where are you, Tucker?

With slow and majestic precision the B-17s were changing their formations. Each combat box of eighteen aircraft closed in behind the lead box, so that the formations were no longer a mile wide but a tighter stream that would concentrate the bombing pattern.

The hazy sunlight shone on the dull brown paintwork of their huge wings and here and there bombers in metal finish reflected the sun as they banked gently for the bombing run. There was more flak now, spreading across the sky like a virulent pox. Behind them the gunfire's gray scars raddled the air for miles, but each fresh eruption was an angry red blotch reaching ever closer to the planes.

This complex of aircraft plants was jealously guarded by concentrations of guns. The lead aircraft of the first box was carrying the Air Task Force Commander, a one-star general. The gunners were trying for him, just as so many of the fighter attacks did. Rumors said the Germans gave an immediate Knight's Cross to anyone who downed a task force general.

The lead ship's bomb doors slowly opened. As this plane reached the Initial Point, the sky ahead of it lit up with a box barrage inside which it seemed nothing could survive. Salvo after salvo was fired into the same airspace. All of the planes would have to fly through that great cube of exploding air and flying metal that was now pulsating red and gray like some sort of venomous seabed anemone.

None faltered. Each plane was no longer under the command of its pilot; the bombardiers had taken control and their eyes were pressed tight to the bombsights trying to recognize the hazy target through the mess of cloud and smoke.

The fighter channel was gabbling with faint voices. Tucker was fighting off a force of German fighters that had attacked the bombers from the east. Colonel Dan could see a tangle of tiny dots, swarming like gnats in the distant sky. He hoped Tucker wouldn't allow himself to be drawn too far off that way. Colonel Dan's one remaining squadron couldn't provide protection for this whole bomber force, and east was not the way home.

As he got to the end of the zigzag he banked steeply to see below. A patchwork of fields surrounded the town, its darker gray diluted by the watery clouds and its shape threaded by the silver glint of a river. Across it there suddenly appeared a thousand pinpricks of brilliant light. The lights flickered and disappeared and the whole landscape wobbled like jelly before the shock waves and heat ripples were obscured by smoke. Then his wing tilted back and closed off his view of "the mean point of impact."

Two Forts—*Hot Tamale* and *Prom Trotter*—had taken hits from flak and were slowly falling back from the formation. Colonel Dan tried to find the bombers' radio channel but got only unintelligible voices through the German jamming signal. *Prom Trotter* had lost another engine and was sinking down through the formation, with other bombers skidding and turning to avoid collision with it. She's going; she's going! No plane that badly damaged can stay in the air. There goes the first parachute, then another. Three, four, five, six, floating softly through the smoke-strewn air. Seven, eight, nine. Then the Fort, its rear stabilizer missing, banked very slowly and fell nose-first into a roll that would become a spin from which no B-17 could ever recover. Colonel Dan shivered. Nine parachutes, it was always like that; the pilot never got out, he had to hold her steady while the other kids jumped. No more college proms for that trotter, he'd be pinned to the inside of the fuselage by centrifugal force, thinking whatever men do think in the final few seconds of their sweet and too short life.

They were through the worst of the barrage now, the target was behind them, marked by a column of dirty smoke. Turn! When the hell are you going to start turning—we're still heading east! Soon the German fighters would be back again, and this time the Mustangs would be nursing damaged bombers and wounded crews. He adjusted the throttle, mixture, and pitch to the slowest setting. They would all have to accommodate to the speed of the cripples until the time came to abandon them. Now at last the turn was beginning.

After releasing their bombs the Groups that had followed in file across the target dived gently to lose about two thousand feet of altitude. This increased their speed out of the flak zone and, according to Intelligence, made the gunnery predictors inaccurate.

As the bombers banked for a gentle turn at the Rally Point, the lead Group throttled back to let its accompanying high and low boxes draw abreast until the whole wing, of about sixty bombers, was stepped up across a mile of sky in a formation that would deploy its machine guns to maximum mutual advantage. By that time, some six miles behind them, the next wing had reached the RP and was completing the same intricate maneuver.

Colonel Dan looked at his fuel gauge. He was running low, they all were, but he'd heard no "Bingo" calls. Where the hell was the Withdrawal Support Group? Suddenly he found the bomber channel. Blackwood Leader was calling the radio relay plane to send the strike signal.

"Payoff Leader from Payoff Red Two. Bogies three o'clock. Level."

Colonel Dan clicked his radio button. He'd often told his pilots that it was sloppy procedure, but he sometimes did it himself when he was tired. Hell, he couldn't be tired already, the mission was far from over. Yes, he could see the Germans. They were flying on a parallel course, holding their position twenty or so miles to the starboard side of them.

Colonel Dan pressed the radio buttons. The Fortress pilots were shouting about how well they'd clobbered the target and someone was yelling about a near collision in the turn. Probably there was a ship with wounded pilots or, worse, some engineer or navigator trying desperately to get her home. On the fighter channel he could hear his own pilots, their voices scratchy like knives across a metal plate, but the unintelligible words were unmistakably the breathless staccato cries and warnings that come from men in violent combat. I sure hope you know what you're doing, Tucker, thought Colonel Dan. He called Kevin Phelan again, "Payoff Red Two. Are they twin-engine ships out there, you think?"

"Got to be," said Major Phelan. "You can see they've got fuel enough to bide their time. Over."

Smart-ass. "Tell me if they look like they're coming in, Payoff

Red Two. Just a little more gas and we could have taken a poke at them. Over and out.''

He looked down. *Hot Tamale*, the ship damaged over the target, was holding on. Ships of the low squadron, of the low box, had opened formation to make way for her. The starboard wing was badly holed and half her starboard stabilizer was torn away, so the big bird wanted to go around in circles, but the pilots were determined to fly her westward; its erratic course was a battle of wills.

He looked from his clock to his fuel gauge. Where the hell was the Withdrawal Support Group? His fuel was almost down to where he'd be forced to take this squadron directly home and abandon the bombers. Tucker, who'd taken the rest of the Group to fight off attacks from the direction of Magdeburg, would have even less gas, for combat burns gas more quickly.

He flew on for another few minutes and then called Blackwood Leader to tell him the bad news.

"So long, Blackwood Leader. Sure wish we could stay. Good luck. Over.''

The bomber formation leader was also watching the Messerschmitts out on the flank, but there was no way of knowing that from his voice.

"Thanks, Little Friends,'' said the formation leader in a flat, emotionless voice. Like a child playing out a scene from some Saturday matinee, pretending indifference to the fact that the fighter jocks were going back to hot showers and a steak supper, leaving them to be shredded by those Messerschmitts patiently tailing along. Colonel Dan took one last melancholy look at *Hot Tamale*; she'd never get home. The lead squadron position in that low box was called Purple Heart Corner. That was where those hungry Messerschmitts would sink their teeth, and a cripple was a choice tidbit for some German kid who wanted to paint a victory on his tail tonight.

He set a course for home and tried to forget about the charges he'd abandoned. There were times when flying a desk didn't seem so bad after all, and this was one of them.

Over Holland he heard Tucker trying to raise base on his radio, but there were still storm clouds to the north and the electricity crackled in his ears, a sure sign that no radio message would be heard in England. And that meant that no one in England would hear any calls for help from Blackwood. Over the Channel, Major Phelan, with his phenomenal eyesight, spotted Tucker's depleted formation and they joined up.

"We have casualties, Payoff Leader," said Tucker. "And Spark-plug Green Leader took his flight and left formation against my orders."

"Roger. Over and out," said Colonel Dan angrily. Sparkplug Green Leader was Lieutenant Morse. And with him were Wein, Farebrother, and that other pilot . . . Koenige.

It was raining by the time they arrived at Steeple Thaxted. Colonel Dan jealously guarded the Group Commander's privilege of landing first and, as they formed into the landing pattern, he waited to see if Major Tucker would assume Slingshot's role to the end. But he was far too smart, and called Colonel Dan on the radio to suggest that he be the first to land.

"You'll go a long way, Major Tucker," said Colonel Dan as he sideslipped in for a neat landing. Tucker didn't reply.

Colonel Dan taxied *The Wild Goose* around the perimeter track to the blast pens where the headquarters aircraft parked. He saw the line chief's jeep there as well as the airfield controller's jeep.

"Butch" Walton, Colonel Dan's crew chief, climbed on the wing to help unclip the harness and unplug the ganglia of wires and tubes that provide the life-support system which makes it possible to ride through the upper atmosphere.

"You got a visitor, Colonel," said Butch. "A one-star general." The rain was drumming on the wings and hissing like a bagful of snakes as it hit the hot exhausts.

"In the airfield controller's jeep?" Generals were seldom to be seen in open-sided jeeps getting splashed with muddy water.

"That's him, sir. Landed here in a C-47 with three-star insignia on the nose . . . real top brass."

Colonel Dan turned stiffly to see the General, knees up under his chin, cramped into the front seat of the jeep. He looked as if he was enjoying it.

The Colonel eased himself out of the cockpit. He was stiff and sore and dehydrated, and needed a meeting with a general the way he needed three rounds with Joe Louis. He used both hands to haul himself out of the cockpit. "Sounds like he impressed you, Butch." He hit the snaps of his parachute, dragged it around to take its weight on his shoulder, and clambered down.

The line chief, who'd been listening, added, "This general's got a guy who just stands around writing notes for him . . . and goes and gets him coffee and doughnuts. And even he's a major."

"That goddamn heater's on the blink, Butch," said Colonel Dan. "I damn near froze, and the windshield keeps misting over."

"I'll get onto that, Colonel," said Butch, his forehead wrinkled as if the Colonel had complained about the table manners of his favorite child.

"And for Christ's sake, do something about these relief tubes. Once they ice up you piss all over yourself."

The tarmac was rainswept, and the jeep was mirrored in it so clearly that the vehicle and its reflection were one. The General, in a beautiful white trenchcoat, got out of the front passenger seat and waved the jeep away to its duties.

Colonel Dan could see the Group Exec's jeep speeding across the apron in the distance, trailing fountains of spray as it hit puddles. Duke Scroll was holding tight to the windshield, trying to get to Colonel Dan before the General got there, but he didn't make it.

"Colonel Badger? I'm Bohnen from High Wycombe."

Burdened by his parachute, Colonel Dan came to attention and gave the General a salute. Bohnen smiled and touched the visor of his cap in a more casual acknowledgment of the military courtesies.

"Any casualties, Colonel?"

Colonel Dan pulled off his flying helmet and let it dangle around his neck. "All my pilots went into combat, sir. This squadron got a couple of German fighters without incurring casualties." He looked up to where the rest of the Group were still in the landing pattern. "One of my Squadron Commanders was leading the Group today, sir. They got into a big fight and were scattered. We'll have to wait an hour or so to know what's happened to everyone. Even then someone might phone from another airfield. When the weather's like this . . ."

"I know," said Bohnen sympathetically. His white trenchcoat was going dark with the steady drizzle of rain.

The Exec's jeep screamed to a halt in a locked-wheel skid that made Colonel Dan flinch. The General didn't flinch; maybe he was deaf.

Duke climbed out of the seat almost before the vehicle stopped moving. There was another officer with him, but Colonel Dan didn't recognize the face and guessed that it must belong to the doughnut major. Scroll waved an imperious hand at Butch Walton to signal him to stow the Colonel's parachute in the jeep. Then he gave the General a perfect salute.

"Let's get out of this weather," said General Bohnen. "You got somewhere we can talk?" He didn't have to add "in private."

"There's a Squadron Briefing Room," said Colonel Dan, who kept his yellow Mae West on to remind the General that he'd just completed a hard day's work.

"Just fine," said Bohnen, climbing into the back of the jeep. Duke got in front and told his driver to go to the 199th Squadron's Briefing Room. Colonel Dan and the doughnut major squeezed in on either side of the General. Duke's jeep had no side screens; the fine rain soaked Colonel Dan's leather jacket and trousers and mud splashed onto the doughnut major's sleeve, but the General stayed dry in the middle. Colonel Dan began to think this general was not so dumb. He watched Duke twisting in his seat to light Bohnen's cigarette and smile at him from time to time. Duke's West Point training had left him with a great respect for rank—those Academy people treat generals the way high school cheerleaders treat football heroes—but Colonel Dan had never been to the Academy. He'd come into the Air Force from flying mail routes, and generals didn't mean a thing to him. For him the world was divided only into pilots and passengers. He waved away Scroll's offered cigarette.

"This British weather is really something," said Bohnen.

"We've asked for building materials to put up a gymnasium," said Duke. "We can't even play football in this stuff; we've got volleyball teams but nowhere to play." Duke turned to Colonel Dan, looked him full in the eye, and nodded sagely. Duke wanted to be quite sure that Colonel Dan understood what this conversation was all about, and Colonel Dan did understand. Duke was building up a defense against what both men expected the General to start talking about at any moment—the riots outside the Crown in Long Thaxted.

"The men get low in spirits," said Duke to the General. "We see it reflected in the sick-call reports. They go to the dispensary complaining of minor, maybe nonexistent, problems—headaches, chills, and stomach upsets."

"I hope you're not asking me to provide an improvement in the climate," said General Bohnen.

Duke smiled politely at the General's joke. "We need better entertainment facilities, sir. At present, the men either sit in their tents thinking about home or go down to the Club for a beer."

Nice going, Duke, thought Colonel Dan. Long Thaxted wasn't even listed as a contender.

"Did you think of using a hangar?" said Bohnen. "For volleyball and boxing."

"We did that until October," said Duke. "But when the weather got worse we couldn't spare the space anymore, we've got so much equipment that has to be kept dry and under cover."

"Make a note of that, Major Price," said the General. The doughnut major plucked a notebook from somewhere under his layers of clothes and, while the jeep stopped to let a newly landed Mustang taxi clear, managed to make a note in it. "We've got to attend to these things *before* trouble arises," said Bohnen, as if that was some kind of command decision that only generals were capable of.

"I *will* have that cigarette, Duke," said Colonel Dan. Duke turned around and gave it to him. They smiled at each other, relieved at the knowledge that their visitor hadn't come to investigate the fistfights in the village.

The jeep stopped outside the 199th's headquarters hut. There was no one there but a duty clerk, and Duke sent him off to make coffee while he himself hurried ahead to turn on the lights in the Briefing Room. It was a small room, used only on the rare occasions when the squadrons were briefed separately. There were soft leather seats and kerosene heating that kept the temperature comfortable, and there were bright lights, writing pads, maps, and telephones. Colonel Dan had no idea of what the General had come to tell him, but he might as well say it here, a mile away from all those keen-eared loudmouths who staffed Group HQ. Duke told the clerk to take down the shutters from the window. Now that the raid was over, the map and briefing boards were no longer secret and the room badly needed a change of air.

The General undid his fine white trenchcoat and the doughnut major took it from him. Colonel Dan's guess was confirmed: there was a large expanse of tunic without flying badges. But there were no ribbons either. Whatever his specialty, he was no Academy man, as a look at his ring finger confirmed. "Did I hear you ordering some coffee?" said the General. Colonel Dan got a better look at him without his hat and coat. The General was a tall man in his middle forties with wavy gray hair and a gray mustache. While the two men stood warming their hands at the stove, he was watching Colonel Dan as though he was an applicant for a high-paying job. Duke nodded and, with the major, slipped discreetly out the door to leave the two men alone. "Tell me about your Group," said Bohnen.

"Good kids," said Colonel Dan, "but they spent too long back home learning how to fly P-39s and P-40s against the Japs at five thousand feet. Suddenly they're changing ships again and tackling the worst flying weather in the world, while learning how to fight a different kind of war, six miles up."

"This board current?"

"Today's mission," affirmed Colonel Dan. He pulled the curtains aside to reveal the map with its ribbons stretching to Brunswick. "We keep all the Briefing Rooms ready even when we know we're doing Group briefing. I figure you never know when there'll be a change of plan that needs a squadron separately assigned."

The General nodded and went to the board and rattled the slats that each bore a pilot's name.

"The colored airplane shows the call color for the mission," explained Colonel Dan. "The airplane on the compass rose shows which runway to use. The blanks are for take-off time, and the number is the compass course from base. We didn't use this room, so the briefing wasn't set up with final details."

"You don't leave much to chance, Colonel."

"My headquarters staff are very experienced officers, sir."

General Bohnen was reading the names of the pilots. "You realize what happened today?" he asked over his shoulder.

"The Second and Third Task Forces were recalled. I heard the order go out."

"Except for the lead wing of the Third. They were close to the target and couldn't verify the signals. What was it like, Colonel?"

"Pretty rough, sir. The weather was clearer over the target and the Krauts were even throwing their night fighter units at us."

"This is their Battle of Britain, Colonel. That's what I told the Commander in Chief yesterday. This is their Battle of Britain. We're bombing them in the Fatherland. They'll throw everything at us and they won't count the casualties."

"My boys are ready for that, sir."

"I don't doubt it, Colonel."

He turned away as if to look at the Flight Operations Board again.

Colonel Dan said, "We stayed with the bomber force as long as we could, sir."

Bohnen turned back to fix the Colonel with light blue eyes which were opened wide, as if to express surprise or bewilderment. Colonel Dan was discomfited by the stare. "Eight aircraft returned early," said the General. "Tell me about that."

"Over Holland on the outward leg, sir. We spotted enemy aircraft. Major Tucker detached two flights to investigate. . . . I would have made exactly the same decision had I been leading, sir."

"Very loyal of you, Colonel Badger." There was a knock at the door and the coffee arrived. Duke had even discovered saucers and spoons, but the sugar was in a tin that looked suspiciously like a carefully washed ashtray.

Bohnen stirred his coffee and said, "But your people didn't get close enough to identify them, so we'll never know if they were enemy. Might have been a couple of British Spitfires returning from a mission. Might have been one of our weather flights."

"I don't have the details yet, sir."

"But I do have them," said Bohnen. "I attended their debriefing. I take it those jettisoned tanks were almost full."

"Yes, almost full, General. We'd only been using them for a few minutes."

"So wouldn't it be more expedient to use fuel from the drop tanks right from the time of take-off?"

"We always draw from the fuselage tank behind the pilot first. When that's down to about thirty gallons, we switch."

"Why?"

"It's standard operating procedure, General. The weight of fuel in the fuselage tank changes the ship's center of gravity. It's like carrying a passenger on a motorcycle—the weight's in the wrong place. We can't engage in combat with that tank full and we can't empty it in a hurry either."

Bohnen pursed his lips. "Were they really Germans over the Dutch coast?"

"I don't know, General."

Bohnen took a leather cigar case from his pocket. "Rey del Mundo." He held out the case to Colonel Dan. "Coronas. You can't get a better cigar than that. They say Winston Churchill smokes that same cigar."

Colonel Dan took one. He didn't care if Groucho Marx smoked

them—a good Havana was hard to find. Both men went through the ritual of smelling them, cutting them, and lighting them. Colonel Dan wondered if the General was expecting him to chew the end off and spit it on the floor; he was eyeing him with wary interest.

"Let me ask you again," said Bohnen, peeling the band off his cigar. "Were those planes over the coast really Germans?"

"Is it important, General?"

Bohnen didn't answer immediately. He got his cigar going with that kind of concentration that only fanatical devotees of good tobacco can muster. Colonel Dan knew the signs—cigars were just about the only weakness his father had ever shown. Only when he'd tasted a little smoke did the General look up. "Eight ships might have made a difference today." He was silhouetted against the window. The daylight was almost gone. Now, as he exhaled, smoke enveloped him in a shimmering box of bluish-gray light. "Eight ships held back out of combat might have afforded the bombers another thirty minutes of escort time. No need to tell you what that would have meant to those boys out there." Bohnen watched Colonel Dan smoking his cigar as though making sure he didn't ill-treat it.

"That's right, General."

"Suppose the Germans put a fighter force on that coastline. Suppose they make just one feint attack on every fighter escort group we send over there."

Colonel Dan looked at Bohnen with a new respect. "I don't think they were Germans, sir. But if they were, I'd say they weren't in the kind of tactical disposition necessary to stage an attack of the sort you describe."

Bohnen nodded and smoked contentedly. "It just needs one bright Kraut to see that weak spot and it could mean the end of deep-penetration bombing missions into Germany. The Eighth Air Force might just as well pack their bags and go home, for all the use they'd be in winning the war." Colonel Dan nodded, and the General walked around the room. "And that would mean the end of any chance of us becoming a separate service after the war."

Colonel Dan said, "Sure," and tried to look as concerned as Bohnen seemed to be, but in fact he cared nothing about the color of their uniforms and the chain of command in Washington; he just wanted to be allowed to fly.

"You think your Group spent too long training in the ZI?" said Bohnen, employing the Army's fancy name for the U.S.A.

"That's not exactly what I meant, General."

The General held up the hand holding his cigar as if he were stopping traffic in Times Square. "I like a man with balls enough to be frank. You said these boys were overtrained and, up at headquarters, my boss is inclined to agree with you."

"Some of my pilots have changed airplanes four times since they were assigned to this Group, and now in spite of this lousy winter they've learned most of the tricks of high-altitude combat. I'd say we have an exceptional bunch of pilots here, General. They're combatready, and raring to go."

General Bohnen went on walking around the room, his head bent and brow wrinkled. Colonel Dan stayed silent. Then the General went across to the window and looked out across the airfield. The light was fading fast and the whitewashed farm buildings that marked the far side of the field glowed unnaturally bright and the chimneys were smoking. "It's like a Christmas card," said the General.

"How's that, sir?"

"The British landscape—it's like a Christmas card. The rolling hills in the dusk, those thatched cottages and the cows . . . Did you ever read any Wordsworth at school, Colonel?"

Colonel Dan knew very little about poetry, but he knew when he was being patronized and he didn't like it. "There are more white farm buildings beyond that rise. When my boys come back they pitch out over that spot. As they break, they bring the throttle back and drop a little flap and the gear to bleed off airspeed on downwind. They turn base leg abeam of that main runway and let the flaps go fully down so they have a hundred and forty on the dogleg to final— that way they come over the fence with a nice one hundred indicated. They glance up quick to be sure those white cottages and the farm beyond are exactly lined up and they touch down real nice at eighty IAS." Colonel Dan tugged at his ear, but Bohnen took no advantage of the pause. "You see, General, these Mustangs are unforgiving SOBs. They stall at seventy-five—it's the torque that flips you over on your back at the last minute. You don't walk away from that kind of crack-up. So I tell my boys to make wheel landings. They keep their tails up—better visibility that way, and you're all ready to slam full power on and go around again." Colonel Dan scratched his arm. "Wordsworth? Was he some kind of poet or something?"

The General looked at him with those wide blue eyes and held his gaze until Colonel Dan began to fidget with his life jacket. "I read you loud and clear, Colonel," the General said quietly. "You want me to know that you expect flyers who understand about 'Indicated Air Speeds' and 'doglegs to final' should be calling the tune. Wingless wonders like me should go back to my nice comfortable HQ and read my Wordsworth and leave you to fight the war, lining up the farmhouses and dropping neatly onto the runway."

Colonel Dan didn't deny it; they both knew that that was exactly what he meant. "I guess you didn't come all this way to check out my poetry, General."

Bohnen smiled good-naturedly. You didn't know where you were with a character like this—he wasn't like any of the other brass Colonel Dan had ever met.

"You're right in thinking I wouldn't know how to line up my farmhouses and land a P-51 on your runway out there," Bohnen admitted. "But you'd better start thinking that maybe you wouldn't be any kind of hotshot behind my desk at High Wycombe."

"I don't know what sort of work you do at HQ."

"Then I'll tell you," said Bohnen with more than a hint of malice. "I'm a troubleshooter. They send me along to sort out problems—problem airplanes, problem Groups . . ."

"Problem colonels?"

At that moment the sound of a Merlin engine rattled the furniture and made them both turn to the window in time to see three Mustangs of the 199th Squadron flying fifty feet high across the field and then climbing gently to go into a circuit. Three aircraft—a bad sign. Colonel Dan stood biting his lip as he strained his ears for the missing one, and finally it came, the engine coughing a little. The fourth man didn't try any fancy stuff, he went straight in and landed while the others were circling. The Colonel looked at the phone but decided against calling to find out if they were all home.

"I was going to say problem flyers."

"We've got none here, General. These pilots are as good as any you'll find in the Air Force. My Group is fully operational. We can handle any assignment you want to give us."

"Good," Bohnen said, and smiled, taking his time. Colonel Dan had the feeling he'd played right into his hands. "The new strategy is to hit the enemy air force wherever he is found, Colonel Badger. We're hitting his factories every way we know how, and our formations are retaliating against his attacks with considerable vigor. But there's still a feeling that we're leaving the initiative to the enemy. There's the feeling that we should be seeking him out in his own backyard."

"Bomb the airfields?"

"*Strafe* his fields," said Bohnen, pausing to draw on his cigar. "Air reconnaissance photos have shown us that high-altitude bombers, and even mediums, aren't causing the Hun any lasting damage on his airfields. He jumps into his bomb shelter, and when we've gone, he repairs his hangars, throws dirt into the bomb craters, and is back in business within a day or two. But a low-flying pursuit plane can hit a field while the crews are resting and the fitters have still got their heads under the engine cowlings. Before anyone knows what's happening, machine-gun bullets are hitting his parked planes and the huts. Incendiary bullets are igniting gas tanks. We kill his air crews and his technicians and clerks. And from that time on everyone around the place is scared shitless, so that they're running for cover every time a Messerschmitt comes in to land. No need to draw you a diagram, Colonel—you know what kind of damage a couple of Kraut fighters could do to your airfield if they came over the horizon in the middle of a working day."

"Damn dangerous," said the Colonel quietly. "When I was flying mail out of St. Louis, back in the twenties, the dispatcher had flown with Frank Luke, the balloon-busting ace. The Germans had lined their guns up on those balloons. Flying through that kind of barrage was a damned sight more dangerous than flying a dawn patrol. How are we going to arrange your strafing attacks?"

"We're not going to arrange anything," said Bohnen. "We're going to let the fighter pilots seek out targets of opportunity as they're returning from their escort assignments."

"They already do that," said Colonel Dan, "and none of my boys are dumb enough to go after a Kraut airfield."

"They'll go for them," said Bohnen, "when they hear that you'll give them a victory for every German aircraft destroyed on the ground as well as those destroyed in the air."

"What's the catch?"

"No catch," Bohnen said. "A plane destroyed either in aerial combat or on the ground will mean an officially credited kill."

"You mean a virgin pilot could strafe five German planes lined

up along the apron at Calais-Marck airfield just across the Channel
and come back half an hour later—an ace?"

"That's exactly what I mean," said Bohnen. He looked at Colonel Dan and nodded to emphasize his meaning.

Colonel Dan walked closer to him, but didn't raise his voice
even though he was angry. "These are good kids," he said, "the best!
They fly and fight and they take their orders and they don't complain. They don't know a damn thing about Hitler or the Nazis or
any other kind of politics, they do what they do because they've been
told it's for America. From the time you climb into your airplane,
your ass belongs to Uncle Sam—that's what they say."

"No one's being ordered to attack—"

"You're right. You're not ordering these kids to attack enemy
airfields. What you're doing to them is worse—you're going to use the
very spirit that brought them here to make them send themselves out
to get killed."

"Correction," said Bohnen. "*You're* going to use it."

"It won't work."

"It'll work, Colonel Badger. Your boys will cheer to the rooftops
when they hear about this new way of picking up kills, and they'll
kick shit out of the Luftwaffe, Colonel, so that when a quarter million other American boys are landed on some French or Belgian
beach this summer, they'll have a little less lead flying around their
ears."

"When will the official order be promulgated?"

Bohnen moved his cigar gently through the air so that it made
small zigzags of smoke. "We're not going to do it that way, Colonel.
You'll just start crediting kills after seeing gunnery films of aircraft
destruction, and soon the other Group Commanders will start doing
the same thing."

"So that's what this is all about . . . You came down here to
take a look at me and decide if I was the kind of guy you'd be glad to
throw to the wolves if this thing goes sour."

He didn't deny it. "It won't go sour, Colonel."

"But why this Group?" said Colonel Dan. "Why not one of the
more experienced Groups—the 4th, the 56th, or the 355th—why a
Group like this?"

Bohnen stared at him but didn't reply.

"Did you pick us with a pin?" said Colonel Dan. "I'd like to
know, General. I really would like to know."

"I have a reason," said General Bohnen. "A personal reason."

11

Brigadier General
Alexander J. Bohnen

"You're a general!" said Victoria Cooper. "You didn't tell us about this."

"These arrangements can foul up, Victoria. I never count my chickens before they hatch. I learned that in the banking business."

"You mean you wait until the check has been cashed?"

"That's exactly what I mean, Victoria." She took his hat and coat.

"What about your driver?" she asked.

"He'll be okay," he told her. "I told him to take an hour off in Cambridge before going back to Steeple Thaxted. I'll phone the motor pool later on if I may use your phone."

"You had to go to Jamie's aerodrome—was that by chance?"

He smiled. That word "aerodrome" was like something out of Jules Verne. "There were technical developments and I could choose any fighter Group that suited me, so naturally I chose Steeple Thaxted. That way I could invite myself for dinner."

"My father and mother were delighted, Alex." She frowned. "Is it still all right to call you Alex?"

He laughed and bent forward to kiss her cheek. "It certainly is, Victoria." She turned her face so that he kissed her on the lips.

"Congratulations, General," she said. "Did you see Jamie?"

"The squadrons were separated. They were still coming in when I left."

She pressed her hand to her mouth and grew pale. "Jamie flew today? And they were in battle? Is Jamie safe?" Her hand gripped his sleeve tightly. "Is he all right?"

"How did you know the Group was in combat?"

"This is Cambridgeshire. Everyone knows that when the planes arrive home in ones and twos it means they've been dogfighting."

"Jamie's safe. He'll join us in time for dinner, as arranged." He smiled and prayed to God that he was speaking the truth.

"You saw him?" she persisted.

"Victoria, I'm not sure Jamie would like everybody to know he has a father on the staff, and I'm darned sure he wouldn't want me sticking my nose into his locker space while his buddies stand around saluting me."

"Of course you're right, General. Forgive me."

"Nothing to forgive," he said. But he noticed that he was no longer Alex.

Victoria's father was an untidy red-faced man with white hair a little too long and sad brown eyes that ill-matched his friendly smile. He was the eccentric British professor—looking exactly the way so many of General Bohnen's countrymen imagined such men to look. But there was shrewdness too. One could imagine him in cotton shorts and safari jacket, striding through the bush and waving his walking stick to quell a native uprising. His study was a comfortable book-lined room with some sagging, chintz-covered easy chairs and a reading light that had been repaired with pink-colored adhesive tape.

"So you are Jamie's father," said Bernard Cooper in a voice that was at once high-pitched and resonant. "He's a fine lad, Colonel Bohnen. You must be very proud of him." He searched the pockets of his ancient woolen cardigan until he found a silk handkerchief to clean his spectacles.

"*General* Bohnen, Daddy," Victoria called over his shoulder as she closed the door.

"What? I say . . . General, yes." For a moment he showed the anxiety the British reserve for the social gaffe. Then, as his eyes came to the single stars that adorned Bohnen's shoulders, and perhaps detected the marks where the colonel's rank badges had been removed: "*General* Bohnen! My dear fellow, how wonderful. This calls for a celebration. A bottle of champagne . . ."

Bohnen desperately wanted to stop him—he knew what a bottle of irreplaceable French champagne represented to any British household. "No, please, Dr. Cooper. Just a glass of whatever you are drinking . . ."

But it was no use, he was out the door and into the garden before anyone could stop him, and came back cradling a bottle of Krug. "We made the cellar into an air-raid shelter," he explained, and wiped the bottle with a cloth. "And put all the wine into the garden shed."

"A little risky, isn't it?"

"Yes, it will break my heart if a bomb blasts it. But meanwhile the whites need no chilling. By George, it's cold out there tonight!" He eased the cork from the bottle and took half a dozen glasses from a corner cupboard.

"I'm a phony . . ." Bohnen confessed when Cooper asked him about his promotion, and explained how the Air Force had given him his commission. It was always best to clarify the true position. Truth to tell, Bohnen had no wish to be taken for some time-serving army officer who'd spent his life squinting down rifle barrels and organizing battalion boxing tournaments in godforsaken parts of Panama or the Islands.

Cooper listened while pouring two glasses and then picked one up to check the wine's clarity before handing it to his guest. "It's politics," Bohnen added as he took the glass and nodded his thanks.

"In what way?"

"Half my working week is spent at committee meetings," said Bohnen. "Anything my general can't find time to attend. It's probably just the same in your job—senior men have to delegate." Cooper nodded. "As a colonel—and a newly commissioned one at that—I was low man on the totem pole. My commander's views never got across properly."

"But now you're a general . . ."

"And I can bang my fist on the conference table, and everyone has to listen."

Cooper laughed. "Wonderful!" he exclaimed. "Wonderful!"—as if this explanation was some kind of amusing cover story that Bohnen had dreamed up to conceal the fact that he was a war hero. "You were in the financial world before the war, so Jamie told me."

"I still have my office in Washington. My junior partner is looking after things while I'm away. We're investment consultants. We specialize in airplane manufacturing."

"High capitalization," Cooper said.

"Yes. With plant that goes out of date overnight and is worth nothing in terms of collateral."

"Ever run across a chap named Willie Larkin? He put together a company that was to make some revolutionary motorcar engine and went bust owing some five million dollars. He was in Washington."

"You mean Lord Lorcain?"

"A frightful rogue," said Cooper. "His grandfather took the name Lorcain—he discovered that Larkin was derived from Lorcain, an old Irish name. . . . He thought Lorcain was more suited to a lord . . . even a lord who'd made a fortune out of laxatives, what?" Cooper grinned.

"He had two Canadian partners," Bohnen said, dredging the few facts he knew from his memory. "The designs and patents he showed us were laughed at by the technical people we talked to."

"As I say, a resourceful ruffian but always a most amusing man at the dinner table. He got a double first at Oxford. I must have you both to dinner sometime. He works in the Ministry nowadays. He's a distant cousin of my wife's, but she doesn't much care to be reminded of it."

Social get-togethers with the British were like taking an evening stroll across the Mato Grosso! Had Cooper waited to see what Bohnen said about his wife's cousin before revealing the score? But what Bohnen never was able to figure out about them was how much they enjoyed springing these devious traps. Had he expressed his contempt for Lorcain, would Cooper have joined in, and would he still have added that rider about his being a distant relative?

And yet Bohnen found a lot in common with Victoria's father. They'd both studied in Germany. To serve the six months' factory work required of engineering students in Germany, Bohnen had gone to old Professor Junkers at his main plant at Dessau. At this same time Bernard Cooper was studying psychology in nearby Leipzig. Both men spoke the language with some fluency, were interested in German history, and had made many good friends there. They talked guardedly; it was not fashionable, or even wise, to say much in favor of Germany, even pre-Hitler Germany, but Cooper was an amusing storyteller and soon they were exchanging memories of Berlin bars, ski runs, and day trips on the Zeppelin.

"Is Adolf Hitler crazy?" Bohnen asked eventually—the sort of damn-fool question too many people ask as soon as they hear a man is a psychologist. But Bernard Cooper answered it in good faith.

"No sign of that, Bohnen. The fellow's devilish clever. I'd say he could teach Freud a thing or two about psychology!"

Bohnen sipped at his drink. "I feel bad about inviting myself to dinner so shamelessly, and now drinking your delicious champagne, Dr. Cooper."

"Don't give it a thought, old chap. Your Jamie is most generous and gave us a memorable evening out. And in any case, these non-vintage champagnes lose vitality very quickly . . . not much pop when I opened it, what? I've learned my lesson, Bohnen. I had two cases of Richebourg 1923 laid down, thinking that a great Burgundy, well looked after, must go on improving. I opened one of them on Christmas Day 1941. The war news was grim—Leningrad surrounded, Hong Kong about to fall, your Pacific Fleet battered—and that damned Richebourg had faded to nothing. I could have cried, Bohnen."

Bohnen laughed. He supposed it was a joke, although you can never be quite sure with the British. "What could Hitler teach Freud?" he asked. Cooper was one of the big names in psychology; he looked forward to a memorable quote.

Cooper grabbed something invisible out of the air and rubbed it into his hair; it was a lecturer's mannerism. "Freud showed us that man is not rational. Man is governed by emotion, by instinct, by images of himself that often prove quite unreal. Hitler has provided the greasepaint and fancy costume complete with Wagner music so they can act out this Grand Guignol. . . . It's all so alien to the Germany you and I know, but it's damned good psychology."

"You've touched a nerve," said Bohnen. "I feel I'm a fraud in this uniform, but I enjoy it just the same."

Bernard Cooper sipped his champagne. "You were at Steeple Thaxted today? Your first visit?"

"My first visit to any Fighter Group in England," the General admitted.

"What were your impressions?"

"I had a difficult decision to make today, Dr. Cooper . . ."

"Bernard."

General Bohnen nodded. "I had to assign a dangerous task to any one of a dozen Fighter Groups . . ." He stopped. He was surprised to hear himself confiding his doubts to a stranger, but it was more a measure of his own anxieties than of Bernard Cooper's sympathetic ear.

"And you chose your son's Group," said Cooper.

"I could see no other way," Bohnen told him. "It's an old-fashioned attitude, I suppose, but there it is. The damnable part of it is that I'm not sure the order is a wise one. I found myself arguing with a man who expressed many of my own doubts."

"The people you work with, your commander and so on, do they know you have a son flying on operations?"

"It's better they don't know."

Cooper took the bottle and refilled the glasses. "Are you quite sure?"

"I'm quite sure," General Bohnen said, and drank some champagne too quickly, almost coughing on it.

"If, in peacetime, I came to you for financial advice, would you conceal any special relationship you had with one of the contending parties?" Cooper stepped back, held the bottle high, and raised an eyebrow before pouring a measure for himself.

Bohnen didn't answer; it wasn't a fair comparison and Cooper must have known it. "I'm not *favoring* the party with which I have a connection, Bernard. I'm selling my own son short rather than use the special information I have to favor him."

"I know, I know," said Cooper. "A rotten position to be in. But I'm sure you did the right thing."

"Yes, I did," Bohnen said, but Cooper guessed that his morning phone call, inviting himself to dinner, had been made partly to make changing his mind about coming to Steeple Thaxted that much more difficult.

"Dinner will be ready in half an hour," called Victoria from the doorway. "And Jamie phoned to say he's landed and on his way over here." She looked at the bottle of champagne and the glasses. "You beasts!" she said. "What about some champers for me and Mummy?"

12

Captain James A. Farebrother

The Germans came out of the sun, and Tucker's formation was being clobbered before any of them realized what was happening. Farebrother saw lines of tracer going past his wing tip, and all he could think of was that the Coopers would be waiting for him at dinner that night and now it looked as if he wouldn't be showing up.

Radio discipline went all to hell; he recognized Tucker's voice calling "Topkick Leader," the commander of the 191st Squadron and part of Tucker's formation, but his voice was blocked out by curses and shouts of "Break!" as the Germans came in among them like tiger sharks through a swimming class.

They were Focke-Wulf 190s, mottled gray, almost white, and flown by hotshot pilots, judging by the way they rolled through them and climbed away still in some ragged semblance of a formation. There were twelve of them—a *Staffel,* according to the intelligence notes—and on their first run-through they shot two of the up-sun squadron out of the sky and left Tucker's wingman—a kid named Baxter flying *Whore Weary*—trailing a thin white stream of coolant.

"Stay with me," Tucker shouted, abandoning all radio discipline. There was no way to be sure whether he was talking to his wingman or to the whole formation. But before anyone could ask him, Baxter had rolled his plane onto its back, unlocked his harness, and was dropping out of his cockpit head first.

Tucker—shaken by the loss of his wingman—opened his throttle, and they all chased after him as he took them up in a steep climb that was calculated to avoid the next devastating onslaught from the Fw's above them. Farebrother turned his head and saw them glinting in the sunlight as they came around for another attack. They were re-forming into line now, figuring that their next pass would break the Americans up for individual combat.

Tucker held tight and took them up and over in what would have been an Immelmann turn had the Germans not come in to attack before it was completed. Farebrother stuck close to Earl Koenige, as any good wingman must, and Earl gave him a chance to put a German into his sights. Farebrother fired a short burst, but the German touched his rudder without banking and slid away with no visible damage. Earl hung on to his own target long enough to put a few holes in its tail. Then they were out the other side, and Earl tipped his wing and took them into a tight turn that brought them back into the fighting again.

The radio was still an unintelligible clamor. There were three parachutes below them—Farebrother guessed the yellow one was German; the two white ones were American, one probably Baxter's. Earl found a stray Messerschmitt 110. These twin-engined fighters were slow, and Earl turned gently for a perfect deflection shot from three-quarters above, but the German seemed to sense he was there —or perhaps he heard a warning on his R/T—for he banked steeply away too quickly for Earl to follow him. But the German passed right across Farebrother's sights. It was matt black all over; probably a night fighter summoned to this big daylight battle over the Fatherland. He had no rearward gunner, the Messerschmitt's back cockpit was packed with radar gear for night interception. Farebrother held tight to the stick grip, gave him the prescribed three rings of gunsight, and gently pulled the trigger. After the first gun-camera pressure, he felt the gun's recoil kick the airframe. With mixed emotions of elation and horror he saw his bullets eat through the thin metal airframe like a buzz saw through a bundle of kindling.

Earl slid neatly back to Farebrother's wing, their roles reversed. Farebrother eased the stick to port and followed the German, still shooting. There was no way that any man could have stayed alive inside it. First the wings went shiny as the bullets burned silver dollars out of the paintwork, then the port engine stopped and trailed smoke as the transparent hood shattered and she went nose up to stall, and dropped away her port engine, flaming fiercely.

But Farebrother's world had gone suddenly black as the Messerschmitt's smashed engine dumped its oil over him and smothered his canopy.

From the radio, Farebrother could distinguish one voice, louder than the others—"Break, Cap! Break! Jesus!"—and as *Kibitzer* shuddered under hammerblows of hits, he realized that he was the "Cap" and it was Earl Koenige warning him about a German on his tail.

Blindly he kicked the rudder and turned away. It threw the German off his aim, but as Farebrother turned, he knew his pursuer was right behind him, no doubt his finger tightening on the trigger as he followed into the turn and tried to bring him back into his gunsight. Now the airstream began to streak the oily canopy enough for Farebrother to get glimpses of the world outside.

Probably Farebrother would have become a Luftwaffe statistic right then had the cloud top not been so close. He dived into it and, after a last burst of fire that put some holes in *Kibitzer*'s wing tip, his streaky world went dark again as the cloud pressed close upon the cockpit cover.

Farebrother checked his gyro horizon and eased back the stick until the rate-of-climb indicator steadied up. He continued straight and level for a moment or two, his hands trembling and his heart beating so fast that he could feel the blood pounding in his temples.

"Jesus, Captain, where are you? You hit?" It was Earl's voice out of nowhere.

"Earl . . . Sparkplug Green Three, I mean. Are you above the cloud?"

"Sure am, Cap. Come on up here, all the other kids have packed up their toys and gone home."

Farebrother took *Kibitzer* up out of the cloud to find three P-51s circling lazily with the kind of confidence that the close proximity of cloud cover provides. Earl was slotted against Mickey Morse, with Rube Wein in *Daniel* on his other side.

"Sorry, Earl," Farebrother said breathlessly. "I should have seen that one."

"You did swell, Cap," said Earl. "You did swell for a rookie, sir. Can you see okay? You're smothered in oil."

MM's reaction was more restrained; he checked with Farebrother for the course home. By now the whole squadron knew that Farebrother was the conscientious one at taking notes at briefing and providing himself with homeward compass bearings from landmarks that might be spotted en route. Farebrother peered through the oil-streaked canopy to see where they were. The cloud was broken cumulus, a legacy of the frontal system with endless altostratus riding on the cold air. To the north, over Hannover, the horizon was still dark with rain clouds.

From this height, low enough to avoid trailing long white tell-tale fingers of condensation behind, Farebrother could see the light gray double line of the Autobahn etched into the wintry landscape of dark green forest and bare brown earth. He knew that road from before the war; he remembered his father driving him at some crazy speed in order to dine with friends in a big mansion near Gütersloh. His father had hit a dog and refused to stop and go back. Even now he couldn't forgive his father for it.

"Sparkplug Green Four. You sure this is the way home?" It was MM again.

"I'm sure, Sparkplug Green Leader." There was always time for radio procedure when it didn't matter.

Near the German-Dutch border they saw Tucker leading a formation home and joined him. As they eased into position, Farebrother could see no sign of Colonel Dan or Major Phelan or any of the other flights that had gone after the twin-engined Messerschmitts immediately before the first attack. He wondered what had happened to them, but decided against using the radio to ask Major Tucker.

"Push it, Sparkplug Green." It was Tucker's voice. Now that

they were in formation, Farebrother eased the throttle forward to adjust to their speed.

Kibitzer was an old banger, dumped on Farebrother because he was a newcomer, but today she was especially temperamental. Ever since the fight with the Focke-Wulfs, Farebrother had been trying to persuade himself that the plane was behaving no worse than usual, but now that he'd opened the throttle to full cruising power she was objecting.

His first fears were for his coolant. He checked that the radiator shutter was open. That didn't help. Farebrother had to face the fact that his engine had ingested a lot of German oil and the plugs and supercharger were acting up. He watched the engine-temperature needle climb and heard what had been no more than hiccups turn into splutters. Now, as the splutters became coughs, the needle went into the red sector. Farebrother eased the throttle back; the needle steadied, but he lost formation until Earl slowed a little too and closed to wave encouragement. Thanks, Earl.

On the radio Tucker called, "You hear me, Sparkplug Green Leader? This is Slingshot. This is Slingshot."

MM didn't answer Tucker's call; instead MM and Rube throttled back to stay with Earl and Farebrother.

"Sparkplug Green Four. You're making oily smoke." Earl's voice.

Farebrother tried pumping fuel by hand. For a moment it all looked good, even the engine quieted, but it was no more than a temporary expedient.

"This is an order from Slingshot. Sparkplug Green Leader and Green Two, Three, and Four: you're straggling behind, pull in tighter. You're all over the sky."

Tucker had no time to watch over his flock. He was taking a direct course for home instead of skirting the heavily defended towns. As they crossed Hilversum, they could hear the hum of the flak radar in the earphones and the next moment they were buffeted by an uncomfortably well-aimed salvo. More antiaircraft guns joined in, and now that they had confirmed the range, it wasn't only the black puff of the 8.8-cm. gun smoke but the larger brown 10.5-cm.'s too. They were at 26,000 feet, and although Intelligence insisted that eighty-eights weren't dangerous at that altitude, there seemed to be plenty of "little black men" up here and even above them.

"Dammit, Sparkplug Yellow Leader. Will you remember that

I'm leading the Group today. Stay at this altitude until I tell you otherwise." It was Tucker shouting at a Flight Commander who was trying to put a little space between himself and the flak.

If Tucker had had any intention of gaining altitude, Sparkplug Yellow Leader's anticipation of it changed his mind. Tucker steered a few points north, but another salvo proved that radar estimations had been fed into the predictor. There was something uncanny about the way the flak kept coming at them, guessing their intentions with each salvo getting closer. Farebrother could smell the cordite in spite of his close-fitting oxygen mask, and now he was able to see the orange flash of the gunfire, a sure sign that the flak was dangerously accurate.

"Jamie, kid. You're still making oily smoke." It was MM's voice.

The airflow had cleared the oily canopy as much as it was going to. Farebrother waved to Earl, who was twisting his neck to see him. By now they were passing over the outskirts of town and the gunfire was lessening. For a few minutes they flew on peacefully, then there came more and more jamming as they went through the coastal region, where German radar defenses were concentrated. A pulsating whine made Tucker's voice difficult to hear. "Sparkplug Green Leader," he was saying. "This is Slingshot. For the last time, and this is a direct order, pull in close."

"Tucker," said MM, speaking deliberately and distinctly and well aware of the other pilots listening to him. "You take your big yellow ass out of here, and leave me be. I never left one of my boys limping, and this isn't going to be the day I start."

There was no response. Tucker had decided it was better not to have heard MM's call, and soon afterward he was worrying about the intense gunfire coming up at him from Amsterdam, a region shaded in red cross-hatching on all operational maps.

MM didn't fly over Amsterdam. As Tucker and the rest of the formation pulled ahead, the four stragglers skirted the built-up areas. Farebrother saw the Dutch coast with mixed feelings. There was a lot of very cold gray water between here and England. All he asked was that the prop keep turning until he was within gliding distance of the far shore. He coaxed *Kibitzer* along with soft words of encouragement.

. . .

They were the very last to land. The Debriefing Room was empty except for Doc Goldman, the Flight Surgeon, and his medic, Corporal Walker, an "old man" of forty. They were sitting in the corner talking and laughing together. Farebrother wondered if they had been sampling the mission whiskey.

"Is Vince Madigan around?" MM asked Goldman after he'd swigged his whiskey.

"Vince had to get back to his office," said Doc Goldman, a small bespectacled New Yorker who seemed incapable of knotting his tie so that it didn't twist up under his collar.

"Is Vince avoiding me or something?" said MM without expecting any reply. He hammered the side of the machine to dislodge a jammed Coca-Cola and held the ice-cold bottle against his forehead. "He told me the New York *Daily News* reporter wanted to see me."

Doc Goldman made a face and said, "I heard something about that."

The room was hazy with tobacco smoke and littered with Coke bottles and empty paper cups. The Intelligence Officer debriefed the four pilots together. He knew all the missing pilots and played a regular bridge game with Baxter—he was still trying to convince himself that his friend Baxter might be limping back across the Channel, but Farebrother knew Baxter was lost, he'd seen Baxter bail out. He felt sorry for the IO, who was becoming too emotionally involved to stand the strain of the debriefings. When they went into the locker room, Tucker was there with the Chaplain. They were sorting through the personal effects from Baxter's locker.

Both men looked up as the four pilots came in, trailing parachutes and flying gear. Tucker had combed his hair and put on his tie and a carefully pressed jacket. "The wine waiter" always looked ready to go on parade; he'd thoroughly enjoyed West Point. His eyes moved quickly across their faces, and nervously he ran a fingertip along his hairline mustache.

"Thank God you guys are home safe," said Tucker. He turned to the Chaplain. "Farebrother's plane was hit in combat, Father. It's a miracle he got it home."

"Miracles are *my* department," said the Chaplain in mock admonition. He was a ruddy-faced captain of about forty-five, wearing a tan service trenchcoat with the thick woolen liner buttoned into it, so that he was bulgy and shapeless. He guessed which of them was the "miracle" and studied Farebrother with sad gray eyes. "Tell me, Captain, did you pray?"

"I did, Father."

"And God heard you."

"Looks like He didn't hear Baxter," said MM, going over to see the personal effects the men were examining.

"Baxter was lucky too," said Tucker, glaring angrily at MM. "Baxter bailed out unhurt from a damned dangerous—begging your pardon, Father—dangerous mission."

MM fingered Baxter's family snapshots and helped himself to a pack of gum. "Any mission you're leading is dangerous," said MM. "We're all lucky to get back."

Tucker's already pale face went white with fury. "What do you mean by that, Lieutenant Morse?"

MM tossed his parachute onto the bench and it landed noisily as the metal fittings and straps slid to the bare floor. "I mean you always choose to lead the really rugged missions, Major. It's a well-known fact that you are the most intrepid birdman in the ETO." MM turned to Rube Wein and Earl Koenige. "Ain't that right, boys?"

"Shoot!" said Earl, always ready to back MM up, even if it meant crossing his Squadron Commander. "That's just what Rube was saying to me when we were looking through my collection of pressed flowers this morning." He looked at MM and was pleased to see him smile.

The Chaplain scooped Baxter's possessions together into a brown-paper bag, picked it up, and said, "I really should be getting along."

Major Tucker threw his flying boots into his locker and slammed the steel door and locked it. Before he left the locker room, he turned to look at the four of them. "Colonel Dan knows you disobeyed an operational command today, Morse. The Exec will be wanting to talk to you. And I don't want any of you four pilots to try leaving base until I give you personal permission."

"Tucker," said MM, "I shot down two Huns today. That puts me two ahead of any pilot in this Group. Vince Madigan has fixed it so that tomorrow a reporter from the New York *Daily News* does a story on me. How would you like me to tell them I got a yellow-bellied Squadron Commander?"

This threat seemed to amuse Tucker. He smiled and said, "I wouldn't advise anything like that, Morse, not with the reporter from the *Daily News*."

Disconcerted by Tucker's response, MM rubbed his face reflectively and persisted with his joke. "Come to think of it, that might be just what you need for a job on the staff. The Japanese staff, for instance. I guess they've all got yellow bellies there. No one would notice."

Earl laughed nervously, as if desperately hoping that Tucker would join in the fun. Rube Wein shook his head and said, "Jesus, MM. You sure have got a sense of humor."

"You insubordinate bastard," said Tucker to MM. "I would have made mincemeat out of you at the Point."

"Yeah," said MM affably, "but I would have made mincemeat out of you at Flying School. Right, Major?" Tucker banged the door and left.

"He'll get you, MM," Earl warned. "He's a real mean SOB, that Tucker. He'll find a way to get you."

"That's what they told me about Hitler," said MM. "But he's still trying, ain't he?"

"I don't like the way Tucker smiled when you told him about the *Daily News*," said Rube. "That bastard's up to something."

"Forget him," said MM. "I already have."

Farebrother buttonholed MM as they dumped their flying gear into the equipment racks. "Thanks a lot, MM. I sure appreciate it."

"What for?" said MM, turning away as if expecting no answer.

"Staying with me out there. Maybe I should go and explain what happened to Major Tucker."

"Forget it," said MM. "You think I'd leave you out there in the big empty space? Shit, you're the only dope who'll lend me money."

After Farebrother had showered and changed, he phoned the Coopers to tell them he was on his way. There was no problem in borrowing a jeep for the evening, none of the other pilots wanted to leave base. Several had claimed victories at the debriefing, and now they were sitting in the bar, waiting for the photo lab to finish processing the gun-camera films that would settle any arguments.

But the prevailing mood was one of despondency. The 195th Squadron pilots were particularly low—they'd lost two pilots on that first pass. One of them, Boogie Bozzelli, the noisy kid from Tallahassee, Florida, who played piano like a pro and on Sundays provided music for the chapel. The other casualty was captain of the softball team. Both men were popular and there were arguments about whether they'd been seen to bail out safely, as their friends insisted, or whether both ships had tumbled, out of control, as other eyewitnesses reported to the Intelligence Officer. Either way, their absence was keenly felt and, after a few drinks at the bar, there were some insisting that Major Tucker had led them into a trap.

Farebrother arrived at the Coopers' house in time for dinner. It was a rather ugly red-brick mansion in a beautiful part of Cambridge not far from The Backs. There was a large garden and at the front a few trees and a gravel drive in which he parked the jeep, having removed its rotor arm as the regulations stated should be done to guard against theft.

Victoria opened the front door even before he rang the bell and embraced him with great ardor. "You were flying, Jamie," she said, almost choked with emotion. "Thank God I didn't know. I would have died of worrying. Was it terrible?"

He took his time before answering. "It wasn't terrible," he said. "I shot down a German plane."

"Jamie!" She stepped back and stared at his face as if expecting some change in the way he looked. "You did what?"

"I shot down a German plane," he said.

"Where?"

"Somewhere between Hannover and Bielefeld . . . it was cloudy."

"Will it be confirmed?"

"Give me a kiss," he said, and embraced her again. He hadn't expected her to be like this; he hadn't understood the British cold-blooded determination to win the war at all costs.

They kissed for a long time, then nuzzling against his shoulder, she said, "Will it be confirmed, your victory?"

"No one can deny it," he said. "My film will show him breaking apart."

"That's wonderful." She hugged him—a schoolgirl's gesture, the hug given to the girl who won the netball match. "Daddy has champagne open to celebrate your father's promotion to general. Now it will be a double celebration."

"Tomorrow, Vicky," he said. "Or maybe the day after. But for today let's keep it between you and me."

"But why, darling? Isn't this something to celebrate—something you'll want to tell your children?" In anyone else he might have found this insistence unattractive, but Victoria could say such things with the innocent curiosity of a child.

"I killed a man today, Vicky. I saw him burn. It's not something I want to celebrate, and I doubt if it will ever be something I'll be proud to tell my children about."

"I love you so much, Jamie. Don't ever leave me!"

"Are our fathers getting along together?"

She laid her head against his shoulder for a moment, then looked up at him. "You said you were a wingman. You said your job was just to protect your leader. You said it wasn't dangerous. How did you come to shoot down the German?"

"It was an accident," he said flippantly.

"Don't treat me like a child, Jamie."

"It's just geometry—three-dimensional geometry—sometimes the two planes turn tightly in an attempt to get a sight on an enemy. And the wingman, inside the turn, becomes the leader and the two pilots change roles. It's difficult to explain . . . I guess it's like dancing."

She pushed him away to arm's length, holding on to his sleeves while she looked up at his face. "Let's hope it's not too much like dancing, darling," she said mischievously; having already tried to improve his ballroom dancing, she'd abandoned him as unteachable.

"And are our fathers getting along together?" he asked again.

"Jamie"—it was a different voice now—"it's quite amazing. I've never seen Daddy quite so relaxed as he is with your father. They've even been telling dirty stories."

"Have you been eavesdropping?"

She blushed deep red. "Yes. I listened at the door."

"You terrible girl! Let's go and say hello to your mother."

She held onto his arm so that he couldn't move toward the kitchen, where he could hear her mother working at the stove. "Jamie," said Victoria, "you make me ashamed." He stroked her hair. "Suppose that tonight there was some young German in Hannover opening a bottle of champagne to . . ."

He kissed the top of her head. "Exactly, Vicky," he said.

Captain James Farebrother looked around the dining room. Nothing had changed since the last time he'd visited the house two days before, to share dinner with them and play bridge. The dark mahogany sideboard held the same collection of antique silver that had been in the family for several generations. An oil painting of Victoria's grandfather still dominated the room, and the same bone-handled knives were as blunt as he remembered them being. The Coopers too were unchanged, her mother's wavy hair was no less and no more gray at the temples, and she was still a rather beautiful middle-aged lady with the same nervous smile as she apologized for their wartime food. Everything was the same, and yet everything had changed; he had changed. He'd been strapped tight into the narrow confines of a P-51, flown it across western Europe, and come back again—a thousand miles. He'd killed a man, come close to dying, and been more frightened than he'd ever dreamed was possible. Of course everything was different; the boy who'd played bridge with the Coopers the other day would never return again. For better or for worse, he was a different man.

"It's a young man's war, Bernard," his father was saying.

"All wars are," said Cooper. "We teach our children that life is a trial of strength, and then we're surprised to find that they believe us." Cooper was an amiable old card, the sort of figure Hollywood casting agencies sent to play eccentric professors.

Jamie's father would never grow old gracefully the way Victoria's father was able to do. Alexander Bohnen resisted the onset of middle age as he'd resisted so much else in his life; as he'd resisted so much of what marriage and fatherhood demanded. He was lean and handsome and energetic, and above all, he was smooth and charming. Giving Victoria a smile, he said, "Your father's too erudite for me, Victoria. Did I teach you that life was a trial of strength, Jamie?"

"You *showed* me it was." Jamie Farebrother was too tired to think of some polite evasion. It was simpler to speak the truth. "You always won. You got the best deal, the bigger margin, or the shrewdest investment."

"Did I?" said Bohnen, genuinely puzzled. His son had hurt his feelings. On the one hand, he was pleased to believe that what Jamie had said was true, and yet he recognized that his tone of voice was reproachful. "For you," said Bohnen defensively. "I did whatever I did for you, and for your mother."

"Sure," his son said, and tried to heal the wound.

"Why do you say a young man's war?" said Cooper. Jamie saw Mrs. Cooper frown to show that she did not want to talk about the war, but Bohnen didn't notice and Cooper paid no attention.

"Jamie's colonel—commanding the Group out there at Steeple Thaxted—is thirty-six years old. A youngster as age is measured in the world of commerce. But already he's too old to command a Fighter Group."

"Colonel Dan's a fine flyer," said Jamie Farebrother.

"No doubt he is," his father replied. "Flew the mail routes back when Lindbergh was doing the same thing. Sure, I looked up his record—no doubt about his flying ability. But by the Army's standards, too old to command a combat Group."

Jamie Farebrother found some element of retaliation in his father's description of Colonel Dan Badger. Jamie had no doubt that Colonel Dan's failings were social rather than operational. Alexander Bohnen would not appreciate the gum-chewing, rough-spoken airman who flew more missions than any Group Commander had to, and who had recently offered an insubordinate staff sergeant a chance to fight him in the boxing ring. "He's not exactly West Point," said Jamie.

"I'm not exactly West Point myself," said his father. "But that doesn't mean I fail to see the value of the sort of professional training men from the Point have behind them."

"West Point training is just fine for infantry officers, for the Signals Corps and the Ordnance Department, and the cavalry officers who have to calculate how much hay to feed to their tanks, but the Air Force is something else again. Pilots have to be able to improvise, to think quickly. I worked many long months trying to teach men to fly airplanes. The Point doesn't produce many natural pilots."

"There are plenty of exceptions, Jamie," his father said. He looked around the table. "Jamie's Squadron Commander—a young West Pointer named Tucker—is an example of a career soldier who's carved a name for himself as a fighter pilot. Right, Jamie?"

He had already resolved never to discuss the Group personnel with his father. It was surprising that the General didn't see what a slippery slope that would be for his son, but his entire business career had benefited from whispered confidences in smoky rooms. "Does he have a reputation as a fighter pilot?" Jamie asked, keeping his voice level.

His father put his fork down on his plate. "Major Tucker will end the war with a star on his shoulder." Bohnen pointed at his own shoulder, just in case there was any doubt in their minds about what Tucker was going to get. "A cadet makes friends and now some of Major Tucker's West Point classmates are rooting for him in Washington and at High Wycombe too." Observing the unenthusiastic look on his son's face, he turned to Cooper. "Do you see anything wrong with that, Bernard?"

Cooper was cautious. "It's the way the world is, Jamie," he said apologetically. "I've been grateful for favors from old school friends of mine. It's asking too much of human nature . . . I mean, we ask men to give their lives for their friends in war. Shall we then punish them for granting friends a favor afterwards?"

"I guess not, Dr. Cooper," said Jamie Farebrother. His father always got the better of such arguments. He remembered the time, so long ago, when his father had explained why it was impossible to turn back to attend to the dog they'd hit. It was miles to the next Autobahn exit and against the law to stop a vehicle on the road. Perhaps his father was right; perhaps the hostility was in Jamie's heart.

"You're no longer married to Jamie's mother, General Bohnen?" Jamie had watched Mrs. Cooper wrestling all through dinner with what he now realized was this opening. Now she raised her linen napkin to her lips as if regretting that she'd blurted it out, and kept her eyes averted from her husband, whose face had stiffened.

Of course his father didn't mind her direct question. He smiled and took a deep breath as if he relished the opportunity to talk about Jamie's mother. "You and Dr. Cooper will love Jamie's mother, just as I still love her. She's gentle and kind and understands music and art, and has all those priceless gifts that Jamie inherited from her. We separated and divorced long before the war, but I write to her still."

Victoria glanced at Jamie and he winked at her. Cooper said, "I hope this is not . . ."

He didn't finish telling Bohnen what he hoped it wasn't, but he got an answer anyway. "Not at all. She's a wonderful woman and she deserves the happiness her new husband—Bill Farebrother—has provided for her." To Jamie, his father's obvious distaste as he mouthed the name of Jamie's stepfather was almost comical, but apparently he had conveyed to the others a heartfelt sincerity. The General looked around the table, his glance lingering a moment on Jamie, who nodded his approval of these sentiments.

Reassured by his son's response, he enlarged upon his former wife's affluent lifestyle and the big house overlooking the Pacific Ocean near Santa Barbara where the Farebrothers now lived.

"It's simply wonderful," said Mrs. Cooper.

"What is wonderful, Mother?" Victoria asked her. Was her mother admiring Jamie's father or the prospect of being divorced from him?

"That you can all remain such good friends," said Mrs. Cooper. She touched her hair. "I've always wanted to go to California," she added inconsequently.

Was Victoria such a complex creature as her mother? Jamie wondered. Mr. Cooper was straightforward enough, always allowing for the fact that he was not only a Britisher but also the father of a girl Jamie was having an affair with, but his wife was less easy to understand. Essentially feminine, she was able to chatter but say nothing, ask questions and require no reply. It was as if she had already decided whether Jamie Farebrother was a suitable match for her daughter, but not yet prepared to reveal her decision to anyone in the world.

13

Bernard Cooper

"Your rabbit pie was delicious, dear," Bernard Cooper told his wife after their guests had departed.

"Thank you, Mummy," added Victoria. "It was a wonderful evening, and you worked so hard."

"And what about me?" said her father. "Didn't I work hard too?"

"Opening the champagne and telling your joke about the drunken air-raid warden." She kissed her father and put her arm around him with a sudden movement that surprised him. "Of course. Thank you both."

"Your father hates rabbit," said Mrs. Cooper.

"It's not a dish I would hunger after when this wretched war is over," admitted Dr. Cooper. "But General Bohnen called it a 'chicken pie,' so I think it must count as a culinary triumph."

"Well, when after the war we return to having a full-time cook and housemaid, you'll not be asked to eat my rabbit pie or any of the other dishes I slave over."

"No offense, dearest," said Cooper, who secretly doubted whether they would ever again be able to afford domestic servants. He wondered to what extent his wife realized that she was sentenced to cooking and house cleaning for the rest of her days.

"To think of that poor man managing without a wife all these years," said Mrs. Cooper. "It's not fair on the children, I've always said that. I know nothing of psychology, but I'm sure there's no greater gift for a child than a happy and harmonious home life. What scars it must have left on Jamie."

"He seems normal enough," said Victoria.

"In his lectures your father says that any sort of trouble in childhood leads to emotional breakdowns in later life. Isn't that so, dear?"

Bernard Cooper was tempted to simply nod, but no expert can tolerate hearing his theories distorted and misrepresented to such an extent. "Genetic or environmentally induced neurotic conflict initiated in childhood is often repressed and forgotten forever, causing no problems in adult life. It's the combination of childhood anxieties *plus* adult stress that triggers physical and emotional symptoms severe enough to require treatment."

Mrs. Cooper's face had tightened as her husband provided his explanation. She'd heard enough psychology to last her a lifetime; she stopped listening, waiting patiently for him to finish, knowing that her departure now, or a deliberate change of subject, would make him bad-tempered for days.

"War brings such *extremes* of stress," Cooper went on, speaking as much to himself as to his wife and daughter, "that even the mildest of childhood anxieties are enough to produce clinical neurosis. I was bound to notice young Jamie's physical fatigue tonight, as well as the way he sought his father's approval, often the sign of insecurity of a kind that can lead to problems."

Mrs. Cooper waited politely to make sure her husband had finished before beginning to gather up the unused cutlery from the table. "Why don't you make yourself comfortable by the fire while we're washing up? I'll put the milk on and we'll have a cup of cocoa before going to bed."

Bernard Cooper took her advice, pleased that she didn't expect him to dry the dishes. His wife's question had started him thinking about both guests. General Bohnen was a compulsive, if not to say

obsessional, personality, conditioned by the business world in which
he found the sort of peer-group respect that such men need. But now
his "duty" had become a rationale for demanding too much from
others, and far, far too much from his own limited emotional re-
sources. Was there within him some deep-felt desire to sacrifice what
he loved most—his son—upon the altar of war? And did the son, in
some dreadful fashion, perceive it, as all sons instinctively share the
mental state of their fathers? Bohnen loved his son, as every father
must love his child, and the son could not respond with equal love,
for that is the fundamental and tragic truth of human biology. For if
children did love their parents with that same consuming passion,
they would never leave home, and the world would end.

Cooper stared at the flickering fire. He wished he could help his
wife reconcile herself to their daughter's need to leave home, but he
could not. The relationships between mothers and daughters are un-
fathomable, even for a psychologist of note. Men compete with their
sons, but mothers devour their daughters—devour them; there was
no other word for it.

From where he was sitting he could hear his wife talking with
Victoria in the kitchen. They were washing up, or clearing away, or
performing some other household task, the tedium of which was
echoed in the listless tone of their voices. And yet Cooper had lived
in a household of women too long to miss the meaningful undercur-
rent that so often runs beneath such undramatic tones.

"I adore Jamie, darling, you know I do," he heard his wife say.
"But I was surprised to notice that he wears perfume."

"It's not perfume, Mother," said Victoria patiently. "It's called
after-shave lotion. Most of the Americans use it."

"And talcum powder on his face," continued Mrs. Cooper, as if
she hadn't heard Victoria. "I can't imagine an English boy using
cosmetics, they'd think it rather effeminate."

"And I can assure you Jamie is not effeminate, Mother."

"And that large gold wristwatch," continued Mrs. Cooper, anxious lest Victoria enlarge on her testimony to Farebrother's mas-
culinity. "And the gold identity bracelet he wears. I'm surprised you
can't see him as something of a mother's boy."

He heard Victoria put the potato peeler, or whatever it was,
down on the wooden drainboard with a loud bang. Women spoke to
each other by means of these abrupt actions. He'd witnessed the same
sort of thing among his office staff.

"I love Jamie," said Mrs. Cooper again, "you know I do, darling. I'd hardly have gone to all that trouble cooking for him if I didn't."

Later that night, as Dr. and Mrs. Cooper prepared for bed, Bernard Cooper mentioned Jamie's obvious deep affection for Victoria.

"Victoria behaves like a slave to him," said Margaret Cooper.

"They're in love," he told her.

"For him it is nothing but a fling!" She pronounced that final word as if it was an obscenity. "He'll go back to America and forget her just as soon as the war is over."

"Why do you think that, darling?" he asked her mildly, hoping for a more reasoned answer.

His wife flared up at him as if she'd been bottling up the answer all evening, as in fact she had. "And if he takes her away with him—will that be better? We'd never see her again. Do you realize that? Your precious daughter will be six thousand miles away!"

Cooper sighed. Poor Margaret, she could foresee only two alternatives: either her daughter would be the spurned plaything of an effete foreigner or she would leave them forever. Perhaps it was just as well that Margaret had a husband upon whom she could vent her anger.

14

Captain
Vincent H. Madigan

In civilian life Vince Madigan had held many different jobs; an English lit. degree from NYU is not a passport to the Pulitzer Prize, or even to a well-paid job on a newspaper. After college, Madigan sold lawn mowers, delivered laundry, and caddied for a swank golf club before getting a job he liked on a good newspaper. At last he was happy; his coverage of the opening of the Queens-Midtown Tunnel—"Mayor Cuts Ceremony; Lady Guest Cuts Tape"—got him a by-line. So it was unfortunate that his dismissal came so soon after-ward as a result of an affair he had with the advertising manager's daughter. On that newspaper the ad manager had some of the biggest advertising accounts in his pocket, and when the editor had to choose between them, Vince Madigan wasn't a serious contender. It was 1940. Madigan was twenty-nine years old and there was an Army recruiting office next door to the sandwich counter where he regu-larly had lunch.

His eventual assignment to the European Theater of Operations as a Public Relations Officer with the 220th Fighter Group was just as casual. When, at Fort Benning, he saw the request on the bulletin board for "officers with experience with the press or public relations for training and assignment to the Air Force," he put in his applica-tion without even finding out what a PRO had to do. The Army sent the volunteers away on a course of instruction during which it be-came increasingly clear that the Army wasn't too certain what a PRO was supposed to do either.

When he arrived at Steeple Thaxted he found a PR office al-ready functioning. A technical sergeant had opened files on all per-sonnel and had cockpit photos taken of the pilots. Press releases were produced regularly. Much of the smooth functioning of the office was due to the efforts of a thin assertive private first class named Fryer. A graduate in journalism from the University of Maryland, Fred Fryer was young enough to believe he knew more about public rela-tions than anyone else on the base, and was foolish enough to try to prove it.

But there were many jobs that the Pfc. was not permitted to handle. With an operational Group such as the one at Steeple Thaxted, Captain Madigan knew it was important to be present at the debriefing when the planes returned from a mission. His sergeant took a photographer around the hardstands to cover any battle-damaged planes or pilots re-enacting their victorious combats. Pfc. Fryer remained in the office to answer the phone "in case Hitler suddenly surrendered."

It was standard operating procedure—SOP as the Army calls it—that fighter pilots got a shot of whiskey on landing after a mission. This came courtesy of Uncle Sam and was issued by the Flight Sur-geon. But when Doc Goldman was on duty at debriefings, he allowed Vince Madigan to pour it for the boys. He knew it gave him a chance to get stories from them.

On that dark January afternoon, after the long flight back from Brunswick, the boys needed that shot of whiskey as few of them had ever needed a drink before. The Group had lost three planes, and Morse's flight—with Wein, Farebrother, and Koenige—wasn't back yet. The strain of the flight was evident in the hollow eyes and drawn gray faces. There was none of the usual shouting and laughing during the debriefing session. The voices were high-pitched—a sign of fatigue—and tinged with hysteria. Harry Costello had seen his roommate, Boogie Bozzelli, shot to pieces. The two boys had grown up together in a small town in Florida. They found Harry sitting in the latrines, sobbing his heart out and incoherent with grief. Doc Goldman gave Harry a shot that quieted him down, and then two of his friends half carried him back to his quarters.

"How did it go today, Spurrier?" Madigan asked Major Tucker.

"It was rough, Vince," Tucker said, taking a whiskey and drinking half of it in one gulp. "With most of the heavies called back, the rest of them took a lot of punishment. We were flying on fumes by the time we landed."

"Is Bobby Baxter here yet?" said Madigan. "I've got some beautiful air-to-air photos of him."

"You'd better send them General Delivery, Berlin," said Tucker. "Baxter took to his chute while we were still over the target."

"Poor Bobby," said Madigan. Baxter had been Tucker's wingman since before Tucker began to lead his squadron.

"It's these Merlin engines," said Tucker. "Baxter was spewing coolant. It had never happened to him before. He got scared."

Tucker was trembling. He saw Madigan watching him and drained the whiskey from his paper cup. "Farebrother had worse trouble," said Tucker. "But Farebrother nursed his ship along. And that *Kibitzer* is a shitty airplane."

"Where is Jamie?"

"I left the rest of the flight with him," said Tucker. "He'll be here soon." He crushed his empty paper cup and said, "Baxter got scared." He threw the paper ball into the wastebasket with violence enough to show them he didn't want to talk about it anymore.

Madigan liked Major Tucker and yet he could never resist needling him. He said, "I hear Mickey Mouse got another Nazi today —someone said they think he got two."

Tucker grunted.

"We're bringing the Group total up toward the hundred mark now, Spurrier," Madigan told Tucker.

Tucker didn't answer, and Madigan turned to watch the room. One day he would write about this—a series of articles for a newspaper or magazine. But would he ever be able to convey the tense atmosphere of this scene? The room was big, made dark by the rain clouds and gathering dusk outside. Half a dozen electric light bulbs hung low over the pine-top tables, shedding warm yellow light onto the papers, pencils, and maps. Discarded scarfs, flying gloves, and helmets were pushed aside as pilots argued, demonstrated, and contradicted each new account of the mission they'd flown.

At the other end of the room the pilots waiting to be interrogated stood around in small groups, not talking, just staring and thanking whomever it was they prayed to that they were back in one piece. Even the ones who'd finished their debriefing didn't leave immediately. It was as if they gained some comfort from standing with their friends in that room.

"One hundred!" said Tucker. "Is that what you publicity hounds are telling them?"

"We're getting real close," said Madigan.

"*We're* getting close?" said Tucker. "How many of those Huns did you knock down with your typewriter, Vince?"

Madigan smiled. "Jesus, it's a good thing I understand you, Spurrier. Some guys would take offense."

Tucker touched his thin mustache. Madigan wondered if he dyed it to make it so black. He said, "I'm sorry, Vince. That little bastard Morse has been handing me a lot of shit lately."

"You don't have to take anything from that creep," Madigan said. "You're the Squadron Commander. Make him toe the line."

"Easier said than done," said Tucker. For the first time, Madigan felt sorry for him. The flyers were a collection of ill-disciplined individualists; there was no way they would respond generously to Tucker's old-fashioned West Point manners and methods. And Tucker just couldn't unbend enough to join in the knock-down, drag-out exchanges that came naturally to most fighter jocks.

Madigan smiled to show he sympathized with him.

Tucker said, "You're the guy who gives him these big ideas."

"Who are you talking about?"

"You know who I'm talking about—the guy you've been writing up as if he's Baron von Richthofen reincarnated."

"Don't get mad at me. I've got a job to do. I just write up the publicity, I don't give anybody special breaks."

Spurrier Tucker scowled. "Well, Morse sure gets his picture in the papers."

"You're talking about his scrapbook? Name me a pilot here who hasn't been mentioned in some Stateside newspaper. Hell, I know *you* have, I've got the cuttings on file in my office."

"And Colonel Dan never gives me any proper support. Last night I went out to the Operations Room to talk about the field order and he bawled me out in front of the whole HQ staff. He does everything he knows to make me look like a damn fool, and he's the Group Commander, so I have to stand there and take it."

But Madigan wasn't going to let Tucker change the subject so easily. He never played favorites with his publicity releases and he wasn't going to let Tucker get away with his beefing about it. "You think Morse is a vain, boastful little creep," said Madigan, "and I agree with you. But he can be a charmer too. He poses in front of that ship with the big Mickey Mouse painted on its nose, and he stretches out his hands the way press photographers like fighter pilots to show how they shoot down Messerschmitts. And he holds a smile while they focus up, and he's always happy to give them one more shot, the way every photographer always wants one more shot. And he tells them how he used to be a night watchman at an eastern women's college . . ."

"No one believes all that crap . . ." Tucker was exasperated.

Madigan grabbed Major Tucker's sleeve and tried to make him understand a few of the facts of life. "No one believes all that crap, Spurrier, but it makes a good story! And reporters live on stories, so stories give MM a lot of extra column inches."

"You mean I should start making up stories?"

"I don't give a damn what you do, Spurrier. But you're complaining about the kind of news exposure MM is getting, and I'm trying to explain it to you. But you'd better remember one more thing: MM is knocking down Krauts, and that's why reporters are interested in him. If he's really added two more today, he'll be the biggest scorer of this Group. If anyone else wants to better his score, I'll happily write up the releases."

But Madigan's efforts to make Tucker see reason didn't have much effect. "Is it true that you fixed up an interview for him with a reporter from the New York *Daily News*?"

"It's true I fixed it up," Madigan admitted, "but I got a message to cancel it. New York cabled their London office that they're up to their armpits in fly-boy features. The reporter's off to do a story on a Liverpool mother who's given birth to quints."

Tucker, who had been hugging himself in an unmistakable gesture of anxiety, now bent forward and laughed shrilly. "Quints!" he yelled. "I can't wait to tell that little bastard what's elbowed him off the feature page! Quints, that's just great!"

By now the interrogations were almost finished. The IO was beckoning to Tucker. "All ready for you, Major Tucker," he called, and as Tucker went across to him he said, "Well, Major, and how did Lady Luck treat you this afternoon?" He smoothed the report pad with the edge of his hand and held his pencil poised. That IO said the same thing to every pilot he interrogated.

Tucker slapped his helmet onto the table. "Did you hear what the *Daily News* is going to feature instead of Morse?" he demanded. Madigan knew that within a couple of hours the story would be all over the base and felt a little guilty at the malicious pleasure this thought gave him.

You don't stand visible to the public gaze holding a fifth of bourbon without soon attracting the attention of Kevin Phelan, the Operations Officer. His face was dirty and his cheeks still bore the red marks that the molded oxygen masks left. "You call that a drink?" said Phelan, throwing a generous measure of whiskey down his throat and offering the paper cup for another.

Phelan had already been with the IO; as one of the Group's senior officers he was always among the first to be debriefed. "How was it?" Madigan asked him.

Phelan reached for the whiskey bottle and twisted it so that he could read the label. "Real good!" said Phelan. "About time we got some sour mash—it's a man's drink."

"The mission, I meant."

"Colonel Dan shot down a Messerschmitt. I hope your photographer got a good picture of him climbing out of the cockpit just now. It's about time you put Colonel Dan's photo in the papers."

"I'll do what I can," Madigan promised.

"Do better than that, Vince," said Phelan. "And that's an order." He reached for the neck of the bottle and tilted it down to provide himself with more whiskey.

"You'd better take it easy on the juice, Major," Madigan warned him. "A one-star general hit town while you were gone. Colonel Dan is with him now—could be he'll need you."

"Take it easy on the juice," said Phelan scornfully. "What kind of talk is that from an Irish boy with a name like Madigan?"

"As one Irishman to another," Madigan joked, "I sometimes wonder what the hell either of us is doing here, fighting England's war."

Phelan swallowed more whiskey and said, "My dad said the same thing. He'd fought the English all his life, he told me, and his father before him. He said he never thought he'd live to see the day when a son of his would be going off to fight for the British. But I told him that a good Irishman shouldn't be so darn choosy when getting into a fight."

"Leave a little of that stuff for the others, Kevin," Madigan said, and Phelan grinned and moved on.

Watching fighter pilots at such close quarters had taught Madigan a lot about the resilience of the young. By early evening of that day of the Brunswick mission, most of the pilots looked fresh and relaxed enough to be newly arrived replacements for those shattered-looking boys he'd seen being debriefed only a couple of hours earlier.

But that was only the youngsters; the men over twenty-five didn't bounce back so easily. Even Farebrother—only a little above average age according to his file card in the PR office—couldn't shrug off the aftereffects of the mission as easily as the younger kids could.

The Officers' Club bar was where they congregated after a mission. The blackout shutters were closed and the electric fans didn't dispel the faint perfume that the U.S. Army's kerosene left on the warmed air. The long mahogany bar top and the shelves of glittering bottles shone in the light of small colored bulbs, like a stage at the end of a darkened auditorium. The rest of this large room was lit only by heavily shaded wall lights. It was too dark to see the cheap gilt ornaments, except as a glint of gold, and too dark to see the large stains on the heavy drapes, the spilled drink and cigarette butts that littered the floor. But this warm dark room—"the Stork Club"—with its virtually unceasing sweet music, provided a substitute every evening for the New York night spots of which they all constantly spoke but which few of them had ever visited.

Farebrother was in the bar when Madigan arrived. He was waiting for a chance to use the phone—after a tough mission the pilots liked to phone girlfriends before the losses were announced over the radio. Jamie had dark patches under his eyes and he was fidgeting endlessly with the large gold Rolex that was coveted by one and all. "Hello, Vince," he said. "Do you have any pennies for the phone?" Madigan found the necessary coins and Jamie insisted on giving him a threepenny bit. Farebrother was like that. "Cheer up, Vince," he said.

Vincent Madigan was not the fun-loving Irishman he liked to be taken for. His mother was from a Swedish family named Carlson that lived in Wisconsin. It is a fact of life that a man with a Swedish father and an Irish mother will be called a Swede throughout his life, but although Madigan had inherited much of his mother's humorless ego, he remained an Irishman; he preferred it that way.

His gratitude to Farebrother for giving him a warm billet far away from the tents had now faded. As he was beginning to see it, Farebrother had needed someone to share the room and Madigan had obliged him. Madigan's opera records, which sometimes kept his neighbors awake, were, in Madigan's view, a cultural benefit that his fellow officers badly needed. And the way in which Jamie Farebrother and Mickey Morse had never properly thanked him for introducing them to their girls would have saddened him, except that by now he had grown used to the way in which the world never treated him with the respect and courtesy he deserved.

"I hear you got your first Nazi," said Madigan.

"Let's wait until the movies are ready," said Farebrother.

Madigan waved a hand at the barman. "Two beers," he said, and they came immediately. He made it a top priority to get along with the Officers' Club staff; a few packs of cigarettes worked wonders. And so his beer arrived in his personal pewter mug, hand-engraved with his inititals inside a winged crest. He saw Farebrother staring at it, and guessed incorrectly that Farebrother's amazement was covetousness. "MM is claiming two," said Madigan.

Farebrother picked up his beer. "That's what I hear," he said. "*Slainte*, Vince."

"Mud in your eye," Madigan countered in a very British voice, holding up his beer.

Farebrother grinned. "*Touché*," he said, and they both drank. Behind them MM was bellowing into the pay phone. "I'll meet you at the Blue Boar. . . . Well, tell your boss you can't work late tomorrow. Tell him you'll be raising the morale of a fighter pilot." There was a pause while he listened, then: "Please, Vera honey." Some architectural genius had put the Club's only pay phones right outside the Rumpus Room, by far the noisiest place in the building. MM took a minute or so to catch his breath, then bellowed again into the phone. "I'm counting on you, Vera baby."

Madigan put his beer down on the counter and wiped his mouth. He watched MM struggling with the British telephone network and shrugged at Farebrother. "I guess MM doesn't realize we can hear him," said Madigan. Farebrother didn't reply, and Madigan said, "I've always had good hearing and I've always been interested in people, ever since I was a kid. I'm something of a psychologist really —in my job, you've got to be." Farebrother smiled as though Madigan had said something funny.

MM yelled, "I'll pick you up at the Blue Boar. . . . I mean, I'll wait for you there. . . . Sure, I know a lady doesn't want to wait around in a bar alone, but I'm promising you I'll be there."

Madigan said to Farebrother, "Vera is a great piece of tail. I sure hope MM appreciates what I did for him."

"I thought MM got you out of a tough spot, Vince. The way I heard it, MM was doing you a favor taking Vera off your hands just when that little brunette was going for your balls with a bread knife."

"At the Christmas party, you mean . . ." Madigan grinned nervously. He was never sure when Jamie Farebrother was kidding him. But behind the smile Madigan was irritated. Jesus, he thought, is that all the thanks I get? Maybe I should remind Farebrother who introduced him to his own broad. He swallowed his resentment, but it was at times like this he remembered his mother telling him he wasn't pushy enough.

"I told you I'd be there," called MM into the phone. He reached for his drink from where it was balanced on the coin box. "Listen, Vera baby, I love you. So be there. Just be at the Blue Boar, will you do that for me, sweetie?" The answer was apparently in the affirmative, for MM went into a series of endearments.

"Sounds like MM's got the hots for Vera," said Madigan to Farebrother. "Well, that's not so surprising, she's quite a number, right? I learned a thing or two from her, I'll tell you that!"

"Is that so," said Farebrother, looking at his watch.

"I wonder if MM knows she's married. She never wore that goddamned gold ring when she was out with me. We were in bed the first time she got around to telling me she was hitched." Farebrother seemed not to have heard what Madigan was saying. Maybe he was too fucking well-bred to eavesdrop.

"Has MM been clowning around with Tucker again, Jamie?" Madigan asked. "I noticed your flight came in long after Tucker got home. Was MM screwing around again?"

"Is that what Tucker says?" Farebrother asked.

Madigan held up a hand and balanced it in a gesture of equivocation. "It's what I hear."

"And did this source from which you heard it tell you that Tucker ordered MM and the rest of them to abandon me with engine trouble in a part of the world where the natives are even less friendly than your average Limey, and not so well-spoken?"

"And MM disobeyed?"

"The whole flight stuck with me," said Farebrother.

Madigan shook his head to show that he couldn't understand MM's behavior. "If MM learned how to keep his big mouth shut, he could easily wind up leading the squadron."

"We're not running him for membership in some fancy country club, Vince. He's the best damn fighter pilot here, whatever the size of his mouth. And when MM wants to kick, he talks man to man. He doesn't go behind Tucker's back spreading stories about him."

"Listen, Jamie," Madigan said, "I'm not rooting for Spurrier Tucker."

"You could have fooled me, Vince."

Madigan hunched his shoulders and grimaced. "I'm the PRO," he said. "I've got to live with Tucker."

"That's the way we all feel," said Farebrother. "We don't want to die with him—that's all."

"How's it going with Victoria?" asked Madigan to change the subject. "Did you score?"

"We get along," said Farebrother, evading the question.

"How well?" said Madigan with a suggestive grin.

"She likes opera," said Farebrother. Before Madigan could think of a reply, the pay phone was free and Jamie finished his beer and turned away.

"If you feel like a change of pace, I can fix you up with a sure thing for Saturday," Madigan called after him. "A lively little blonde, a sweet kid. And a sure thing, I guarantee it." Farebrother didn't look back. There was so much singing in the Rumpus Room by then that perhaps he hadn't heard.

Madigan watched Farebrother on the phone, but he couldn't hear what was being said. Then Farebrother waved good night after finishing on the phone. He didn't say where he was going, but Madigan could guess; he knew Jamie had borrowed Doc Goldman's jeep. Madigan liked to know everything that was going on; he considered it all part of his job.

Things got more hectic in the Stork Club as the evening wore on, and it was about nine o'clock when a short fat man in civilian clothes came pushing his way up to the bar counter. He had a strong Bronx—or maybe Brooklyn—accent, and he was asking for Lieutenant Morse. Madigan suspected some kind of gag, but the newcomer was serious enough to be convincing. Mickey Morse was holding court before half a dozen cronies down at the end of the bar. There was a table there, tucked away under an old airplane propeller and some posters in which airplanes and movie stars were depicted in primary colors. MM regarded it as his regular place in the bar, and woe betide anyone who was sitting there when MM wanted it. He stood up and leaned over the end of the bar counter when he heard his name being called.

"Are you Lieutenant Morse?" said the aggressive little man. He was wearing a new civilian belted raincoat from the pocket of which he produced a note pad and pencil.

"That's me," said MM.

"Mickey Morse, the guy I've read about in the *noospapers?*"

"One and the same," said MM, smiling nervously. There was no way out of it now, gag or no gag. All conversation in the bar had stopped, and even the noisy crowd in the Rumpus Room had drifted in to see what was happening at the bar. The civilian bartenders had stopped serving. They stood back and were watching the exchange with that dour solemnity with which the British workers on base treated everything "the Yanks" did.

The man in the raincoat threw his hat in the air and shouted, "And where's the young lady who's given birth to those five babies, sir? I want to interview her. Congratulations on a top score!"

The civilian—who was really a master sergeant from the Air Service Group's Ordnance Supply and Maintenance Company based near Thaxted Green—found his final words drowned by the roar of drunken cheers going up from the crowded room. He was lifted up by two pilots and handed a bottle of whiskey as a reward while they carried him shoulder-high around the Club. Needless to say, one of the shoulders belonged to Spurrier Tucker, and well in evidence nearby was Major Tarrant, the officer in charge of the Military Police Company. Some people said he almost smiled.

But Madigan was watching MM as he flushed to the roots of his hair, gripped the edge of the counter, and tried to smile. Even Madigan felt a little sorry for him.

"Quiet everyone, please." It was the voice of Duke Scroll, the Exec, just about the only voice that could have quelled that racket in so short a time. "The Group Commander has something to say to you."

Colonel Dan leaped up onto a chair in what was meant to be a demonstration of their commander's youthful fitness. In fact he stumbled and nearly knocked the chair over, and had to suffer the indignity of being helped into position.

Everyone was quiet now, and all faces were turned toward him. "We drew a tough mission today," he said, and cleared his voice before continuing. Colonel Dan was only thirty-six, three years older than Madigan, but he looked like a man of fifty. "And we'll go on drawing tough missions, some of them a lot tougher than the one we flew today." He took his time looking around the room. "But I just came back from looking at some combat film and I want to tell you that, subject to confirmation by HQ, the Group shot down six German planes today and badly damaged four."

"Who?" someone shouted amid the cheers and shouts.

"Captain Farebrother knocked down a Bf 110 so neatly that it flew apart with his first burst. Major Phelan also shot down a twin-engine Messerschmitt. Lieutenant Dittrich got an Fw 190. Special congratulations, Dittrich, on your first victory." He raised a hand and touched forefinger and thumb in a high sign of congratulation. "You too, Farebrother . . . Where's Captain Farebrother?"

"I think he went to bed, Colonel," shouted Madigan, who had an idea that Colonel Dan would not be pleased to hear that Farebrother was off base without permission.

"Reading his training manuals, no doubt," said Colonel Dan. It raised a laugh. Jamie Farebrother was reputed to be a pilot who learned all the regulations by heart.

"You said six," shouted MM.

"Don't worry, Lieutenant," said Colonel Dan. "I wouldn't sell you short. You got two kills today." He looked around the room. "And that makes Lieutenant Morse the highest scorer in the Group." There was a loud cheer. The same pilots who'd been so delighted to

celebrate MM's recent humiliation were just as ready to shout congratulations; exactly as Madigan remembered teen-agers at high
school parties.

"Six!" shouted Major Kevin Phelan, Group Operations Officer.
"You said six, Colonel. Who got number six?" He was smiling as he
asked his question, and Madigan decided he must already know the
answer.

"You're just looking for a free drink, Major Phelan," said
Colonel Dan. The pilots chortled. Just like schoolboys, they enjoyed
best these familiar jokes in which each one of them had an appointed
role. Happy to play the part of town drunk, Kevin Phelan responded
by putting his tongue out thirstily.

"Yeah, I got that last son of a bitch," said the Colonel hurriedly.
"Drinks on me for the rest of the evening." There was a pandemonium of congratulations and war cries and whistles. The little
"civilian" had departed, and the joke played upon MM was forgotten by everyone except MM himself.

Madigan looked around the noisy room—drinks spilled on the
floor and the air blue with tobacco smoke and ribald song. The
wounds of that day were beginning to heal, or at least were harden-
ing to scar tissue. By that time Madigan was one of Steeple Thaxted's
oldest American inhabitants. He'd seen the Group change airplanes
and he'd seen them change Group Commanders. Maybe he didn't
know enough about planes to have an opinion on them, but as for
Colonel Dan, Madigan preferred the guy he'd replaced. As far as he
was concerned, Colonel Dan was a selfish and opinionated man who
openly admitted that he had no interest in anything but his planes
and his flyers.

Colonel Dan couldn't be bothered with the problems of the
service units or interest himself in the terrible conditions in which
the ground crews lived. Don't ask Colonel Dan to present prizes at
the sergeants' Rocker Club party or suggest that he pose for a publicity photo in the bakery early one morning and show the boys that
their work was appreciated. Colonel Dan was always too busy molly-
coddling the goddamned pilots, who, in any case, got extra pay, more
leave, and shorter working hours than anyone else on the base.

This meant that the Exec was overworked, and Duke Scroll was
a man who thought everyone should do everything by the book.
Well, Madigan could tell him that you can't run a PR office by the
book the Army wrote; and certainly not at Steeple Thaxted.

15

Captain
James A. Farebrother

The cold front that had brought havoc to the Brunswick mission passed across Britain, so that by the following morning there was the usual west wind and the blue sky that is a legacy of such weather systems. Farebrother got up early and bicycled across to the technical site in search of *Kibitzer*.

He found her in number two hangar. She was a sorry sight, fuselage and half the port wing black with German oil which in places had baked on in a shiny finish. Her port wing was supported by a heavy tripod jack so that two mechanics could kneel under the wing to work at the disk brakes. One of them threw a wrench into the open toolbox with enough noise to awaken MM's dog, which stood up, stared, yapped unconvincingly, and settled down again.

Farebrother walked around and touched the sharp edges of the alloy from where the sheet-metal workers had removed a wing tip and taken it away to the machine shop. The engine covers had been removed to reveal the entrails of the engine, and up by the nose of the aircraft there was a pulpit-like metal rack. On it stood three men bending close to the Merlin's innards.

"How is it?" Farebrother called up to them.

The men at the engine looked down and he recognized Tex Gill and Mickey Morse. The third man, wearing master sergeant's stripes painted on his leather jacket, was the line chief.

"You were lucky to get this heap home," said MM. He was wearing the olive-colored herringbone twill coveralls that the fitters wore and a fleece-lined leather jacket, a painting of Mickey Mouse filling the back of it. "Looks like three cannon shells went through her without exploding."

The line chief tugged the large visor of his fatigue cap as if embarrassed by what he had to say about Farebrother's plane. "We're going to talk to the Major about making her a category E, sir. The sheet-metal shop never patches ailerons or flaps, and maybe the

Major will think it's not worth fitting her out with new ones." He grimaced. "But you know how short of planes we are right now. My guess is that the Major's going to want her fixed up right here."

"Could you do that?"

"Sure. We could give her a new engine, we've got plenty of those. We'd patch the holes . . ." He looked at Farebrother and then at MM, hoping they'd try to argue him into getting a new plane. "Could be I'll have enough guys to polish her back to the bare metal and wax her." The line chief paused and unconvincingly added, "She'd be as good as new, Captain."

"Run the end titles on her," said MM as he climbed down from the engineering platform. As he wiped his hands on cotton waste, he told Farebrother quietly, "The line chief is waiting for you to offer him the price of six bottles of whiskey. Then he'll sign her off as a category E."

Farebrother knew what the line chief was after, and he also thought of all the things he'd promised *Kibitzer* if only she brought him home. "She's been a lucky ship for me," he said.

"Let's get coffee over at the dispersal shack," said MM.

"Do what you can, Chief," said Farebrother. He got on his bicycle and looked away from the forlorn *Kibitzer*.

"Films will be screened at eleven," said MM, looking at his wristwatch. Farebrother guessed that he had got up early to pester the photo section into showing him his gun-camera films before the regular screening. He'd left his soft-topped officer's cap on his bicycle —it was greasy and battered, and now he stuck it onto the very back of his head, making himself look as unmilitary as possible. "You did all right yesterday," he said. It was a mighty accolade coming from one so reluctant to praise anything or anyone. As if to prevent Farebrother from replying, he turned away and gave a short, earsplitting whistle that brought Winston running.

MM threw a leg over his bike and cycled off, knowing that Farebrother would follow him, just as Winston did. He cycled fast, stabbing at the pedals with that angry energy with which he did almost everything. He went around the back of the huge bitumen-coated steel hangars, their doors clanging mournfully in the wind.

All was still and silent. The planes were parked like monuments on the skyline. A faint yellowish haze drifted across the airfield from the potbellied stoves in the corrugated-iron huts where the airmen lived. Farebrother cycled fast to catch up with MM.

"Track in that lousy sun! When's it going to get warmer?" said MM as they turned onto the perimeter track and faced the full blast of the cold westerly wind.

Farebrother should have realized that it was a rhetorical question, but he answered anyway. "It will stay cold. Temperatures stay steady following the passage of a cold front."

"You ever think of going on one of those radio quiz shows? *Doctor I.Q.* gives away eight hundred and fifty silver dollars on every show. Even a wrong answer gets you a carton of Milky Ways."

"Candy is bad for your teeth," said Jamie. "How are things with you and Vera?"

"She gets kind of moody at times. I guess all women are like that."

"Why don't we make up a foursome for a movie some night?"

"That would be great! I think I made my peace with your Vicky."

They cycled in silence. Apart from the damp cold wind it was a beautiful day. The Cambridgeshire countryside was green under a cloudless sky, and birds were singing in the trees that surrounded the firing butts. There were rabbits too, plump with winter fur and unfrightened enough to scuttle across the perimeter track ahead of their wheels. Winston made halfhearted attempts to chase them, but his regular treats of PX candy made him no threat to the local wildlife.

Mickey Morse was not athletic in build, and his cycling was inexpert. After that first burst of energy, his speed slackened, so that Jamie had pulled alongside him easily.

"Vince was sore about me not going to London with him. He says it's left him in a spot."

"Screw him!" said Farebrother. "Vince is always in a spot with his women. It's his way of life."

MM studied his friend with renewed interest and wondered whether this uncharacteristic anger was a sign that Vince was becoming too much for even the imperturbable Farebrother. "Did he tell you I hadn't finished college?"

"Why should I be talking to Vince about your days at college?"

"I lied when I filled out that questionnaire he gives out. I wrote down I finished college. If he writes to them . . ."

"Forget it, MM. Vince has other things on his mind. Without us he'd still be in one of those tents. There are still some officers over there."

"Without *you*, you mean. You invited him, not me. Anyway, Vince doesn't have a long memory for favors people do him—only for things he does for other people. By now Vince has probably convinced himself that he moved into your room to do *you* a favor."

"Vince is okay," said Farebrother. "Everyone's got faults, I guess."

"You heard what he did to me last night? Made me look like a dummy in front of everyone at the bar. I didn't go to breakfast this morning, I knew I'd have some smart-ass gags waiting for me."

"I heard about it. But hell, MM, you can take a joke."

"Vince deliberately screwed up that *Daily News* interview."

"Vince did? Never! Vince would love to get a crackerjack newspaper reporter down here to see you—it would make him feel like a hotshot himself. And it would get him noticed by the PR department at Wing, or in London even. No, Vince wouldn't fuck it up deliberately."

MM turned his head and smiled his relief. "I guess you're right, Jamie."

"But if you want to meet newspapermen, why not ask Vera?"

"She's not a reporter, she's just a typist or something."

"But reporters work out of that office. I met one old guy when I was picking up Victoria—he wants to do a story about the air war."

"A British reporter does?"

"Australian. A tough old bum, fifty, maybe sixty years old. White hair, curly mustache, sideburns, but he's no Santa Claus. He's a big man, Victoria told me. I'd guess you would fit right into his plans."

"Could you find out about him?"

"Sure thing."

As they passed the firing butts, Jamie Farebrother saw a car moving on the far side of the airfield. This part of the field was a little higher than the technical site, so he could see men around the C-47. His father had probably spent the night on the base in the hope of seeing his son in the Officers' Club this morning at breakfast. He knew how much his father wanted to be near him, but he couldn't respond to this love the way his father expected. And yet, seeing his father depart, he was afflicted by a sick feeling of guilt. As quickly as the scene had appeared it was hidden by the uneven green surface of the airfield. But the feeling of guilt remained.

Mickey Morse took his hands off the handlebars to show his skill at balancing, but he wavered uncertainly and had to give up his demonstration. There was the distant sound of the C-47 revving up its engines; then they cut and it fell silent again.

They reached the place where *Mickey Mouse II* and *Happy Daze* were parked. There was an empty place, marked by oil slicks—that was where *Kibitzer* usually stood. These loop-shaped hardstands were macadam surface, added to the airfield after the concrete loops on the south side. But the asphalt had cracked with the winter frosts and had broken to reveal loosened stones, so that planes had to be guided around the potholes to get to the taxiway.

Near *Happy Daze* two bicycles were resting against the shack that the ground crews had improvised from huge packing crates and sheets of corrugated metal. They were not the heavyweight old-fashioned bikes the Army provided; these were lightweight models with low-slung handlebars—the BSA racers that Rube and Earl had bought in Cambridge. Rube and Earl had become enthusiastic cyclists.

MM pushed open the door of the shack. It was bright and warm inside, garlanded with light bulbs and warmed by a homemade electric fire. The walls were plastered with pinup girls from *Yank* and *Esquire*. The photos were so close together and so numerous that they looked like wallpaper with a pattern of repeated buttocks, breasts, and toothy smiles.

Rube and Earl were inside, sitting on broken chairs and talking with a middle-aged corporal from the dispensary.

"I thought you guys were racing around the perimeter track."

"We dropped by for a cup of coffee," said Rube although there was no sign that the dented electric percolator was in use.

"I could use a cup myself," MM said, and picked up one of the cups from which the men had been drinking. "This is no coffee. Are you guys boozing?"

"See you around, Corporal," said Rube. The middle-aged medic took the hint, nodded to MM, and left.

MM was poking behind a broken airplane seat that the corporal had been sitting on. He reached down, produced a bottle, and shook it so that the clear liquid sparkled. "Some bastards are manufacturing moonshine out here." Rube and Earl said nothing. Jamie touched the percolator in search of coffee, but it was completely cold.

MM uncorked the bottle and wet the palm of his hand so that he could lick it. "Hooch! I knew it."

"Are you going to tell Major Tarrant?" asked Earl, shifting uncomfortably.

"Raisins, I'd guess," said MM, savoring the homemade alcohol. "And that old medic is from the dispensary. Are you two in on this racket?"

"Don't pretend you're some kind of Boy Scout, MM," said Rube. He smiled scornfully.

"Is this what you two are up to when you go off on your bike rides?"

"It was just for kicks," said Earl.

"Kicks! And that's what makes me so sore. I can understand the enlisted men maybe get desperate for some liquor, but you guys have your whiskey ration."

Rube had his arms folded tightly and wore a scowl on his face. "Cut it out, MM," he said quietly.

"I'm the lousy Flight Commander around here. Don't tell me to cut it out, buddy!" MM found a piece of tubing that was part of the disassembled still. "Shut up, you fuckhead! You know what the penalty is for making illegal liquor on a military installation? It's death! It's a capital offense under Section Three hundred and ninety-five of the Military Code!"

Although both Earl and Rube were certain that MM was inventing all this on the spur of the moment, there was a sufficient residue of fear for them both to go very pale. MM pressed his advantage. "Ask Jamie," he said. "We were talking about it only the other night." Such was Jamie Farebrother's reputation as a man with an encyclopedic knowledge of law and science that both the lieutenants began to believe MM's nonsense. They stood stiff and out of breath as if drenched with a bucketful of icy water.

MM relished the sight of them for a moment before saying, "And next time you break the law, don't do it in collusion with enlisted men. Some of these guys will put the arm on an officer, given a chance like that."

"You mean officers wouldn't?" said Rube, who seemed to want to prolong the argument.

"You know what I mean," said MM.

Farebrother broke into the silence that followed by apologizing to Earl. "Say, Earl, I promised to help you with that letter to your brother-in-law. What say we do it now, before the screening?"

Earl brightened at so easy an escape from MM's wrath. "Let's go, Cap. I looked up the date of my check and I kept copies of the letters."

This subterfuge did not deceive MM, who only grudgingly let Earl go, but Earl appreciated it. Farebrother and Koenige cycled off together and left Rube and MM to their wrangling. As they cycled past the firing butts, the duty armorers were positioning Tucker's *Jouster*, with its garishly painted knight in armor, for gun synchronization. There was a large audience of village children—they'd climbed through a gap in the fence. Testing guns was rated second only to a forced landing as a spectacle for the local kids.

"How did you get into flying, Earl?" Farebrother asked, more to make conversation than because he had a great curiosity. On the other side of the field his father's C-47 began taxiing out. The main runway was blocked by the work detail of the Engineering Battalion who were filling the cracks with mixed concrete. The C-47 would have to come past the two cyclists before taking off.

"My dad bought two old Curtiss Jennys, war surplus, a hundred bucks apiece. He wrecked one teaching himself to fly. We cannibalized it to keep the other Jenny going."

"Your dad sounds like quite a guy, Earl."

"My folks are German," explained Earl. "My grandparents are still living in Germany, and so are some aunts and uncles and cousins. Sometimes it gives me a funny feeling flying over there. Especially when I see the heavies toggling their loads. I figure, gee . . . Well, you know."

"Sure, Earl."

"My dad's a great guy," said Earl. "I sure miss him. My mom too . . ." he added loyally. After a pause he said, "I never talk about my relatives in Germany. Someone might figure I wasn't to be trusted flying missions."

"No one would feel that way, Earl," said Farebrother, even though Rube Wein's accusations were fresh in his memory.

"Mickey Mouse wouldn't," said Earl. "MM sticks by his guys. That's what's so great about him."

"You can say that again. You all stuck by me out over the water when *Kibitzer* was coughing bad."

"MM's afraid of his dad," said Earl. "That's why he won't let anyone share his room. He has nightmares. He keeps the light on all night."

"I noticed that."

"His old man used to come home late at night and pull the boys out of bed and beat them up."

"Drunk, you mean?"

"Beat them up real cruel. Sure, he was a bottle-a-day man. Then, when MM's mom died, his old man got religion. Really got it—he preaches and all that. You see all those letters on the shelf in MM's room? All in the same writing, all from his father. He never opens them."

"But he never throws them away, huh?" They stopped and watched the C-47 trundling around the taxiway toward them.

"I guess you're right," said Earl. "I never thought of that." The big transport plane got to the end of the runway, turned, and then sat there waiting for permission to take off. "Fire's the only thing really scares me," Earl admitted. "I used to have bad dreams about it, then I got a civilian to let me have some sleeping pills—didn't want to see a flight surgeon, those guys write everything into your record—and it kinda settled me."

Suddenly the C-47 roared its engines and went rolling off down the runway, wobbling as it gathered speed on the uneven concrete. Like an invalid negotiating dangerous steps, it climbed cautiously into the bright blue sky. The two fliers leaned on their handlebars watching the big bird take to the air. When it was airborne, Earl rang his bicycle bell and started off again. But he stopped to look back and found Farebrother still watching the plane, his face green.

"You okay, Cap? You sure look bad."

Farebrother nodded to show he was all right, but quickly brought a handkerchief up to his mouth. Earl reached out to put a hand on his shoulder, but Farebrother laid his bike down, bent over, and vomited onto the grass verge.

Earl rested on his bicycle, watching his friend but saying nothing. Farebrother vomited again as the plane returned across the airfield in a rather sedate buzz job that brought it no lower than eight hundred feet. He retched until there was nothing left in his stomach, then wiped his mouth, tasting the sour acids of yesterday's food. When he'd cleaned himself up as well as he could, he explained, "I had dinner with friends last night . . . rabbit. I've never been crazy about the idea of it."

Earl said nothing but mounted his bicycle with exaggerated care as if to avoid his friend's eyes.

"Maybe I should have eaten breakfast," Farebrother added, demanding that Earl assist in his self-deception.

But Earl Koenige was a country boy. "It's yesterday's combat," he said. "It leaves you knotted up inside. You hold on, laughing and joking and drinking, you hold on and hold on. Then suddenly, for no reason you can figure, something happens to trigger it. Your brain tells your body it doesn't have to hold on anymore, and you puke, or you cry, or you shout at someone . . ." Earl shrugged. "Or you get shipped home on a Section Eight." It was quite a speech for Earl; he must have thought about it a lot.

"Is that what Rube does—shouts?"

"You mean like the other day? Oh, sure. He gets mad and calls me a Nazi and stuff like that. I don't care about that. I used to get it at school. Rube's going through a big thing about being taken POW. Everyone gets some kind of nutty worry like that. I told him, but he still worries."

"Did he tell you that?"

"I'm the only one he talks to," said Earl. "We get the bikes out and take a couple of circuits around the taxiway and Rube gets it out of his system. That's why I went into that moonshine thing—it takes his mind off his other worries, you know what I mean?"

"Sure, Earl, sure." From the firing butts behind them they heard the sudden burst of machine-gun fire. Birds rose into the sky, screeching and flapping their wings in alarm.

16

Lieutenant Colonel Druce "Duke" Scroll

"You get out your little old notebook, Duke," Colonel Dan said over his shoulder as they watched the C-47 climb away into the sky. "And you write in red ink, block capital letters: 'General Alex'—because he likes to be called Alex, he told me that—'Bohnen.' That's B-o-h-n-e-n."

"Yes, Colonel," said the Group Executive Officer with a sigh. "I have already noted the General's details."

"And if he comes here again when I'm flying a mission, you go out on that goddamned main runway with a bucket of white paint, and you write 'Bohnen' in letters ten feet tall. You got that, Duke?"

"You've made it quite clear, Colonel." The Exec addressed the Group Commander by rank, in the third person, when trying to distance himself from his anger. "And what exactly is the Colonel proposing to do should this eventuality arise?"

"What am I going to do?" Colonel Dan shouted incredulously, pushing his short unruly hair back. "I won't land here, Duke, I'll fly right back to Germany—that's what I'll do."

"I'm sure they have generals like Bohnen there too."

"You bet your ass they have them." The two men watched the C-47 coming back on a reciprocal course across the airfield. "What's the old bastard going to do now?" muttered Colonel Dan.

"Perhaps toggle some high explosive onto us," the Exec suggested.

"Very funny," said the Colonel, who considered it the Group Commander's privilege to make jokes. "You didn't have him chewing your ass out. I took it for the whole Group. Those guys up at HQ live in a different world, Duke."

"Indeed they do, Colonel." The Exec busied himself with some papers while the Colonel went striding around the office like a newly caged lion. He was an uneducated, untidy, aggressive loudmouth, but Duke Scroll had grown to like him during the time he'd worked for him. He flew too much, and neglected his desk work—the Exec could see the brown folder he'd placed on top of his tray; it was still unopened—but his concern for his pilots was profound. He worried about his flyers in a way that must sometimes conflict with his duty to send them into battle. A failing as a soldier, it was to his greater credit as a man. But Duke Scroll was an Academy graduate; he knew that top brass would never see it that way if it came to a showdown.

Colonel Dan was angry after his session with the General. Now that he'd gone, Colonel Dan was determined to fight a return bout, but this time his Exec was to stand in for the General. So now he stabbed the air and said, "You ask me the difference between a P-47 and a P-51, and I'm likely to tell you that the Thunderbolt has twice as many guns and fewer stoppages, Mustangs have coolant leaks and heater failures. And I'd tell you that the T-bolt is a tough baby—that Jug will take more punishment than any other plane I know and still bring you home for supper. You get into trouble in air-to-air combat and she'll outdive anything that tries to chase you. Take her down onto the deck and she'll swallow all the ground fire they can throw at you."

"I don't imagine that those opinions were well received by the General. You were sent here to convert the Group to P-51s."

"He asked me for a frank and honest opinion."

"Come on, Colonel. You don't imagine he meant that literally."

"I don't know how he meant it, Duke, but I gave him my honest opinion. The Jug is an easygoing plane with unbreakable landing gear. My pilots are still learning the light touch these temperamental little Mustangs need." He stopped striding up and down, reached over the desk for a pack of cheroots, and shook one loose. "But the real difference between a P-47 and a P-51 isn't any of those things," said Colonel Dan sarcastically. "General Bohnen told me the real difference, so button your ears back. The P-47 costs Uncle Sam 115,434 dollars and these P-51s are only 58,546 dollars apiece. For less than two thousand lousy bucks added on to the price of a Jug, you can get two Mustangs."

"But there are other cost factors—maintenance, stocking spare parts, and . . ."

"Don't think that HQ hasn't got fingers enough to work that one out, Duke. I told him the way the Merlins are wearing out at under two hundred hours. He tells me the air war is hotting up and we're not going to have many ships lasting anything like that long in operational use."

"Did he say that?" It sounded callous expressed that way. Duke Scroll took off his eyeglasses and, holding them up to the light, tried to find some dust on them.

"He said the Jug cost too much, drank too much gas, and was overweight with it. I said, you've just described my wife, General, but I love her dearly."

"What does its weight matter?" The Exec put his glasses on and stared at him. Less than two hundred hours! How many of the pilots would survive a tour if that was the life expectancy of their planes?

"Weight matters to HQ. That old bastard is trying to move us out of here, Duke. He says, and he's got it printed in the manufacturer's handbook," Colonel Dan added sarcastically, "the P-51s are only seventy percent of the weight of a Jug. He says our Mustangs don't need these concrete runways—they could put bombers here. The planners at HQ say we could manage on a grass field, and to hell with the mud. The better weather is coming, and that's official."

The Exec shuddered at the prospect of moving the whole Group to some other, even more primitive, airfield. "What did you say?"

"I offered to show him the god-awful accommodations I'm putting officers into. I told him he'd need a series of shots and a dusting of DDT before the doc would let him near the squalor the GIs endure."

"Would they really move the Group?"

"You move 'em, I told him, and you'll be needing a new Group Commander." He laughed and lit the cheroot he'd been waving in the air. "He won't move us, Duke. I sent him away with a flag waving from his ass."

"Could you be more precise about what you said, sir?"

"Hah! I told him about the way those thieving British contractors had put no proper foundation under the perimeter track. I told him the way our hardstands are cracking just under the weight of our lousy little Mustangs. I told him about stone and flint in the runway concrete, and how it was ripping our tires to pieces even now that we've increased the pressures beyond regulation settings. You put some heavies into this dump, I told him, and you'll see real trouble. Forget it, General, I said. Go back to where they fly desks and the flak is made of paper."

The Exec looked at him doubtfully. Well, Colonel Dan always exaggerated, but this time he must have put up a firm stand since they hadn't sent for the kind of facts and figures the General would need before finally deciding to move them. "In my experience, generals like Bohnen—civilians in uniform—like some spit and polish, it bolsters their egos. You should have let me put an honor guard out there for the send-off. A dozen men with white equipment and rifles . . ."

Colonel Dan blew smoke at him. "A firing squad, you mean?"

"We could use a few friends at headquarters," Duke said.

Colonel Dan shrugged. "I wasn't at the Point like you and Tucker and the rest of them. The guys I wasted my youth with were flyers. Nowadays, they're running bankrupt airlines or working on some production line making aero parts. They're not smooth enough to rate a job at HQ." He scratched his arm nervously. It had been reset clumsily after a bad crash a decade or more ago and sometimes it pained him. "Those jerks at HQ stopped being soldiers long ago, and they never *were* flyers—they're all bankers and stockbrokers and mathematicians, Duke, fighting the Germans with slide rules."

"It's that kind of war, Colonel."

Colonel Dan smiled. He didn't want to think so. He took his leather jacket from the chair back and looked out the window as he put it on. "Look at those two, cycling on the apron in that icy wind. Some of these kids don't seem to feel the cold the way the rest of us do."

"We're getting old, Colonel." Duke looked out the window. "Captain Farebrother and young Koenige," he said. It was his habit to identify to Colonel Dan men he didn't recognize.

"I wish I had your knack of remembering all the names," said the Colonel.

He was still watching the two officers cycling toward the technical site, probably heading for the gun-camera screening at 11:30 a.m. "What do you make of Farebrother?"

"You said he shot down a German yesterday."

"How many times have we had headquarters phoning up to inquire about that guy? What kind of pull has he got, or does he just have solicitous buddies?"

The Exec didn't know and made no attempt to guess. Colonel Dan put on his battered cap and leather jacket and tightened the knot in his tie, while watching his reflection in the framed photo of his wife and children that stood on his desk. It was too early for the screening, but Duke knew the Colonel wanted to escape from his desk.

"I'm going over to the screening, Duke. I've got to tell these boys that strafing enemy airfields will get them kills from now on. But I don't like it, Duke." He zipped up his jacket. "Stand down next weekend. Tell squadron orderly rooms to issue as many passes as possible. The weather has got to change for the better this month. We're going to have a long, hard summer, Duke, building up to the invasion."

"Before you go, sir . . ." Duke got up and reached across him for the brown folder that he'd placed on his desk. The Exec knew he was determined not to look inside it. "I've written the actual letters on your behalf, sir. All I need is your signature."

Colonel Dan knew what was in the folder, of course. Duke Scroll laid the three typewritten letters on his desk. They were addressed to the parents of the three pilots posted "missing in action" after the Brunswick raid. He scribbled his signature hurriedly onto each. He didn't read them.

17

Victoria Cooper

Only two young people very much in love could have endured so cheerfully that train ride to Wales. They sat on a big suitcase in the corridor and did not complain about the dim blue bulbs prescribed by the blackout regulations. They huddled close, not caring about the lack of heating, or noticing the servicemen jam-packed into every compartment or the rifles and equipment that were piled on every side of them.

Jamie Farebrother and Victoria Cooper were the only passengers to alight from the train at their destination. It was dark and beginning to rain. The railway station—actually no more than a halt constructed for the transport of milk from neighboring hill farms—was staffed by a harridan who scarcely glanced at their train tickets but treated their inquiries about the whereabouts of a public telephone with narrow-eyed suspicion. She looked at Jamie's trenchcoat and at the huge leather suitcase he carried. It belonged to Victoria's father and now contained her two changes of clothes, stout walking shoes, three books—G. K. Chesterton, *A Farewell to Arms*, and *The Murders in Praed Street*—a frilly nightdress newly bought, expensive pre-war soap, her mother's silk slippers, and a large-scale hiker's map.

Over her shoulder Victoria carried Jamie's field bag. In it, tucked between shirts and underwear, there were a canned honey-smoked ham, two hundred cigarettes, and a bottle of bourbon.

"We're not Germans," said Victoria petulantly.

"You can never be sure nowadays," said the woman, pulling her collar up. But she let them use her telephone to call "Evans, car hire; funerals and weddings."

They sheltered in the loading shed until the car came. It was a large Daimler with confetti from some long-forgotten wedding to be found on the floor and in the buttoned leather seats.

The driver, a small man with a smart peaked hat and formal black overcoat, had an accent Jamie couldn't understand. He opened the car door for them and saluted as they climbed into the back seat, but the effect was spoiled when he sneezed and in reaching for his handkerchief revealed a stained roll-neck sweater.

At Lower Hill Farm their reception was not a warm one. Mrs. Williams, a short muscular woman with a black woolen shawl held together under her chin by a white-knuckled fist, showed them up to their room. The stairs were steep and narrow, and Jamie, in avoiding damage to the wallpaper, almost overbalanced. "I don't allow drink in my house," said Mrs. Williams.

Even by the soft flickering light of the brass paraffin lamp they could see that it was a tiny room. A huge curlicued brass bedstead occupied most of the space. It seemed ridiculously high—piled with underlays, mattresses, blankets, and down quilts so that it almost reached the ornate light fitting. The bedcover was of intricate crochet work and the linen sheets, turned down over it, were rumpled, as if the woman had turned the bedclothes hurriedly at the sound of the car coming up the steep rocky path from the road.

"I'll be bringing you a jug of water," promised the woman. "Hot water," she added.

Jamie Farebrother looked at the old washstand; an enormous patterned jug stood in a matching bowl. Beside it there was a china soap dish with a folded facecloth and a tiny sliver of soap—soap was rationed. Under the bed he glimpsed a chamber pot with the same raised blue flowers of the washstand set. It was all like a museum; he'd never realized before what a primitive country Britain could be. He felt a surge of panic at the thought of being forced to use the chamber pot in the night with Victoria in the room. He looked at her, and whatever it was that she saw in his face made her look away hurriedly as if trying not to laugh.

"Thank you, Mrs. Williams," he heard Victoria say, "we both need to wash. We've had a long journey." She was twisting the ring on her finger. The woman noticed this and looked at Jamie and frowned.

"Breakfast at eight o'clock," said the woman. By now Jamie was growing accustomed to her singsong accent. "In the kitchen. Bottom of the stairs and turn right through the parlor."

They waited for the footsteps to go downstairs before they spoke again. "It's nearly midnight," said Victoria, as if to account for removing her coat and then her jacket.

Jamie said nothing. He took off his cap and trenchcoat, then opened his bag and took a swig from the bottle of bourbon. He held it out to Victoria, but she shook her head.

From just outside the door the woman suddenly said, "Your hot water is here."

"Thank you, Mrs. Williams. Good night," said Victoria. She nudged Jamie.

"Oh, sure . . . good night, Mrs. Williams," he said dutifully.

It's going to be a complete fiasco, thought Victoria. All her misgivings had come back to her. Whatever was she doing here in the Welsh countryside at midnight, with a man who was virtually a stranger, wearing a borrowed wedding ring, and desperate to use the toilet?

She began unpacking the big leather suitcase, putting Jamie's shirts and underwear into the chest of drawers alongside her own clothes. It was raining much harder by now, beating against the shuttered window and gurgling along the gutters before crashing to the ground. From somewhere in the lower part of the large farmhouse there came the sound of a stiff broom being energetically used on a stone floor. Victoria guessed that downstairs the rain was getting into the house, but she kept this guess to herself.

Jamie went to the empty fireplace and looked for a moment at the carefully pleated piece of dusty pink paper that had been used to decorate the grate. He touched the wall to see if there was any warmth coming up the flue from downstairs. The wall was cold and the wallpaper crackled as he dislodged loose plaster.

"Are you cold, Jamie, darling?"

"Sweetheart, I've never been so cold and wet in my whole life." He shivered. "I've forgotten what it's like to be warm and comfortable."

She didn't reply. She could hear a measure of homesickness in his voice and knew there was no answer to it.

"It's Saturday night," said Jamie Farebrother. "In California it's still afternoon. By now the ferryboat to Catalina will be loaded with college kids and their dates. You can look over the side and see clear through fifty feet of Pacific Ocean—watch the fish and see the sea floor. Tonight they'll be dancing to one of the big-name bands. Maybe there'll be a moon and boys will be stepping out onto the balcony of the Avalon ballroom with their favorite girls. The air will be warm, there'll be a million stars and the moon's reflection in the dark water of the bay."

"It sounds like heaven," said Victoria.

"It sure beats this part of England, honey."

"We're across the border here—this is Wales."

"Listen to that rain!"

Jamie sat on the chair. His trenchcoat with its thick woolen lining was still buttoned up to the neck. He looked around the room. "I remember another place like this," he volunteered suddenly. "Two rooms, no heating, and furniture so big you have to stand in the hall to open the wardrobe. My poor old nurse ended her days in a place like this. I loved her. She meant more to me than my mother." Victoria said nothing; he wasn't speaking to her so much as telling himself something. "She was the one my sister and I always went to if we had troubles, or a grazed knee—if we wanted an appreciative audience for some new joke or just felt like being hugged. Nanny was always there to put things right. I sure missed her when I was sent off to school."

"She must have missed you too."

"It broke her heart, I guess. I remember her crying. I'd never seen her crying before—I'd never seen any grown-up crying before. I didn't know they *did* cry. I said, 'What's wrong, Nan?' and she said she was crying because she was so happy to see me in my school clothes."

There was a long pause. Victoria said, "What did you say?"

"I said it was nothing to cry about. I told her about the pool with a high board, and the microscope I'd seen in the physics lab when my father took me to look the place over."

"You mustn't blame yourself, Jamie. You were just a child."

"The following Christmas—without telling my parents—I took a bus up to Hartford, Connecticut, from this beach house my father had rented on Long Island Sound. I found her . . . it was in a tumbledown house that smelled of boiled laundry and cat pee. I was a fastidious kid and I wouldn't sit down because the sofa was covered with cat hairs. She had a big ginger cat and she cuddled it and said, 'This is my little boy now that I don't have you anymore, Jamie.' I promised to go back and see her again, but I never went. Then my father told me she'd died and had left me her commonplace book full of poems she'd copied out in her neat handwriting and quotations from the books we'd read together in the nursery and her special recipe for seed cake."

The wind howled. He stood up and swigged a little more

from the whiskey bottle. Victoria watched him but said nothing.

"I never got the book. My father burned it. He was worried about germs, he said—my father hates germs." He licked his lips to taste the whiskey on them. "Jesus, that wind will take the roof right off this place."

"I'm sorry, Jamie. I should never have brought you here."

"Got any idea where I should start looking for a bathroom?" From his bag he took one of the Army's curious right-angled flashlights and switched it on to test it.

"There are no bathrooms in these old places. They probably put a tin bath in front of the kitchen fire once a week and boil up water on the stove."

"You know what I mean," he said testily.

Hastily she put her coat on, took the flashlight from him, and went downstairs to seek out Mrs. Williams again. She had invested all her hopes and wishes in this adventure, and remaining confident that it would be a weekend of blissful happiness, she'd found strength enough to disregard the pain and distress it brought to her parents. But now that confidence was ebbing away as she realized that Jamie Farebrother found nothing blissful here. For him perhaps such illicit weekends were no more than routine, and this one notable only for the squalor and discomfort of the journey and the accommodations. Would this be something he'd joke about at the bar of the Officers' Club?

She was still wondering about this as she made her way through the garden in search of a toilet. She scrambled past some wind-tormented bushes and heard close by the screech of an owl. It frightened her. She shone the flashlight and through the slanting scratches of driving rain she saw a ramshackle outhouse. By the time she got back to the room she was thoroughly wet and disheveled.

"Find it?" he asked.

Men were so damned selfish. He had no word of sympathy or affection. "Out in the jungle. Follow the path from the kitchen. It's on the left . . . twenty or more yards. You'll need the torch." He took it from her with a perfunctory kiss on the cheek. "Look out for the snakes," she said with just a hint of ill humor, and he grunted to acknowledge her joke and went downstairs.

She was in bed by the time he returned. She heard him washing in the big bowl and caught a glimpse of him, stripped to the waist. His body was still brown from the California sunshine.

The sheets were icy cold and he gasped as he slid into bed beside her. Their embrace was decorous. Cold, weariness, and disappointment are not conducive to physical love.

At breakfast time they got a view of the countryside. Behind the farmhouse the hillside was sudden and steep and strewn with large boulders. The intense green of the grass was interrupted by livid outcrops of rock and then, on the higher slopes, muted by a garland of mist that hid the summit.

Mrs. Williams was nowhere to be seen and their breakfast was carefully arranged on the bare table. There was a small freshly baked loaf, two eggs beside a small saucepan, a fraction of homemade butter, and half a jar of black-currant jelly.

"It's a feast," said Victoria.

"It sure is," said Jamie, who by now had grasped the austerity of British rations.

Victoria poured boiling water over the eggs and put the pan on the stove top before making tea. "She's very trusting," said Victoria. "The tea caddy is filled with what must be a month's ration."

"She's probably running the local black market," said Jamie. "Maybe we'd find the barn filled with caviar and champagne."

"Shut up, you fool," said Victoria, looking around in case the old woman was within earshot. But she laughed.

"I'm sorry . . ." said Jamie. "If I was in a lousy mood last night, I'm sorry."

She blew him a kiss as if she hadn't heard him properly. "How do you like your eggs, buddy boy?"

He looked up sharply: "buddy boy" was not one of Victoria's usual terms of endearment. "Any way they come." He reached out to embrace her, but she deftly avoided his hands.

"Down, boy, down."

"You'll be sorry," he said.

"I'll take a rain check."

"Rain check!" Jamie screwed up his face in horror and said, "You must 'ave been consorting with those bleedin' Yanks."

"Just one Yank," Victoria said, and came around behind him and stroked his closely cropped hair. He turned and embraced her tightly.

"I love you, Vicky," he said.

"I love you," she whispered. "I love you, I love you, I love you."

He kissed her, and as they remained locked together the sound of aircraft engines broke the silence of the countryside. There were three twin-engined Mosquitoes flying up the valley, passing close over the farm with so much noise that the chinaware vibrated on the dresser.

"My God, they're low," said Victoria.

"There's a bombing range about fifty miles north of here," said Jamie. "Maybe they're practicing for some special high-precision target."

"Even here one can't get away from the war."

"It will all be over soon."

"We've been telling ourselves that every day since 1939. Now it's 1944, and it's not so easy to believe anymore."

"How are the eggs doing?" He wanted to change the subject.

She looked at her watch. "Just about ready." She scooped them from the boiling water and put them into the egg cups. They ate in silence for a few minutes. Then Victoria said, "Vera just can't stop talking about your friend Mickey Morse. They see an awful lot of each other."

"Love at first sight," said Jamie flippantly. He looked at Victoria for a moment before deciding to confide further. "MM's talking of getting hitched."

"Not to Vera!" exclaimed Victoria.

He looked at her, trying to understand why she was so emphatic. "Sure to Vera—who are we talking about except Vera and MM?"

"Vera's married."

"That's what Vince said."

"She's married to a perfectly wonderful man named Reg Hardcastle, the Duke's butler. Nearly everyone in Cambridge knows Reg. He's fighting in Burma and has won a chestful of medals."

"Don't get mad at me, honey." He raised his hands in supplication. "I didn't know she was married. And I'd bet a month's pay to an old underwear button she's never told MM."

"Vera likes a good time. She's convinced the war is going to last until she's fifty." Victoria laughed to indicate how ridiculous this idea was, but her laugh was unconvincing. "Vera's determined to have a good time."

"With MM?"

"With Vince, with MM, and with anyone else who doesn't take having a good time too seriously."

"Well, MM does take it seriously. He's making all kinds of plans —he's got it bad."

"You'd better drop a word to him, Jamie. Vera will never divorce Reg Hardcastle. I've heard her say so, not once but many times."

"She's a Catholic?"

"I don't know what religion she is, but she's one of those women who get married for ever and ever. It wouldn't make any difference what Reg did or said, or whom she met—she's Mrs. Reg Hardcastle till death do them part. Some women are like that."

Jamie Farebrother took the long wire toasting fork and made toast at the open stove while he thought about the effect this news would have on his friend.

"I'm sorry, Jamie . . . about Vera and MM, I mean. Perhaps I shouldn't have said anything."

He shook his head. "He'll take it badly," he said. "And when guys feel bad they fly bad."

"He doesn't look like the sort who would take Vera so seriously."

"Most of these kids have never been anywhere or done anything on their own. They like to tell everyone what hell-raisers they are, but they're just college boys from small towns where two drunk drivers constitute a crime wave."

"Is MM from a town like that?"

"He grew up in a gas station in Arizona, miles from the nearest little town. He makes a lot of noise, but that's just a cover-up for his shyness."

"Vera treats him like a little boy."

"MM's mother died a long time ago—he's never had a proper home life. I guess that's what Vera provides."

"Poor Mickey Mouse—poor Vera. It can't last, can it?"

"Who knows?"

"I like him now that I've got to know him better."

"All that 'track in the soft focus' stuff is just to hide his shyness. Get past that and you get to the real MM."

"And what is the real MM?"

"Nerves of steel, never frightened to say what he thinks, and totally loyal to his buddies."

"Those are very masculine virtues, Jamie."

"He won't make Vera pregnant and then abandon her, if that's what's worrying you."

"I didn't say he would."

When they finished eating she washed the dishes before they went out for a walk. The air was cold and, judging from the way the stunted trees were bent, the fierce wind down the valley was no worse than usual. It flapped their coats and tangled Victoria's long dark hair. It crooned in the telegraph wires and howled through the trees.

Victoria looked so English in her green tweed suit with her pearls and her flat-heeled shoes. Her hair blew across her face as they ran like children up the hill that loomed over the little farmhouse. Only by a narrow margin did Jamie win the race to the summit and the curiously shaped "green stone" which local legend said was the last remaining part of a great medieval abbey. He rested against it and mocked her. But there was no mockery in their embrace. "Let go of me, you fool," she said. "We can be seen for fifty miles in every direction," but she laughed and made no great effort to escape his hug. Below them they recognized the railway station and the farm and the narrow country road that connected to the main Shrewsbury one.

They were coming down the hillside, their walk hastened by its steepness, when they saw the long transport truck edging its way cautiously through a narrow cutting. The "Queen Mary" was loaded; its long trailer held the fuselage and wings of a badly damaged Mosquito. The nose of the plane was crushed and its Perspex shattered. One of its wings was broken enough to spill its entrails— ganglia of colored wires, ruptured hydraulic piping, and fuel lines.

"It's a Mosquito," said Farebrother, gripping her hand. They went closer and watched the two RAF men maneuver the vehicle inch by inch through the gap in the granite. "It's not one of the ships we saw, of course. This one is RAF Training Command, and she's been out in the weather for a couple of weeks or so." Farebrother said it hurriedly and tried to distance himself from the machine, and what had happened to it, but it was no use. The broken aircraft's shadow darkened them.

The pub in the village was closed, a "no beer" notice propped in the window. There was nowhere else to eat and, still hungry, they walked back along the road to the farm.

"Will you get a lot of flak when you get home?" Jamie said suddenly.

"Flak?"

"Will your folks be mad at you?"

"I don't know," she said artlessly, "I've never done anything like this before."

"No . . . sure."

She laughed at his embarrassment. "I'm no longer a child, Jamie."

"Neither am I, but I wish someone would explain that to my father."

"Do you want me to try?"

"How would you start?"

"I'd tell him a few interesting personal details about your performance in bed."

"Well, listen . . ."

"You're blushing, Jamie. I do believe you're blushing." Aren't men extraordinary, she thought; even the most dedicated lecher could be made uncomfortable by such casual references to his sex life; she'd noticed this at the office where she worked. "My father will act hurt, my mother will sulk, but eventually they'll get used to the idea that I have a life of my own."

"I'd hate to think I'd caused you a quarrel—you're such a happy family."

"Is that the way it looks to you? I'm glad. But we're not a happy family. Once long ago we were, but now we're just three people sharing accommodations."

He shared the pain he heard in her voice. "If you don't want to talk about it . . ."

"He was the best father anyone could wish for. He told me stories and made me toys—a huge doll's house complete with dressing room for the lady of the house and a book-lined study for the man— and my mother was always there when I wanted to boast or wanted to cry."

"What happened?"

"What indeed? Now my father spends as much time at work as he can, and my mother sits listening to *Hometown* on the radio."

"What kind of show is *Hometown*?"

She looked at him wishing that he hadn't asked. "Nazi radio propaganda. 'Hometown' is the song they use for the signature tune."

Jamie Farebrother said nothing. They walked in silence for a few minutes.

"My brother was much, much younger than me . . ."

"I didn't know you had a brother . . ."

"It's difficult for a boy to endure an older sister. Boys with big sisters feel intimidated . . . they feel they've got to prove something."

"And you were very bright."

"I got high marks at school and did well at university . . . yes, that made it worse for him."

"Where is he now?"

"Nick wanted to impress us all. He joined the merchant navy when he was still only a child. He was torpedoed somewhere off the coast of Africa last September. It was an oil tanker. None of them survived. A naval officer—a member of my father's club—saw it go up in flames. My father never told me, I overheard him on the phone. Then I found out more from the files at the newspaper." She ran out of breath and stopped.

"And now your mother listens to the German radio."

"They read out the names of prisoners of war, Jamie. My God, it's horrible. Those German broadcasters must be sadists—they know mothers and sweethearts will keep listening to the names, keep listening and hoping. I used to sit with her, but I couldn't bear to see my mother's face."

"I'm sorry, darling. I had no idea."

"We never talk about him. It's as if Nick had never been born. One day my father went up to his room and took away the clothes he'd left there and his toys and the sports equipment. And he locked the room up and hid the key so that my mother would never go in there and think about it all."

"It's a lousy war," said Jamie, well aware of how inadequate it sounded.

"And it's turned my mother against me. Sometimes I catch her looking at me and I know she's wishing that Nick had survived and that I was . . ."

"No, no, no. That's just being silly, darling." He put his arm around her.

"Nick was her favorite, but I loved him too. We all loved him—he was such a sweet boy."

"I know."

"Nick was only a child, Jamie."

"I know, darling. I know." He hugged her as they walked; she was trying not to cry.

To change the subject and dispel her grief, he started talking animatedly about Frank Sinatra. A onetime vocalist with the Tommy Dorsey band, he was now on the way to becoming as famous in Britain as he was already in America.

"My sister lives in New Jersey," said Jamie. "She wrote and told me about seeing him at the Paramount Theater in New York. She said the audience goes crazy—teen-age girls, she said—it was like a riot, the show she went to."

"The paper said he earned a million dollars last year."

"You should know better than to believe what they say in the papers," he told her.

She smiled. "Anyway, I like Bing Crosby best." They walked hand in hand along the valley road until they came to the stony track with the sign that said "Lower Hill Farm (Williams)." He opened the gate to let her into the field. It was more enjoyable to walk on the grass. She stumbled on the uneven ground and he caught her around the waist. She hadn't hurt herself, but she couldn't resist the temptation to limp in order to keep his arm about her.

"It's strange to rediscover someone you thought you knew so well."

She knew he was talking about his father. "I'm glad, Jamie."

"My mother never lied to me . . . I don't mean that. But I saw him through her eyes."

She touched his hand in response.

Jamie said, "I used to hate him, really hate him."

"And now?"

"I feel kind of sorry for him, I guess."

"But your father is wonderful, Jamie. He's so entertaining—I've never met anyone with so many stories. And he adores you, Jamie. I could forgive him anything because of the way he loves you."

"He was disappointed when I didn't go through with my law studies, but I would never have been any good at it."

"But surely you realize that your father is prouder of your being a fighter pilot than he ever would have been of your achievements at law school."

"Do you think so?"

"Oh, Jamie!" Men were so slow to understand anything that was unspoken, and far too reliant upon things that were actually said.

"I remember one Christmas a neighbor gave me a big box of magic tricks. I practiced all day and did them all for the kids at my party, then my father took them all out of the box and showed everyone how they worked. I was furious. I never forgave him."

Victoria laughed at the intensity of his emotion, and Jamie joined in her laughter, but the memory still rankled. "He's got to be in control," he said. "He's got to be running things."

"Don't get angry with him, Jamie."

He kissed her hair as they walked. "I get mad at him, and then I feel guilty as hell about getting mad at him. Either way it's bad."

"Why sorry for him?"

"He's a loner, and loners aren't ever happy. What's he got? His cronies, his club, his stocks and bonds, the star on his shoulder. He wants nothing and he's got nothing."

"He wants you, Jamie." She said it with no feeling of competition.

"But I don't want him. I'm not going to spend my life trying to get his approval for everything I do."

It made no great demands on her feminine intuition to discern when men were speaking heartfelt truths and when they were wishing for things that were evidently not so. Jamie Farebrother had some deeply felt desire to please his father. She noted this fact, and wondered whether it could affect her relationship with Jamie, but she did not contradict. She said, "I love you, Jamie."

The lace curtain moved, and she knew that Mrs. Williams must be watching them embrace as they strolled through the field. Mrs. Williams was not the sort of woman who would approve of such flagrant gestures of love, but it didn't matter. Why should she care? She was young and deeply in love with a man who loved her. "If I got pregnant, would it matter very, very much?"

He stopped and swung her around to look into her eyes. "You wouldn't get rid of me that easily," he said. "Are you . . . ?"

She shook her head; it was too soon to be sure.

18

Lieutenant
Stefan "Fix" Madjicka

Officers' Club
280th Bombardment Sq. (H)
Cowdry Green
Norfolk, England

Dear Captain Farebrother,

I should have written before to thank you for that really great evening and a delicious dinner. It was swell of you to let me tag along at a get-together for close friends. And meeting Vicky and her folks was a real pleasure.

I guess I'm no good at writing this kind of letter, but on account of the things I told you that night I figure I owe it to you to tell you that Captain Stigg is dead. And I thought maybe it would come better from me than you hearing about it any other way.

We were wrong thinking we wouldn't be flying another mission before we got our leave. Our ship was still being repaired, but the Group was assigned to one of those milk runs against the missile sites in the Pas de Calais, and all incomplete crews were assigned to other planes to bring the Group up to full strength.

So we were a patched-together crew. Waist gunners from the replacement depot, a navigator reassigned after a spell in the hospital, a radioman who was two trips behind his crew and wanted to catch up with them, and an engineer who couldn't get along with his previous pilot. The plane came complete with bombardier and ball gunner, the rest of their crew having completed their tour and gone home. She was called *The Little Yellow Bird*, and I asked the ball gunner if his crew didn't know that the song was called "*Goodbye*, Little Yellow Bird," and he said, "Yeah, and the rest of them have already said goodbye to her." I guess I should have kept my mouth shut.

Anyway, none of us were too worried about how the crew would shape up together. Even the kids from the replacement depot knew that a "no-ball mission" was a milk run and liked the idea of marking up an easy one.

We went out to the ship real early because we wanted to look her over, on account of this being one we'd never flown before. We sat down in the cockpit, and while I read off the pre-flight checklist, Charlie carried through the checks. And I said to him, "Charlie, you're going to fly this one—really fly her."

He looked at me and smiled in that way he had. "How's that, Fix?" he said.

For a moment I almost chickened out. I felt maybe I should just smile back and make it into some kind of joke. but I made myself say, "You're the airplane commander. It's better you strap in and stay that way on this mission, Charlie. No need to go back to check out the gunners and stuff like that."

He didn't say anything. He went on looking at the clocks and switches, but I saw him moisten his lips and I knew I'd got to him.

"Were you talking about me with Jamie the other night when you went back upstairs?"

"No, sir!" I said. I felt I had to lie about it—I couldn't see any other way to handle it.

He didn't seem angry, he was just as calm as he always was before a mission. To see him going through his pre-flight you'd think Charlie Stigg didn't know the meaning of fear. No white knuckles, no twitching face—none of those things. "You told Jamie," he said, as though making up his mind definitely that I really had. "I sure wish you hadn't done that, Fix, old buddy."

"It's a milk run today, Charlie. Tough it out. It's not so bad. Close your eyes when the shit comes up, that's what I do."

Charlie tried to smile. "Can't hold formation with eyes closed," he said. "I know, I've tried." His face was pale.

"You're going to take her all alone today," I told him.

"From the time we cross the coast I'm hands off. Anything needs checking, I do it."

"You got a deal, Fix," he said, and he really seemed to be in good shape. I thought he'd decided that he could overcome his problem and that I was helping him. But later I realized he was worrying about what I might have told you.

There was still plenty of time, and it being a new crew, I figured we should get to know each other and clarify the way I wanted the sightings of enemy fighters called just like the book and the intercom chatter kept to a minimum. After we'd gone into a huddle on that one, Charlie told the crew that this was a milk run and we'd only be over enemy territory for a few minutes for the bombing run against the coastal sites. He got the bombardier to confirm all this and the boys were pretty cheerful.

I looked at my watch and told them all it was twelve minutes to "start engines." Guys usually like to have a couple of minutes to themselves before climbing aboard for a mission. I notice they wander off a little to be alone. I guess some of them say a prayer, and for all I know maybe others empty their hip flask! Some take a leak, some fix a good-luck charm on their hat or check their parachute one last time. We all have to get ourselves adjusted to the idea that we're about to be flying straight and level for a long time while the Germans are throwing various kinds of lethal hardware at us. Believe me, Captain, that's a tough thing to adjust your mind to.

So when I didn't see Charlie I didn't think anything about it. "Start engine time" on the board still gave us ten minutes taxiing out. There were some scrubby little trees behind the hardstand where crewmen would go to urinate out of sight. No one seems to have heard the shot. The navigator found Charlie there with the gun in his hand. He'd half fallen into the ditch. By the look of it, he put the muzzle into his mouth, but it's on the record as "accidental death" and that's the way it will be. As you heard the other night, Porky's the best Group Commander anyone could hope for. Porky came racing out in his jeep and gave us all a quick pep talk about being careful with our side arms. "There's too much fooling around with these Colt automatics," he told us. "The next man found taking potshots at rabbits will be court-mar-tialed." Man, he nearly got *me* believing it was an accident!

And then Porky took Charlie's parachute and climbed into the left-hand seat to fly the mission—no electric flying suit, no body armor, just his class A uniform. What a guy!

The irony of it was that it *was* a milk run. A few lousy puffs of flak miles off on the port beam and no fighters anywhere. I tried to reach you by phone in time for Charlie's funeral, but you were on leave and no one knew where you were, not even Victoria's folks. I sure hope I didn't put my foot into it with them. Anyway, Charlie got a real military send-off and Porky read the prayer:

> *But the souls of the righteous are in the hand of God,*
> *and there shall no torment touch them.*
> *In the sight of the unwise they seemed to die:*
> *and their departure is taken for misery,*
> *And their going from us to be utter destruction:*
> *but they are in peace.*

There are a few of Charlie's personal things that I've kept for you. I know he would have wanted you to have them. He was always talking about you and the great times you'd had together, and he hadn't had time to make any real close friends here. You'll be getting the package in a few days. I didn't want you to open the package not knowing, and I figured I better tell you soonest because you might be talking with your father about Charlie and so on.

I sure am sorry. I've got an idea that if I'd got to know him really well I would have liked him a lot. I guess it was a tough decision and I respect him for it in a way.

Yours sincerely,

Stefan Madjicka (Lieutenant)

And who the hell was Lieutenant Madjicka to stand in judgment on Charlie? If he'd got to know him really well . . . All of Farebrother's misery was transformed into dislike for this hard-nosed copilot who'd humiliated Charlie and almost sounded proud of the way he'd driven his captain to destruction. Farebrother read the letter again, all his thinking colored by the idea that if he'd been sitting in that seat next to Charlie, it would all have come out differently.

"You feeling all right?" said Rube Wein. "You sure look rotten."

"Bad news," Farebrother said. He folded the letter and put it into his pocket.

"You've gone white. Sit down there and I'll get you a scotch or something."

"A guy I grew up with," said Farebrother. "A bomber pilot."

"Dead?"

Farebrother nodded. He was sitting well forward on the hard little chair that stood under the letter rack in the lobby of the Officers' Club, and he found himself rocking backward and forward, as if his grief had dealt him a physical blow that had literally unbalanced him.

Rube Wein came back with a whiskey. Jamie felt the harsh taste of it in his throat. "You were quick."

"I helped myself. I figured this was an emergency."

"Thanks, Rube."

"Let the folks at home do the grieving. Plenty more guys will buy the farm before we're through."

"The big glass mountain in the sky, you mean?"

Rube smiled coldly, surprised that Farebrother knew the phrase. "The big invisible glass mountain is waiting for us, feller. You'd just better believe it."

"I do," said Farebrother. "I do."

19

Henry Scrimshaw

Henry Scrimshaw was tall and broad with a big white mustache and luxuriant sideburns. He had staring eyes and a large shiny bald crown to his head, and his huge freckled hands held a silver-topped walking cane. His clothes were old-fashioned—highly polished ankle boots made for his outsize feet, a raglan tweed overcoat, and a matching tweed cap. His voice was hoarse from the strong tobacco he burned in his meerschaum pipe. And yet the pipe was more play than addiction, for he toyed endlessly with it, tapping down the filling, relighting it, pushing and prodding and sucking and sniffing as though it were a musical instrument upon which he was giving a virtuoso performance.

"You should have come out to Steeple Thaxted," Lieutenant Morse told him. "This place is a dump." Morse consulted his wristwatch with an imperious sweep of the arm.

"Yes, it is a dump," Scrimshaw agreed cheerfully. Once, this part of Cambridge—not too far from the river—had been an attractive neighborhood. Edward VII was said to have danced in the ballroom of this hotel under the crystal chandeliers that were now dismantled and packed away in the air-raid shelter. But the war had brought factory workers who now crowded into the elegant old turreted mansions of the streets nearby. They earned enough to pay handsomely for shared rooms, and each evening this hotel was packed with horny-handed workers, still in their grimy overalls, buying endless rounds of the watery wartime beer and arguing, singing, and sometimes fighting in the empty car-park.

The saloon bar was shabby—cracked linoleum on the floor and cigarette burns on the tables. Morse shifted about uncomfortably on the hard bench. Some of his countrymen would have thought it a picturesque glimpse of "merry old England," but Morse cared nothing for the fact that there had been a tavern on this site before Shakespeare was born. Morse cared only for himself, Scrimshaw decided; he had that sort of flashy manner so many country boys wear to hide their fears of the big town.

It was Friday lunchtime, and this little "private bar" was dark and empty but for the two men. The hotel was quiet except for the voices of some women workers in the public bar who were cheering the competitors in a darts tournament. There was an occasional glimpse of them through the racks of polished glasses over the counter—florid-faced women with bright cloths tied over their hair and cigarettes stuck in their scarlet lips.

Morse was cold; he hadn't unbuttoned the heavy military overcoat he was wearing. Every now and then he reached out to touch the cold metal of the central heating as if hoping that it would start getting warm. "So why didn't you come out to the base?" Morse persisted. "The colonel announced a stand-down. Everyone's on pass in London."

"Don't tell your granny how to suck eggs, sonny Jim. I've been a newspaperman since before you were born. I was writing up the weddings and funerals and floods and fires for my hometown paper before I was fifteen years old." Scrimshaw sipped at his whiskey and then gulped some beer. "And I've learned a thing or two."

Morse offered his cigarettes, but Scrimshaw declined; he didn't like the sweet American tobacco, it made him cough. He picked up his pipe and looked at it as if evaluating an antique. "I learned not to see people on their home ground, not the first time anyway. Not when I'm trying to decide whether they're good copy." He looked up from his pipe to stare at Morse.

"Is that so," said Morse, putting a cigarette into his mouth directly from the pack and striking a match with a casual tough-guy mannerism that he'd picked up from gangster films.

"Too much going on," explained Scrimshaw. "Too much 'background.' " From the public bar came the steady thud of the darts and occasional shrill cheers. He waited for an argument, but Morse just smoked and said nothing. He'd told his story and now he was waiting for Scrimshaw's reaction. The old man hesitated. He had no great love for the Americans: "overfed, overpaid, oversexed, and over here," as the British kept saying. But the U.S.A. was a hungry market, and another good story with a North American slant could get him signed on to one of the really big syndicates.

The door banged and a brewery deliveryman came through it, wrestling with a barrel of ale. Outside in the street the horses of the dray fidgeted nervously on the frosty road and breathed ferocious white clouds. Morse shivered at the draft from the door and tucked the skirt of his overcoat under his legs like an old lady at the seashore. "Jesus, what a dump," he said again, but Scrimshaw didn't sympathize. He took a large flask from his hip pocket and poured a measure of scotch into his own empty glass. "What have you got in the way of photos?"

"The PRO at the base is a friend of mine," said Morse. He'd described everyone else as "a very good friend of mine," and Scrimshaw wondered what the PRO might have done to occupy this lesser rank in Morse's affections. "We can get all the pictures you want." Scrimshaw pushed his hip flask toward him and he poured himself a little whiskey, then he cradled the glass in his hand and held it up to smell it. It was good stuff, better than the rot gut the pubs rationed out to each customer, and better than was sold at the Officers' Club.

"Pictures of you as a child? Playing with a toy plane or something?"

"Maybe," he said, and shrugged. "I'll write to my aunt and ask her."

"You said your father's still alive," Scrimshaw reminded him. Morse looked up from his drink as if surprised. "This is what I do for a living, old bean," Scrimshaw told him. "You'll need a better memory than that, if you're intending to tell me a pack of lies."

Morse's face reddened. "My father doesn't have any pictures," he said. "But you can tell your magazine that I'll get some for them."

"I am not employed by any newspapers or magazines. I'm a free lance: I write the stories and then sell them where I can."

"Well, I don't want to waste my time working on something that won't get published."

Scrimshaw laughed. "Don't you worry your pretty little head about that, sonny boy. My time's more valuable than yours." To underline this contention he looked at his watch and sighed in the self-important way he'd learned from editors. "And I've already spent half an hour chatting, when I might have been earning some money."

Scrimshaw watched the young officer carefully, half expecting him to show some signs of ill temper, but he saw no pent-up anger in him. He'd said nothing against the Germans, he wasn't of Jewish or Polish extraction, he was motivated by drives that were less reasoned but more fundamental even than hatred: simply, he wanted to be a success. Scrimshaw had seen that look in the eyes of film stars and shipping tycoons, he'd seen it in the faces of bishops and bomb throwers, and it made him cautious.

Morse must have glimpsed his misgivings. He said, "But you promised. Farebrother said you promised . . ."

"Promised to meet you, promised to hear what you have to say," Scrimshaw told him.

"Well, you've heard all about me, Pop. But how do I know you're the hotshot who can write it?"

Scrimshaw grinned sardonically. "I'm a professional," Scrimshaw said. "Before the war I was a news agency man in Vienna, before that Berlin. I'm good—bloody good. My stuff is published everywhere . . . South Africa, New Zealand, Australia. Everywhere."

"What about the States?"

"I brought some clippings with me."

Morse became more animated as he unfolded those yellowing cuttings, the fragile, tangled evidence of Scrimshaw's past successes. "That's great!" he said with an earnest admiration that even the cynical old man found flattering. "They've printed your name," he said, fingering the by-line as if trying to detect some irregularity. "You're famous."

"No, I'm not famous," said Scrimshaw. "I'm not aiming for a Nobel or determined to write a serious novel. But Henry Scrimshaw is known in every bar where journalists hang out, from Chungking to Addis Ababa and from Guadalajara to Warsaw. And if that list doesn't include any towns in your part of the world, then thank your lucky stars, pal, because I've spent most of my life watching men blow each other apart." He took another bite at his cheese sandwich. The cheese content was minimal and the gray-colored "National Wheatmeal" bread was spread thinly with margarine that was now being made from palm oil. Morse picked up his half, inspected it carefully, and put it back on the plate untasted.

"You walk into any of those bars," Scrimshaw went on, "and those reporters will tell you Scrimshaw is a pro. They'll tell you that if Scrimshaw thinks a lead is worth following up, the chances are that no sub-editor is going to spike the story. Because this big nose of mine, Mickey Mouse, old friend, can sniff out what sells papers. Maybe it's not always big news—I'm getting a bit too old for dodging bullets and I've never claimed to be a scoop merchant—but the stories I write have got 'human interest' and that's what newspapers and magazines need these days. So don't you worry about wasting your time."

"And do I have 'human interest'?"

Scrimshaw looked at him. It was going to need a lot of work. "Why do you want to be in the papers, son? Strictly off the record, why?"

"After the war maybe I could start a little bar, or a restaurant. People would come there to meet me. Maybe some airplane manufacturer would make me a vice-president . . . there could be all kinds of opportunities."

Scrimshaw finished off both halves of the sandwich. That was the difference between them, thought Scrimshaw: this kid wants to be an opportunist, and I am one.

"What do you think, Mr. Scrimshaw?" he said. "From what I've told you?"

"I think you're going to get yourself killed, son. That's what I think. If you want my advice, I'd forget all this about attacking German airfields just to rack up a few extra Jerries. Those Luftwaffe bastards have been fighting this war since 1937. I saw them in Spain. My oath! They're not going to be sitting down there on their asses waiting for you to sail over and blow their planes to buggery."

Morse grinned, tossed back his whiskey, and said, "You may be a big-shot writer, Pop, but what you know about air fighting could fit on the head of a pin and still leave room for the Lord's Prayer. You stick to the writing, I'll do the fighting, okay?"

"I'm going to need a lot of help. I'll need to spend time with you . . . lots of time, I work slowly. And I'm going to tell you how to handle other reporters so that we goose up the market and get it ready for the three-parter I'm writing. Do you understand?"

"Sure. It's a deal."

"And don't forget—I've got the exclusive. That means you give stories to other writers only if I give you permission. And I won't give you permission."

As Scrimshaw was saying this, a tall old man came into the bar. He was elegant in dress and manner, with an unnaturally white face in which, as he smiled his recognition, his teeth seemed long and yellow.

"That's Peter Colfax. He's the butler for the Duke—he took over from Reg Hardcastle," Scrimshaw whispered. And when Morse made no response: "He took over from Vera's husband . . . your Vera."

"Vera's husband?" said MM. "Is Vera married?"

"Don't pretend you didn't know," said Scrimshaw. "You go to the house. Don't tell me you thought she'd furnished it like that just for herself."

MM didn't answer. Scrimshaw had hit the nail right on the head. Vera's place was obviously arranged for a married couple—he'd had misgivings about that the first time he visited her there.

"Everybody around here knew Reg," Scrimshaw told him. "He was the Duke's butler and a sergeant in the Terriers . . . he knew everyone." MM went cold; he hated the thought of Vera with another man.

Old Peter Colfax came over to the table where the two of them were sitting and waited while Scrimshaw made the formal introductions.

"How are things going at the house these days, Peter?" said Scrimshaw.

"The venison has helped eke out the meat ration. Cook has found a thousand ways of preparing it, but you still can't make it taste like beef." He looked at Morse. "You're a flyer, are you?"

"He's an ace fighter pilot," Scrimshaw told Colfax. "One of the best. I'm writing a big story about him."

"I'm proud to meet you," Colfax told Morse with that sincere but distant deference that seems to come naturally to traditional domestic servants. "It's a young man's war," said Colfax.

"Or so all us old 'uns keep saying," Scrimshaw said, and laughed. Colfax had sewed his old campaign ribbons to the chest of his blue Melton overcoat. Despite his age, he felt self-conscious at being out of uniform.

"I had a letter from Reg the other day," Colfax said. Scrimshaw watched Morse out of the corner of his eye, but the young man remained impassive.

"Still in Burma, is he?"

"I wish I had the letter with me," said Colfax, patting his pockets. "Yes, Reg was in the Arakan fighting. Our boys fought the Japs man to man and pushed them back yard by yard." Colfax looked at Morse. "And I don't have to tell an American that Johnny Jap doesn't give ground easily."

Morse didn't respond. Scrimshaw said, "I heard Reg was going to get a battlefield commission."

"Recommended for it," said Colfax, "but it never came through. I suppose he was disappointed but he gave no sign of it in his letters."

Scrimshaw pressed the old man to join them for a drink, but he wouldn't stay. He'd come in only to settle the Duke's monthly account. It wouldn't do, Colfax said, to be breathing alcohol while helping the Duke with his tie. He laughed at the thought of it.

Colfax readied himself for the street with a studied care, buttoning his fine double-breasted overcoat and inspecting each sleeve for dust, hair, or ash. "Yes, salt of the earth, Reg Hardcastle," he said, as if he'd been thinking it over. Holding a pigskin glove in his left hand, he nodded to Scrimshaw and extended his hand to Morse. "I'm proud to shake your hand, Lieutenant," he said. "After this damnable business is over, it will be chaps such as you and Reg Hardcastle who will shape what comes next. Good luck to you, my boy."

"Thank you, sir," said Morse, shaking his hand gravely and remaining standing until Colfax had gone out into the street. "What a crazy old guy," he said.

"Would you believe he's seventy-five years old?" Morse raised his eyebrows. "Peter was batman—personal servant—to the Duke's father. They were at the battle of Paardeberg and at the siege. South Africa I'm talking about, back in 1900."

"So how old is Vera's husband?"

Scrimshaw chuckled. "Reg is just a kid compared to old Peter Colfax, but he got the plum job—butler—because he knows about wine. The Duke's very particular about wine, and old Peter couldn't tell a corked claret from a flat Guinness. God knows what a cock-up he's making of the butling. But there's a war on . . . ."

"Yeah, so I heard," said Morse. He stubbed out his cigarette and drained his whiskey to indicate that he was about to go. "I promised to phone Vera," said MM. He stood up and began to look through his change for pennies.

"Are you annoyed about something, kid?" Scrimshaw asked, stretching out a handful of change.

"Don't snow me, buddy," Morse said, taking the pennies he needed for the phone.

"What do you mean?"

"Getting the old guy to meet us in here, so you could hand me the propaganda about Vera's husband."

He began to turn away, but Scrimshaw reached out and took his arm. "Wait a minute, pal," he said. "You're not dealing with your average dozy old Pom now, you know." Scrimshaw gripped his arm tighter. "Peter came in just by chance."

Morse wrenched his arm free, but he didn't walk away. "You wanted to make me look like a heel. It was a setup."

"And I say it bloody wasn't. Now take that back." Scrimshaw tossed his notebook onto the table. It went into a puddle of beer. "Or you can take your life story and stick it up your ass."

Morse took a stick of gum from his pocket and put it in his mouth, chewed for a moment, and then said, "Okay, Hank. If you say so." Scrimshaw nodded, retrieved his notebook, and wiped the beer from it with a grimy handkerchief. Morse said, "Maybe I'd pull the same corny routine if Hardcastle was a buddy of mine."

"You'd better realize that Vera could make things difficult for you," said Scrimshaw.

"How?"

"You may not find her so easy to shake off. I know Vera—she can cling."

This ruse of Scrimshaw's didn't work. "I don't want to get rid of her," explained MM. "Vera's just great." He tossed the coins in the air, caught them, and then went off to phone.

Scrimshaw watched him go. He was a cute little bastard. Was there a brain behind that unpromising exterior or was his skepticism just primitive cunning? Either way, he had been correct. Scrimshaw had arranged for Peter Colfax to come along and "accidentally" run into them and tell MM the kind of a man Reg was. They'd thought it was subtle when they planned it. Scrimshaw's real inclination, and Colfax's too, was just to throttle the dirty little bugger. God! Cambridgeshire was packed with unattached women. Some evenings you had to elbow your way through the ones standing outside the Red Cross Club in Trumpington Street, and there were still more outside the Officers' Club in Market Square. The pubs were full of easy women, and so were all the other regular haunts of the Yank soldiers. So why did this bastard have to take Reg's wife to bed? Damn the bloody war!

20

Vera Hardcastle

It was the following week. Vera Hardcastle was three-quarters of an hour later than usual getting back to her little house on Michael Street. She'd worked an hour overtime, and now it was getting dark, with a steady drizzle of rain. She knew MM was there—his motorcycle was propped inside the wall of the minuscule front yard. There was a piece of oilcloth tied over it to keep the saddle and the engine dry; MM was uncharacteristically fussy about the engine. He'd let himself in—the key was hanging inside the letter-box—and made a fire. By now they had fallen into a regular routine.

"I'm sorry, darling," she said as she kissed him. "Three buses went by, all crowded. I thought I'd never get home."

"You're cold, honey. Is it still raining?" He held her very tight, like a little boy awakened from a bad dream.

Vera hugged him and ran her fingers through his lovely wavy hair. "You gorgeous man," she said into his ear. The gaslight hissed and the air in the pipes made a popping sound. After the brightness of the electric lights in the office this light was rather romantic. They stood embracing for what seemed like an age before he let go of her. She never got used to having him waiting for her—it was like some scene from a Hollywood film.

She slipped the scarf from her head. She hardly dared look in a mirror, knowing that her hair was in a tangle. And her makeup—so carefully done before leaving the office—was now a mess. She said, "I'll make you some coffee . . . there's still some of that tinned ham left. I can make fritters. You must be hungry."

"Take the weight off your feet, sweetie. Get yourself warm at the fire. I phoned the base—I'm not on the board. No need to be back until tomorrow roll call."

"Roll call." She repeated his words while worrying in case he made a noise in the morning and the people next door heard him. The husband was an engine driver and was up and cooking breakfast by 5 a.m.

"When they say roll call . . . for officers that means right after breakfast, just in case there's some kind of panic, or some lousy lecture on aircraft recognition or something . . ."

He looked at her as if seeking her approval, so she just said, "That's wonderful, darling," and kissed him again, on the tip of his nose, and then stood there warming her hands at the fire. He'd used a lot of coal; Americans never seemed to realize that it was rationed.

"That photo on the bookcase," said MM, "is that your father?"

Vera looked at the man in the baggy khaki uniform. He had been killed in France when she was little more than a baby; the photo was all she knew of him. "Dad never came back from the war," she said. "My mum passed away soon after him." The glass of the photo was covered with a film of soot. She felt guilty about that, as she did about never visiting his grave. She wiped the picture with her hand. "These coal fires make such a mess," she grumbled. The dirt was everywhere in the air, her clothes became soiled after an hour or so. People said it was the war factories—they tried to blame everything on the war. "My aunt looked after me for a year, but then she had to put me into the orphanage. She took me home for holidays sometimes. She was always saying she would take me back home with her for good, but she never did."

"Poor Vera," said MM. "Growing up in a lousy orphanage. That sounds tough."

"Lucky Vera," she said. "Most of the kids didn't even have visitors. They didn't have *illusions* even."

MM leaned forward and took the kettle from the hearth and jammed it into the hot coals so that it balanced on the top bar of the grate. Her aunt had had a kettle like that. Vera remembered so well those nights when she'd watched the kettle, waiting to hear it sing, knowing that when it boiled the hot-water bottles would be filled and she'd have to go to bed. How many nights had she gone to sleep in the rough orphanage blankets—only the girls in the top class got sheets—dreaming of what she would do once she was back with Aunt Edna. How hard she was going to slave for her, how much love she was ready to give.

"I was sixteen when I left the orphanage to work for the Duke," said Vera. "There were twenty servants there, not including the gardeners or chauffeurs."

"Oh boy!" said MM. He touched the kettle with the toe of his shoe to make sure it wouldn't topple. She paused, not knowing whether he wanted to hear more. He said, "Sweet sixteen, and never been kissed."

She knew he wasn't being sarcastic or nasty. With her he was never sarcastic or nasty. "Not much chance of being kissed up at the house," she told him.

"No amorous house guests?"

"They were all past it," she said. "Foxes were all they wanted to chase."

"So what about your husband . . . what about Reg?" said MM. It was the first time he'd ever referred to Reg by name. She realized that he must have been thinking about their future, and she knew then that MM was really serious. In a way that frightened her.

She laughed, making light of it. "It was all my doing," she admitted. "Reg seemed quite happy without any women in his life." She could remember the day she'd followed the newly appointed butler into the wine cellar. It was gloomy and the dust got up her nose. She pressed close to him as if trying to see the bottles on the rack. He didn't step back, so she moved herself against him. Then, suddenly, he grabbed her roughly and kissed her hard on the mouth. But the dust from the wine bottles he was moving must have gone up his nose and he sneezed. She giggled and then he laughed too. "He was such a toff, MM. I couldn't believe it when he asked me to marry him."

"Why don't you have any photos of him?" said MM. The kettle began to croon.

"I do have a photo of him," she said, "but I have to have the frame repaired." She got to her feet. "Did you say you wanted the ham fritters?"

"How long is it since I first talked to that Australian newspaperman? How long can it take to write one lousy piece?"

"That Harry Scrimshaw is a funny old codger. He takes his time about everything. Did he tell you about all the wars he'd been to?" Vera tittered.

"Is that all baloney?" said MM in alarm.

"No, it's true. I asked one of the subs at the office. He said old Harry used to be a top name until he took to the bottle."

"He puts it away real fast, I noticed that. Hell, Vera, I've shot down three more Krauts since the first time I talked to him."

"You're too easygoing, darling. You should give him a good talking-to. Does he realize that you're one of the top scorers now?"

"He knows."

"But don't cross him, darling. He can be a spiteful old devil if he's put out."

"I'll give him another week. I've spent hours and hours talking to him—I couldn't start all over again. And he does spend a lot of time working on it, I've got to admit that."

"Spends a lot of time cadging free drinks at your Officers' Club bar," she said. She enjoyed reminding herself that MM was an officer.

MM smiled. "Jamie can handle him, that's for sure. At the bar last week, Scrimshaw made some crack about 'Yanks' and Jamie took him apart."

"Hit him, you mean?"

"Jamie never hit anyone in his life. He just asks Scrimshaw a couple of questions and makes him look like a jerk. He's really something, that Jamie Farebrother."

"You're getting real thick with him lately. I get sick of hearing how wonderful he is."

"Jamie's okay." He said it reflectively, as though he was still making up his mind about it. "He's so very cool about everything. We get back from a mission and he steps out of his ship like some railroad tycoon stepping down from his private Pullman car. And Tex Gill, his crew chief, just loves it. Tex is intelligent, but he worships the guys Jamie Farebrother treads on."

"I can't imagine him treading on anyone, he's so gentlemanly."

"Maybe he doesn't always mean to, but he's awful good at giving people an inferiority complex." The fire was burning more brightly now, and MM took his coat off and threw it across the sofa. "I've got to admit I was a little rough with him when he first arrived."

"You never told me that."

"A new captain set back my chances of getting promoted. The Table of Organization allows each squadron so many guys of every rank. Captain Farebrother's arrival was all Tucker needed to make sure I never made captain, but that's not Jamie's fault. He doesn't give a damn about rank—doesn't give a damn about anything, as far as I can tell."

"Except Victoria."

MM looked at her for a moment before replying. "Except Victoria, I guess." He smiled as he remembered something. "You should have been there the other day when we were watching the gun-camera films. He got another German plane. It was good shooting, Vera. He opened fire at exactly the correct range and gave it the right deflection, and the strikes were on the cockpit, just like the textbooks tell you. That Nazi was really clobbered by just one short burst. Enough is enough, right? He takes his finger off the trigger and saves his bullets for the next one. Right? So slow dissolve and next morning we're in the film room with the rest of the guys and Jamie's got a definite kill up there on the screen. I turn to him and say, 'Nice work, kid, you sure creamed that son of a bitch,' and Jamie looks at me as if I'd just spit in his mother's eye." MM sighed and loosened his tie.

"Victoria told me he won't talk about the planes he shoots down. She said it's somebody's son or husband or brother. Do you think that's something Jamie said to her?"

"Nuts! Everyone gets a kick out of shooting down an enemy plane—the Germans get their kicks out of shooting down ours. My guess is that Jamie didn't want us riffraff to see him gloating."

"And you just said you liked him," she said reproachfully. "Listen, do you want something to eat? It will have to be grilled, I've used up my fat ration, so I can't fry anything."

"Make that Spam and canned spaghetti, will you? Sure, I like Jamie. He's a straight guy, and he told Vince that I should be leading the squadron because I was the best. We're not sitting on the membership committee of some goddamned country club, he told him. I overheard them. Then Dixie Doppelman in the 191st Squadron said Jamie had told him the same thing. What are you laughing at? It's true."

"The names you boys have—Dixie, Earl, Brandy, Red . . . Those are names we give to our dogs in England."

"That's an anti-American remark likely to lower our morale and give comfort to the enemy," he said, grinning.

"And there are plenty more where that came from," she told him, and ducked into the kitchen as he grabbed a cushion to throw at her.

"Switch the wireless on," she called from the kitchen. "Let's have some music."

He switched it on and poured a drink for both of them while he waited for the radio to warm up. He couldn't find the American Forces Network, but there was dance music on the BBC. Then he went into the kitchen and watched her prepare his meal.

"Do you nick all this grub, MM? I wouldn't want you to end up in prison."

"You can eat it with an easy conscience, Vera. They were 'hospitality packs.' We've got official instructions not to accept too much food from British civilians."

"Not much chance of accepting too much," she said. "Those two slices of ham you're going to have for supper must weigh four ounces. That's the whole ration for us civilians."

"That's only one meal a day!"

"You twerp!" she said, ruffling his hair. "Four ounces of bacon or ham a *week!*"

"Gee, Vera, I didn't know things were so tough."

She got some perverse sort of pleasure from reciting her hardships. "Each week, two ounces of cooking fat and two ounces of tea. Three ounces of cheese, and I love cheese. And my grocer says the cheese ration is going down when the next ration period begins."

He put his arm around her shoulder. "That's not enough to keep alive on, sweetheart. I should have brought you more."

"I'll only get plump," she said.

"This weekend I'll get a jeep and fill it with PX goodies."

She turned to him and kissed him. "Go and sit down, there's a good boy. It's too cold in this kitchen." It was no more than a scullery really, a narrow little place with a broken door and an ill-fitting window that looked out on a dark yard and outside toilet.

"I'd rather be cold with you, honey."

She wiped the lipstick marks from his mouth. She used his handkerchief, holding it up for him to moisten, just as she'd seen mothers do for their infants. It would have been a good time to remind him that she was nearly ten years older than he was. She could have told him that he should be looking for some young girl of seventeen who could look up to him and see him the way he wanted to be seen. But she didn't say anything like that; perhaps it was her vanity that stopped her. He must have realized that there was a big difference in their ages, but he never said anything about it. She told herself that she looked younger than she really was, and that was true enough, but MM had fallen for her because she *was* older, because she mothered him, and because he could confide all the fears and shortcomings that no one else must know about. He'd even admitted being frightened of his father.

She straightened the collar of his shirt. "You shoot down lots of Germans, MM."

"Do you love me, Vera?" He said it lightly, and smiled as if it was no more than banter.

"Sometimes I do," she said. "Do I have to keep saying it over and over?" She gave all her attention to the Spam and spaghetti.

"I want you to tell me every hour, on the hour. Maybe every thirty minutes on our anniversaries."

"So we're going to have anniversaries, are we?"

"We've got to do it right, Vera. You've got to write to your husband and tell him about us. I want to take you back to America with me."

She looked at him before answering. They'd had a violent scene after MM first learned she was married. He'd called her a whore, thrown plates across the room, and twisted her arm. Such physical violence frightened her, but it also revealed the strength of his passion and she was flattered by that. She smiled. "They say that on these dark nights you can't walk far across the grass at Parker's Piece without falling over sandbags." She pushed the food onto their plates in an offhand way. "And when you fall over them, you always hear one of them saying, 'You will take me back to America with you after the war, won't you?' " She picked up her plate and walked past him into the parlor.

MM didn't move. "I've heard all those jokes, Vera," he said. When he went to get his plate, he saw a curled photo that had fallen down behind the big wooden plate rack. Straightening it out, he found Vince Madigan, dressed in flying gear, posing by a Mustang fighter. "Thanks for the memory" he'd scrawled across the sky; some nerve, that Vince. MM pushed the photo back out of sight and picked up his plate.

"Pick up your supper and come sit by the fire." She had seen him looking at the photo and she half expected him to start ranting again. But she was ready for him—Vera could shout and swear with the best of them, as MM had discovered. They had fights regularly, but Vera didn't mind too much; she quite enjoyed a really noisy argument as long as nothing got broken.

Coming in to join her, MM said, "And after we've eaten, I'll fix that vacuum cleaner for you. I went over to the engineering shop and got the washers I needed."

And that's the way they spent their evenings, sitting by the fire in that cramped parlor, with corny comedy shows on the wireless and MM mending a chair or painting a door or fixing up a new shelf. While Vera was knitting sweaters that were lopsided because she couldn't read the knitting pattern without glasses and she'd never wear them when MM was with her. And after the first week or so even their sexual life was restrained because Vera said she had to be so very careful. Eventually they made love only when it was "a celebration," and the only event they ever seemed to celebrate was MM shooting down another German plane.

21

Major
Spurrier Tucker, Jr.

Spring was creeping over northern Europe. The continental land-mass had warmed enough to form dome-shaped cumulus, the sort of clouds artists use to depict a perfect summer's day. Above the formation of Mustangs, the sky was a vivid cerulean blue that in a painting might have seemed a vulgar overstatement.

Down through the clouds Major Tucker could see the fields and forest, their angular patterns distinctively German. It was mid-day, the sun was high and was making tiny disks of light in the polished Plexiglas of the canopy. Tucker shifted in his seat; despite the cushion, three hours of continuous flying had stiffened his muscles and made him tired and restless. Over his shoulder he saw his wingman constantly fidgeting with his throttle to hold his position. It was customary that brand-new pilots flew as the Squadron Commander's wingman for the first couple of missions—it was reputedly the safest place in the formation—but Tucker hated having a rookie pilot to nurse.

He eased his goggles up on his forehead and rubbed his cheeks where the rubber had been, feeling the trapped perspiration dribble down his cheeks. He checked his instruments to be sure that all was well. The Group's task—"penetration target withdrawal support" for the mission to Magdeburg—had been uneventful. Now the squadrons were to return to base independently, seeking "targets of oppor-tunity" en route. Tucker watched the other two squadrons losing altitude as they pulled away to the north of his track. They were diverging sharply, soon they would be mere specks on the white clouds below. He twisted against his harness to make sure his own planes were holding formation.

Up here in the sky Tucker never felt completely free, in the way so many of the other flyers claimed to. A man was never his own master here, not even on a fine spring day like this. It was not only the complex, turbulent, and unpredictable weather systems, it was

the machine in which he flew. The failure of some insignificant-look-
ing piece of metal was enough to bring the whole roaring power
plant to a halt, and then gravity called the tune. Again Tucker eyed
his instruments. Flying a heavier-than-air machine had never ceased
to be a miracle for him. In that sense, he was an old-fashioned romantic about airplanes in a way that none of the more enthusiastic
pilots were; they all seemed to take it for granted.

It was absurd to find himself riding through the sky. Tucker was
a soldier. Four generations of Tuckers had been through West Point.
His great-grandfather—Spurrier—had marched into Savannah with
Sherman. Tucker's father had come close to getting a star in 1918,
but the war ended too soon and he finally retired still a colonel. Now
it was Tucker's chance. So far all his father's advice had been sound.
The Air Force had expanded at an unprecedented rate, and provided
him with a rank he'd never have gotten with the infantry or the tanks.
And if the Air Force was to become a separate service, it would have
its own staff in the Pentagon. Its top brass would all be men who had
earned silver wings and had air combat experience enough to lend
authority to their orders and weight to their opinions. So he had to
be here riding a tin bird through the upper skies and, on a day like
today, almost enjoying it.

The worst part of his job was trying to make the flyers understand their responsibilities. These fighter pilots were not like Academy men, and not even as disciplined as the "ninety-day wonders"
who were now taking command of platoons, and companies, of infantry. Even educated men like Farebrother were unable to adjust to
the Army's way of doing things. That morning, prior to the mission,
Farebrother had demonstrated his unhelpful attitude.

"Say, Major . . . Earl would like to give this one a miss."

"For God's sake, Captain! Can't you see I'm up to my eyes in
work?"

"Okay if I get one of the spares to fill his slot?"

"Wait a minute, Captain. I'm still commanding this squadron. I
don't want my subordinates rewriting the field order to fit into their
social life."

"Earl has good personal reasons for missing this one. He's never
asked before, Major."

"No, he's never asked before." Tucker smiled knowingly and
tapped his pencil on the desk. "I guess you figure we should all have
at least one chance of neglecting our duty."

"I didn't say that."

"And is this 'personal reason' something that Lieutenant Koenige will eventually confide to me, Captain? And if so, why is he skulking about out there in the hall while you plead his case for him?" Tucker smiled. It had been a lucky break to spot Koenige through the partly open door.

"He asked me to come."

Tucker nodded. "And you're his wingman, so you came."

"I'm his buddy, so I came."

"I suppose Koenige felt he'd have more chance of pulling it off if he sent in a captain. Too bad he couldn't turn up a major or a colonel."

"Lieutenant Koenige has relatives living in Magdeburg. He doesn't want to be part of a bombing mission on their hometown."

"Get Koenige in here—I know he's outside the door. Koenige! Come in here!"

The door opened, and Koenige entered Tucker's office looking down at his flying boots. "Now, what's all this crap about trying to duck the mission?"

"It's like Captain Farebrother said, sir. I don't want to bomb Magdeburg. My folks were born there . . . grandparents too."

"You're not going to be bombing anyplace, Koenige. You fly a fighter plane, you don't fly a B-17."

"I know that, Major Tucker," said Earl Koenige.

"You fly the mission, Lieutenant. Try not to think about the target. Concentrate on your job. Can't you see how this kind of thing could upset everyone? Why, the next thing we know all my pilots will be selecting the targets they want to fly to. And what about the enlisted men? A great example of war-winning determination this would be!"

"You don't understand, Major."

"I understand better than you think, Lieutenant. I don't know who's been putting you up to these crackpot ideas." Tucker rested his eyes on Farebrother for a moment. "But forget it. As I say, concentrate your mind on your job." Tucker tidied the edges of an envelope. "Maybe your family has moved. Maybe they're already dead. Hell, we've bombed shit out of Magdeburg in the last few weeks."

"You callous bastard, Tucker," said Farebrother.

Tucker looked up, both surprised and hurt to see the contempt on Farebrother's face and the horror on Koenige's. These guys sure could be sensitive when it suited them! "Well, I'm sorry. I didn't mean it like that, Lieutenant. Can't you see I'm trying to help you?" To Farebrother he said plaintively, "I'm trying to help him."

"I'll fly," said Koenige.

"Good," said Major Tucker. "Once you get into your plane you'll stop brooding on all this nonsense."

"I think Lieutenant Koenige should see the Flight Surgeon," said Farebrother.

"Come on, Captain! You know standing orders say no pilot can report sick after briefing."

"Tucker, it was the target announcement . . ." began Farebrother, but he gave up with a snort of exasperation.

"I don't want the doc to say I'm unfit to fly," said Koenige. "I don't want that written into my record."

"You're talking sense," Tucker agreed. "Keep the pill pushers at arm's length unless you're trying for a Section Eight or something."

"I'll fly," said Koenige.

Tucker met Farebrother's eyes and registered the disapproval there. But how would Farebrother have handled it if he'd been Squadron Commander? Koenige had already been briefed; substitute a spare and the squadron would fly one plane short. And if the Group Commander started asking questions, would it be Farebrother's neck on the chopping block? It would not. It would be the neck of Major Spurrier Tucker, and a blot like that on his record could ruin a career officer's chance at top rank. . . .

Tucker eased the nose down and watched the altimeter needles unwinding as his wings cut the tops from billowy cumulus and then plunged into it.

"Sparkplug Leader from Yellow Two. There's an airfield . . . ten o'clock." It was Rube Wein's voice.

"Yellow Two. Roger. Out."

Tucker led the squadron into a gentle diving turn to port and then the flights separated. He could see the German airfield now—a large one with three long runways and some transport planes lined up on the apron. He eased the stick forward until the dive was steep. The ground came rushing up at him, buildings and roads twisting as he went into a wing-over and flattened into a wide turn that brought him straight across the field. He glanced in his mirror as he corrected his heading to bring them across the airfield from the north. By now the rest of his flight had pulled up and were flying line abreast.

He came across the apron low enough to get a shot at all five transports. They were three-engined Junkers Ju 52s, painted in gray and green mottled patterns. As his gunsight moved up to the first one he fired a long burst and saw flashes as his bullets hit the metal airframe. He held the trigger and let his gunfire move along the whole line of aircraft, then he banked steeply and came around in a tight turn that gave him a chance to fire at a twin-engined Heinkel being refueled at dispersal. His strikes, like big white flowers, suddenly blossomed on the wings of the Heinkel and its attendant tanker. A jet of flame preceded a roar as the tanker's contents exploded with a blast that lifted Tucker's plane and tilted it over into a steep bank. He wrenched the stick over to level off. He kept low, trees almost brushed his wings. He felt himself break out in a cold sweat. For a moment he had thought he was going to hit the ground.

He looked over his shoulder. Yellow flight was down on the deck and coming in from the east. One of the Junkers was well alight as Yellow flight all opened fire.

"Green Leader from Sparkplug Leader. Go up to ten thousand and give us cover."

"Roger. Wilco." They might curse but they would go.

He saw that his wingman had fallen back. "Pull in, Red Two. Sparkplug Red Two. Do you read? Pull in."

"Roger. Wilco."

Tucker came around a little wider to give the new pilot a chance to draw up to him. It was bad enough having to hit these Hun airfields without having to wet-nurse some new kid while doing it. Now the flak really started up. Great arches of colored lights were being lobbed over him as the gunners swung around wildly to shoot at Blue flight, who were coming in from the south.

There are those who say that the only true courage is in overcoming fear, and by that definition Major Tucker was not courageous. He had no fear about being shot down because he simply couldn't envisage it. Tucker's fears were social. He went cold at the idea of being humiliated by his superiors, held in contempt by his peers, or disrespected by his subordinates. His relationships with women had been marred always by his fear of being spurned. But in the face of the enemy Tucker had the cold and clinical mind of the professional soldier. Today these two contrasting aspects of his mentality were to be put to the test.

To go in again or gain height and head for home—that was the big question. On the one hand, his squadron had suffered no casualties, was positioned for the second pass, had enough ammunition, and was psychologically prepared. Arguing against it was the German flak, increasing second by second. The gunners were getting the range and deflection and knew exactly where they must come.

He looked at the airfield—there were plenty of undamaged targets. If he headed for home, he'd no doubt face jeers from MM, and yet if they went in again, Tucker's Red flight would have the best chance of escaping in one piece. It would be Blue flight's final pass that would catch the worst and most accurate gunfire. For an instant he thought of sending the final section up to join the top cover, but MM was flying Blue Leader and he'd complain that this was a deliberate way of preventing him from getting more kills; he'd complained before of being "restricted."

"Sparkplug Leader. One more time and home."

This time Tucker went in a little higher to give his wingman a chance to get in a quick burst. There was a fighter plane coming down the runway; some plucky little German bastard was coming up to have a shot at them. Tucker touched the rudder and brought the gunsight pip down so that he could stitch him to the runway. He could see strikes as the German fighter passed through his gunfire, then he pulled his nose up and climbed away.

He looked around the horizon. If they were bounced now they would be decimated, but he relied on his top cover to give them warning. Come on! Come on! It seemed to take hours for the orbiting planes to come in, one by one, across the airfield. The antiaircraft defenses were now at peak performance. The air behind him was an arcade of colored lights through which each plane had to fly. Pale gray smoke was drifting across the airfield from the guns and from two burning aircraft, one of which had collapsed on the ground. A line of red flame was suddenly drawn across the scene—a Mustang had been hit. Too low to escape, the pilot tried to put it down, but a wing tip touched a parked plane and the Mustang cartwheeled into a spectacular explosion. Tucker turned to see better and a second Mustang was hit. Its nose went down as the pilot slumped across his stick and it plowed into the burning transports, its fuel spurting fountains of fire. Their line-abreast formation had grown ragged. Two Mustangs lagging behind banked away rather than face the concentrated gunfire, but the flak followed them. The last four planes pressed their attack home and, benefiting from the distracted flak gunners, came through the towers of black smoke that now covered the wreck-strewn apron.

"Sparkplug Leader to Green Leader. Form up on me." Tucker led them up toward the clouds. Climb, climb, climb away from it all. There was a double click as Green Leader acknowledged the command.

"This is Sparkplug Leader. Who is missing? Sound off. Blue Leader?" This was the part he hated. He deliberately put his mind to other things, as he always did when faced with situations he hated. He remembered his days at the Point—marching marching marching. The icy wind up the valley, the gray uniforms, the gray slabs of ice floating on the sluggish water of the Hudson. The gray Gothic buildings, the faces blue with cold; "Duty, Honor, Country."

"Sound off, Blue Leader. Who did we lose?"

22

Captain Vincent H. Madigan

"Every last officer on this base knows more about public relations than I do," said Vince Madigan. "I get advice from the captain in charge of the fire-fighting platoon, I get hints and tips from the Flight Surgeon and endless complaints from the pilots . . . the other day I even had the Chaplain telling me the best way to handle what he called 'the moral paradox of Christians fighting the war.' It's enough to make me puke."

That wasn't the way Captain Madigan usually spoke to lieutenant colonels from the Grosvenor Square PR office, but this one seemed different—smart, friendly, and very relaxed; before the war he'd been a senior executive with a West Coast talent agency. This whiz kid was nothing like the West Point stuffed shirts who regularly came on the phone telling Madigan to straighten out his paperwork. Or, what was worse, complimenting him on some piece that the insufferable Pfc. Fryer had written. Madigan's visitor, Lester Shelley, had been made a "leaf colonel" because he was a hotshot agent and publicist, and when the war ended he was going right back to take up his career exactly where he'd left off. "Take it easy, Vince," he said. "You're going to get plenty more of that kind of shit. Just give them a big smile and thank them warmly. That's all part of the job, kid."

Lieutenant Colonel Lester Shelley smiled. It was a broad smile of the kind that he himself prescribed. His teeth were white, even, and perfect, as only Beverly Hills dental mechanics can make them. His skin was olive, despite the sunlamp he'd carried across the Atlantic in an effort to hold on to his California tan, but he still looked more like a movie star than the "small-town lawyer" he liked to say he once had been.

"Don't give me that 'plenty more' stuff," Madigan said, and laughed to make a joke of it. Madigan's laugh, like his voice, was deep, manly, and assumed.

Shelley looked over his shoulder to make sure there was no one within earshot. "We're in the same racket, Vince," he said, "and you're the kind of pro I like. And when I like someone I put it on the line." He smiled again, and Madigan could recognize the cosmetic surgery that had been employed to tighten the muscles of his face and make him look younger. "But I'm going to need you in my corner. Can I count on you?" He fixed Madigan with his clear brown eyes, and when Madigan nodded he slapped his arm. "Great, Vince! You and I are going to make a hell of a team."

"A team to do what?" asked Madigan, knowing that Shelley was only at Steeple Thaxted for a brief visit.

"You're not kidding me, are you, Vince? You've been around. You saw the PR potential in Lieutenant Mickey Mouse a long time ago, unless I'm very much mistaken. All that Mickey Mouse crap! I've got to hand it to you—you put that story together out of nothing but a bunch of paper clips and a phone book, as we say in Hollywood."

"I just did what I could," Madigan said modestly, and was about to enlarge on it, but Shelley waved a manicured finger in the air, so Madigan took another sip of his whiskey and waited.

"Handled in the right way," Shelley went on, "Lieutenant MM —or whatever we decided to call him—should be a really big story. And my general agrees with me that it's time Fighter Command hit the headlines. The public's getting a little tired of hearing how the Heavy Bombardment boys never falter while the Luftwaffe kicks the merry shit out of them. I have a hunch that John Q. Public is looking for something new in stories about the war, Vince. They want something spirited, something vigorous and optimistic. Nineteen forty-four's going to be the year we shaft the Axis, and that's got to be our theme."

"Fully agreed, sir."

"For Christ's sake, call me Lester." He looked at his watch and told the bartender that the clock over the bar was two minutes fast. Without waiting for a reply he added, "I've got a busload of reporters arriving here in half an hour. These are top writers from the big papers and syndicates. They'll want to file all kinds of junk, but we've got to make sure they all get an eyeful of this kid Morse. He's the big story—they'll all latch on to that." He looked at the clock again, sniffed at his martini as if it might have gone bad, and then said, "Morse is flying today, that's right, isn't it?"

There was no need to confirm it, they'd already been in the Briefing Room. Madigan had shown him the tapes stretched across Germany to Magdeburg and waved Morse's nameplate at him. "I think I can claim I've started the ball rolling on this one already, Lester," Madigan told him.

"That's great, Vince," Shelley said, and took a puff at his cigar.

"An Australian writer named Henry Scrimshaw is doing a big story on MM for us. Over the last few weeks the two of them have been putting it together. Scrimshaw is here almost every day. I've alerted the photographers, so we're maximizing our photo coverage of MM, with plenty of backup shots showing the way the ground crews—armorers, crew chiefs, and parachute packers—play a vital role."

"That's great, Vince," Shelley said again, but there was even less conviction in his voice this time. "Can you tell me a little more about . . . what was that name? . . . Scrimshaw?"

"I don't know a lot about him," Madigan admitted. "But I do know he's sold some big stories to Stateside papers and magazines."

"Australian, eh." Shelley scratched the tip of his chin with his thumbnail before taking a puff at his cigar. "Have you got a copy of the contract handy?"

"Contract?"

"Scrimshaw and MM . . . what did they sign?"

"I didn't know Army Regulations would permit it," Madigan said. "I'd need a ruling on that."

"Well, you've got it, Vince," he said, fixing Madigan with a cold stare. "A man doesn't lose his basic rights as a citizen when he joins the Army. I'm happy to tell you I've signed a lot of contracts since joining the Army. There are a number of Hollywood stars who'd be sitting on their butts for the duration unless I could authorize their employment."

"I'm pretty sure MM hasn't signed a contract," Madigan said, and drank a little of his whiskey. This "friendly" bastard was making him sweat. Madigan wiped the palm of his hand on his pants. Shelley smiled as if Madigan was only pretending to sweat. "So I think we're okay on that one, Lester."

Colonel Shelley sighed and riffled through his briefcase. Then he looked up and smiled that warm friendly smile that he'd recommended to Madigan. "If you'd studied law, instead of whatever it was you did study . . . you'd know that Scrimshaw has acquired far more contractual rights by not signing anything than by drawing up a proper contract."

Madigan drank more whiskey. "How so?"

"Lieutenant Morse has been sitting down talking to him with a view to publication of that material. There is an implied contract existing. The law is going to give the Lieutenant the same rights that the subjects of Scrimshaw's previous stories enjoyed. In other words: zero."

"I see."

"Now, I don't intend to tolerate that situation . . ." He scratched his chin. "I'm afraid we'll have to get rid of this Australian guy."

"Perhaps we should talk to Scrimshaw. I think he might cooperate."

"It's not the kind of risk we can afford to take, Vince." He showed his teeth again. "We've got to have someone we know doing the big story, someone we can trust. We'll want to have the typescript well before publication, so we can get rid of errors and maybe add some important material that's been missed."

"But a big-shot reporter won't do it on those terms."

"I don't know how many big-name reporters you've had close dealings with, Vince," he said icily, "but I don't anticipate any great difficulty. Scrimshaw and all these other newshawks have to play ball with the Army or we strike them off the accredited listing and they never get into an army post again." He puffed at his cigar. "We won't have any problems, Vince."

"I guess you're right."

"It's not a question of censorship, Vince," Shelley said, noting Madigan's lack of enthusiasm. "It's a question of winning the war. Don't let's get our wires crossed on this one, Vince. This will come out a whole lot better for the kid. We'll fix up a proper contract. No reason why Lieutenant Morse couldn't earn two thousand dollars or more for an exclusive."

"I'm with you all the way, sir."

"Lester," he said. It was little more than a murmur that seemed to come automatically to his lips as he kissed his cigar.

"We've had a lot of reporters visiting the base lately."

Shelley pursed his lips. "London is jammed full of press people. Some mornings I can hardly push my way through them to get to my office. And not only Americans—Brazilians, Russians, Swiss, Portuguese, Spaniards, Turks . . . You'd find Hottentots and Eskimos too, if you looked close." He smiled to show Madigan that although being nice to them all was part of his job, he had no intention of looking *too* close. "The reporters are all waiting for the goddamned invasion, Vince."

"When will that be?"

"It's not even decided yet," Shelley said, as if to imply that the moment it was, he'd be among the first to know. "But the smart money says it's got to be May. The British have already suspended steamer service between Britain and Ireland for all civilians. They've designated a coastal zone around southern England and are going to prohibit entry to it." He looked at his watch again and decided he had time to finish his story. "You ask me why we've got to go in May? Well, I was with a very dear friend last week—he's at Supreme Headquarters on Eisenhower's planning staff. He tells me that any invasion will require hazy moonlight, cloud ceiling at least three thousand feet, less than twenty-mile-an-hour winds in the Channel and even less on the beaches. A century of meteorological records shows that June averages only two and a half days when all those conditions prevail! And after June the weather gets worse and worse, with the fall gales blowing up the Channel."

"Can't the Germans figure that out too?"

"Sure they can, but SHAEF hopes maybe they won't. Allied correspondents have been requested not to speculate about the date of the attack, but it looks like May, Vince, so you tell Lieutenant Morse he hasn't got a lot of time left."

"Because of the invasion?"

"These news guys are sitting around with their brains in neutral, peering into whiskey bottles for something to write about. But once the invasion gets going, every reporter worth a damn will be with the Army on the Continent. The dogfaces will be getting all the headlines, and you and I are going to be enjoying that long siesta we've been promising ourselves. And if your Lieutenant Morse comes up to scratch, you'll maybe find yourself eating and drinking your way across the U.S. of A. on a savings bond tour. Which would also give you a jump in rank."

"Sounds good to me," Madigan told him. It sounded like typical Hollywood bullshit, but maybe this little guy could swing it. "Where do we start?"

"You find some way of keeping Scrimshaw off this airfield, while I try to think of some way to keep Lieutenant Morse confined to it."

"For how long?"

"Just long enough for him to sign a postdated contract with a more suitable writer. We've got to look after this boy, Vince. He's risking his neck for us."

"It won't be so easy keeping him on base," Madigan said. He didn't mention the existence of Vera Hardcastle; that would make things a lot more complicated.

It was late that afternoon before the planes started arriving back. Southern England was overcast with gray cloud and the light was already failing, so the photographers had all fitted their Speed Graphics with shiny reflectors and flash attachments. The bus that had brought them from London was parked behind the firing butts, not too far from the hardstands where MM and the other three flyers of his flight regularly parked. It was very cold and most of the correspondents stayed inside the bus. The driver kept the motor running to provide some warmth. The sky to the west was a sulfurous yellow and the billowing clouds were tinged with pink.

Captain Madigan stood at the front of the bus, explaining as much as he could tell them about that day's mission. The Group had been assigned to "target penetration withdrawal support," and the target was Magdeburg. He didn't add that the sight of the route map had produced a low groan at briefing that morning. Instead, he proclaimed that February 1944 was already a legend, and the "Big

Week" was being described as one of the greatest battles in history. Eighth Fighter Command flew 2,548 sorties in that month despite the consistently terrible weather. During February it had been the bomber crewmen who had suffered the casualties; the fighters had come through with comparatively light losses. Now they were entering a different phase of the war—at least the Hollywood leaf colonel was right about that—and the Fighter Groups had slogged their way through March toe to toe with the Luftwaffe. Missions were penetrating deeper into Germany, and fighter pilots were earning their flying pay as they'd never earned it before.

It was only a few minutes after he'd come to the end of his little pep talk that the first of the returning fighter planes was spotted. They arrived back in a long, straggly formation. Colonel Dan in *Pilgrim*, leading the 195th Squadron, was the first to land. Then, fifteen or twenty minutes later, came Tucker, leading the 199th Squadron across the airfield at about four hundred feet before they pitched out for their landing pattern. It was obvious that they'd been in combat, and not just from the torn patches over the gun ports or the dark stains that streaked back across their wings. It was obvious from the ragged flying and careless approaches, the sideslips onto final, and the lopsided touchdowns that sent the planes bouncing along the runway while the ground crews winced at what was happening to "their" hydraulic systems. Madigan made a face. These boys were shook!

He looked around to see how the correspondents were taking it. They seemed happy enough. They'd forgotten all their little worries about telephones, toilets, and hot coffee. They were all out of the bus now, necks craning upward, animated and smiling foolishly at each other. What a comical bunch they looked; chubby, red-faced men, with ill-fitting army trenchcoats that bulged with notebooks, gloves, motion-sickness pills, candy bars, and the inevitable hip flask. Every one of them was trussed up with straps supporting gas mask, binoculars, camera, and knapsack. Some of them even had pencils tucked into their army caps.

Mickey Mouse II landed, with *Daniel* and *Kibitzer* right behind it. They taxied around the perimeter track while the reporters grew more and more excited at the prospect of meeting the young ace pilot who'd been so ballyhooed to them. The three planes didn't keep to regulation taxiing intervals, and for one moment it looked as if Jamie Farebrother was going to chew the tail of the plane ahead of

him. Madigan swore—it would be just his sort of lousy luck to have
an accident happen with the press there. But the moment of danger
passed, and he smiled at Colonel Shelley to indicate his relief. Shelley
hadn't registered the incident; it was Henry Scrimshaw who, having
arrived mysteriously and attached himself to the party without permission, grinned at Madigan and nodded. That old Australian buz-
zard missed nothing. Madigan didn't relish the prospect of warning
him off the Lieutenant Morse story. He was a tenacious old-timer,
and Madigan had met such men before; they invariably defied authority and weren't easily intimidated.

Madigan had arranged to have MM's dog with them, and as soon
as *Mickey Mouse II* was parked he heaved Winston up into the
cockpit. It was just the sort of stunt the press enjoyed. The camera
shutters were going like machine guns. MM was grandstanding, of
course, even to the point of putting his flying helmet on Winston's
head. When MM had milked that one, Madigan had a can of paint
and a brush ready so that they could get shots of the crew chief
painting another swastika on the nose of his plane while MM stood
by, smiling.

Jamie Farebrother's plane was parked by this time. Madigan
went across to the adjoining hardstand to say hello, but Jamie didn't
seem to hear his greeting or notice his wave. He was sitting in his
plane with his hands outstretched to the metal uprights of the windshield. His face was as white as a corpse and drawn tight, so that his
cheeks were hollow and his eyes dark-ringed. "How did it go, Jamie?"
Madigan called, but there was no movement, and the eyes stared
straight ahead.

"Stand back, Captain," said a voice behind him, and Staff Sergeant Tex Gill, Jamie's crew chief, elbowed Madigan aside. "The
Captain's having trouble getting out of his seat. Can't you see he
needs help?" The sergeant said this over his shoulder as he stepped
up on the wing of *Kibitzer* and began unclipping Farebrother's
shoulder harness.

It wasn't until that moment that Madigan realized what these
missions took out of a man. Jamie Farebrother had been in that
cramped cockpit for nearly five hours. Now he was numbed, both
psychologically and physically. He had to be helped down like some
sick octogenarian.

"Did you get anything, Jamie?" Madigan called to him. He
looked around to find Colonel Shelley, and was disconcerted to see

him frowning. Madigan had never had so many really important press people to look after and with Shelley watching every move he was getting very edgy. "Get anything, Jamie?" he called again.

Sergeant Gill shook his head, but foolishly Madigan went on trying to make conversation. Glancing over at all the razzmatazz still going on around *Mickey Mouse II*, he could now see that even MM was looking off-color, but there was a lot of Barnum and Bailey in that kid and he was determined to put on a show for the press. None of them realized what a bad day the Group had had; none of the reporters spared time to look at Rube Wein or Jamie. Perhaps that was just as well.

"Where's Earl?" Madigan asked Jamie. He could see that *Kibitzer* had fired its guns—the plane reeked of powder, warm oil, and spilled coolant. He'd grown to hate the smell of those planes, and he hated the sound the cooling engine made, clicking and pinging with the sounds of the contracting metal. Whatever he did for a living after the war, he'd stay as far as he could get from aviation.

Sergeant Gill eased the parachute harness off Jamie's back, and Madigan steadied him with a hand as he jumped to the ground.

"Where's Earl?" Madigan asked again. "Where's Earl Koenige?" It occurred to him that perhaps the sound of the engine hour after hour had made Jamie deaf.

Jamie pulled his flying helmet off and shook his head as if to clear his mind. "Earl bought the farm." He said it as if he was angry with Madigan.

"Shot down? Earl? Did he bail out? Shit! How did it happen, Jamie?"

Jamie Farebrother put his hand on Madigan's chest and pushed him violently away. "He burned, Vince. What do you want out of me, an eyewitness account for a press release?"

His push almost made Madigan lose his balance, and he had to steady himself against the edge of the wing. The metal skin was icy; the planes were cold after flying so high. Madigan rubbed his hand. "I'm sorry, Jamie. I'm really sorry. You were good pals, I know."

Everything he said seemed to make matters worse. He looked around to make sure that Colonel Shelley hadn't noticed this exchange, but he needn't have worried, the Colonel was talking to the men from the big syndicates. Jamie turned away and walked to the waiting jeep. Rube Wein was already sitting in it. The two men barely looked at each other. They sat staring straight ahead as if hearing and understanding nothing. The seat beside the driver remained empty.

Madigan turned back to join MM's circle of admirers. "Do you want to see the one thing a fighter pilot's got to do after coming in from a long mission?" MM called out to them. In response to the affirmative noises, MM said, "Cameras ready, guys, and hold the front page!" And he unbuttoned his trousers and urinated on the ground.

Madigan looked around to see how they were taking it. There were smiles and a whistle and some sounds of encouragement. MM had judged his audience well. Madigan looked at Colonel Lester Shelley, and the Colonel winked back.

After looking at his watch, Madigan said in an authoritative voice, "We must let Lieutenant Morse go to the debriefing now. But you gentlemen will have a chance to talk to him again after that."

"Can we go to the debriefing too?" one of the reporters asked. The others paused to await the decision.

"No such luck, I'm afraid," Madigan told them. "The mission today involved specifics that have to remain secret." There was the sudden flare of a match in the gathering gloom of the afternoon. "No smoking!" he called. "Now I'm taking you to a beautiful old English pub." And as an afterthought he added, untruthfully, "It's a favorite hangout of the pilots and you'll pick up a little local color. We have food and drink waiting there for you." They began to move toward the bus.

Colonel Shelley edged up to Madigan and whispered, "What goddamned specifics about the mission are secret?"

"The secret is that the Group has been shredded," Madigan told him. "You take this bunch across to the debriefing and you're going to wind up with some fighter pilot sobbing on your shoulder or vomiting in your hat."

"How do you know they've been shredded?" Shelley asked.

"While you've been watching that clown MM performing his act, I've been counting the ships coming over the fence. We've got a lot of NYRs, Lester."

" 'Not yet returned' doesn't mean dead."

"Right, sir. But I'm afraid your reporters might not fully grasp such a subtle distinction."

Shelley slapped Madigan on the shoulder to show he agreed. By the time they reached the bus the reporters were all seated and waiting to go. No one had gotten lost, which was surprising; it must have been the mention of food and drink that did it.

As Captain Madigan climbed in and slid the door closed, the bus lurched forward. In the gathering gloom Cambridgeshire looked mysteriously beautiful. At short notice he had arranged for the press contingent to eat at the King's Head Hotel in Lower Collingwood. American airmen had been involved in some noisy brawls in Long Thaxted, and until the villagers became more friendly it was expedient to keep the press away from there. Anyway, reasoned Madigan, Lower Collingwood was a prettier village and exactly what newspapermen fresh from the United States expected England to look like. Just to make sure that the food and drink were equally up to the expectations of the fourth estate, he'd sent his PR sergeant ahead with canned food and a case of scotch.

As the bus passed Hobday's Farm, which was in a direct line with the runway, a P-51 came in low over the fence. Its engine was wheezing asthmatically in the cold air as it hung, flaps down, poised over them, predatory and colorless in the failing light. Then, with a thunderous roar, it flashed overhead and was gone behind the ash trees that marked the edge of the farm. For a moment there was silence in the bus. Then everyone began speaking at once. "Would that be a late arrival?" said a voice from the gloom.

"Yes, sir," said Captain Madigan. He walked down the aisle of the bus; he didn't want to be sitting up front like some down-at-the-heels tour guide. "And running a little low on fuel, judging by the sound of his motor."

Madigan picked his way past the seated reporters and their equipment. Henry Scrimshaw, who had gate-crashed the party, was alone in the back seat, smoking his evil-smelling pipe. Madigan went back to him, and Scrimshaw gathered the skirt of his old tweed overcoat and moved aside to make room.

"Jesus, but England is beautiful," Madigan said.

They were going through Thaxted Green by that time. Its thatched timber-framed cottages around the neat little village green were enough to bring a gasp from even these tough hacks. There were a few coils of gray smoke from the cottage chimneys. The smoke drifted through the stark leafless meadow elms that could be seen against the watery pink sky. The bus groaned on its springs as the driver took the humpbacked bridge a little too fast. Some idiot, trying to snap a photo, hurt his nose and complained loudly about the excessive speed. Others, more desperate for liquid refreshment, remonstrated. Madigan looked out the window and pretended not to notice the disagreement. Under the bridge, ducks were fidgeting to make ripples on a pink brook that was swollen by rain and tangled with willows. How could anyone who'd studied English literature be less than enchanted, thought Madigan.

"Ever think of going back to Australia?" he asked Scrimshaw.

Scrimshaw took the pipe from his mouth and said, "Is that in the nature of a suggestion?"

Madigan laughed. "Not at all, Mr. Scrimshaw. I'm delighted to have you join us today. I would have sent you an invitation except that this whole visit was arranged by my London HQ at very short notice."

"I don't need any invitations for this kind of junket, thanks," said Scrimshaw. "I have my own car and a supplementary petrol ration. I manage to see what I want to see."

Madigan decided this was a perfect opportunity to lay the facts on the line for him. "Security is getting tighter all the time," he told him. "On account of preparations for the invasion. From now on you may find it a whole lot harder to get past the gate without showing the sentry your pass. Better be sure you have it with you at all times."

"What pass?"

"Haven't you got a gate pass from Group HQ?" Scrimshaw just stared at him. "Or a letter from Eighth Air Force?"

"You damn well know I haven't." He took the ancient pipe from his mouth and prodded inside it as if to demonstrate that the conversation was not holding his attention.

"I've seen you on the base two or three times, Mr. Scrimshaw. In our conversations about Lieutenant Morse you never requested official facilities. I thought you'd fixed everything with my people in Grosvenor Square. If not, you'd better do that right away." Captain Madigan took off his glasses and began polishing them. "Orders say civilians have to have an area pass and must be accompanied by an officer at all times." Only when he'd finished cleaning his glasses and put them back on did Madigan look into Scrimshaw's face again.

"So you turn a blind eye to reporters strolling through the gate," said Scrimshaw, smiling to reveal his long yellow teeth, "because escorting them around would give you hours of extra duties?"

"There's a big notice at the gate, Mr. Scrimshaw. 'All visitors must report to the guardroom'—'all visitors' includes reporters."

Scrimshaw leaned closer. Madigan smelled the tobacco, the breath, and the damp overcoat that had never been cleaned. "Are you threatening to kick me off the airfield, Captain?"

"No, of course not, Mr. Scrimshaw. It's my job to help the press in every way I can, that's what the Army pays me to do. If you will ask your editor to submit an official request in writing to my office, I'll expedite it at maximum speed."

"I told you I haven't got an editor—I'm a free lance. I went through all that with you." He tapped his pipe out on the heel of his shoe. He was speaking very slowly.

Madigan recognized the signs of anger and wanted to placate him. "I guess I misunderstood . . . but no matter. Being a free lance will delay things a little—the Army will want to run a security check on you—but all the more reason why we should submit your request as soon as possible."

"You listen to me, pox-brain," said Scrimshaw, not bothering about the Australian accent he usually tried to eliminate from his voice. "You give me the runaround, and I'll give you a story that will have your air force generals in Washington screaming for your blood."

Madigan chuckled politely, pretending to think it was all a gag. "What exactly would you do, Mr. Scrimshaw?"

"I would write a story—a long detailed story—about a top American air force fighter ace who is screwing the wife of a British soldier on active service overseas. It would be a big story, Captain."

"It happens," said Madigan. "It's lousy luck, but it happens all the time. You know that." He began to feel uneasy but tried not to show it. The bus was filled with reporters.

Scrimshaw gave one of his bleakest smiles. "If you don't see that you're sitting on a powder keg, Captain, you must be an even bigger idiot than I took you for."

Madigan got up from his seat without replying. He had to steady himself as the bus turned off the road. In a loud voice he said, "Okay, gentlemen. We're just coming up to the King's Head in the beautiful little English village of Lower Collingwood." He cleared his throat, knowing it was a way of getting attention from an audience. "A bit of history, gentlemen. English public houses named after the Pope soon changed their names and their inn signs after King Henry the Eighth quarreled with Rome back in the sixteenth century. Most bar owners were smart enough to put up a portrait of Henry himself . . ." Madigan paused for the inevitable titter. "And that's why still today most 'King's Head' pubs have Henry the Eighth on the sign. The present inn was built in the sixteenth century and it's said that Oliver Cromwell once spent the night here." He looked at them and smiled at their wide-eyed trusting faces. No matter what tough-guy airs these "top writers" might adopt, they were just tourists at heart; they didn't want scoops, they wanted stories. Except for Scrimshaw, who was a troublemaker.

Madigan decided to leave him alone for an hour or so. A few refills of scotch would probably mellow him, and Madigan was confident that a friendly chat near the log fire with a bottle close by would calm Scrimshaw down and convince him to wait for an official pass. The man must know that writing that kind of muckraking story about Morse and Vera would get any reporter barred forever from all U.S. bases—and maybe British bases too. He cursed Vera; why in hell did she have to tangle with *two* medal hunters? It made his life so fucking difficult.

By the time Captain Madigan had made sure that all the Americans had refreshments, and had answered questions about everything from drinking British tap water to how many pennies there were in a shilling, Scrimshaw was nowhere to be seen. Madigan didn't go looking for him; he told himself it was all for the best.

Bernard Cooper

To a casual observer, the pair might have looked like a club member forced to play a round with his elderly caddie. The taller man had the calm, confident manner that wealth sometimes bestows, while the ruddy-faced man with him trailed along, his white hair ruffled by the breeze and his attention shared among the golf, the countryside, and the conversation.

"Change is a young man's pleasure," said Bernard Cooper, his voice still imbued with the pride of his last stroke and the pleasure of being outdoors on such a fine morning. "Travel, meeting new people, tasting exotic foods, learning a new language—young people thrive on such variety," he told General Bohnen. They were playing golf at Cooper's club, where wartime changes were everywhere evident. The greens were neglected, the staff were elderly or infirm, and most of the members not away at the war were sporting some sort of uniform. Worse, the most unlikely chaps seemed able to get a game here nowadays; noisy, back-slapping fellows who threw money about and bought drinks for everyone in the bar—behavior that the pre-war committee would never have tolerated. Half of them didn't even have their own clubs. "If I were younger, I would probably be tickled to death to think of Christ's College being used by clerks from the Ministry of Food, and King's letting an RAF Transport Wing use The Backs as a lorry-park. Now I'm old enough to find it disturbing. At my age a man wants food he's accustomed to, at set hours. I don't want Britten when I can listen to Mozart, and even the journey to London has become a trial to me."

"Are you trying to provide me with a typical example of British understatement?" asked Bohnen with a grin. "You English exhibit a flexibility that makes us Americans pop-eyed. Sometimes I make believe all this is happening in Washington." They were on the fairway, and he was taking his time selecting a wood for his drive. Bohnen had fine clubs that he'd brought from America, a typical example of his foresight. "I wonder if we Americans would have endured an overpaid foreign army taking us over." His clothing—other than shoes—was entirely military, but such was the variety of the U.S. Army officer's wardrobe that, even so, he was attired more suitably than Cooper for the game. He was wearing pinkish-beige trousers, a light zipper-fronted rainproof field jacket, and a close-fitting cap with a very large visor.

"Your people are also adaptable, judging by the way they're making themselves at home here. My work takes me to London two or three times a week, and I've seen how Mayfair has become a 'little America.' But you must know all that better than I do."

Bohnen wondered to what extent Cooper was being deliberately caustic about the Americans in London. He didn't reply until he'd played—he had an amazing ability to concentrate his mind on one thing to the exclusion of everything else. He watched the ball land on the far side of the casual water and realized he'd have to be very careful with his next stroke. But then he was careful about everything he did. Now he smiled at Cooper and said, "I'm afraid we've even put the 787th Military Police Company into the Junior Constitutional Club." A palpable hit.

"I saw them yesterday morning," said Cooper, and after one quick practice swing he hit the ball with just enough force to bring it down the middle. For the first time he began to have hopes of beating the invincible General Bohnen. Casually, with scarcely a glance at the carry, Cooper went on talking. "Your 'snowdrops,' you mean. They were marching about in Green Park and a shepherd had to move his flock to make space for them. Sheep! In Green Park. I ask you."

"We were lucky, you and I," said Bohnen. "We were able to travel and see Europe while there was still something to see. I wonder how much will be left standing by the time young people are free to travel again." He took the cover off the head of a spoon, or what Cooper heard was called a "No. 3 wood" nowadays. He realized that Bohnen was going to try to get that long shot over the puddle of rainwater. Bohnen began swinging around. He used a most unusual grip that Cooper would have liked to learn, but he had the feeling that Bohnen would not readily help an opponent to play a better game. The General played to win—he said so in as many words. It was the American way, he said, when they'd discussed it the last time they'd played. Cooper suggested that it was perhaps more sophisticated to play for the sake of the game. Nothing sophisticated about that, Bohnen told him, it's decadent. "Decadent to play for the sheer pleasure of the game?" Cooper asked him. "Decadent to rationalize one's defeat before it has even taken place! That's what happened to the French in 1940," Bohnen had replied.

"Come along," said Bohnen impatiently now. He was pushing the curious, but most convenient, wheeled cart that he brought along to carry his clubs. "You were talking about changes," he prompted, and Cooper envied him his ability to remember conversation. One had the feeling that Bohnen could, and did, commit to memory every conversation he had.

"But I'm no longer young," Cooper said. "And I have to confess to you, Bohnen, I do not enjoy what's happening."

Bohnen smiled as they reached a place where he could study the lie of his ball. He used the spoon, but he hooked the ball and the shot was not up to his usual standard. "You're a dark horse, Bernard," he said. He pronounced the name in the French style, the accent on the second syllable. It sounded strange. "I met a young officer at our club in Stanhope Gate last night. He remembered some of your lectures from when he was at Cambridge in 1938. He told me you'd studied with Freud and knew Adler."

"I heard Freud lecture a few times in Berlin and Vienna. I used to join the crowd with Adler at a café he frequented."

"He also told me that you've been doing some damned important work for the psychological-warfare people."

"I help where I can," Cooper told him. "Most of the top specialists are in demand for clinical work . . . the war is burdening the country with a fearsome problem in mental health. RAF bomber crews have been the subject of some recent studies . . ."

"But you don't take patients?"

"That's not my line. No, I write and lecture. I never wanted to be an analyst or set myself up in some sort of confessional. Lately I've made a comfortable little niche for myself advising various committees, and the forces, about propaganda."

"Cloak and dagger, this fellow said you were."

"Then he exaggerated. Of course, the fact I'd lived in Germany in my younger days, and have pretty fluent German, makes me of interest to the intelligence people. I've even spent some time talking with the German prisoners of war, bringing myself up to date with German attitudes and ideas."

Bohnen looked at him quizzically. "Do you want me to introduce you to any of our psy-war people?"

"My goodness, no," said Cooper, embarrassed to think that Bohnen might believe he was looking for more fees.

They walked on in silence. When they got to Bernard Cooper's ball he scarcely had a chance to take out his putter when Bohnen picked up the ball. "You've got it," he said.

"That's very kind of you, Bohnen," Cooper said. "But I'm not sure that my previous display of putting justifies your confidence."

"I just can't wait any longer."

"Wait for what?"

"Bernard," he said. It was an interesting sidelight on their respective backgrounds that he indicated his friendship by using the first name, while Cooper kept to the university-educated Englishman's style of addressing intimates by their last name. "You've been huffing and puffing and preparing to say something to me ever since you got out of your car." He tossed the ball and Cooper caught it. "You've talked about everything from your school days to the civilian meat ration, but I still don't have the slightest idea of what you want to discuss."

"Well, I'm not sure . . ."

"Now don't go all British on me, Bernard. Is it about your daughter?"

"Victoria is thinking about going to stay with her aunt, but nothing is arranged."

"Your wife's idea, was it?"

"Not at all."

"Come now, Bernard. We're men of the world. Your wife doesn't approve of my son, isn't that the problem?"

"No," said Cooper. "At least . . . she approves of Jamie, but she feels they should wait before getting engaged."

"That's better, much better," said Bohnen approvingly. It was the sort of thing one said to a drunk who has just vomited. "We can help each other, Bernard, no point in fooling around. If Victoria wants to give Jamie the air, it's no business of ours."

Cooper was about to say that Victoria had no wish to give Jamie "the air," if that was the sort of rejection he surmised it to be, but he didn't want to reveal that the whole idea was his wife's. "My wife's sister, in Scotland, hasn't been too well lately. Victoria is rather fond of her aunt and wants to have a look after her."

"Scotland eh?" Bohnen putted his ball neatly into the hole. Cooper had a feeling that the General had given him his shot as some kind of self-imposed penalty. "That should really break up the romance. Your wife pitches a mean curve, Bernard." He smiled, as if the deliberate attempt to separate his son from Victoria didn't bother him at all.

"It's not that . . ." said Cooper, but he'd never been very good at lying.

"What did she do—get her sister to write and say she was sick and lonely?" Bohnen used his iron to mime a violinist playing an adagio with half-closed eyes. "We're no match for them, Bernard. We're just humans—they're women!"

"All parents are tempted to destroy their own children, Bohnen. It's a fact of life."

"You want to clarify that a little?"

"Human offspring have to be fed and protected for fifteen years or more before they're ready to leave the nest."

"Maybe that's just a consequence of our complicated civilization."

"You think a fifteen-year-old would have been capable of felling a marauding lion or killing a bison for meat during the Stone Age?"

"You've got a point there."

"No other animal cossets its young for such a long period. Fifteen years would be more than half Stone Age man's adult life. Even today, with our increased life expectancy, parents have immense influence upon the minds of their children."

"I could maybe show you a few instances where they didn't," said Bohnen cheerfully.

"You mean rich parents whose children have become dedicated communists?"

"And kids who insist upon making every mistake their parents warned them of."

"The influence in those cases is even more marked than in cases where the child accepts the parent's advice."

"No action without reaction." Bohnen looked at Bernard Cooper with a measure of cynical amusement. It seemed a typical "scientific answer"; whatever happened, the theory remained valid.

"I can see I haven't persuaded you, but no matter. The thrust of my argument is the effect the child has on the parent. After fifteen years or more of caring for a child, parents find it difficult to relinquish their role. There is temptation to cripple the child and thus keep the child dependent."

"And what form does this mutilation take?" said Bohnen.

"Mothers tell daughters that they'll never attract a husband, and if they do attract one, the mother is likely to pick him to pieces."

"Or say she should wait a little longer," said Bohnen, who now began to understand what Cooper was trying to tell him. "Maybe you should explain to me how fathers cripple their sons."

"By telling them they're stupid or lazy or inadequate ..."

"Or should have been studying law instead of flying fighter planes."

Cooper shrugged. "We all do it." He remembered telling his own son that he wasn't old enough or fit enough to get into the Army; so, to show his independence, he'd falsified his age and joined the Merchant Marine.

They went on with their round of golf, speaking only as much as was necessary for the game. It was a wonderful morning to be outdoors. The ground was still hard from the winter's frosts, and there were bald spots of bare earth polished shiny by the winds. From the hillock where precious grass seed had been expended on the big bunker near the Cambridge Road, they could see the hunt going hell for leather. The hounds were bunched tight and swerved suddenly toward the river. The horsemen quickened the pace, knowing that the hounds might lose the scent at the water. They made a stirring sight, most of them dressed in hunting pink and the horses dashing forward. Even the Italian prisoners of war working in the beet fields cheered them on.

"It's spring," said Bohnen, as if passing judgment on the day. "I wish Adolf Hitler could see that hunt. He'd realize that you British can't be beaten."

"It smells like spring," Cooper agreed. It was a day that brought to his mind no end of school-book poems that extolled the power of nature awakened in slumbering earth and bud. And yet the arrival of the time for the seeding of the land brought also the inescapable reminder that before Europe's crops were gathered, there was to be a terrible bloodletting that would bring a harvest-time of tears. The infantry battalions were moving south, concentrating near the seaports where they would embark for the invasion of the mainland of Europe. Already there was a quickening of air activity, so that the steady hum of aircraft provided a continuous background to their game.

"B-17s . . . Fortresses," said Bohnen as they raised their eyes to a formation of twenty or so planes flying east. He looked at his wristwatch. "That's a Bomb Group heading for its wing assembly point. From there the wings go on to form divisions at an assembly point on the coast, and finally the whole damn task force will be on its way to Germany."

They remained standing there long after the aircraft were out of sight, relishing the view. Here the peat fens gave way to a chalk ridge, so that the land changed at every step. "I'm very fond of the view from here," said Cooper.

"It's worth fighting for," said Bohnen.

The skyline was broken by the tall brick chimneys of Thaxted Hall. From the fifteenth hole there was a fine view of this Jacobean mansion and the Dutch-style outbuildings added nearly a century later. The long drive, flanked by a hundred mature elm trees, shone in the sunlight, and the man-made lake, with its absurd little ornamental bridge, reflected the clear blue sky. Cooper noticed the way Bohnen was looking at it all. "That's Thaxted Hall," Cooper told him. "The Duke still lives there."

"It's an impressive spread."

"At the turn of the century the property was much bigger. They owned the land that's now Steeple Thaxted aerodrome, and this golf course and everything as far as the London Road. Death duties forced the family to sell off a lot of it."

"What it must be like inside!" said Bohnen.

"It's magnificent. The Duke's father sold land rather than part with his pictures and furniture. He owns Holbeins that any museum would covet. Are you interested in antiques, Bohnen?"

"I have a small collection—Chinese jade, Japanese swords . . . a Dutch marquetry escritoire I could never part with." He admitted it reluctantly, as if he'd been asked about his personal habits. Despite his obvious affluence, Bohnen never talked of his possessions; it was one of the things that Cooper liked about him. "So you've been inside, Bernard?"

"The Duke was at Peterhouse with me—we're good friends. He has an amateur interest in psychology. He reads a lot and then has me over to a dinner which tends to become a tutorial, but I don't mind singing for my supper. I dined with him just a few days ago. He's preparing a celebration to welcome home one of the staff on leave. Everyone on the estate will be invited. There'll be a pipe band and dancing in the great ballroom."

Bohnen walked along the fairway to get a sight on the next hazard. "This is a tricky one, as I remember."

"The Duke's butler is returning from Burma, with medals galore."

"Good for him," said Bohnen, who was showing no interest in anything except addressing the ball. He took a couple of practice swings using that interlocking grip which served him so well.

"The problems will begin when the hero gets home, I'm afraid."

"Why?" Bohnen was still swinging his club, but he was no longer concentrating on the ball. He was gazing downward, but Cooper knew he was listening.

"The poor fellow is likely to find his wife in bed with another man. An American officer, as a matter of fact."

Bohnen stopped practicing with his club and looked up. "Does he have to find out? Sometimes it's better not to know the truth. There are lots of people on both sides of the Atlantic who are going to have to come to terms with that one, Bernard."

"It's gone too far, I'm afraid. A newspaper johnny has got hold of the story and seems determined to publish." Cooper didn't mention Henry Scrimshaw by name, or say that he played an occasional game of billiards with him. And he certainly didn't describe Scrimshaw's fury about the way "the bloody Yanks" had encouraged him to write his story and then suddenly reneged to the extent of kicking him off their airfield.

Bohnen stared at Cooper, his face twitching nervously as he tried to understand why he should be interested in such gossip. "Is this something to do with Jamie?" And then: "This is what you really wanted to talk about, isn't it? Not your daughter going away, but this . . ."

"The young officer is a close friend of Jamie's. His name is Morse, Lieutenant Morse."

"The ace? The one who looks as if he's becoming top scorer in the ETO?"

"The husband is a sergeant major and he's coming home from Burma. 'The forgotten army,' those men in Burma call themselves."

"I don't like the sound of that," said Bohnen with the manner of a man conceding something to a plaintiff. He tapped his wood against his toe.

"Our political-warfare people are broadcasting propaganda to German soldiers. We know that the most demoralizing theme is that wives, sweethearts, sisters, and daughters are being seduced by foreign laborers working in Germany."

Bohnen looked at Cooper and rubbed his chin. "Then we must prevent publication."

"Difficult," said Cooper. "There are two stories, good stories— the Englishman coming home and the pilot's success. A good journalist covering either story in any depth would come upon the infidelity, and Jamie tells me there are a dozen reporters out there at Steeple Thaxted whenever they get back from an operational flight. The journalists are shouting at Morse about any Germans he may have shot down even before the lad is out of his plane."

"Back home the papers have been drumming up interest in who's going to be the first American to shoot down more Germans than our top scorer of World War I."

"Yes, Jamie mentioned that."

"Our PR experts have been doing all they can to keep the pot boiling. The Air Force needs that sort of publicity. We like to have Mr. and Mrs. America opening up their morning newspaper eager to find out who's the top-scoring ace."

"Well, speaking as an expert, Mr. and Mrs. America are not going to be very pleased to hear that their innocent young boys are being seduced by married women in foreign climes."

Bohnen smiled ruefully. "I guess that's the way our papers would angle the story."

"Frankly, the mums and dads don't worry me, Bohnen. But if this story is given the kind of exposure I think a human interest story like this merits in editorial terms, there won't be a British or American soldier who doesn't know about it by the time the invasion is launched. It's an emotive issue . . . the sort of story that every soldier likes to argue about. Everyone will take sides, and to some extent the lines will be drawn between nationalities rather than personalities. It will be the easiest trigger for a fight between our soldiers in every pub in England, and it will be a gift for the German propaganda services, at the moment they most need one. The Germans virtually *invented* propaganda—they'll know how to squeeze the last drop out of this."

"And that is your considered opinion? The advice you would give to your people . . . or have already given them?"

Cooper nodded. "Battlefronts are vulnerable where two allied armies join flanks. When American and British units are fighting shoulder to shoulder on a beachhead, subjected to every weapon the enemy can bring to bear upon them, we'll need every last atom of mutual respect."

"But where do I come in, Bernard? Why are the two of us talking about it? Can't it go through channels?"

"The newspaper writer talked to the Duke. The Duke had a word with his House of Lords chums. The feeling from our side is that it can all be settled 'out of court.' No written complaints or meetings that could leak to the press. The Duke roped me in, Bohnen. It's not the sort of task a man volunteers for."

Bohnen nodded sympathetically, but there was still a trace of anger in his voice. "So I'll assign Lieutenant Morse to Honolulu . . . orders with immediate effect. I could have him out of Britain by tomorrow evening."

"I must advise caution, General Bohnen. The Lieutenant might protest loudly. If the press think you're victimizing him, they could make it into an even bigger story."

Bohnen slammed his club into the trolley in a gesture of exasperation. Quietly, unnaturally quietly, he said, "So what do you suggest?"

"Remember that Morse is a war hero too. You mustn't give the press a chance to say that the brass hats are deliberately preventing him from shooting down more Germans."

"Hot damn! Why does that little cocksman have to be a fighter ace?" He picked up his golf ball. "I'm going to ask you to excuse me, Bernard. You were going to win anyway and I'm due back in London early. I'll have to think about this, and maybe consult our PR people. Will you be home if I call you this evening?"

"Of course. I'll help in any way I can."

He tugged at the visor of his cap in what might have been a salutation. "Well, thanks for the exploding cigar, pal."

Cooper smiled. It was obviously a joke. He supposed Bohnen was referring to the situation with Hardcastle and Morse.

"By the way, Bernard, isn't Victoria making any difficulties about being shipped off to Scotland? That doesn't sound like your daughter. She seemed like a very spirited girl to me."

"To tell you the truth, Bohnen, that's been surprising me too."

24

Lieutenant Colonel Druce "Duke" Scroll

"Did you notice the date, sir?" asked Kinzelberg, Lieutenant Colonel Scroll's sergeant clerk.

"How could I miss it," said Duke Scroll. It was the second anniversary of the day the 220th Group had been born, "activated" by a typewritten order that made Captain Scroll and Pfc. Kinzelberg its only personnel. They shared a dilapidated office near the flight line at Hamilton Field, California, and were being buried under an avalanche of military paperwork as they prepared to receive "cadres" from other Groups. They knew exactly what to expect: the misfits, the disgruntled, the hypochondriacs, the troublesome, the drunks, and the cripples. And, by God, that's what they got, as orderly room staffs joyfully dumped upon them all the personnel they wanted to be rid of. "Kleenex," Sergeant Kinzelberg called them, because no one wanted to use them more than once. He put a K on the covers of their personnel files and, using any possible excuse, passed them on to other Groups. "You and me, Sergeant Kinzelberg, are the Group's oldest members. How are you enjoying it?"

"I like it in England, sir. When we get a little sunshine I even like the weather."

The sun was bright that day. The frost had gone and there were signs of new grass and buds on the trees. "I was thinking about all that Kleenex," Scroll told him. "Do you think those goldbricks are still being reassigned from place to place?"

"I figure they are," said Sergeant Kinzelberg solemnly. "I figure that few of them lasted long enough with a combat outfit to get sent overseas, so when the war's over, the Kleenex will be the first ones out of uniform."

"There are times when you depress me, Sergeant Kinzelberg."

"Yes, sir, I know."

"And I'm as depressed as any man deserves to get on any one day in this man's army. Did you guess that that phone call I just had was from General Bohnen? And could you guess he's coming back here again tomorrow? And Colonel Dan's got to be here because he wants a special word with him. I mean, could you guess that all that could happen just because I pick up a phone?"

Kinzelberg didn't answer. He'd worked for a bookie in Trenton, New Jersey, before the war. A rumor said that his scarred face and twisted little finger were inflicted by a cop when he refused to give a precinct captain evidence enough to nail his employer. In short, Kinzelberg was a man who knew how to keep his mouth shut. "I didn't hear the phone ring, sir."

"You know who General Bohnen is, don't you, Sergeant? He's the man HQ sends to visit this base from time to time, to make sure Colonel Badger doesn't become too easy to live with."

Kinzelberg permitted himself the briefest of smiles. "Should I call the sergeant at the Officers' Club and make sure they get the VIP quarters ready?"

"Let's pray the General will have urgent business elsewhere before nightfall, Sergeant. But, yes, tell them to fix up room number three—that's the one with the adjoining sitting room—with some books, magazines, fruit, flowers, and a bottle or two of whatever the PX has available."

Kinzelberg moved toward his office so that he could use his own phone. "And, Sergeant," Scroll said, "we'll need another room in the BOQ for Colonel Shelley. He's that high-powered PRO from London. And the General asked for the use of an office. Put a couple of those wicker armchairs in Major Phelan's office. It has a good view of the airfield and just may remind them that we're trying to fight a war around here." Scroll frowned as he thought about it. "And you'd better police up that office. I don't want the General looking for a scratch pad and opening a drawer filled with . . ." Scroll stopped, deciding it would be bad for discipline if he voiced his suspicions about what might be found in a field officer's desk.

"I understand, sir," said Kinzelberg. "And do you want me to try and find Colonel Dan, and tell him the General's coming?"

"Men have been awarded the Medal of Honor after volunteering for tasks less dangerous than that."

"So I'll just arrange for the two rooms." Kinzelberg was making quite certain that there was no margin for error. Giving him an order could sometimes be an ordeal, like going through a lease with a lawyer. "And I'll do nothing about telling Colonel Dan?"

"Colonel Dan is on his way over here," said Scroll. "He was test-hopping *Pilgrim* and I saw it land ages ago."

Colonel Badger came into the Exec's office by kicking the door open. It swung around to hit the bookcase with enough force to make the plasterboard shake. This did not startle Scroll; Colonel Dan usually entered his office in this manner, but today he seemed more agitated than usual.

"There's something I must tell you, Colonel," said Scroll, determined to break the news of Bohnen's arrival immediately, but the Group Commander wouldn't let him begin.

"And there's something I've got to tell you, Duke. Pin back your ears and get ready for this one, because I'm good and mad!"

"Yes, Colonel, I can see you are."

"I took that plane up for a test hop—and goddammit, I'm still having trouble with that engine—and after landing, I went in to wash up. Can you believe this, Duke . . ." Colonel Badger was leaning on the Exec's desk, quivering with rage. "One of my officers prevented me from going into the can! One of my own officers . . . right here in the goddamn Officers' Club."

"Which officer was that, Colonel?"

"The guy was obviously straight out of the sack. He was standing there in the corridor—blue chin, hair uncombed, towel over his shoulder and wash kit in his hand. 'You can't go in there, Colonel,' this son of a bitch says to me."

"Which officer was it?" Scroll asked again.

"He's standing outside the door of the latrine stopping me from going in there."

"I understand, sir. Which officer was it?"

"You understand, do you?" the Colonel roared. "Then you'd better explain it to me right now!"

"I don't claim to understand what motivated this officer," Scroll said. "I'm simply telling you that I understand your description."

"No need to shout at me, Duke," said Colonel Dan.

Duke Scroll hadn't been aware that he was shouting at anyone, although in the heat of the discussion it had become necessary to raise his voice in order to be heard. "Did he give any reason for this action?" Scroll asked, although he'd already guessed what had happened.

Colonel Dan pulled out some cheroots and a box of matches, but his hand was shaking so hard that he broke several matches without having lit the cigar. Finally Scroll leaned over and lit it with his lighter. "Thanks, Duke," said the Colonel. He inhaled and stood for a moment blowing out the smoke. This seemed to calm him a little. Scroll was holding a pencil over his note pad and he fidgeted with it in the hope of prompting Colonel Dan to provide the officer's name. After that he might get something more in writing—he'd found that taking a statement from anyone in a state of high excitement could be a way of lowering the temperature. But the Colonel ignored Scroll's gesture. "This officer says, 'The girls are in the bathroom right now, Colonel,' and he gave me a sickly kind of smile. And I could hear those English broads in there, giggling and laughing . . . it sounded as if there were a dozen of them in there." The Colonel shook his head in disbelief. "He told me I couldn't go in."

"Who did, Colonel?"

"I keep *telling* you . . . the Group PRO . . . that jackass of a captain who walks around with the camera around his neck . . . the one I saw wearing the jacket with flyer's wings and decorations at Christmas."

"Captain Madigan," Scroll said, and wrote the name on his pad.

" 'What goddamn girls?' I asked the son of a bitch, and he says, 'The girls who came for the dance on Saturday.' Well, I've got to tell you, Duke, I blew my lid. 'Saturday? Saturday! It's now Tuesday, you whorehound,' I told him. 'You get these women off my airfield and then get back to your quarters and consider yourself under open arrest.' "

Duke Scroll wrote that down without comment.

"I want that officer off this base, Duke, and I mean right away."

The Exec looked at Colonel Dan and waited for him to cool another degree or so. "Maybe you should let me go across to his quarters and speak with him, Colonel."

"When I say get him off the base, I mean exactly that!"

"Colonel Badger," Scroll said, "may I suggest we speak more quietly? My sergeant clerk is the soul of discretion, but we can probably be heard in the hangar." He pointed to the brick wall which separated the headquarters offices from the big steel building where the aircraft were repaired.

Colonel Dan sighed and sat down. He put his feet on a stool and puffed at his cigar. "Now don't tell me *you've* got a woman in *your* quarters, Duke."

"No, Colonel, but I suspect that a dozen or more officers regularly have women staying with them in their quarters on the Saturday night after the dance. Mostly it's the junior officers, the pilots in particular, but I believe Major Phelan's girlfriend doesn't usually leave the base until late Monday morning, and one of the flight surgeons also has regular companions . . . both those officers have rooms to themselves, of course."

"Kevin Phelan? That mad Irish bastard?" Colonel Dan smiled. Scroll knew he'd been right in mentioning Phelan; he could do no wrong in Colonel Dan's eyes. "And I didn't realize this was going on?"

"But Captain Madigan knows it's going on, Colonel, you can be quite certain of that. Any Group PRO always knows everything . . . in a manner of speaking, it's his job to know what's going on."

The Colonel's brow wrinkled like that of a small child asked to calculate a sum. "Is there a lot of this going on, Duke? I mean, I knew that the occasional girl stayed over . . . but . . ."

"Airfields are difficult to police, Colonel. Keep them out of the main gate and they come strolling back across the perimeter wire, jump the ditch near the fuel-storage area, or find a way through the back of Hobday's Farm. The previous commanding officer got a complaint from the civil police, after a father told them his daughter hadn't come home. Wing sent a whole Military Police Company to turn the base inside out, and they found one hundred and eighty-nine civilian women on the base that Sunday afternoon."

The Colonel looked at his Exec and pursed his lips as if to whistle, but no sound came. "You're telling me to forget the whole thing?"

"At Narrowbridge, and most other places, I guess, they post notices saying that all women civilians have to be off the base by Monday morning. But we don't dare put that kind of thing in writing, now that the place is seething with reporters. Why don't you let me pass the word around?"

"Sometimes, Duke, you make me think that maybe you're the guy who went broke barnstorming his way around the world, and I'm the West Point stuffed shirt."

Duke Scroll smiled gratefully, knowing that this was Colonel Dan's idea of a compliment. "And, Colonel," said Scroll, "General Bohnen phoned. He's coming over here tomorrow. He wants to have a word with you."

25

Brigadier General
Alexander J. Bohnen

General Alexander Bohnen could see the control tower, the nearest dispersal, and an RAF rescue amphibian that had brought a pilot back after he had ditched in the Channel. The atmosphere was tense; crew chiefs, mechanics and armorers, crash crews and men on flying control duty kept watching the eastern horizon where the returning Mustangs would eventually be seen. A dozen men were playing ball, others were bent over a card game, the Duty Flight Surgeon was standing by the ambulance throwing a ball that was dutifully retrieved by Winston, but all these activities were only pieces of bad acting. When the Group was flying a mission, no one really relaxed.

Bohnen turned away from the view of Steeple Thaxted airfield. "From the windows of my London office you can see that barrage balloon crew in Grosvenor Square," said General Bohnen.

Lieutenant Colonel Lester Shelley noted not only that the General had a London office, in addition, presumably, to other offices elsewhere, but that his London office faced out onto the Square and had at least two windows. It was an unmistakable mark of power and prestige. Shelley's office was shared with his sergeant clerk and had a window on a light well. "Sure," replied Colonel Shelley. "The balloon is crewed by women and they call the balloon 'Romeo.' "

"And don't think that's just by accident, Colonel. That way, the British provide every man jack of us with constant evidence that even their womenfolk are fighting the war. That's why the RAF assigned their Women's Auxiliary Air Force unit to Grosvenor Square, slap in the middle of all our offices."

"I guess you're right, General."

"Don't underestimate the English. When it comes to loading the dice, they wrote the book."

There was a polite knock at the door and Sergeant Kinzelberg came in to ask if they wanted coffee or something else. General Bohnen was not deceived by this solicitude. "You can tell Colonel Scroll that we'll be ready to see the base commander within the hour." General Bohnen did not consult Colonel Shelley on his feelings about coffee. Kinzelberg saluted and withdrew.

The two men, although not greatly divided by age, and both wearing the uniform of the United States Army, personified radically different aspects of successful America. General Bohnen was an eastern conservative, tall and muscular; his uniform came from a Washington tailor who'd dressed many generations of professional soldiers. Lester Shelley's uniform was more modern in style. It bore the silk labels of a Beverly Hills tailor who catered to the needs of some of the movie colony's wealthiest stars. Shelley had all the mannerisms of a studio executive. He used his hands as he spoke and waved his cigar around in the air. He smiled readily, and he even grabbed the General's arm in a way that was commonly regarded as a friendly gesture in the world from which he had come. General

Bohnen did not resent this behavior the way most senior officers would have. They were both civilians in uniform, and he knew that, like himself, Shelley had been selected to do a job he'd already proved he was good at. He'd had dealings with many such men—tough, boisterous, confident, calculating men. And he knew that, like salesmen and merchants, they depended upon their energy to overcome social resentment. But Bohnen did not greatly admire such self-confidence, for he'd spent most of his life among richer and more powerful men who demonstrated the greater confidence of not caring whether they were liked or not.

"Primarily," said Bohnen, "and throughout . . ." He paused again for emphasis. "We must consider the interests of this young pilot . . . Lieutenant Morse."

"Exactly," said Shelley, examining the ash on his cigar. "He's newsworthy." The reply had come too quickly, and General Bohnen had the uncomfortable feeling that Shelley had guessed everything he was about to say. Guessed too that the concern about Morse and the married woman originated with the British. And guessed that Morse was about to be made "un-newsworthy."

"And yet," said Bohnen, "I'm not sure that it would be in his interest—or in the interest of the air forces—if Lieutenant Morse became a widely publicized figure."

Shelley nodded. Aware now that his previous answer had been precipitate, he leaned well back in his wickerwork chair and smoked in silence, admiring—and noting for his own future use—the plural form "air forces." That was the way the Pentagon talked. He closed his eyes as he'd seen writers do in script conferences when deep thought was indicated.

"As I understand it," continued Bohnen, "Lieutenant Morse needs only a few more victories to beat Rickenbacker's World War I score and become the ranking ace in the history of American air power." He waited, but Colonel Shelley didn't open his eyes, so Bohnen went on. "The way the fighting's going, Lieutenant Morse could rack up the necessary wins on his next couple of missions, perhaps even on his next."

"So you're going to have him removed from flying duties, with immediate effect," Shelley said, his voice giving no indication what he thought of that idea.

"It will be your task to support, and justify, any decision headquarters makes about Morse. And I don't only mean draft a suitable press release."

Shelley opened his eyes and stared at Bohnen with his lids half closed as if trying to see into the glare of a bright light. "Strictly off the record, General, do you mean you want me to help you concoct a reason for grounding the kid? Something I think the press and radio boys might swallow?"

Bohnen stiffened. "We haven't yet reached a stage in our history when a commanding general has to explain to reporters the reasoning behind his operational orders in wartime."

"Is that a fact?" said Shelley.

"Yes, it is." Bohnen leaned forward as he said it and knocked a cushion to the floor without noticing that he'd done so.

"Trouble is, a lot of the bloodhounds out there wouldn't classify this as an operational decision. They'd sniff its ass, and say it's just the kind of victimization they're here to expose."

"Are you . . . ?" began General Bohnen.

Colonel Shelley raised his hands in supplication. "Just playing devil's advocate, General." He smiled. "You can count on me, I'm with you all the way." His eyes were still screwed up, so that the smile with which he accompanied this assurance was strained. "But you'd better understand what we're up against. The press won't be too thrilled about HQ grounding their favorite boy. There will have to be a little give-and-take."

Bohnen was surprised to find a cushion at his feet. He picked it up and tossed it into an empty chair. "Give?" he said. "Give what, to whom?"

"The only way we could extricate this boy from the arrangement he'd made with an Australian free lance was to sign him up with a big syndicate, the kind of big outfit the Australian wouldn't dare tangle with."

"Signed, you say?"

"Two thousand dollars paid on signature. They'll squeal bloody murder. We'll have to wheel and deal and give them some kind of exclusive in compensation."

"Let them squeal," said Bohnen. "They put their money on the wrong horse."

Colonel Shelley moved his jaw so that his upper lip stretched tight against his bared teeth. It was a mute gesture of hostility from a man who didn't permit himself vocal ones. "Maybe they'll think they put it on the winner, but that you came along and fixed the result."

Bohnen touched his face. "Squeal how?"

"A syndicate like that places stories in magazines and papers all the way from the Yukon to Rio. Get into a slugging match with them and they could roast us. I mean you and me, General. Roast us personally."

"Then you'll have to find a way out." Bohnen was careful not to specify exactly what he wanted done, and this reluctance was not lost on Shelley. The General was going to keep his hands clean.

"You ever meet the sort of hard-nosed bastards who get to manage a syndicate office? Concocting a story to convince them won't be easy. I know what we're up against, General. This same son of a bitch gave me a tough time with Morse's contract."

Alexander Bohnen had never liked California, or the people who lived in that soft-living, slow-moving region that Easterners called "occupied Mexico." He'd opposed Jamie's going to college there, and he'd been right to do so. Moreover, Mollie's marriage to a Santa Barbara oil engineer had done nothing to moderate his prejudice, and neither had this meeting with Colonel Lester Shelley. General Bohnen heaved himself out of his soft chair with the kind of weary determination with which an Olympic champion climbs out of the pool. "We are not here to *concoct* stories," said Bohnen in his low, carefully measured voice. "Neither will you be required to *fix* any results." The General towered over Shelley, who was still sprawled in an armchair. "Fact!" said the General, grabbing a finger of his left hand. "Lieutenant Morse has been credited with German aircraft destroyed on the ground, as well as air-to-air kills." He paused and took two fingers in his grasp. "Fact! His actual score of aircraft shot down *in the air* is far from equaling Rickenbacker's total. Fact!" By now he had three fingers. "Lieutenant Morse still has combat film submitted for appraisal. Until the results of that film are officially judged, his score cannot be revised, no matter how many crosses Morse paints on his ship, and no matter what the newsmen have already printed."

"Hold tight, General!" said Lester Shelley. The wicker chair creaked as he shifted uncomfortably. He was losing control of what had promised to be a game in which he held the trump cards. Until now, senior officers had always deferred to Shelley's Hollywood expertise. This one didn't, so now Lester Shelley fought back. "The way I've heard it, you were the one who told the Groups to start crediting ground kills. It was your idea—you can't pull this kind of switcheroo."

"Switcheroo?" said General Bohnen, as though encountering an obscenity for the first time. "I'm simply telling you something that must be obvious, even in Hollywood. If you are going to compare the number of planes shot down by Rickenbacker with the number of planes shot down by Lieutenant Morse, you can't rig the result by adding in Morse's strafing kills. The kind of victories Eighth Air Force acknowledges, apart from that comparison, has nothing to do with it."

"That's just going to sound like double-talk to reporters."

"Then you break it down into words of one syllable, Colonel. That's why the Army handed you that uniform. Go out and get shot at."

"Public relations is not just for reporters and radio commentators. We've got to think of how the pilots are going to take it. They're going to see it as a slap in the face."

"And what about the pilots in other air forces? What are the pilots in Ninth Air Force and Fifteenth going to say if we let this boy inherit Rickenbacker's mantle? And what about the Pacific Theater and the navy pilots shooting down Japs? In case you don't know it, Eighth is the only outfit crediting ground kills."

Colonel Shelley bit his lip to demonstrate concern. He nodded and then looked up at the General. He knew the real reason for getting rid of Morse as leading contender for the ace of aces spot, and he knew General Bohnen had prepared his arguments at short notice. He admired such rationalization; it had the ring of inevitability that convinces. He liked that "what else can we do—we don't like it, but there's no other way" line of argument. It had worked for Lester Shelley in the past, when he was a studio lawyer. A movie star, declining in popularity, still wanted to keep to the terms of a big fat contract signed in his heyday. They'd brought a poet from New England and paid him a thousand a month to write the worst script the studio had ever commissioned. The star waited nearly two years for this masterpiece to take shape; then he'd finally caught on and settled for a rewritten contract. Two years at a grand a month was peanuts for wriggling out of a two-million-dollar contract. Yes, General Bohnen would have done well in Hollywood. "Count on me, General," said Shelley, getting to his feet and stubbing out his cigar.

"Tell your office you'll be sticking close to me over the next few days, Colonel. We'll need to confer as this situation develops."

"Yes, sir," said Shelley. He picked up his cap and came casually to attention.

Bohnen looked him straight in the eye. He didn't trust Shelley, who was not the sort of man he'd choose to do business with. But in the Army as well as in civilian life one had to play the cards one was dealt. He suspected that Shelley not only had arranged every detail of Morse's contract with the press syndicate but had also taken a percentage or a handling fee. If he ever got a shred of evidence to support his suspicion, he'd have the Colonel court-martialed, but he knew enough about show-business lawyers to have little hope of uncovering such a deal. "I have no doubt that you and I will work this out together, Colonel Shelley."

"This Group Commander—Colonel Badger—has a terrific record both as a flyer and as a fighting man," said Shelley. "He flies lots of missions and gets kills. No one has a right to tell him who flies on his wing."

"I take your point, Colonel Shelley. You think Morse's grounding must remain a low-echelon decision that Headquarters says it can't countermand."

"I do, sir. The press won't dare attack a fighting man like Colonel Badger."

"Excellent," said Bohnen. "I knew a man with your experience would find a way out of this. I'll make sure you get full recognition." He reached for the phone. "Now we'll go along and explain what's needed to Colonel Badger."

"Are you sure he'll play ball?"

"Colonel Badger wants to go right on leading this Group into action. Sure he'll play ball, or he'll find himself flying a typewriter the rest of the war."

"And you'll put another commander in here?"

Bohnen tapped his briefcase. "I took the precaution of having his orders cut before I left London."

Shelley nodded his admiration. Not since the first few minutes of their meeting had Vera Hardcastle, or her home-bound soldier husband, been mentioned.

"Mr. and Mrs. America deserve clean-living young men as heroes," said Bohnen. "These are the men our next generation will admire and model themselves upon."

"In a way," said Lester Shelley, "and I mean this very sincerely, creating heroes in wartime is a lot like creating movie stars."

26

Captain
James A. Farebrother

"Break! Break! Je-susss! Break!"

The up-sun squadron was getting it. Farebrother heard the shouts of joy and terror on the radio, but he was keeping close escort on the bombers. The other squadron was somewhere beyond the cumulus clouds. Nervously he twisted around to scan the sky. His wingman was a nineteen-year-old uncommissioned flight officer who'd just arrived from the replacement depot. It would be rash to depend upon him to spot attackers. He realized how Earl must have felt when first nursing Jamie along.

There were plenty of Germans in the sky, and about five miles away to the south he could see more climbing out of the clouds. He looked below; the Forts were droning steadily on as if they hadn't noticed the impending attack, although he knew that all eyes would be on those swarming midges.

As the Germans came closer he recognized them as Focke-Wulf 190s, "formation destroyers" equipped with a big 21-cm. mortar under each wing to break up the bomber boxes. How long before . . . ? Surely Kevin Phelan had seen them? Ah, here we go. *Phelanski's Irish Rose* was leading the Group today, and he began a steep turn that would give them an interception, but not before those long-range mortars had fired at the bomber formation. That's the price paid for the really close escort the bomber crews liked. Now that they were on a collision course, the Focke-Wulfs grew bigger every second. They were in line abreast, and about a thousand yards away, when their wings flickered with flames as the rockets lumbered away.

Big black clouds of smoke appeared amid the bombers as the rocket shells exploded. The Germans were now close enough to rake the bombers with cannon fire. The nearest Fort took hits right from the first. *Scrapbook*, an aged B-17 with weathered green paintwork and a shapely blonde on the nose, reared and bucked. Slices of aluminum flaked off her body, flashed in the dull sunlight, and then folded back into the slipstream like the discarded skin of some great green snake. Only when the stream of cannon shells got to the Plexiglas did the Fort swerve. The top turret's clear glass turned white and shattered. The hammerblows inched along to the cockpit windows and the glassed nose, so that for a moment she disappeared in a snowstorm of broken plastic. Amid the whirling snowflakes, like the tiny Santa Claus in an inverted glass paperweight, men could be glimpsed, arms and legs flailing as they tried to find support in the thin blue sky. The snow flurry melted but the men remained. They twisted and, arms stretched, floated in the Fort's surrounding air before falling away, cartwheeling into the scattered confusion of broken wreckage.

Pilotless, the huge Fort slowly careened and tilted further and further until she rolled right over, breaking in half as her tormentors —the blue-painted Fw 190s—screamed past, twisting through the flying debris.

A Focke-Wulf came through Farebrother's gunsight. He fired and saw strikes near the cockpit, but the German, at full deflection, twisted away and was gone. Another plane charged at him. Instinctively his finger tightened on the trigger, but just in time he recognized the white stars and held his fire. It was huge as it slid toward him. The two planes almost collided, and as the German passed, with only a few feet to spare, *Kibitzer* rocked and wallowed in its turbulent wake.

He turned again to bring another German into view and moved his head to see his wingman, Luke Robinson, still with him. Good boy!

The gunfire was bright in the gray sky. Bang! Bang! His plane shuddered and the stick jerked as bullets plucked the elevator. He dived away. Where was the kid? Yes, he was still following. An explosion to port as a chance shot turned fuel and ammunition into a brilliant orange ball and the subsequent white flash that consumed the aluminum airframe in instantaneous combustion. No shortage of targets; the sky was full of Germans, but as fast as he got one in his sights he'd see the gunfire of another streaking past his wings. Break! He turned away so tightly that he felt the juddering that warns of a high-speed stall; gently does it.

Another German came into his view. Anyone who'd been tempted to believe those intelligence assessments about the Luftwaffe at its last gasp could revise that estimation! The Messerschmitt was still there: a Bf 109G with the big 30-mm. cannon designed to smash up the heavier structures of the bombers. One such shell striking a single-seater is enough to blow it apart. A touch of stick, keep turning. Faster, faster! Slowly the Messerschmitt grew in the ring sight. The German turned, and Farebrother eased the stick and held on to him, pressing himself forward against the harnesss with the insane feeling that he could actually increase his speed by leaning forward. The sun swung gently into his windshield and everything disappeared in the blinding furnace of its light. Eyes closed, keep turning, range and deflection are narrowing. He took a hand off the throttle long enough to unsnap his harness. The risk of smashing his face against the panel was outweighed by the freedom it gave him to look around the sky.

He craned his neck to see around him. He'd done the same thing only half a minute ago, but thirty seconds was time enough for a speck to become an attacker and blow him to blazes. Still the German ahead hadn't seen him. Drop the nose a little to bring the blue aircraft up into the lighted orange circle, a touch of rudder to ease the deflection. The German was careless, all his attention on his own gunsight. He was stalking; ahead of him, and just below, a crippled B-17 sliding back out of formation, its gunners not at their stations. More rudder. Mustn't make the same mistake—a quick look around for attackers. Good, the wing tips of the Messerschmitt stretched far enough to touch the circle. He squeezed the trigger and felt the kick of the guns. Long smoky trails of gunfire touched the wings and erupted in bright yellow strikes that made the German tip over into a roll and dive, the usual Luftwaffe evasive tactic. Farebrother, ready for it, stuck close on his tail. The Messerschmitt was still in his sights and still taking hits. The prop slowed and stopped. The canopy opened and a black bundle tumbled out, cannoning off the wing and slamming into his own stabilizer before bouncing away spread-eagled. His pale flying coveralls now mottled with red blood, the German pilot sailed past over Farebrother's head.

Farebrother turned his head again to see Luke Robinson. His neck was getting stiff and his back muscles were tired from all this twisting about. If only the kid would stay close enough to be seen in the rearview mirror. Parachutes! There were parachutes—white, American parachutes—above him. Above him! If there were chutes above him, he was below the bombers and that was lower than he wanted to be. Stick back and start climbing; altitude means salvation to a fighter pilot until the last desperate tactic of running for your life at zero feet. Climbing. Luke was still there. Now he saw the bomber boxes sailing through the sky above him. The bombers were trying to tighten formation now that so many had gone down or fallen behind. More parachutes. A Fort trailing smoke, two dropping out of formation, poor bastards. Another explosion seen only out of the corner of his eye, a gigantic flash of yellow light that filled the whole sky. It left no more than a shape of gray smoke, a spider shape, its ever-lengthening gray legs made of smoking debris falling to earth. The unmistakable sight of a fully laden bomber exploding!

"Break! Jamie, break!" MM's voice, where did he come from? Farebrother threw his plane into a violent skid and tumbled inverted into an uncontrolled fall that became a dive as the weight of the Rolls-Royce engine pulled his nose toward the earth. Luke Robinson was still there and the German attacker high and to the left. Good—his shooting is wide! Luke fired a burst but was not positioned for getting hits.

It was dark as they dropped into the billowing cumulus where the world was made of gray jelly and pressed close upon his Plexiglas. Then immediately out of the bottom of the cloud—stratus therefore, not cumulus; even the infallible Farebrother is permitted a mistake now and again. Here under the cloud Germany was sunless, a muted pattern of fields and forest. The only relief from this gray world was the long glittering white wires that came from behind and lit his path. Shit! The Kraut was still on his tail and firing. You bastard! Turn and dive. The bullets are still coming, more throttle. And where the hell was Luke Robinson, what's a wingman for anyway? Farebrother gripped harder on the stick, trying to stop it from vibrating. The wires, curving gently like telegraph lines swaying in the sunlight, came nearer to his port wing. "Break!" Someone's still shouting—Luke or MM. No, it's Rube Wein's voice. So come on over here and heave on the stick and you'll find out!

The throttle was against the fire wall; emergency power. Dive steeper, and steeper still. The white airspeed needle chased around the clock. Faster—350, 400, 450—the white needle caught up with the slower red danger line and Farebrother knew that his airframe was in jeopardy as he used all his strength to pull at the stick. Both hands couldn't hold it still. He braced his feet and pulled so hard that he expected the column to break in his hands. He could feel a dull pain in his belly, his legs were as heavy as lead. There was an insupportable pressure on his head, forcing him down in his seat until he thought his spine would snap. His vision clouded and darkened as the centrifugal effect drained the blood from his brain. He felt the airframe shaking; just a vibration at first and then a pounding, now it was jolting him about in his seat as the wings tried, and failed, to deflect the engine from its chosen trajectory toward the earth. He looked out and saw his wings flapping as if to break off.

No "wires" now, the German was no doubt wrestling with his own controls and waiting for the Mustang's wings to rip off. Farebrother was still trying to pull out of the dive as he lost consciousness.

"Sparkplug Blue Three from Sparkplug Blue Four. I repeat, where are you?" It was the nervous high-pitched voice of Luke Robinson, but eventually his fear overcame the discipline of his radio procedure. "Cap! For Christ's sake. Where the hell are you? It's Luke."

Farebrother was unconscious for only a few seconds, and when the blood pumped back up to his brain and restored his dimmed vision, he saw trees and rooftops flashing past. A small lake, a factory chimney, a farmyard with a dozen people staring up at him. He overtook a train, its smoke trailing across the fields like a long streamer of shiny black silk. He shook his head and only with a tremendous effort of will throttled back and resumed full control of himself and his machine. It seemed so much easier, so much more comfortable, so much more sensible to sit and watch the world rush past. He looked at the instruments and then gently tried the ailerons and rudder.

When he was straight and level, he searched the horizon: not a plane in sight. He checked his wings and looked again to his instruments; all back to normal, but his compass showed him heading east and his fuel was low. By now he must be somewhere near the Polish border. He looked down to find a landmark, but from this height the agricultural land of Silesia seemed flat and featureless. He turned until he was headed northwest, climbed gently up into the overcast, and called up on the radio. Only when he'd tried all the channels did he hear MM's voice, patiently calling him. He answered, "Jamie here, MM. Over."

"Thank Christ. I thought they'd got you, Jamie."

"I blacked out. I think my ears are blocked. I can't hear so well."

"Where the hell are you?"

"Southeast. I'm coming up to find you. Is Luke there?"

"He's here. We're circling till you come. Hurry up, we're all low on gas."

Farebrother broke out through the cloud cover and saw MM, Rube, and Luke Robinson, his wingman, describing lazy circles two or three miles to the west of him. The sunlight was brighter now, the sun was full and frosting the clouds with a blinding white topping. To the north he saw long trailing white threads—the condensation trails of the bombers—the threads bending now as the task force skirted Frankfurt an der Oder. They'd come a long journey to these bleak borderlands of the east, and many of them would never see home again.

Two more single-seaters were skimming the cloud tops by the time *Kibitzer* reached MM and the others. He watched the two strangers suspiciously. Only a week before, a couple of Bf 109s had joined a formation of look-alike Mustangs and clobbered the rear element before getting away scot-free. But these were Jugs, two fat T-bolts who preferred flying home in company. They slid into position behind Luke Robinson, who was flying *Sue-perlative*, one of the newest of the Mustangs; factory-fresh, it was still in natural metal finish. From now on it was to be air force policy to leave aircraft unpainted; it saved a few man-hours in the factory and increased speed. Even old *Kibitzer* had gained ten m.p.h. from her new engine and polished metal finish. For the bombers, locked into their huge formations, the shiny finish seemed a logical modification, but many of the fighter pilots disliked the mirror-flashing attention the new planes got as they turned in the sunlight. Farebrother raised a hand to Luke in salutation. The boy, thankful for a sign that he wasn't going to be blamed for losing Farebrother in the dive, waved back.

After MM set course toward the bombers, one of the Jugs pulled up closer to him, and its pilot ran a finger across his throat to show he was low on fuel. MM made a gesture of acknowledgment and tried again to find a common frequency on the radio, but couldn't reach them. The Jug fell back into battle formation, with about three hundred yards between fighters.

The bombers were stretched out across the river Oder, their target—the sprawling Focke-Wulf plant at Sorau—almost in sight. The air commander, in the lead plane of the task force, had throttled back to accommodate the cripples. Even so, the outermost planes in the formation, which had to keep jockeying the throttles to hold position, had a difficult task. It was little wonder that these outermost planes were subject to so high a proportion of mechanical failures, and little wonder that these were the ones to suffer most from the German fighters. . . .

As the six fighters reached the bomber formation, they could see half a dozen Messerschmitts making concerted attacks on the high squadron of the top box. The fighter pilots could sense the feeling of relief that ran through the minds of the men in this huge task force as they spotted the American fighters. The formations tightened and there were gunners waving from the open ports of the waist positions.

The Messerschmitt pilots saw the American fighters too, and abandoned the damaged Fortresses, with their windmilling props, idly swinging unmanned guns, their wings and bodies shiny with spilled fuel and leaking hydraulic fluid, their shattered plastic and torn alloy. They abandoned them, but they didn't go far; they circled like sharks some ten miles off to starboard. They didn't seek fighter-to-fighter combat. Their orders were strict: it was the American bombers that had to be destroyed!

MM turned sharply and, to their great credit, the nervous Jug pilots followed him trustingly. Together the mixed formation made for the Messerschmitts, but they didn't go to full throttle, their fuel was too low for that, and far too low for combat. The Messerschmitts climbed away unhurriedly, as if they guessed this was no more than an empty gesture.

Farebrother turned his head to see the bombers plodding on toward their target, searching the horizon for the escorting Fighter Groups which hadn't yet arrived. Who could see the bomber crews without admiring the phlegmatic determination which makes other kinds of courage seem no more than temporary lapses of judgment? They were the real heroes, the ones who came up here day after day as human targets for every weapon an ingenious, dedicated, and tenacious foe could use against them. So in life itself the true measure of courage is to fly on despite the tragedies of accident, sickness, or failure.

"One more time!" It was MM, turning away from the Messerschmitts for one last pass right down the miles of bomber formations. They tucked in tight behind MM, who was now cruising for minimum fuel consumption. Farebrother had his prop at 1,700 revs in fine pitch; now he gave the engine all the manifold pressure he dared. Poor *Kibitzer*, she took it like a lady and didn't complain.

They steered west after leaving the bombers, and no one looked back. Some three thousand feet above them they could see a lone Junkers Ju 88, the "contact holder" following the American bombers and talking all the time to German ground control. Soon the Messerschmitts would go back in to finish their meal.

Below him Farebrother recognized, from the map on his knee, the junction of the river Oder and the Hohenzollern Canal. Not far beyond that were the suburbs of Berlin with all the flak and fighter defenses concentrated around the capital. It was not a healthy place to linger. The bomber force had been routed in from the Baltic, but the six fighters would have to get home by a more direct route if they were to make it across the Channel with props still turning. To the south of Bremen they were met with an untidy cannonade of flak. At first it was eighty-eights well wide of their track, but then came some big 10.5-cm. bursts much nearer. They could hear the radar humming in their earphones, and MM climbed and changed course.

Near Holland's great inland sea, the IJsselmeer, the clouds were less billowing and soon stretched beneath them like flat gray concrete, all the way to where they touched the bottom of the big red disk that was the dying sun. Sandwiched between the strips of pink cirrus overhead and this unending colorless carpet, the six airplanes seemed suspended in space, halted at some great red traffic light hanging in the sky.

"Sparkplug Blue Three from Blue One. You want to take a look at my tail plane? The controls are getting real stiff."

Farebrother narrowed the space between them and went high enough to see properly. "Looks okay to me, MM."

"What do you think, Rube?"

Rube Wein brought *Daniel* in closer, but he too could see nothing wrong with MMs' tail. "But you're holed aft of the cockpit, buddy. Could be the control runs or something." Wein's academic prowess was exemplary, but his knowledge of aircraft anatomy was sketchy.

"Are we over the sea, Jamie?" As usual MM had abandoned radio procedure. "Sure I know about the holes, Rube. She's screaming like a banshee—the wind's playing on her like a flute." MM was careful to make his inquiry about the sea sound casual.

Farebrother looked at the map on his knee and then at his clock. "In about four minutes, MM. Over."

"She's giving me real trouble, Jamie. Get up, you bastard . . ."

This last remark to his plane, which was becoming more difficult to hold in the turbulent coastal air due to the airflow sucking at the curled edges of the gaping holes. "I'm not bailing out," said MM in response to the silence. "I've got two sure kills on my gun camera and I'm not leaving it."

"For Christ's sake, MM," said Farebrother. Even if it was a joke it didn't amuse him.

All four Mustangs had taken hits; it had been a tough one. And yet there was no pleasure in their victories and their survival. Their last sight of the unprotected bombers was one they couldn't forget, and they felt sullied by their own good fortune. Rube Wein's plane wobbled a little and belched black smoke as the supercharger cut out. He gave it a little throttle to bring him up level with the others.

"You okay, Rube?" said MM. "No glass mountain?"

"I'm okay," said Rube Wein, irritated that MM should reveal and scoff at his reluctantly confessed fears.

"So let's go home," said MM, and all the aircraft pulled in tighter together. The six pilots, alone in their single-seaters, couldn't help each other over the cold dark sea, but some atavistic feeling made them want to fly closer together and MM got comfort from that.

The formation had only just passed over the Dutch coast when Rube Wein came on the radio. "Blue Leader from Blue Two—I can't make it to England." His voice was as calm and matter-of-fact as it always was.

"What in hell do you mean, Rube?" demanded MM indignantly. *He* was the casualty, everyone knew that, so why was Rube trying to steal his thunder?

"I'm out of gas. It's this goddamned blower."

"Shit, Rube, we're practically there now."

"It's no use, MM. I've been nursing her, but the needles are out of sight."

"Have you switched left and right a couple of times?"

"For Christ's sake, MM, I'm not fresh out of Primary Flight Training. It's the blower, like I told you. I'll bail out over Holland. The Resistance guys will maybe smuggle me out or something."

"Now listen, Rube . . ." But MM's advice went unheeded as Rube's wing tip tilted steeply and he began a wing-over that dropped him out of formation belly-up like a dead fish.

Farebrother twisted his head to see how far back Rube would

have to fly for a landfall. There were condensation trails high over the coast—Germans fighters responding to the radar tracks made by the six Americans. As the German planes reached the higher atmosphere, the air condensed to leave a white plume. One after another they became visible against the deepening color of the eastern sky. Rube Wein would be easy meat for them.

"Tell the Colonel I'm sorry." It was Rube Wein's voice again, fainter now and scratchy with static. "I can't swim, see? Explain that, will you, MM?"

"We can't come back, Rube. We're all low on gas."

There was some sort of reply, but it was swallowed up in the rhythms of the German jamming. They listened all the way back over the sea, but they never heard him again.

"Just you and me left now, Jamie," said MM as they crossed the English coast.

"And Luke," said Farebrother hastily. He realized how the new boy must be feeling.

"Oh, sure," said MM. "Sorry, kid. . . . Rube should have high-tailed it home long before his gas got so low," said MM, ignoring all radio procedure.

"He'll be okay, Blue Leader," said Farebrother. "I'd say he bailed out long before those fighters got anywhere near him."

There was a double click on the radio as MM jiggled the switch to acknowledge the message. Soon the Thunderbolts waggled wings and dropped out of formation to find their own base.

It was clear at Steeple Thaxted, or relatively so; some puffy stratocumulus, pink-lined to dramatize the lowering sun. The grass was shiny with recent rain, and the reddening sky was reflected on the wet runway. MM took *Mickey Mouse II* into the landing pattern, moving jerkily into finals as he manipulated the stiff controls. He went in a little high, but MM knew the field well enough to effortlessly slip off fifty feet or more so that he was just right as he went over the hedge. Children playing in the paddock near Hobday's Farm stopped their game to watch him, and were surprised at the sudden increase of power that made the engine roar to bursting point, and the little lurch the plane gave as it teetered on the edge of stalling and, wheezing and bawling like an angry old woman, staggered inch by inch back into the air again.

"My gear's jammed," said MM on the radio even before the red flares were fired from the flying control truck. "You guys better go in first. I'll have to belly in, I guess." Retaining control to the end, he added, "Luke first, Jamie next."

Tex Gill jumped up onto *Kibitzer*'s wing as she came to a stop on the hardstand. "We were getting a little worried, sir," he said, looking at his watch and at the bullet holes.

"I got one," said Farebrother. Unlike most other crew chiefs, Tex never asked. "I saw him bail out. But we lost Lieutenant Wein." Farebrother heaved himself out of his seat and stayed there to watch *Mickey Mouse II* come around the circuit. Tex was watching too, but neither of them admitted his concern. "He ran out of gas and turned back to bail out over Holland." Farebrother pulled up the sides of his helmet and prodded a finger in his ears, but he was still a little deafened.

"Everyone liked the Lieutenant," said Tex Gill, still watching MM.

"Ran out of gas," said Farebrother. "His supercharger was on the blink. He came right out over the water before turning back."

Tex Gill looked at his pilot and nodded. Farebrother's face was deeply lined, his eyes bloodshot and darkly underset. Where his oxygen mask had been pressing against his face there were red "scars" curving from nose to jaw. "The stupid bastard should have turned back at the first sign of trouble." To anyone but Tex Gill, Farebrother's voice might have seemed angry, but a pilot had no secrets from his crew chief. He could see in Farebrother's face the desperate bitterness we save for loved ones who die.

"I guess he didn't want to leave Lieutenant Morse without a wingman," said Tex Gill. "Seeing how you had to look after the new young officer." He jumped down from the wing, and Farebrother followed, steadying himself on Gill's shoulder.

"I shot down a Messerschmitt, Tex. The pilot bailed out." Farebrother winced with pain and sat down on the trailing edge of the wing.

"You hurt, Cap?"

"Just cramp." He felt like a fool, but he had to wait until the circulation came back to his leg. "I saw this German pilot, Tex. He sailed past me close enough to touch." Tex Gill said nothing. Farebrother said, "I guess he was dead. He hit his stabilizer, and there was a lot of blood."

"You got some leave coming up, Captain? You sure deserve some."

"A lot of hardware under him. I guess they're tough to handle with cannons and all that junk strapped under the wings."

"There comes Lieutenant Morse," said Gill, easing the parachute harness off Farebrother's shoulder. "He's going to do that real nice, I'd say."

"I can't leave MM now, Tex. And we've got Lieutenant Robinson to think of too."

"You need a rest, Cap," said Tex Gill, deciding there was no point in being too subtle with a man so clearly in a state of shock. "Sometimes . . ." He shifted awkwardly, wondering how to continue. "Sometimes a guy out here on the line sees things the Flight Surgeon misses. You and Lieutenant Morse, you both need a rest."

"You're a good buddy, Tex," said Farebrother, handing him the chute. "And there he goes!"

The main runway was still under repair, so MM had to use the shorter one. He came in wheels up and settled *Mickey Mouse II* gently onto the concrete with plenty of room to spare. He kept its nose up so that the air intake hit first. The plane tilted a bit and made a lot of noise as it slid along, tearing alloy off its underside. Men standing on a nearby revetment saw the Mustang disappear into a cloud of white smoke, but the "smoke" was a spray of rainwater thrown into the air as the plane waltzed down the concrete, and their gasps turned into sighs of relief as the plane came to a standstill and the ambulance and crash wagons went chasing after it.

Farebrother walked to the jeep that was waiting to take them to debriefing. Luke Robinson was already sitting in it. "You want to get in the back seat, Luke?" said Farebrother. The driver looked around but said nothing.

"I'm okay."

"Get in the back seat," said Farebrother, climbing into the back himself and dumping his parachute on the floor.

"I'd rather . . ."

"Get into the back seat, you stupid son of a bitch," said Farebrother in a voice that made Robinson shoot out of his seat as if it was red hot.

"Gee, Captain, I'm sorry," he said as he climbed into the back of the jeep.

Farebrother took off his helmet and wiped his face with his hand. To the driver he said, "Drive down the runway and pick up Lieutenant Morse."

"You'd need permission from flying control to drive out there across the airfield. Anyway, this jeep's not marked for it."

"Get going," said Farebrother. His voice was soft but even more intimidating than his previous burst of bad temper. "And that's an order, goddammit. We didn't ride all the way across Europe so you could leave him to walk back from his ship."

The driver turned in his seat to argue, but when he saw Farebrother's face he did exactly as he was told.

27

Colonel
Daniel A. Badger

The Group Commander looked around at his office—the cracked lino, the cluttered desk, and shabby furniture. His father had warned him that a serviceman's life is one of poverty and humiliation. "Faith without miracles" was his father's description of a military career. "Redemption without atonement, penitence without spiritual reconciliation." His father had never dwelt upon the heartfelt pacifist convictions that had subjected the family to so much local criticism during the first war and long after. Had his father ever suspected that the snubs of certain neighbors played a part in Danny's long-deferred decision to get into uniform? When he was finally "ordained" a second lieutenant with the Air Corps, his father was not in the congregation.

Colonel Dan took out his handkerchief and blew his nose loudly in a defiant trumpet. Well, even his father hadn't warned him about the chances of having a couple of dressed-up civilians telling him exactly how to do the job he'd been doing since long before they'd learned how to salute. The trouble was, if it all went wrong, these two bastards would be back here telling him that he'd fucked up. He picked up a chair by its back and swung it high into the air before letting it crash back into place.

These guys come on real strong, thought Colonel Dan a few

moments later, watching his two visitors arranging their chairs and lowering the blinds and making sure that poor little Lieutenant Morse wouldn't manage to see the faces of the senior officers in case they revealed their feelings. Not much chance of these two blank-faced paddlefoots revealing their feelings—they didn't seem to have any, except for an irrational hatred and contempt for one of his best pilots, who'd committed no crime more heinous than jumping into the sack with a married woman. Well, "he that is without sin among you, let him first cast a stone . . ." Dan Badger decided to put his foot down about one thing. He'd insist upon seeing Lieutenant Morse without these two in the room. They could wait in the clerk's office and put their ears to the lock if they wanted to be sure he was obeying their crackpot orders.

At first Colonel Dan had thought the flashy little lieutenant colonel was from the Judge Advocate General's Corps; he had some of the imperious arm-waving mannerisms Colonel Dan associated with trial lawyers, but most of his knowledge of such men had come from Hollywood films. Now it transpired that the little creep was no more than a flack in uniform, a PRO.

General Bohnen seemed to sense Colonel Dan's dislike of Lester Shelley and did his best to keep the preparations for this so-called interview between the Group Commander and Lieutenant Morse as brief as possible.

"Let Dan decide about the position of the telephones. We don't want it to look like a courtroom."

"Just trying to help," said Lester Shelley. He replaced the telephones—black for internal numbers, green for scrambled line, and red for operations—on the desk and spent a few minutes trying to disentangle the wires.

"Let it go, Lester," said Colonel Dan. The little PR colonel insisted upon being addressed by his first name. "Those wires are always snarled up." He waved away his jacket that Lester Shelley had politely removed from the back of a chair and was offering to him like some kind of hotel flunky. Colonel Dan always worked at his desk in his nonregulation short-sleeved khaki shirt; everyone around here knew that.

Lieutenant Morse strolled into the room so casually that it was clear he had no suspicion that Colonel Dan was about to ground him. And he listened carefully to some rigmarole about a recommendation for a Distinguished Flying Cross. That didn't excite him very much—they were giving out lots of DFCs lately; he was after greater glory. His mind was dwelling upon the thought of Colonel Dan, some time soon, calling him in to announce that he'd been given the Congressional Medal of Honor. . . . It was then that he realized he was being grounded.

"Shit! What for?" said Morse. "You mean because I cracked up my ship? Listen, Colonel, she was shot full of holes, and the salvage crew will confirm it. You get on the phone now to the Mobile Reclamation and Repair Squadron. One of their tech sergeants said he didn't know how I'd got her back."

Colonel Dan decided not to deny that the crash landing was connected with his decision; he was relieved, in fact, that Lieutenant Morse had found some kind of basis for it. "The Exec has some jobs for you, Lieutenant, so for the time being I want you to remain on base. You'll find that officers working here at HQ don't have as much free time as flying personnel."

Morse didn't like that little speech, it sounded too much like a permanent assignment. A couple of days off the flying roster was one thing, but a permanent office job was his idea of hell. "How long's this grounding likely to last, Colonel?"

"I've been looking through your file, and your flying hours are adding up, Lieutenant. You're getting awful close to going home."

"I'm getting awful close to being the top ace in the ETO, Colonel, and you know it."

"I don't intend to argue with you, Lieutenant Morse. You are grounded and that's it. The Flight Surgeon and I both think you need a little rest. Doc says you were hysterical when they hauled you out of that wrecked ship."

"Don't give me that crap about needing a rest! I get a full night's sleep every twenty-four hours and I'm not standing here reporting for sick call. I'm not asking for phenobarb and a double shot of mission whiskey—I'm in A-one shape and as fit as anyone in the Group. And I wasn't 'hauled out' of my ship—I brought her in real careful and I climbed out in my own good time."

"Take it easy, son," said Colonel Dan. "You convince me you weren't hysterical when you were swearing at the doc and deliberately disobeying his order to get into that ambulance for a checkup. You could find yourself facing charges."

"Did Doc Goldman report me then?"

"Come on, Morse, you know Doc Goldman better than that. I

saw it myself. I saw you standing on your ship, and I could hear you shouting 'Horseshit!' right here at the apron where I was watching you come in."

"Oh, sure, I get it," said Morse sarcastically. "Heads you win, tails I lose. Either way I get grounded. Who talked you into handing me this raw deal—was it Major Tucker?"

"It's nothing to do with Tucker," said the Colonel.

Lieutenant Morse had grown excited, and Colonel Badger got to his feet as a natural reaction to this hostility, then realized immediately that he should have remained seated; that's what Duke Scroll would have done. Instead, Colonel Dan leaned forward and shook a finger in Morse's face. "You get this, and get it good, kid: I call the shots around here, and if I say you're benched, you're benched." He sat down again and rubbed his bare arms nervously. "Now get out of here and tell Major Tucker I don't want to see your name on the board until further notice. Tomorrow morning at eight-thirty you'll report to Colonel Scroll in class A uniform and be told your new duties. Meanwhile you are relieved from assignment and duty, effective as of now. Got that?"

Morse's face contorted. The muscles of his jaw bunched and a vein on his forehead grew visible so suddenly that, to Colonel Dan, it seemed as if the boy had aged right before his eyes. With the same rigidity Lieutenant Morse swung his arm up in an exaggerated salute and stamped his feet as he turned about-face. "Dismiss!" called Colonel Dan, but already Morse was striding toward the door. He slammed it after him with enough force to shake the building.

General Bohnen, Lieutenant Colonel Shelley, and Lieutenant Colonel Scroll came into the office as soon as Morse had departed. "I think the noise of that door slamming is going to have everyone in earshot wondering what that was all about," said General Bohnen, but he smiled to show he wasn't really worried.

Duke Scroll said, "Colonel Badger always shuts his door like that, General Bohnen. *I* don't think it will attract any comment." He also smiled.

It was an attempt to cheer up Colonel Dan, but it didn't succeed. Sadly he said, "I intend to write up that young officer's efficiency report in such a way as to undo a little of the damage I've just done him."

Duke Scroll was the only person on the base who realized how closely Colonel Dan identified with Lieutenant Morse. The two personalities had little in common really, but Colonel Dan remembered that in his youth he had been a failure at everything except flying, and he knew that this was also true of Lieutenant Morse. But there was envy there too; envy of a top-scoring fighter pilot of the kind who'd taught Colonel Dan hów to fly after the first war.

"I'd advise caution, Dan," said General Bohnen in that fruity avuncular voice that had commanded the full attention of so many anxious businessmen. "Give him 'superior' as an efficiency rating, but let Duke here take care of the report." He touched Colonel Dan's arm in a congratulatory gesture. "Well, I think we must get out of your way now, Colonel. The weather's good—every chance your Group will fly tomorrow. I'm sure you have a lot to do."

Duke Scroll held the office door open for the two visitors and insisted upon taking them over to the Officers' Club for a "cup of coffee and a sandwich." The footsteps of the three men echoed down the corridor, and Colonel Dan swung his chair around so that he could watch the softball game on the grass behind number one hangar and the Stars and Stripes flying from the mast at the parade ground. These simple evidences of American life reassured him—he felt in control of his life and his job again. He was about to pick up the phone and ask his clerk for coffee when footsteps came hurriedly along the corridor and the door opened without Duke's usual polite knock. It was Colonel Lester Shelley, the PRO. He entered the room holding a cigar aloft in a gesture that was both salute and apology. "I came back for my glasses," he said.

"Well, I . . ."

"As a matter of fact, I wanted a word with you, Colonel." Lester Shelley artfully pulled a leather eyeglass case just far enough out of his pocket to show that he really had them. "You and I may have to work together on this tricky problem." He smiled and blew smoke. "Half the trouble in this world could be averted if women smoked cigars. My father said that, and I believe it. You can sit down and talk with anyone who appreciates a good cigar. Cigar smoking is contemplative, see."

"Right, Lester," said Colonel Dan, who had no idea what kind of response his visitor expected.

"That's why I know I can talk man to man with you, Colonel." Lester Shelley looked quickly over his shoulder to be sure no one else was in the room. "I'm going to do you a favor now, Dan, because I figure I might need one in return someday."

"Anything I can do . . ." muttered Colonel Dan.

Shelley looked around again, then pointed a finger at him. "For your private ear, Dan. For your *very* private ear." He held up his hand to emphasize the confidential nature of this disclosure. "General Bohnen has his son right here on this base."

"His son!"

"His only son, and he's very very attached to that lad."

"I've got no one on the roster named Bohnen . . . a commissioned officer or an EM?"

"I keep my ears open, Dan, otherwise I would never have discovered it myself." He tapped his nose. "A word to the wise, right?"

"On this base? Named Bohnen?"

"Farebrother, a captain, I think. A bright young man from what I hear. Do yourself a favor, Dan. Cultivate the kid. No telling what could come from being in the General's good books, right? Sure, a captain—name of Jamie Farebrother."

"Well, thanks, Lester."

Colonel Lester Shelley pulled his briefcase up tight under his arm as if he was about to crash through the opposition for a touchdown. He waved his right hand in what was almost a military salute, and hurriedly left the room.

So that was it. Farebrother! Now Colonel Dan knew why his Group was so frequently honored with visits from the General, and he understood all those polite phone calls asking about Farebrother. Colonel Dan turned to the window to look at the airfield—*his* airfield. He watched the softball game for a moment or two. It wasn't the team playing, just guys from the workshops taking a break. They were white-faced, listless, and obviously in poor physical condition. The men servicing and repairing the planes had been working day and night through the last few weeks. They needed rest and some properly organized physical exercise, but there was no letup in the operational requirements, and there was every sign that things were going to get even hotter. More engine changes, more bullet holes to repair, more guns to clean, and more of those lousy letters to inform next of kin that a brother, son, or husband was MIA. That was the formula: missing in action. That gave some tormented mind an opportunity to come to terms with the loss before receiving the final, fatal certainty of death.

So Farebrother was General Bohnen's son! Come to think of it, there was a certain physical resemblance. Did Bohnen have double standards—would he have grounded his own son if "the reputation of the service" was at stake? Yes, decided Colonel Dan, the General would have done it just the same. Bohnen had the same damned inflexible self-righteousness that Dan Badger's own father displayed. But it wasn't the way Colonel Dan liked to do things. He thought back over his interview with Lieutenant Morse and felt cheapened by it. Who the hell were those two that they could come in here and make him do such things to his own men? And to a flyer!

Colonel Badger noticed that the door to his clerk's inner office was partly open. He could see Sergeant Kinzelberg in there, filing papers at an open drawer, and wondered if he'd heard the conversation with Shelley. For a moment he was going to ask, but then decided he wouldn't get a straight answer; Kinzelberg—and his boss Duke Scroll—were birds of a feather: "hear nothing, see nothing, and say nothing." He kept meaning to buy a "three wise monkeys" statuette and put it on Scroll's desk as a surprise present. A solid-gold one wouldn't be too much to repay Duke for all the times he'd covered up his errors and smoothed over his arguments and generally kept the Group running while Dan Badger was having a good time, flying his fighter plane and making believe he was fifteen years younger than he so obviously was.

Badger closed the door quietly and then scratched himself and stretched his tired arms. Hanging around here all day at General Bohnen's disposition was more tiring than flying a mission, even a mission like today's. Colonel Dan sighed. For the first time he was ready to acknowledge that maybe he was too old to be commanding a combat Group, if part of the job meant nurse-maiding those tinhorns. He looked out the window and tried to decide if the weather would hold; still uncertain, he phoned to ask Kevin Phelan, but Major Phelan was nowhere in the Operations Building and his staff had no idea where he was or when he'd be back. Colonel Dan banged the phone down. He wanted an excuse to talk to Kevin Phelan. Maybe they would have gone over yet again the football game when the Bears beat the Redskins 73–0 in the championship playoff. Daniel Badger enjoyed telling Kevin Phelan about it. If the Major was bored by this recital, he'd been in the Army long enough to know that it was a commanding officer's privilege to bend the ears of his subordinates and, apart from interjecting the necessary expletives into the commentary, he never interrupted.

Unable to find Phelan, Colonel Dan did something that for him was almost unprecedented. He took one of the keys that he kept at the end of a thin gold chain in his trousers pocket and unlocked his liquor cabinet. Then he poured himself a triple measure of bourbon and locked up the cupboard again. Only after the General's C-47 climbed into the sky did he drink his whiskey. He didn't sip it or run it across his tongue to get the flavor; he felt a strong need for alcohol in his bloodstream and tipped the glass up and emptied it in three long gulps.

He was sitting behind his desk, a warm glow in his belly and euphoria in his heart, when a tap came at the door. Only officers of field rank were permitted to bypass his clerk's office. "Come in," shouted Colonel Dan. The door opened and Major Tucker entered.

For a moment Colonel Dan thought that perhaps his whiskey was responsible for what he was seeing. For this was a new Major Tucker, bristling and bellicose. He saluted with that punctilious style that marked all the West Pointers, but his manner was as near as Tucker had ever come to being insubordinate. "I encountered Lieutenant Morse on the flight line, Colonel. He told me you'd grounded him."

Major Tucker waited for confirmation of this. "You got it right, Major," said the Colonel, speaking a little more slowly than usual in case he should slur his words. He was well aware that drinking so early in the day did not agree with him.

"Then I'm going to ask you to explain that, sir."

"All in good time, Major."

"I'm afraid that I cannot accept that answer, Colonel."

"You'll accept any damn answer I give you," said Colonel Dan, speaking far too quickly.

"Perhaps I should remind you that Lieutenant Morse is the finest pilot, and the most successful one, in this Group."

"And perhaps I should remind you, Major Tucker, that I am its commanding officer."

"You have no occasion to speak to me in that tone of voice, Colonel Badger. You certainly are the Group Commander, but you seem to have overlooked the fact that I am a Squadron Commander, and as such I'm Lieutenant Morse's commanding officer. It may well be that you've had some 'lawyer' discover that you're within your rights, but I would like to tell you, Colonel, that I consider such lack of courtesy demeaning to me and inexcusable. Lieutenant Morse is a more successful fighter pilot than you are, and a better flyer than I can ever hope to be. Whatever his infraction of the Military Code, we are at war and we need the best pilots flying missions. Assigning this highly trained officer to administration duties is disgraceful. I'm prepared to take personal responsibility for his future behavior and I'll prepare a report about his crash landing that completely exonerates him."

Colonel Dan leaned back so that his swivel chair tilted on its springs. He smiled and shook his head in disbelief. "But you hate Lieutenant Morse. You were in this office only last week complaining about his insubordination."

"Insubordination is not something to be punished by keeping the Lieutenant on the ground. Sure, I hate the little bastard, but he's helping win the war and there's no one I'd sooner have flying my wing when some Kraut fighters are on the horizon."

Colonel Dan rubbed his face in a futile attempt to be rid of the effects of the alcohol. "Is this all part of the West Point philosophy, Tucker? All this 'there's a bitch in the chorus but the show must go on' stuff? They teach you that at the Point?"

Tucker looked at Colonel Dan and decided it wasn't sarcasm. He thought a moment and then nodded his head in affirmation. "I suppose you could say it is, sir. The Academy instills in a cadet the belief that a skilled commander uses his men and his weaponry to best advantage." Major Tucker sufficiently forgot himself to touch his hairline mustache as he tried to remember what else he'd learned at West Point. "I'm convinced that Lieutenant Morse is a good soldier and should be on the fighting line."

Colonel Badger looked at his Squadron Commander respectfully. He felt shamed by Tucker's reproaches and suddenly wished he'd taken a tougher line with Bohnen. "Tell me, Tucker, is that why you want a staff job? You think maybe you'd be better running an office at Wing than you are at leading a squadron in the air?"

Major Tucker pursed his mouth for a moment. When he answered there was an unmistakable nervousness in his reply. Major Tucker knew that he was not as quick-witted as the Colonel, and now he was frightened that he might say something that could damage him. But finally he decided that for someone like himself it was easier to speak the simple truth. "Yes, sir. I don't have the right temperament. Lieutenant Morse should really be leading the squadron."

Colonel Dan nodded and moved some papers on his desk.

"Okay, Major Tucker. Get lost! I'll think about what you said. Your objection has been noted . . . noted officially. You want to object in writing?"

"I don't think that would be the proper thing for a loyal subordinate to do, Colonel."

"Dismiss, Major Tucker."

He watched the way in which Major Tucker performed the about-face. He even had a special West Point way of opening the office door. "And, Tucker . . ." Colonel Dan called as he stood there in the doorway.

Major Tucker turned and waited.

"You're all right, Major." He said it weightily. "Maybe West Point's got something after all."

"Thank you, sir."

28

Major
Spurrier Tucker, Jr.

Major Tucker hated his first name, Spurrier. It was all part of that family tyranny that had forced him to go to West Point at a time when he had a secret ambition to be an actor. His father and his grandfather, as well as old man Spurrier, on his mother's side, had all done well at the Point, or had subsequently risen to high rank. Now his father never stopped trying to get Major Tucker a staff job, and this involved letters written to old friends and congressmen and any other influential person the old man could find a way to. That morning's mail delivery had brought a letter from his father. It was an unusual letter, his father telling him that if he decided to leave the Army after the war and take up any other sort of work—his father had underlined "any other" with the green ink that he always used for emphasis—no one would stand in his way. Had his father read between the lines of Spurrier's letters home and realized that his son was desperately unhappy? Had his mother known all along that her son felt burdened by the family's military plans for him? And was the ultimate tyranny despising yourself if you fell short of expectations?

There was enough moonlight for Major Tucker to pick his way past the parked trucks and civilian buses that filled one side of the parade ground. Guests were still arriving for the "payday dances" at the Officers' Club, the Aero Club, and the Rocker Club, where the senior noncoms usually had the best food, the best music, and the prettiest girls. There were soft greetings and low wolf whistles as girls were helped down from the trucks that brought nurses from local hospitals, "land girls" from nearby farms, and females of all shapes and sizes from the regular liberty run to Drummer Street, Cambridge.

Tucker followed the whitewashed stones that lined the path to the Club. In his hand he had his whiskey ration, a bottle of Johnnie Walker. He'd already had a stiff drink before setting out for the dance. It wasn't a celebration; he was trying to forget the way he'd argued with his Group Commmander. It was a damned stupid way to wreck a career.

Tucker had no partner for the evening. He'd never picked up all the fast talk and superficial joviality that seemed necessary to attract women. He recognized himself as a staid and neurotic personality who found it very difficult to relax. And this evening he was wound up very tight. Tense and jumpy, he was no longer sleeping properly—he should have asked the Flight Surgeon for some sleeping pills, but such requests always got back to Colonel Dan. Tucker was determined not to be grounded. If he just held on, he knew the staff job would come through. Meanwhile he was wound up like a mainspring. Maybe he should get drunk—half the officers in the Club were flying one wing low already.

Lieutenant Mickey Morse was at the bar wearing his pearl-gray Stetson. He was waiting for the bartender and holding a tin tray of glasses with some mixers and a bowl of ice. "What are you drinking, Tucker, old sport? The barkeep seems to have been written out of the script." Rumors said Tucker had protested about MM's being grounded and MM appreciated that.

"The hell with him, MM," said Tucker. "I've got a bottle of scotch here to start us off." He put his bottle on the tray.

"Attaboy!" It was rare for Tucker to call him MM, and unprecedented to be offered a share in his liquor ration. "Come and sit down here." Morse took an extra glass from the bar and pointed to

the table under the old propeller and movie posters where he regularly sat. The new pilot—Luke Robinson—and other officers of Tucker's squadron were already there. "Major Tucker's treat," Morse
announced, banging the bottle of scotch on the table and tipping ice
into the tumblers.

"Thanks, Major," said Luke Robinson, the only man present to
regard Tucker's action as normal. The other pilots were warmer in
their gratitude. "This is real nice of you," said MM. Vera, who was
sitting next to him, took her drink only after giving Tucker a kiss on
the cheek.

"Where have you been hiding this man?" Vera asked MM.
"He's gorgeous!" Tucker blushed.

They had a good view of the stage. The twelve-piece band was
the best the Army had this side of London. They were from the
Strategic Air Depot, where badly damaged planes were repaired. The
depot had countless personnel to choose from, so some of the musicians had been professionals and they played without letup. The
vocal group was British, from London, and they were good too, but
their American audiences never got used to hearing the lyrics sung in
that English accent: "Those icy fingers up and down my spine. The
same old witch-*crahft* when your eyes meet mine."

"Is your buddy Jamie here?"

"He sure is, Major. He's dancing past the table where Colonel
Dan's sitting." Vera took MM's Stetson and placed it carefully on
Tucker's head. Tucker smiled.

"With the tall beautiful girl? Is that the Victoria I keep hearing
about?"

"She works with Vera," said Morse, caressing Vera's arm as if to
be sure she was really there with him.

Major Tucker noticed the affectionate gesture and was touched
by it. He smiled at the men around the table and the girls with them.
They weren't a bad bunch of kids, he decided. Suddenly he was
seeing them in a new light—maybe he should come to the Saturday
dances more often.

Vera had an arm around MM, but her eyes were on Victoria and
Jamie. Tonight Victoria was planning to break the news that she was
pregnant. Vera had said a prayer for her, and now she was watching
Jamie to see if it was going to be answered.

Vera was in top form that evening, not only interjecting her
acid comments about American manners and mores, but contradict-

ing MM's account of the Christmas party in Cambridge and providing her own version of that evening. Without cruelty—although Vera had a cruel sense of humor—she impersonated Colonel Dan's dice throws, poor Earl waving his Confederate flag as he fell off the piano, and Vince Madigan hiding behind MM when the girl went after him with the bread knife. Her mimicry was spare and effortless, and even if her American accent was less than perfect, she exactly captured Colonel Dan's happy, drunken eyes as he won six hundred dollars on a roll of the dice, and the collapse of Vince's self-confident smile, and Jamie's constant look of bewildered embarrassment as he found himself the host to a gathering that got more lunatic with every moment until he had to face an angry policeman who had been deluged with fruit punch from an upstairs window.

Major Tucker swirled the ice in his glass as he realized what Vera's narrative was leading up to. He wet his lips as they all followed Vera's gaze and turned to look at him accusingly. "It was Jamie," he explained. "He said I was to get rid of the fruit punch immediately. He said it was making people sick."

Vera roared with laughter. "That copper had cucumber slices sticking to his helmet." They all laughed and Tucker realized that the nervous way in which he'd delivered the line was all part of the story. He laughed too. MM slapped him on the back appreciatively. They were all beginning to think that Major Tucker might turn out to be one hell of a good raconteur.

Another large scotch appeared in front of Major Tucker. He began to protest that he already had a drink, but noticed that it was almost finished. "The next bottle's on me," he said, and waved a hand at the bartender, who nodded his understanding and in spite of the crush around the bar reached for another bottle of scotch.

"It's good to see you letting your hair down, Major," said Jamie Farebrother as he danced slowly past with Victoria in his arms.

Major Tucker got to his feet. There wasn't much room to move in their cramped corner, but he extricated himself from between table and chair and unsteadily presented himself. "May I dance with your young lady, Captain Farebrother?"

Jamie smiled. He'd never seen his Squadron Commander tipsy before. "I'm sure Victoria would be delighted," he said, glancing at her. "I guess I'm never going to get the hang of dancing.'" Farebrother introduced them in the same solemn manner that Major Tucker had employed.

"Where did you learn to dance, Major?"

"I don't often find a good partner, Victoria. And please let's make that Spurrier." It was not merely politeness; Tucker was good at ballroom dancing, and Victoria's compliment made him all the better. "Where did I learn? It all started when I used to cut history class to take tap lessons. That was in high school, back home in Augusta, Maine. In those days I wanted to be an actor."

Victoria looked at Major Tucker and tried to decide whether this was a line he took with girls, a joke, or a simple answer to her question. "But you went to West Point, Major. You went to the Military Academy. You mean that you really wanted to be on the stage?"

"Oh, you saw the Academy ring. Sure, I'm a career soldier. My folks made me realize what a lousy life I'd have in show business."

Victoria felt sorry for him. "It's never too late, Spurrier."

"You could be right, Victoria," he said, and smiled. He was rather handsome, with his flashing eyes and thin mustache. When he smiled it was easy to visualize him as a matinee idol. He held her closer and danced just a little more boldly, not caring if other couples turned to watch. "After what I said to Colonel Dan yesterday I might well be looking for another job after the war."

"I can't believe you were rude to him," said Victoria truthfully. "I can't imagine you being rude to anyone."

"That's the funny thing about it," said Tucker. "I can't believe it either, but I was."

Major Tucker danced with all the girls seated at MM's table. And then he danced with all the other attractive girls he could find in the Club, careful always to ask their partner's permission in the polite, formal manner he'd used with Jamie and Victoria. To Tucker's surprise, to his *amazement*, he encountered no hostility whatsoever. On the contrary, everyone he spoke with seemed to be smiling at him and he was plied with drink even by officers he scarcely knew.

It was still only ten-thirty when the band began the "South American medley" that was a renowned feature of the Air Depot musicians. Major Tucker wasn't daunted by the rhythms of South America—he delighted in them. When his partner let go of his hand with a laugh of dismay, he stepped back and danced alone with ever more sinuous grace. Now the band was picking up on him, and the other dancers formed a circle to watch. Most of the British visitors accepted his performance in the same way they accepted all the other extraordinary things that the Americans did, said, and owned. But his fellow officers were seeing a Major Tucker entirely beyond anything they'd ever seen before. Even Doc Goldman, the Flight Surgeon, who knew very well what acute stress, coupled with physical danger and exhaustion, could do to his charges, watched Major Tucker's wild and wonderful dancing with open-mouthed astonishment.

Mambos, boleros, cachuchas, fandangos, and flings were nothing to Major Spurrier Tucker, Jr., that night. He danced whatever the orchestra offered with style and grace. Hands in his pockets, a lazy smile on his face, and MM's Stetson tipped forward over half-closed eyes, his seemingly effortless soft-shoe "Sleepytime Gal" brought everyone to their feet and an audience response that Fred Astaire might have envied. Spurrier Tucker was born anew that night, and when the band played its final chords, there was a pandemonium of applause. They cheered, whistled, and screamed their frantic appreciation. The noise brought the MPs out of the guard post and stopped the bridge tournament in the faraway village of Long Thaxted. And the clapping and shouting didn't fade away quickly—they were still calling for more when a couple of out-of-breath sergeants arrived from the Rocker Club, anxious to discover what could have happened to their officers. Major Tucker, flushed and smiling, was pointed out to one and all; overnight he'd become the most popular officer on the base. It was an experience beyond Tucker's wildest imaginings and he reveled in it.

Armed with the spurious self-confidence that celebrity bestows, Major Tucker walked across to Colonel Dan's table and said, "Mind if I join you, Colonel?"

"Grab a chair, Major Tucker," said Colonel Dan. "Where'd you learn to shake a foot that way?"

"West Point," said Tucker.

The Colonel smiled and pushed a bottle of whiskey over to Tucker, who took it and poured himself a drink. "You're going to wind up with a thick head in the morning, Major," he warned.

"It will be a new experience for me, knowing it was caused by alcohol," said Tucker.

"You riding me, Major?" said the Colonel with mock severity. He was disconcerted by this confident brashness that Tucker was suddenly displaying, but he was attracted by it too.

"Maybe I am, Colonel. And maybe I'm going to keep riding you until I get Lieutenant Morse back into the air."

Colonel Dan looked around to see who was in earshot. There were two young women at his table—chorus girls from one of the London shows; Kevin Phelan had brought them both. Now they were fully occupied with Kevin's account of meeting Clark Gable in the men's room of the Waldorf-Astoria. Colonel Dan looked around for reporters too, but they were all at the bar, drinking heavily and exchanging stories about being bombed in the air raids over London. Satisfied that no one could hear him, Colonel Dan drew his chair a little closer to Major Tucker. The band was playing a noisy arrangement of "Praise the Lord and Pass the Ammunition." Soon, thought Colonel Dan, the bandleader would have to decide whether the mood was going to require the soft and dreamy arrangements of "My Devotion" and "Dearly Beloved" with muted brass, shimmering strings, and house lights dimmed, or whether it would develop into one of those rumpus evenings, with the girls ignored, percussion and trumpet to the fore, while the men roared their way through "On, Brave Old Army Team," etc., etc., etc. If it was heading for that kind of drunken party, he'd go back to the office and catch up on some paperwork.

The Colonel stared at Tucker and then zipped his brown leather jacket up tight against his neck in some subconscious plea for secrecy. He said, "You find some way of keeping his name off the lousy reports and I'll let him fly."

Major Tucker leaned back in his chair and nodded his head carelessly. He looked around and waved over his shoulder to MM, who was dancing with Vera.

"He's brought that godddamned woman tonight," Colonel Dan said, more loudly than he intended.

Kevin Phelan delivered the punch line of his story—"but mine is bigger than yours"—in time to hear Colonel Dan's angry remark about MM's girl. Phelan grinned lazily and said, "Who did you think he'd bring—one of the Red Cross ladies?"

"So why the hell can't he see her off base somewhere?"

"Because you won't let him out the gate," said Phelan.

"Oh, sure. I forgot," said the Colonel. Phelan got to his feet and asked his girl to dance. The second girl, an eighteen-year-old wearing too much eye makeup and wielding a long ivory cigarette holder, leaned across the table to smile at Colonel Dan.

Major Tucker, who had listened to this exchange with interest, said, "MM and his good lady . . . has that got something to do with Morse being grounded?"

"Where did you get that 'good lady' crap, Tucker? You been listening to the BBC or something?"

Tucker smiled calmly; he knew his guess was the right one. He gestured to the girl and said, "Would you permit me to dance with this beautiful young lady?"

"Morse can fly," said Colonel Dan. "But I don't want any more victories. You got that, Tucker? No more kills are to be credited to him. Headquarters tells me he's not hero material."

Tucker stood up and dusted off his class A uniform jacket although it was already immaculate. He bowed to the girl. "May I have this dance?"

"Charmed," said the girl. Her voice was high and nervous; she was trying to be the sort of highborn lady that Americans liked to meet. She was too young for an old married man with kids, the Colonel chided himself. Too young perhaps for the thirty-year-old Major Tucker, but at least they might speak the same language, which was more than Colonel Dan was able to do with her. He waved Tucker and the girl away with a smile and a nod. "Let the kid fly," he said impulsively. "But I'll send Sergeant Kinzelberg over to show your orderly room people how to fudge the paperwork . . . so I can prove I didn't break orders."

"Suppose he shoots down more Nazis . . . suppose he beats the Rickenbacker total?"

"Don't get suddenly sober, Tucker. I was just getting around to liking you drunk."

"Very good, sir," said Tucker, and he put his arms around the girl and danced off happily onto the crowded dance floor.

29

Lieutenant Colonel
Druce "Duke" Scroll

Lieutenant Colonel Scroll walked past the officers seated with their girls on the low wall under the trees that marked the edge of the Officers' Club lawn. Some of the women wore men's uniform jackets around their shoulders against the chilly night air.

He pushed open the blackout door of the Club and entered the crowded lobby. Blackout shutters sealed the windows and, despite the fans, the air inside was hot and heavy with the smell of drink and tobacco and human bodies. Duke Scroll sniffed the air with displeasure. He went through the Rumpus Room to the dance floor and saw Colonel Dan alone.

Colonel Dan spotted him and came over to where he was standing. "What are you drinking, Duke?"

"Nothing right now, Colonel. I'm just taking a look around."

The band was playing "Smoke Gets in Your Eyes." Colonel Dan said, "You missed Tucker's act."

"I hear it was really something."

"I'm beginning to think Tucker's okay," said Colonel Dan. "You hear that song? They were playing it the night I got my Air Corps commission."

"I know it's a very old song," said Scroll.

"I proposed to Babs that night."

"If you were thinking of going back to the office, Colonel, there's no need. There's no paperwork that can't wait till Monday."

"I'm going back to my quarters and write Babs a really long letter. I miss her and the children."

Scroll turned to watch the dance floor, and Colonel Dan said, "I'm going to let Morse fly, Duke. The hell with headquarters."

Scroll didn't reply. A vocalist had taken the center of the stage. The dancers were moving slowly, but spots of mirrored light raced across them, catching the faces frozen in a chance moment.

"For all we know, this may only be a dream,
We come and go, like a ripple on a stream."

The spots of light caught Tucker laughing, Farebrother whispering into Victoria's ear, and MM turning to call a greeting to some couple dancing past. Duke Scroll said, "Signs all point to a 'maximum effort' for Monday, Colonel."

"So love me tonight, tomorrow was made for some,
Tomorrow may never come, for all we know."

Patiently, Scroll let Colonel Dan watch the dancing for a further few minutes—he knew how much he liked seeing his boys have a good time. But finally he said, "And Major Tarrant would like a word with you, sir. He's out front."

Colonel Dan turned abruptly as if shaken out of a dream, and Duke Scroll followed him out to the front lawn. From there they could see that the blackout was not good. There were cracks of light around the shutters, and upstairs there were curtains carelessly drawn, leaving chinks of yellow light.

Major Tarrant saluted Colonel Dan. As commander of the Military Police Company he wore a short waterproof mackinaw complete with MP armband, pistol belt, and gleaming white helmet liner. He was obviously on duty.

"Everything okay?" said Colonel Dan.

Scroll said, "Major Tarrant reports that there are women going across to the BOQ."

"Should be easy enough to stop them," said Colonel Dan. He disliked Major Tarrant.

Tarrant said, "Women are coming out through the staff entrance and through the kitchen, sir. Some of them even climbed out of that tiny window in the toilet. I'd say there must be fifty women over there by now." He was looking at the houses used as Bachelor Officers' Quarters.

Colonel Dan looked at the quaint English-style houses with their red tiled roofs and neatly fenced gardens, and pursed his lips. But he said nothing.

"You said you wanted it stopped," said Tarrant. It was the sort of irritating reminder that made Tarrant so unpopular, not only with Colonel Dan but with a lot of other personnel.

"Yeah, stopped," said Colonel Dan, looking Tarrant in the eyes. "And you didn't stop it. You let it happen."

Duke Scroll interceded on Tarrant's behalf. "Major Tarrant is stretched, sir. This weekend we are, of course, modifying the gunsights in accordance with new instructions from the Depot. We have men working in the cockpits. The hangar doors are open and there's a lot of equipment lying around. With so many civilians here tonight, I told Major Tarrant to make sure the Technical Site is well patrolled."

"I've known pilots to take civilians across to the dispersals, and even to the hangars," said Tarrant. He put his hands on his hips so that his thumbs were hooked into the white MP belt.

Colonel Dan didn't ask his officers to stand at attention when they spoke with him, but he found Tarrant's stance offensive and insubordinate. He didn't remark on this, but his annoyance could be heard in his voice. "Pilots maybe take their girls to see their ships, Major. Nothing necessarily sinister about that."

"No, sir," said Tarrant, and he let his hands fall to his sides. "And what action will I take with respect to these women in quarters?" Impatiently he fiddled with the flap of his white pistol holster.

"I don't want your cops pulling my officers out of bed and looking in closets, if that's what you mean."

Duke Scroll knew Colonel Dan well enough to know that his former indignation about women in the BOQ was now entirely forgotten. "Major Tarrant and I will take another look around the building and then go and check on his Technical Site patrols."

Colonel Dan put a hand on Scroll's arm. "I smell a field order too, Duke. I got word the next mission will be another rough one. Now that the Krauts have moved their plane factories eastward, it's another long, tough hike for us." Tarrant remained nearby, but tactfully ignored this private aside. Now the Colonel raised his voice a little to include Tarrant. "Maybe tonight will be the last time some of these kids get into the sack with a girl. Bear that in mind, will you?"

Duke Scroll nodded. "I'll get word around that all civilians must be off the base by Sunday noon without fail."

But Colonel Dan had already turned to Tarrant. "Take it easy, Major Tarrant," he said. "Remember this is the only home my boys have got."

After the Colonel had gone, Duke Scroll walked around the

building with Major Tarrant. Scroll said, "We'll have to do something about this blackout, Major. The German Air Force is sending intruder patrols over England at night. Airfields are the prime target for them. I wouldn't want us lit up like the boardwalk at Atlantic City when they're looking for somewhere to strafe."

"See, I talked to Colonel Dan about that last month, but he snapped my head off. . . . He doesn't like me, I guess. Everything I do riles him. What kind of guy is he?"

"The Colonel has a lot of worries you don't get to hear about, Harry," said Duke in a rare moment of informality. "Yet he flies all the toughest missions himself and, in spite of being fifteen years older than some of his pilots, he flies well and gets kills. Then he climbs out of his ship, and when the rest of them are drinking or sleeping or whoring around, the Colonel's shuffling the paperwork, writing reports, and fighting off idiotic interference from the top brass."

"I never figured it like that."

"I'll tell you something, Major Tarrant. I was writing to my wife last night and I said to her that it was my privilege to be working for one of the finest men I've ever met."

Tarrant didn't reply. It seemed an extravagant assessment of a man who was too much like some of the roughnecks he regularly threw into cells. But on the other hand, Duke Scroll was a West Point man, pedantic, precise, and very hard to please. Tarrant prided himself on his flexibility and perception; they were an essential part of a policeman's skills. In the future he'd look at Colonel Dan with a new eye.

"Prickly and restless," said Duke Scroll in a startling indiscretion. "Changes his mind about things, as you saw a minute ago, but he's brave, Harry. Colonel Dan will never get that star. Generals don't stare their superiors in the eye, or get into arguments on behalf of some Pfc. who can't write or on behalf of some lieutenant who can't do anything except shoot down Germans. After the war the Colonel Dans will be eased out of the Air Force just like the kids who are doing the fighting."

"I guess the Colonel's quite a guy," said Major Tarrant, who, with a good wife and a good job waiting for him in Flint, Michigan, couldn't view the prospect of getting out of the Army at the end of the war with anything but pleasure.

They turned the corner to where a long line of trash cans stood at the door to the kitchens. There was a sudden riff of music and a brief flash of yellow light as two people emerged. Major Tarrant stopped in the shadow of the bicycle shed, and so did Duke Scroll. They watched the man and woman walk across the yard and disappear behind a truck. There was a broken piece of fencing there, and the couple could be heard climbing through it to the grass verge behind the officers' quarters.

"Two more," whispered Major Tarrant. "Going over to the BOQ."

"Captain Farebrother, I think," said Duke Scroll.

"And the tall English girl who's always with him," said Tarrant. "I have her name in the visitors' book. You think I should have a word with them . . . ask them where they're going? If we made a real fuss about one couple, the word would get around and maybe discourage some of them."

"Wrong time, wrong place, wrong people," said Duke Scroll, who by now had heard Colonel Dan's alarming news that they had the son of a general in their midst.

"I see exactly what you mean."

"Do you?" asked Duke Scroll, who was quite sure that Tarrant didn't.

"Too late, on account of the girl's pregnant already. Sure, I saw that immediately."

"Farebrother's girl?"

"Not big-bellied or anything. It's something in the way a woman carries herself—it's psychological, I guess. I saw the way she walks. I was eight years on the force. A cop gets to spot things other people miss."

30

Captain
Vincent H. Madigan

Monday was a big one, just as Colonel Dan had predicted. "Bad Monday" the Group called it ever afterward. Reporters always seemed to smell out the newsworthy missions, and Vince Madigan had a big crowd of them on his hands that morning. It was a particularly inconvenient time to be getting cryptic messages from Vera, but he was curious about them just the same. He wondered if she wanted to ask him about MM's trouble with Colonel Dan, of which Vince knew only rumors. His clerk, Pfc. Fryer, who spoke to Vera each time she called the office, got the impression that she was just another of the girls who were madly in love with the Captain. Madigan saw no reason to disillusion him.

Meanwhile, Madigan did what he was especially good at—conducting the press through the base without letting them get in the way of operational preparations.

He stepped up onto a rack of seventy-five-gallon drop tanks so they could all see him. "The ground men climbed out of the sack at five forty-five in the a.m., gentlemen. A mechanic and armorer assigned to each ship cycled out here and began the pre-flight checks. They were later relieved for breakfast by other men. Communications did their pre-flights last night to test the transmitters while the air was clear of traffic."

Some of the newsmen were taking notes. Others were photographing one of the planes as a mechanic leaned a shoulder to its prop blades and turned them to clear the cylinders. Then the crew chief climbed into the cockpit of *Kibitzer*, and the engine coughed, spat, and then started up with an earsplitting roar as flame shot from the exhausts. Tex Gill knew he was the center of attention and he played along with it, gripping the stick as if to hold the tail down and furrowing his brow in concentration as he watched the instruments. Then he chopped the throttle, and there was a moment of silence before the next P-51—*Mickey Mouse III* in brand-new natural metal finish—was started up. The armorer was, at Captain Madigan's urging, checking *Kibitzer*'s guns, feed chutes, and ammunition. It had already been done once, but it made a good picture.

"Gas tanks still have to be checked and oxygen bottles filled, but we'll see that at one of the other dispersals as we go back around the perimeter track in the bus."

The pre-flighting finished, the ground crews would normally have hidden themselves away inside their improvised huts and shelters, but today they were reluctant to get out of the limelight. They did even more checks; for the third time Tex Gill went around his P-51, tugging at the ailerons and shaking the flaps. Then he hunkered underneath to look at the landing struts and examine the tires once more. Even when the men finally sat down to play cards and talk, they did it self-consciously.

"Any of you men from Washington State, Miami, New York City, or the Dakotas?" said Madigan, knowing that certain reporters in the group would welcome stories with regional references, but none of the men responded to his question. They went on posing and posturing and carrying on their contrived conversations and pretended that Madigan and his reporters were invisible.

Captain Madigan turned to his charges and said, "The Intelligence Officers were among the first to know about today's mission. The Duty IO and the Operations people didn't get any sleep last night, you can bet on that. They were preparing the wall map for the mission and getting the Briefing Room ready."

Pfc. Fryer from Captain Madigan's office drove up in a jeep. He hurried over to his captain and, taking him aside, whispered, "That same lady phoned again. I told her you were tied up, but she says it's real urgent she talks to you." Fryer delivered the message in a hushed monotone, but there was a smirk in his voice.

Captain Madigan was annoyed by Vera's insistence. "That dame doesn't know the meaning of the word 'urgent.' Does she think I'm sitting out here waiting for something to do?"

Emboldened by this confidence, Fryer said, "Sure. I said, 'Life and death, you mean, lady?' "

Captain Madigan now had his back to the newspaper reporters. "So what did she say to that?"

"She said, 'Yeah, that's right, it's a matter of life and death.' I said, 'You got to be kidding, lady,' and she gets real mad and says she's got to see you." Fryer rubbed his nose and added, "She sounds real hysterical, Captain. Might be a good thing if you could take time out to calm her down. Could be she'll try to come onto the base or something." The "or something" meant appeal to the Chaplain for instant marriage and the acknowledgment of fatherhood which was required for an unmarried mother to receive a U.S. Army allowance.

"It's nothing like that," said Captain Madigan testily. "I don't know what she wants."

"A confidential message. She wants to give you a confidential message for someone . . . another officer, she said."

"Why didn't you say so in the first place?" So it was about MM. Well, he'd better chase that up or he'd have that damned Colonel Shelley on his neck.

"Sorry, Captain. I thought that was just a smoke screen."

"Think you could take over this junket for me? Take them on the bus to Operations and tell them how the poor old S-2s and S-3s have been up all night, working their balls off pinning red tape on the map and writing up the pilots' course cards?"

"An error of one degree on a course card for a deep-penetration mission could mean a navigational error of hundreds of miles and endanger the whole bombing force."

Madigan smiled sourly at the verbatim rendering of his usual press briefing. "Not too long in Ops, just let them look in the door. I'll take the jeep. Lunch is laid on for them, isn't it? You sent the usual to the King's Head with my compliments? . . . Good. No one is to leave the press party or make a phone call until Operations gives the okay." He looked around him. The reporters were staring at the planes and the airfield with awed fascination. This batch were all fresh from the U.S. and this was their first sight of an operational airfield. "Phone the office and get someone to bring a bunch of those press handouts I did—'The air base is a big town.' It has all the dope you need for the tour. Get the photo boys to run some combat film. Then show them the Link trainer, the laundry, the mail room, the dispensary, the infirmary, the bakery, and anything else you can think of. But make sure the jail's empty before you take them over there. One time I had a drunken machinist lecturing my press party about the lousy deal he got from the cops and the need for official brothels. I don't want anything like that to happen today."

"It won't, sir," said Pfc. Fryer with a superior smile and a brisk salute. Fryer's journalism diploma was not good preparation for the menial role he was all too often given to play.

"If I'm not back by twelve-thirty, I'll take over from you at the King's Head."

But already young Pfc. Fryer was addressing the party. "Gentlemen. Those of you who require a 'photo opportunity' should get ready for the arrival of the pilots. You'll notice that some of the planes are unpainted. This bare metal finish can add five or ten miles an hour to the top speed. No need to tell you that in combat this can"—he glanced across to where Captain Madigan was watching him from the driver's seat of the jeep—"be vital." He smiled nervously and continued. "The P-51s, often called Mustangs, will take off in pairs. This requires a high degree of skill, especially from the wingman—the second ship in each pair—because he has to keep close by juggling his throttle. To make it a fraction easier for him, the leader of each two-ship element won't use full throttle. As the wheels leave the runway, you'll notice the planes wobbling a little. They're unwieldy—all the tanks are full and the wheels and flaps are down, and there's only just enough airspeed to lift the wings into the sky. It's a hazardous moment even for highly trained, experienced flyers. You've no doubt noticed already that our main runway is under repair, so we have to contend with a slightly shorter one, and today we have ground mist to make things even worse. . . ."

The reporters looked across to see how the trees around the service road leading to the fuel-storage area were obscured in a thick gray blanket. The young man was doing a magnificent job, thought Madigan; it wasn't easy to imbue take-offs with such drama. All too often he'd had this kind of press party shuffling their feet and demanding hot coffee, but today they were giving everything their rapt attention.

Captain Madigan turned on the jeep's engine, and its sound blotted out the well-modulated and careful voice of Pfc. Fryer. On the far side of the field the first of the fighter planes was taxiing out. It was *Pilgrim*; Colonel Dan was mission leader again today.

As Madigan turned his jeep, he saw Major Tucker climbing down from a truck in full flying gear. The flyers were laughing and joking with him in a way they'd never done before. Madigan wondered what the hell had come over Tucker, and while he was pondering this, he saw MM climb out of the back of a jeep with Farebrother. Those two had aged in the last few weeks; this was no time to go bothering MM with messages from Vera. Madigan waved to them and they catcalled back; someone gave a piercing whistle, but

Madigan didn't respond with his usual vulgar hand sign because the reporters might see. The boys were in high spirits. Madigan was pleased about that; it was what was needed with a press party in close attendance.

He stopped at his quarters before setting off to see Vera, washing quickly and changing into his best uniform. Then he borrowed Farebrother's brushes and polished his shoes. He looked at his roommate's bed so carefully made and the uniforms clean and pressed and on hangers in the wardrobe they shared. Farebrother was too damned neat and clean; he wished he was sharing with someone more easygoing. He borrowed one of Farebrother's ties; there was a stain on both his own. Now overhead there was the sound of an unceasing succession of airplane engines as pair after pair bellowed at the overcast which echoed the sound back again.

Madigan had no authority to use his jeep off base—in fact, no permission to leave the base at all—so he was a little alarmed when, at the gate, an MP waved him down. "Shit!" said Madigan under his breath, and he got ready to tell the MPs that he was needed urgently at the local newspaper office, which was not too far from the truth. No good asking Major Tarrant to turn a blind eye; Tarrant had never been known to do anyone a favor.

"One of your people on the phone for you, Captain Madigan." The MP touched his white helmet liner. "You can leave your jeep right here, sir."

The sergeant on duty in the guard post handed the phone through the window to the table outside. "Captain Madigan here, what is it?" Madigan smiled conspiratorially at the MP sergeant, but the sergeant didn't respond.

"One of the planes cracked up on the runway, sir. A blown tire." It was the PR sergeant. "The reporters want to go over and look at it. Will that be okay?"

"I don't want them writing that some crooked Limey contractor put cheap fill into the airfield and it's killing our boys. Even if it's true I don't want them saying it. Where are they now?"

"Fryer's keeping them on the bus while he phones. He's on the other line, sir."

"Good thinking, Fryer," muttered Madigan sarcastically. "Is the pilot hurt? I can still hear planes taking off."

"I can't get through to Ops or the tower. I guess they're using just one side of the runway."

Madigan rubbed his face as he thought about it. He could still hear the loud roar of airplane engines as the pairs circled the field before heading up through the overcast. "Tell Fryer to give Ops a miss. Show them some combat film and get plenty of coffee and doughnuts over to the photo section. Then the tour of the base as arranged. Tell the newshounds they'll be taken over there as soon as we have clearance, and that means when we know there are no casualties and no spilled gas or anything dangerous."

"I'll tell Fryer, sir. Will you be long?"

"No, Sergeant. I plan to be back before the lunch at the King's Head. We get a good meal into them, and by the time lunch is over, the wreck will be cleared away. They'll have to do it fast—they'll need that runway for the return. Hell! It's not as if we can tell them it was due to battle damage."

At Vera's house a man answered the door. "Come in," he said. "Vera has been trying to get hold of you."

He ushered Captain Madigan into the tiny parlor and insisted that he take off his coat and sit down in the best armchair. "I'm just having a cup of tea," he said. "Vera would have wanted me to make you comfortable." Vince smiled and looked around the tiny room. The table was set for breakfast, but the cloth was freshly stained with tea, and the milk jug set aside to make room for a can of milk with jagged holes punctured in its top. The fireplace was littered with ashes and cinders and the fire was almost out.

"I'm in a bit of a hurry," said Madigan. "We're flying today."

He poured some tea. "I've been hearing the planes go over. Flying Fortresses, are they? Is that your lot?" He was a gaunt middle-aged man with a soft friendly voice and a close-lipped smile. He was wearing army trousers and a khaki-colored sweater. His black shiny boots were on the sewing-machine case, displayed like an objet d' art. His face was lined and wrinkled, as skin goes so quickly under a tropical sun, and his hands were scarred, with blackened nails that had come from manual labor. Even Vera had had trouble recognizing this muscular, hard-eyed, coarse-spoken version of the husband who'd sailed away nearly four years ago. "Damn cold, isn't it," he said. "I can't get warm."

Vince took the hot mug of tea from him and said, "Are you Vera's husband?"

He shivered. "It's cold here in England."

It wasn't very cold, but Madigan smiled and nodded. "You'll be glad to be home," he said, and sipped some of the strong dark tea.

"Home! It's all you think about out there." The words tumbled out, as if rehearsed a million times, but the voice was low and calm. "Men go crazy . . . the jungle, the malaria, the bloody stinking wet heat all the time. And men need women, Vince. You know that."

"You know my name?"

"Oh, I know your name all right." A plane went over very low. It was probably returning because of engine trouble. Madigan noticed its faltering sound.

The man went into the kitchen and came back with a packet of something and spooned it into his tea. "It's salt," he explained. "It takes a little time to get used to the idea that you're not sweating it out of every pore day and night. It's a craving, Vince. Men have cravings—women too, I suppose."

The conversation was taking a turn that Vince Madigan didn't like. "I should be going," he said, but he didn't get up. He waited to see how the other man would take it.

"Drink your tea, Vince."

"There are some buddies of mine . . ." Vince had some vague idea of saying that his buddies were within calling distance, but the man's dark eyes fixed him with a stare that dried up his words.

"Buddies," said the man, rolling the unfamiliar word around in his mouth as if tasting it for the first time. "Buddies. I lost some fine 'buddies' out there in the jungle, Vince. Fine men. Not heroes, not all of them anyway, some of them scared, Vince. Scared stiff all the time. But men! Men who gave up their lives for their friends, Vince. That sounds unlikely here in Cambridgeshire, doesn't it?"

"No," said Madigan.

The man carried on as if he hadn't heard him. "Yes, it sounds silly here in Cambridgeshire, where men go on strike over tea breaks, where factory workers get double pay for Sundays, and men who want a pint of beer, a shave in hot water, a clean shirt, or a woman go out and grab the nearest one they find. Money must be an advantage, eh, Vince? Being a Yank with a big fat wallet and fine cigars and cheap whiskey, what woman can resist you? They're weak creatures, Vince. You must have discovered that by now."

Madigan got to his feet. "I know what you're suggesting, Mr.

Hardcastle. But there was never anything like that going on between me and Vera."

The man paid no heed to Madigan's assurances. His voice continued in the same unexcited monotone. "And look at the uniforms they give you. Not this cheap rubbish. Not this bloody old rough, itchy, hairy blanket that our people think good enough for soldiers. They dress you up in fine wool with collars and ties and nice brown shoes."

"The flyers are the ones that make the money," said Madigan in an attempt to side with the man. "They *are* rich—overseas pay and then flying pay on top of everything."

"That's right," said Hardcastle. He picked up a photograph of Vince Madigan. It was bent and creased from being stuffed down behind the plate rack, but Hardcastle flattened it with the edge of his large hand. He's spent half the night looking at it. Madigan was wearing flying gear, his arm around the prop of a P-51.

Madigan cursed his bad luck, and he cursed Vera for holding on to the photo after they'd separated. "I know this will sound silly to you," he said, "but I had that photo taken as a joke."

Hardcastle read the inscription aloud. " 'Thanks for the memory, Your darling, Vincent.'" He looked up. "Was that a joke too, Vincent? Not much of a joke, Vincent. Not much of a joke to play on another man's wife, Vince." He tore off the inscribed part of the photo and tossed it on the fire.

Madigan decided to move very slowly. To keep smiling and nodding, but to make slowly for the door. For a time it seemed as if his plan might work.

"Sit down, Vince." Madigan looked up to find Reg Hardcastle holding a huge British Army Webley revolver. In spite of its weight, Sergeant Major Hardcastle had no difficulty holding it steady. The gun looked antique, but Hardcastle regarded it as an old friend. A dozen or more times it had saved his life in the jungle, where quick shots at close range were what mattered. But there were no notches carved into the wooden grips; Sergeant Major Hardcastle was not an ostentatious man.

Vince sat down and felt his body sweating with the heat that his great fear had generated. Suddenly the seemingly dead fire came to life as the torn photo blazed, flickered, and died again. "You've got the wrong man," said Madigan, his voice croaking as his throat went dry.

"You're wasting your breath. Vera told me everything. She told me all about you, Vince."

"Let me talk to her . . . it's a mistake, I swear it is."

"You can't talk to Vera." He gave a brief bleak smile. "I've already dealt with her."

"No . . ."

"She's in the scullery, Vince. I did it with a knife. I didn't want any noise. I didn't want the police coming round asking questions until I'd had a chance to deal with you."

"They're sure to get you," said Madigan. He loosened his tie and undid his collar button. He remembered his father telling him that women would be his downfall. His father had discovered that Vince was having a torrid affair with the wife of one of his best customers, a very dear friend. She was twenty years older than Vince, and after the scandal the woman and her husband had moved to another town. His father had never forgiven him. Even now his father always left the house soon after Vincent arrived to visit his mother. "The police are sure to get you," said Madigan again.

"Of course. After I've done you I shall go and tell the bobbies," said Reg. "I loved Vera, you see. I've nothing to live for without her."

"But why? Why kill me?" Jesus, what couldn't Mozart have done with a misidentity scene like this! Tonight in the Club he'd tell Jamie Farebrother about it, and Jamie would have to admire the way he kept so cool and even managed to think about Mozart.

Hardcastle pulled the hammer back far enough to make the cocking mechanism click, and all thoughts of Mozart went out of Madigan's mind. "Because it will be in the newspapers, and other Yanks who are carrying on with married women will read it. If you'd read about a Yank lover-boy getting murdered like this, perhaps you'd have thought twice before chasing my poor Vera."

"But it wasn't *me* . . ."

"And I agree with you. It's the woman's fault every time. It's the sort of situation you talk about in the jungle, see. And all the blokes agreed about that—it's the woman's fault every time."

"I can tell you the name . . ."

"Don't demean yourself, son. Die like a man. Die the way your friends die over Germany. You must have seen them go. You must have faced the fact that one day it could be your turn."

"I'm not a flyer." Madigan's voice became an ugly little screech. "I'm not a flyer. Can't you get it into your stupid head?"

"It's no use, lad," said Hardcastle in a sympathetic tone of voice. "I'll give you a minute or so to pull yourself together, and say a prayer if you're given to that sort of thing."

"Please," said Madigan. "Please. I'll give you anything, I'll promise you anything, but please . . ."

The two men looked at each other for what seemed like a long time to Hardcastle, and then he squeezed the trigger and blew off the top of Vincent Madigan's head.

31

Victoria Cooper

Victoria Cooper did not get up on the morning of "Bad Monday." She'd heard the sound of aircraft engines from the time it was first light, and she knew that so many planes at that time of morning was always the sign of another big American daylight raid. The heavy bombers circled for hours and hours, so that she couldn't doze off to sleep again, but she remained in bed. She could come to terms with the droning sound, but she didn't want to catch sight of one of the planes; it would trigger off her fears for Jamie.

She didn't go to the office on Mondays; that was one of the benefits of working on a weekly newspaper. Her mother brought breakfast in to her, putting the tray down on the bedside table and announcing, "I've given you as much milk as I can spare until the milkman comes this morning."

"Thank you, Mother. That's very kind."

It did no good; her mother was not ready to forget the harsh words that had been exchanged when Victoria arrived home in the early hours of Sunday morning. Her parents had waited up for her return, her father smoking and coughing and looking apologetic, her mother wringing her hands and deceptively soft-spoken as she voiced all the cruel and bitter things she'd been wanting to say for years.

Her mother had guessed that she was pregnant, of course, just as Vera had guessed: women had a keen eye for such things. Had Mickey Morse also guessed, or had Vera told him? Victoria wished that Jamie had guessed too, then she wouldn't be here in bed trying to decide the best way of breaking the news to him. She'd wanted to tell him at the Officers' Club dance but the words didn't come.

She placed her hand on her belly. Would he be pleased or would he be angry? Would he think it was just her way of trapping him into marriage? Surely not, for in that tentative way of his he'd already spoken of marriage—he'd talked about other American servicemen who'd married English girls. But it was difficult to decide exactly what he thought about their decision, except that it was an additional burden to carry when a man went off to risk his life fighting.

She took her cup of coffee to her writing table and spent the next hour laboring over a letter to Jamie. She told him she was pregnant and happy to be so. She explained that her mother wanted her to go away to stay with her aunt and have the baby there, far from the war. Jamie would know that "far from the war" meant far from her parents' friends and neighbors and far from the influential men who visited the house to talk to her father. It would give her a chance to think, she wrote, but then she crossed that out; it sounded absurd—she was equally capable of thinking here in Cambridge. And yet the physical changes her body was undergoing did affect her mind too. She couldn't think about anything except the baby, and she felt slower-witted and unable to concentrate. She told Jamie about feeling depressed for no reason that she could fathom, and then deleted "depressed"; her father had taught her not to use such clinical terms to describe mere lowered spirits. She reached for another sheet of paper and tried again. She was going away in order to give *Jamie* a chance to think—that was nearer to the truth of it. After that, she found it easier to continue. She told him how much she loved him and that she would go on loving him even if he decided never to see her again. She didn't want him to feel trapped; she expected nothing. He'd given her the happiest months of her life and she would never be able to forget him even if she tried to.

She didn't seal the letter but read it again and again and rewrote it and even managed to add a joke. When finally the letter satisfied her, she sealed it and then carefully disposed of the early drafts. She had no doubt that her mother would read anything she left in her room, and to be sure of avoiding this she flushed the other sheets down the toilet and put the sealed envelope into her pocket.

She was still thinking of Jamie and how he'd react to her news when she went downstairs to help her mother prepare lunch. There was a visitor with her father in the drawing room, and as she passed the door she heard a man's voice saying, "There's no way to be sure who did what first. It might have been the soldier who bumped off the other two." She could hear her father murmur an acknowledgment.

Her mother was in the kitchen washing carrots so as not to waste any vitamins by paring them; it was a "kitchen hint" that the BBC had provided after the morning news bulletin.

"Who's with Daddy?" she asked her mother. "Bumped off" sounded like something out of comic books—she couldn't reconcile such a phrase with any of her father's friends or colleagues.

Her mother turned away from her work at the sink and looked her up and down. "I'm glad to see you're not wearing all that paint and powder," she said peevishly. Victoria's restrained makeup had been mentioned repeatedly by her mother during their fight. There was a subtle implication that makeup and the loss of virtue were two facets of the same dishonor.

This morning her mother was still looking for an argument; the rage was boiling inside her. Her daughter's pregnancy confronted her with facts she did not want to face. She was reminded of her own advancing years, the heartaching loss of her favorite child, the threadbare marriage that remained. She could have endured it all if only her daughter had not rejected her too. If Victoria had confided in her she could have endured even the foolish bliss that now shone in Victoria's eyes.

"Could it be the man about the War Savings Committee?" asked Victoria.

Mrs. Cooper turned on the faucet so that water poured into the kettle noisily enough to drown conversation. Only when the kettle was full did she say, "I'm sure your father doesn't tell me his business." She forced herself to smile—she felt sorry for Victoria, she'd told her husband that not once but a thousand times. Her husband did not reply to such assertions. He knew that in the darkest places of his wife's mind it was not sorrow that fueled her anger; it was envy.

Dr. Cooper put his head around the kitchen door. "Could you

spare a moment, Victoria dear? There's someone here who'd like a word with you."

"Who is it?" said Victoria.

Mrs. Cooper also looked at him quizzically, but Dr. Cooper said only, "It won't take very long."

The visitor was about thirty years old, but his pallid face and small frame made his severe clothes—a black jacket and pinstripe trousers—strangely inappropriate. He looked like a lanky boy dressed up to play the role of a bank manager in the school play.

"Miss Cooper," the man said, "I want to begin by . . ." His voice was hoarse and rather high-pitched. Her father silenced the visitor with a fierce look that revealed a side of him she had never seen before. At once she realized why some of his students went in fear and awe of him.

"Sit down, my dear," her father said tenderly. "I want to introduce Detective-Sergeant Jenkins."

"A policeman?" She watched the detective as he selected a coughdrop from a tin he kept in his pocket.

"CID," announced Jenkins before popping the coughdrop into his mouth.

"May I continue?"

"I beg your pardon, sir." His apology was as ironic as the question.

"The sergeant has brought us some shocking news, Victoria." He was watching her face, and over her father's shoulder she could see the detective watching her too.

"Jamie?"

"No, no, no," said her father. "Not Jamie."

She sighed. She could bear almost anything if it wasn't about Jamie.

"It's your friend Vera," said her father. "There's been some kind of accident."

"Not an accident," said Detective-Sergeant Jenkins, who had no time to waste on these genteel preparations. "Murder! Mr. and Mrs. Hardcastle living in number forty-five Michael Street. Both of them are dead."

"No," said Victoria. She was sure it wasn't true. Surely Reg Hardcastle was somewhere on the other side of the world. "She's coming here tonight . . ."

"Three blows with a kitchen knife," said the detective.

". . . to bring me some cotton for my embroidery." Victoria finished what she had set out to say while her mind came to grips with the news. Poor Vera. And poor Victoria. Vera—such a scatty-minded chatterbox. They'd laughed together and consoled each other, and Vera was the only person she could talk to about being pregnant. It was Vera's irrepressible optimism that had made her pregnancy so easy to adjust to. Vera was the noisiest, liveliest person in the world—Vera couldn't be dead. "I was with her on Saturday," said Victoria.

"And the husband was shot dead," said the detective. "Shot by an American officer."

Victoria felt faint and leaned against the back of the armchair to steady herself. Who could it have been but MM?

"Yes," said the detective, still sucking on his coughdrop. "Mr. and Mrs. Hardcastle are both dead. It happened sometime this morning. The police surgeon thinks we were there within the hour."

"You were commendably quick off the mark," said Dr. Cooper.

The police detective looked at him for a moment before confessing. "A man who said he was Mr. Hardcastle phoned the police."

"A neighbor has already identified the Hardcastles," Dr. Cooper told his daughter. "The police want you to look at a photograph of an American officer. It's no one I've ever met—I've told the sergeant that." While the policeman turned away to take the photo from his briefcase, Victoria looked up at her father's face. He'd met MM twice. Mistaking her open-eyed puzzlement for fear, Dr. Cooper smiled to tell her not to worry.

She looked at the photograph—a badly torn glossy picture of Vince Madigan dressed up in flying helmet and life jacket. There was a Mustang behind him, and Vince had an arm around the prop blade.

The policeman rattled the tin of coughdrops, impatiently waiting for her to speak. Finally he said, "It's the American squadron at Steeple Thaxted. You'll know that from the letters on the plane."

"And you don't know who he is?" she whispered.

"I know who he is, all right," said the detective. "I've got his documents. I need someone to identify him." He looked at Dr. Cooper and with a knowing smile said, "And I don't want the Americans in on this, trying to cover it all up. They always look after their own, you know."

Her father leaned close to her and said, "If you know who it is, you must tell the officer. He'll want you to identify the body, I should think."

The detective frowned. He'd never get any dead bodies identified if he told people they'd have to visit the morgue.

Victoria shuddered. She realized that her father was trying to protect her and she loved him for it. And if she admitted to knowing Vince Madigan, the next question must inevitably be "and what was this American's relationship with Mrs. Hardcastle." And then more questions. "I don't recognize him," she said softly.

So poor Vince was dead. He'd held her in his arms on the dance floor Saturday night. He'd brought a bottle of bourbon up to Jamie's room and he'd argued with MM about the best way to catch soft-shell crabs and won four pounds on a bet about an old baseball score. But what was Vince doing at Michael Street on a Monday morning?

"I understand you know a lot of American servicemen," said the policeman. "Look again at the photo, miss. Are you quite sure you don't know him . . . never seen him before?" She could smell the strong coughdrop on the detective's breath, and she watched her father's face tighten in resentment at his rude manner.

"If my daughter says she doesn't remember seeing him before, she cannot help you. As I told you she's not awfully well. I can't allow you to harass her."

The policeman ignored him. "I must remind you, miss, that there is such a thing as obstructing a policeman in the execution of his duty."

"You've gone too far," said Dr. Cooper angrily.

"Have I?" said the detective. He gulped as he swallowed the remains of his coughdrop. "Well, some might say I haven't gone far enough. Your daughter is keeping company with an American soldier. . . . Never mind how I know." He waved away Dr. Cooper's protest. "This American is dead." He tapped the photo. "He may be a victim, but it looks to me like the husband came home and found the American had been there overnight. The husband killed the wife, the lover kills the husband and then commits suicide. Otherwise what's an American soldier doing there early on a Monday morning?" He jingled the coins in his pocket. "I'm conducting a murder inquiry and there's still a lot to do. Now I ask you again, miss." Tapping the photo, he said, "Have you ever seen this man before?"

"No, I haven't," said Victoria.

"Very well." The policeman reached for his roll-brim hat.

"Then I'll ask you not to leave Cambridge without informing me. I might need to ask you further questions when my investigation has made more progress."

"My daughter is leaving town this afternoon," said Dr. Cooper. "She has arranged to go and stay with her aunt in Scotland."

The policeman looked at both of them. He sniffed. That was the uncooperative attitude you might expect from a family that encouraged their daughter to go around with Yanks. And these were well-to-do people—putting on airs with him—not working class. Such lax attitudes offended him. He'd make sure that no daughter of his kept company with foreign soldiers. "It's not in my power to prevent you leaving, miss. But if necessary I will obtain your address from your father and contact you through the local police . . . wherever you are," he added meaningfully.

He went to get his overcoat. Victoria closed her eyes to hold back her tears. Poor Vera, she'd looked so lovely at the dance.

"You didn't ask him what happened," said her father when he returned from seeing the detective out. "The police expect you to be more curious, darling. It must have seemed suspicious to him."

Victoria nodded. But she knew what had happened. Vera's worst nightmare had come true. She wiped a tear away. The only mystery was Vince—why Vince, why not MM? And then she guessed the answer: Vera had told her husband about Vince. She hated Vince, and it was her last chance to protect MM. How typical of her.

Her father said, "The police found our address in the Hardcastle house. You'd sent her tickets for a dance and put your name and address on the back of the envelope."

She nodded again. What did it matter how they'd found her address? But her father's words reminded her of something. She reached into her pocket and pulled out the letter she'd written to Jamie. "Will you post this for me, Daddy? I have no postage stamps left."

"I'll do it right away. I want to take the dog for a walk before lunch."

"Thank you, Daddy." She sat very still, and he knew she wanted to ask him something. He waited. "You want me to go away?" she asked softly.

He went over to her, but didn't touch her. He could no longer bring himself to embrace her now that she was a grown woman. "Of course not, darling."

"Mother wants me to go?"

"We both think it would be best. And now, with this awful murder, you might find things very difficult if you stay here."

"And I'm pregnant," she said, annoyed that he had avoided saying it.

"Yes," he said. He found some stamps in his wallet and stuck two on the letter to Jamie. He held the letter in his hand, tapping its edge on the mantelpiece as he waited for her to say she would go.

"We love each other," she said. "That's all that matters, isn't it?"

He turned, looked at her, and then lowered his eyes. "I don't know, darling."

"Will you take me to the station in the car?"

He brightened, now that she was being sensible. "Of course. And phone the station and reserve a seat for you. And I'll talk to your editor and explain you're not well enough to go to work . . . it will all be all right, dearest."

She heaved herself out of the armchair. Sometimes she felt heavy with the child inside her; it was only her imagination, but it was a vivid illusion. "Don't forget to post my letter," she said before going through the door. "I'll go upstairs and pack my things."

"I won't forget," he said. But he did forget, and when lunch was over Mrs. Cooper discovered the letter on the mantelpiece. After only a moment's hesitation she tore it open and read it. She read it twice, very carefully, before putting it into the fire.

32

Captain
Milton B. Goldman

The medical staff was stretched on that "Bad Monday." The Group's Table of Organization called for a medical section with four doctors: a Group Surgeon and one captain for each squadron. But there were only two captains, and the major was in Edinburgh, attending a medical services clinic on sulfa drugs. So on Monday the two remaining doctors tossed pennies to see who would go to the sick bay and dispense aspirin for hangovers, an unidentifiable chalky liquid for diarrhea, and fierce talk to the time wasters. Milton Goldman was the better doctor—better, in fact, than most of the flight surgeons in the Eighth Air Force—but the penny came down heads and so he was sitting in the ambulance on the line at the moment the Group took off.

The ambulance driver that day was a balding middle-aged corporal named Walker. He had a large droopy mustache, and large droopy eyebrows, which contrived to make him look slow and sleepy. But Walker was neither slow nor sleepy. The two men had spent many such hours together, and rank was no longer a barrier between them. With that quiet desperation that overtakes people trapped in elevators, mine disasters, or marriages, they politely exchanged small talk. They were discussing the unpredictable temperament of women. Inevitably Vincent Madigan's reputation came up.

"Now that Captain Madigan, he really understands women," said Goldman. Goldman was a short bespectacled New Yorker with quick coal-black eyes and a neurotic temperament that caused him to fidget with keys, jingle coins, or, as now, hammer continually against the dashboard with his fist.

"You said it."

"He's always in love—really in love—that's what swings it for him."

"With a new one every week?" said Walker, who was a family man for whom the sheer effort of falling in love every week was an appalling prospect.

"We had a professor at medical school who reckoned love was entirely chemical."

"Is there really such a thing as an aphrodisiac?" said Corporal Walker.

"You tell *me*," said Goldman, who knew the swanky Madison Avenue drugstore where Walker had worked as a senior pharmacist. "If there is such a thing, then the Captain Madigans of this world have no need for it."

Walker sniffed. "The Captain Madigans of this world do not abstain from using things on the grounds of having no need."

Goldman grinned. "I hadn't figured you for a philosopher. . . . Ah, here they go, that's Major Tucker's ship taxiing out now, isn't it?" He pushed his glasses against the bridge of his nose to see better. Two Mustangs were in position at the northeast end of the runway. With brakes fully applied, the pilots opened the throttles so that the planes jumped about excitedly, like children on tiptoes, as the props clawed at the air.

"That's Tucker," said Walker. As the wheel brakes were released, the plane settled heavily onto the concrete and waddled forward, slowly at first and then gathering speed as the high-revving engines howled like animals in pain. Corporal Walker looked at his watch. "Looks like we'll be okay for the coffee shop this morning, sir."

"It's all right for you guys," said Goldman. "But I might as well order a bottle of iced Bollinger as hope for a cup of fresh coffee in the Officers' Club. Those guys goof off whenever there's a mission flying."

"There's a coffee machine in the Aero Club."

Goldman made a face.

"Will you look at the way those guys tuck up the landing gear before they're over the hedge." Walker gave a low whistle of admiration, but there was no surprise in it. He'd said it before; in fact, he almost always said it when they were watching the take-off. Along the perimeter track the planes were tightly packed in pairs. The noise of the engines was almost a continuous roar as the throttles went forward and the planes already in the air came around the field to form up into flights and then head up into the overcast. "Yes, I'm a philosopher," said Walker, suddenly resuming their conversation in a voice loud enough to be heard against the aircraft noise. "You have to be, to survive in a barrack room without going nuts."

Goldman nodded. "Did you hear what the target is today?"

"The scuttlebutt says Berlin," said Walker in a voice that showed he didn't believe it. "It'll be a tough one. The Colonel never misses a tough one."

"The Colonel shouldn't be flying any kind of mission," said Goldman.

Walker looked around quickly; he'd recognized the voice of the physician. "You mean he's sick?"

"Sure, he's dying of old age, just like the rest of us." Goldman grinned. "No, the Colonel's in good physical condition for his age. But in combat, spots before the eyes, imperfect blood circulation, or a slightly slowed reaction can kill you. A fighter pilot is over the hill at twenty-six, no matter what the book says. I'm telling you."

The next pair of planes was halfway down the runway when one of them suffered a blown tire. The plane slewed around until it was sliding sideways, screaming, as the wheel rim ripped the tire to shreds. The strut, not designed for such strain, collapsed. As the wing banged down onto the runway there was a noise like a buzz saw as the prop blades chewed a series of cuts out of the concrete before bending. The plane shed a section of wing and sundry pieces of engine before coming to rest.

"Christ! There's one for us," said Corporal Walker.

"Hit the siren and let's go," said Goldman, touching his medical box to be sure it was there and slamming the ambulance door all in one action.

The control tower, under which the ambulance, fire engine, and crash tender were waiting, was a small white-painted building with a crude balcony and a tiny glass-sided room on the roof. Staff Sergeant Harold Boyer was checking communications equipment in the tower that morning. He'd gone out on the roof to watch the take-off, and his elevation provided him with a good view of the accident.

Sergeant Boyer had never been trained on airframes, but his many years in the Air Corps enabled him to recognize the way in which the collapse of the strut allowed the wing to hit the ground with such force that the main spar snapped somewhere about midway along the wing. This, aided somewhat by the effect of the prop blades hitting the ground, jolted the engine off its mounting. "Kee-ryyst!" said Sergeant Boyer. He looked down to where the fire truck and the ambulance were parked. "Get going, Doc!" he yelled, shouting more because he desperately wanted to do something than because the men in the ambulance might hear him above the noise. In any case, it was unnecessary; even before his words were uttered, the ambulance was pulling away. But the duty crew of the fire-fighting platoon weren't at readiness that morning. The grotesque white man-shaped asbestos suit was still lying across the front of the truck when the accident occurred, and by the time the ambulance started off, the duty fireman was only just beginning to get into the suit.

"Get into the truck, you stupid son of a bitch," shouted Boyer. "Get your butt off the ground. She's a category E, and if she flames, you'll be in the stockade." His final words were drowned by the noise of a solitary unpainted plane flying very low over the runway. It was a dangerous thing to do under such circumstances, but no one blamed the pilot of *Mickey Mouse III*. Lieutenant Morse was trying to see what had happened to his wingman.

Staff Sergeant Boyer's training and experience had enabled him to recognize the difference between a common "ground loop" from which a pilot could be expected to walk away with no injuries that a shot of mission whiskey and a sleeping pill wouldn't cure, and this cat. E—"damaged beyond economical repair"—with a pilot pinned behind his engine and groaning in spite of the morphine that Dr. Goldman had put into his veins.

"Get those lousy goddamned sonuvabitching clippers . . . the heavy-duty shears!" It was McDonald, a gray-haired lieutenant of the Mobile Reclamation and Repair Squadron. He was standing on the wing, having levered the canopy fully open with a series of heaves that needed all his strength. Now, in spite of being out of breath, he found the energy to shout. He exchanged looks with Doc Goldman. They both knew that he was shouting because, like the others, he was frightened that she was going to burn.

It was a classic fire hazard: leaking oxygen bottles and probably arcing in the electric wiring. And there was gasoline everywhere; they could hear it gurgling softly from the ripped tanks and see the shine of it on the silvery metal of the aircraft. They could smell its heavy vapor in the air and see it running across the concrete and forming pools in the grass. Worst of all was the noise they could hear from beneath the cowling, where liquid dripping onto hot engine parts was sizzling like steaks in a frying pan.

"Now, you guys not on duty, beat it!" shouted Lieutenant McDonald. He threw the wrecked hood to the ground and took the bolt cutters from his sergeant. "We got enough problems here without rubberneckers." In a lower voice, to Goldman, he said, "Where's that stupid bastard Tarrant the one time we need a few cops to clear these guys away?"

"Polishing his buttons," said Goldman, who also wanted a scapegoat upon whom to vent his frustration.

The Exec arrived even ahead of the Group Engineering Officer. Colonel Scroll stood for a moment to read the name painted on the nose of the wreck—*Kibitzer*. So the phone message from the tower had got it right. Pausing only long enough to make sure there was room for take-offs to continue, he clambered awkwardly onto the broken wing. Now he could see the way in which the engine's weight had twisted and corrugated the metal skin. He held on to the warm metal alongside Doc Goldman and watched the shears cutting through the heavy-duty zippers and the wires of the electrically heated suit. Jamie Farebrother seemed to be unconscious. Goldman was holding his pulse and wearing that impassive face that doctors acquire at medical school. His eyes were red from the stinging fumes of glycol and hydraulic fluid that mingled with steamy vapor to cloud the wreckage.

Corporal Walker used scissors to cut through the pilot's flying jacket, sweater, and shirt sleeve and then opened a vein for the tube that he taped quickly into it. Goldman held the plasma bottle aloft until the corporal finished and then handed it back to him.

"Is he trapped?" said Duke Scroll.

"The engine's shifted off its mount, it weighs over half a ton, and the kid's got it pinned against him," said Lieutenant McDonald without pausing in his work.

"How bad, Doc?" said Duke Scroll. He had to lean close and shout a second time because of the noise of the planes passing them with only a few feet to spare. Now he was close enough to smell the morphine spilled on Goldman's hands.

Goldman glanced first at Farebrother to be sure he couldn't hear his answer. "His flying days are over, sir."

Duke Scroll looked at the doctor, remembering the way Goldman and Farebrother had been laughing and joking together at Saturday night's dance, but Goldman betrayed no emotion; he looked sad, but Goldman always looked sad, just as Major Tarrant always looked fierce and Kevin Phelan always looked drunk. Duke Scroll said, "Is there any kind of specialist unit that could . . . ?" He wiped his eyes, the fumes were getting to him.

Goldman shook his head. "No, sir. He's in shock—falling blood pressure, falling temperature, and weak pulse—he's probably hemorrhaging internally. I can't get to him properly. The blood's bloated his abdomen so his seat belt's wedged right into his stomach —we can't get at it. We'll need metal cutters to give us more room to move. McDonald thinks he might have to use winches to rip the fuselage apart."

Having levered open the small rear canopy panel, McDonald reached into the fuselage with the bolt cutters trying to sever the harness from its anchors behind the pilot's seat. He couldn't get to it and he cursed the broken pieces of metal softly as he tried again and again.

Scroll climbed down and found his way barred by a man in class A uniform complete with peaked service cap. The smart appearance of this private first class contrasted with the other men variously dressed in twill coveralls, fatigues, baseball caps, fleece-lined leather jackets, and sweaters. The Pfc. saluted solemnly.

"What is it?" said Colonel Scroll. He'd grown to like Farebrother, and now he needed a moment to resume that impersonal manner that was necessary to his rank and position.

"Pfc. Fryer," the young man announced. "I'm from the PR office, conducting the press party. Okay if I bring them over here, sir?"

"To see the war at first hand, you mean?" Although Scroll paused, the young Pfc. was wise enough not to answer the question. "Is that what you'd advise?" Scroll persisted.

Pfc. Fryer was not easily intimidated. He had long since learned that the power of the press far outweighed that of the generals, and this man Scroll was only a colonel. "The folks back home should see the sacrifices, sir." When Scroll didn't react he added, "Let them see the human story behind the casualty figures, sir."

"This pilot won't even be in the casualty figures," said Scroll. "Accidents on take-off, accidents on landing, even the cripples who go into the Channel are not included with the battle casualties."

"Right, sir," said Pfc. Fryer. There was a note of hesitation in his voice now. He couldn't exactly determine Scroll's attitude. Surely the sight of Farebrother couldn't have upset the man the enlisted men all called "Iron Ass." "I forgot about the way the figures are calculated."

"Keep those people out of my sight," said Scroll. "And we sure don't want them over here getting in the way and taking snapshots for their albums."

"Whatever you say, sir," said Pfc. Fryer. He decided that Colonel Scroll had an ulcer or some other ailment that made him occasionally bad-tempered. Captain Madigan had often said that lectures about public relations should be compulsory for all the officers. Fryer had never felt himself more in agreement.

Scroll got into his jeep. "Take me back to my office," he told his driver. He began rehearsing what he was going to say to General Bohnen when he reached him on the phone.

When Scroll returned to his office he was surprised to see the Group Engineering Officer waiting for him. "No use me being over there. That lieutenant from Reclamation knows more about dismantling that wreck than I could learn in a lifetime," explained the Major. "What I want to know is, how do you feel about having our only remaining runway blocked?"

"What's the alternative?" said Scroll.

"No problem—we elbow the wreckage aside. I've got a bulldozer standing by. It's a five-minute job."

Scroll carefully removed his eyeglasses and stood holding them in both hands. "Before extricating the pilot, you mean?"

"That's the tough part," admitted the Major. "But I already checked with Weather and he says there's every chance it's going to close in. If the wind shifts a little they'll have a crosswind. And with the kind of ground mist we've been having the last few afternoons, bringing their ships in to dodge that wreckage could be fatal."

"You think I don't know that, Major?"

"I'm sorry, sir."

"And is it going to be better for the pilots' morale to hear that we bulldozed an injured man off the runway like so much goddamned offal?"

"I just don't know the answer."

Scroll felt equally ill equipped to answer such a question, but his commanding officer was in the air and with him were his deputy and Phelan, the Operations Officer. "Leave it the way it is until they get the pilot out," he said finally. "Keep the bulldozer crew on standby and leave word with your clerk so I can reach you." He joggled his glasses. "I might talk to Colonel Dan over the radio . . ."

Scroll buzzed for his clerk without dismissing the GEO. "Are we in radio contact, Sergeant?"

Sergeant Kinzelberg looked at his watch. "They should be approaching the German border soon, sir. We could reach them, I guess, but they'd have to reply through the relay ship."

Scroll bit his lip. "Well, let's leave that one for the moment," he said briskly. "Let's not hand them any more problems for the time being."

The Engineering Officer saluted and left the room. When he'd gone, Colonel Scroll turned to his clerk and said, "I want you to find General Bohnen. . . . Find him wherever he is. Right?"

"Any message?"

"I'll speak with them at the other end. Just locate him." Colonel Scroll sat down at his desk and dumped his eyeglasses into the in tray while he rubbed his eyes. He didn't want to worry Colonel Dan, but if he got back here and found General Bohnen waiting for him he was going to be mad as hell. On the other hand . . . Jesus Christ, how could anyone hesitate to send for the boy's father in a case like this?

While his clerk tried to reach the General, Scroll paced the office and worried. Eventually he went along the corridor to the office of the Group's Technical Inspector. Spencer Larsson, a slow-spoken major from Milwaukee, was sitting behind a paper-littered desk puffing reflectively on an antique meerschaum pipe. He jumped up when Scroll came into the room, coughed, and waved the smoke away.

"Spike," said Colonel Scroll, "listen carefully, because I don't want any misunderstanding. You get the 199th Squadron Engineering Officer and all your best people, and you take that damned strut to pieces bit by bit."

"On the ship that crashed?"

Scroll fought down a desire to swear and said, "Right, Spike, the landing gear of the ship that just broke up into spare parts on my only good runway. You'd see it out of your window if it wasn't for the tobacco smoke in here. You hold an investigation of that failure with your best people. And you make sure there's no kind of cover-up, and nothing swept under the carpet."

"What's this all about, Duke? You think it's sabotage or something?" He tapped the meerschaum pipe, and after making sure all the tobacco and ash were out of it, he stood it carefully in the ashtray.

"No, I don't," said Scroll, "and I'm afraid I can't discuss it with you. But my crystal ball says that some tall dark stranger with a star is going to walk into my office anytime now and he's going to ask me if I've started an inquiry into that wreck out there. And when I say yes, I have, and I send for you, I want you holding a big fat file of depositions, technical reports, and close-up photographs. And I want that file to be the finest example of accident investigation that the Eighth Air Force has ever seen, because if it goes all the way up to the commanding general's office and those guys find a split infinitive somewhere in the testimony, or a photo with a spotty glaze, they're going to grind me into hamburger and I'll make sure you're the gravy. Got me?"

"I sure have, Duke. You leave it to me. I take it I can have photographers and stenographers and such?"

"If you want Major Tarrant posed nude on top of the tower, you've got it," said Scroll.

"It may not come to that," said Larsson.

Scroll looked up to find the Major smiling. "Prepare a memo telling me what you're doing, and have it on my desk within an hour, Spike. Drop everything else until this one is completed." Scroll went out hurriedly before Larsson could begin one of his long, slow technical explanations.

Even the resourceful Sergeant Kinzelberg took more than an hour to locate General Bohnen. He was in Lancashire, sorting out a supply mix-up at the vast and labyrinthine U.S. Army supply and repair depot at Burtonwood, near Liverpool.

Colonel Scroll sought out an old West Point friend who was working there and explained his need to find General Bohnen. "It's urgent, very urgent. We have a casualty here . . . someone close to the General. Now, let's go green on this one . . . follow me? . . . Good. He's probably going to want to get here fast, but there's no way we could take a multi-engine, both runways are out of action. I'm going to suggest he fly into Narrowbridge and we'll have a car for him there. And keep an eye on him, he might take it hard. . . . No, that's all I can tell you, pal. Call me back when you get the General. I'll be near the phone waiting."

Colonel Scroll hung up and looked at his watch again. "Sergeant," he called. "Any word from Doc Goldman?"

"One of the clerks has just been over there, sir. Captain Farebrother is still in the cockpit."

"And how long before TOT?"

Kinzelberg was waiting for that question. He'd calculated how long it would be before the mission bombed. "Fifty-five minutes, sir."

When the phone rang Scroll grabbed it immediately, only to find that the caller was Major Tarrant, commanding the Military Police Company. "I'm sorry to bother you, Colonel Scroll," he said. Major Tarrant had a hard metallic voice that Scroll did not like. It was the sort of voice that he remembered cops using when, as a kid, they'd found him necking in his dad's car. "But I was wondering whether you'd had a call from the Cambridge police, the British police?"

"No, I haven't," said Scroll.

"No questions about men on pass?"

"I'm in no mood for playing 'twenty questions,' Tarrant. What's eating you?"

"I had a call from the army lieutenant working as liaison with the civilian cops. He says there's some kind of rumpus in the detectives' room down there. They won't tell him anything, but they've asked for a postmortem . . . could be a murder inquiry. He says they have a photo of a fighter pilot posing in front of his plane. He says the plane is painted with our code letters."

"If one of our guys has murdered someone, it's up to the Limeys to give us the facts as fast as possible. If those cops are trying to cover up, you can bet our guys aren't guilty. Maybe they're looking for someone to pin it on."

Major Tarrant found this attitude toward the British police a reflection upon all police, and he regarded the Exec's suggestion as a personal affront. "I'm sorry to have troubled you, sir," he said coldly, and hung up.

"I think I've insulted Major Tarrant," Scroll told his sergeant. "And that's not an easy thing to do."

The next call was from General Bohnen. He listened to Colonel Scroll's description of the crash without interrupting. "Is Captain Farebrother seriously hurt?" Bohnen asked.

"The Flight Surgeon can't examine him until he's released from the wreckage."

"I think I'll fly down to see you right away."

"I've got accommodations ready for you, sir. Do you need an overnight bag from your London office? I can arrange it from here."

Until Scroll's offer of accommodations, General Bohnen had remained cool and composed, but he detected in Scroll's voice the implication that his son Jamie was mortally injured. His voice cracked. "Thank you, Colonel Scroll, that's most considerate. Please arrange it."

When Scroll put down the phone he pressed down on it for a moment as if trying to keep it from ringing again. "Sergeant! You want to run over and get me a ham sandwich. I think I'd better stay right here for the time being."

He looked out the window. The cloud was breaking up in the west, so that there was a little hazy sunlight dappling the hills behind Steeple Thaxted village, but more rain clouds were coming in to darken the sky overhead.

"Sergeant Kinzelberg," said Scroll when his clerk returned with the ham sandwich. "Do we have any standing instructions about whether an officer should always accompany press parties on base?"

Sergeant Kinzelberg looked at him but said nothing.

"You see," said Scroll, lifting the bread from the top of the ham sandwich to see how much meat there was inside, "there is a Pfc. conducting a big press contingent around the base at present. Is that the normal procedure?"

Kinzelberg fidgeted awkwardly and rubbed his hands on his trousers and tightened the knot of his tie.

"Goddammit, Kinzelberg, are you listening to me? Or is everyone going crazy?"

"I could probably find the section number and so on," said the sergeant, "but no civilian is allowed on the base unless accompanied by an officer at all times. I can't imagine that the War Department classifies reporters as anything but civilians, even if they do wear army-style uniforms."

Scroll nodded and bit into his sandwich before noticing that his clerk had placed a drink in front of him. He picked it up and sniffed at it. "What in hell you bringing me booze for? Did you ever see me drinking whiskey in the middle of a working day? Jesus Christ, Kinzelberg, are you after a Section Eight or something?"

"We lost the Colonel," whispered Kinzelberg.

"Speak up, Sergeant. Did you ever see me drinking whiskey . . . what was that you said?"

"We lost the Colonel, sir." There was a long pause. "I've just come from Operations . . . I thought you might ask me how everything was going, you do sometimes . . ."

"Yes, that's right, I do."

"Kraut fighters came through them in a head-on attack. One of them collided with Colonel Dan's plane."

Scroll drank some of the whiskey.

Kinzelberg said, "There's no doubt about it, I'm afraid—everyone saw him go. The major in Operations said it might be better if I told you . . . and I figured a drink . . ."

"We've got General Bohnen coming in," said Scroll briskly. "I guess you already know that Captain Farebrother is the General's son."

Kinzelberg nodded.

Scroll finished his whiskey and held the glass up to get the final drop of it. When he put it down he said, "We'd better get on the ball,

Kinzelberg. By tomorrow morning—maybe even tonight—we'll have a new commanding officer breathing down our necks. That's the policy, you know—they don't give anyone a chance to get broody about casualties like this."

"I'll find that regulation about press contingents, sir. Shall I draft a memo for the PR office, or would you rather keep it to something you mention in the Officers' Club?"

"I told him not to go today," said Scroll. "I pleaded with him. He needed a rest. He's too damned exhausted to fly."

There was the sound of someone entering Sergeant Kinzelberg's office. "Who's that?" said the sergeant, and Corporal Walker appeared in the doorway. He was hatless and there was oil on his trousers and stains on his jacket. "What is it?" said Kinzelberg in a voice indicating disapproval.

"I'm Corporal Walker of the medical section. I have a message for Colonel Scroll."

"What is it?" said Scroll. He recognized the corporal who had been assisting Doc Goldman at the accident.

"Captain Goldman's compliments," said Walker, "and I'm to tell you that we won't get Captain Farebrother released from that wreckage before the Group's due back."

"How is he?"

"You're asking me, sir?" said Walker. There was no insolence or insubordination in his voice, but Scroll recognized immediately the demeanor of the well-paid civilian who volunteered to fight for his country but wanted to have that amateur status acknowledged in any dealings with authority. Colonel Scroll had always found it expedient to adjust to such informality whenever possible.

"Sure, I'm asking you," said Scroll. "You're a trained medic, aren't you?"

"I doubt Captain Farebrother will last the night, Colonel. I think he's hurt real bad." He held out his hand with fingers splayed, like a farmer watching a handful of soil fall away. "That motor hit him with enough force to break the seat, and that requires a lot of force. He's in shock . . . and with multiple abdominal injuries. You or I would have died of the shock within minutes. He's young and he's strong, but it's not enough." He looked down at his hand and then up at Colonel Scroll. "Statistically, abdominal wounds are more often fatal than even head injuries."

"Did Captain Goldman mention the idea of contacting the medical staff over at Narrowbridge? They have a big base hospital for the Bomber Groups, and those B-17s are bringing back bad casualties almost every mission these days."

"There's nothing those folks at Narrowbridge can teach Doc Goldman," said Walker. "Once we get the Captain out he'll operate right away."

Colonel Scroll decided that it would be unwise to interfere in this matter. Quite apart from the military procedures and the chain of command of Army Medical Services, there was the special relationship between doctor and patient. Any layman fool enough to interfere with that could wind up with the whole medical profession at his throat. "Well, Captain Goldman is probably the best judge of that," said Scroll. "Ask him to phone me when he can spare a moment. There'll be a visitor for Captain Farebrother. He's on his way now."

"He sure as hell better hurry," said Walker.

"March out," said Sergeant Kinzelberg, "and next time you come into the Colonel's office, make sure you're properly dressed. Nothing says medics got some special right to go around without hats."

Scroll went across to his desk and finished his sandwich. There was the English girl—Victoria something. Tarrant thought she looked pregnant. Tarrant was a pain in the ass, but he was no idiot. And last week, at the bar, Jamie Farebrother had casually raised the question of officers getting permission to marry.

Kinzelberg's phone rang and Scroll heard his clerk grunting and okaying to someone. But suppose he sent for the girl—Victoria Cooper, that was the name. Suppose he found her, and sent for her, and then discovered that General Bohnen didn't know about her, or disapproved of her, or wanted her ordered off the base. Maybe he should go over to the wreck. If Farebrother was conscious and asking for the girl, it would be easier to decide.

"That was Operations again," said Kinzelberg.

Colonel Scroll had been staring right through him. "Is that right?" said Scroll.

"They're on their way back. Major Tucker is leading and Lieutenant Morse has taken the 199th Squadron. The heavies were badly hit. We lost five in addition to the Colonel . . . could be more, the Krauts are fighting all the way."

"Ever had the feeling, Kinzelberg, that you shouldn't have gotten out of bed this morning?"

Kinzelberg knew what was expected of him: he tried to smile. "You want me to give any kind of message to the GEO, sir?"

Scroll continued to look out the window as if he might find some solution there. "About dragging the wreck away?"

Kinzelberg waited patiently.

After a pause, Scroll said, "General Bohnen will be here soon. There's a car waiting at Narrowbridge. He'll be the ranking officer."

"The Group could land at Narrowbridge too, sir."

"Sounds like our boys are going to arrive shot up and low on gas. Are we going to hand them a navigation exercise and a new landing pattern?" It wasn't a question for Kinzelberg to answer. Scroll went on. "All the Groups hereabouts are in the air today. Narrowbridge will be expecting their own ships . . . big ships that have taken a worse licking, some of them carrying dead and dying. And look at that weather. Half the fields in southern England are socked in already."

"It's a tough decision, sir."

"And whatever I do will be wrong," Scroll muttered. "I know the General well enough to be sure of that."

"Someone will have to bulldoze the wreck, sir. If you don't give the order, General Bohnen will have to. It's his son, like Colonel Dan told us, and General Bohnen won't dare leave him there and prejudice the whole Group. The press are swarming everywhere these days. They'd be sure to find out, and if they did they'd crucify him."

Scroll turned to face his sergeant. "So what can I do, Kinzelberg?" His tone was shrill, the anger of a man on the defensive. "Shall I tell General Bohnen to go away again? Do I insist on retaining command here because I've got the sort of operational experience needed for this kind of decision?"

"No, sir," said Kinzelberg in the curt emotionless voice that is the enlisted man's only refuge from those in authority.

"Thanks, Kinzelberg," said Scroll. "Now just tell Major Tarrant that we're expecting the General sometime soon. I expect the gate to be properly manned, and his men ready with the proper military courtesies."

33

Brigadier General
Alexander J. Bohnen

There was a moon, but it gave only enough light to throw a little
silver dust onto the outlines of the hangars and the parked planes.
There was no sound except for the occasional plane on its lonely
errand, and the sound of the Steeple Thaxted church clock that
could only be heard on nights like this when the wind was from the
west.

There were four men in the small white room of the base hospital. Corporal Walker had taken extra duty in place of the theater
orderly who'd worked all afternoon. He wore a white cotton coat and
sat on the chair by the bed, reading from a pile of *Yank* magazines
that were on the bedside table.

Lieutenant Morse was grimy-faced and his long hair was disheveled. He'd been here since debriefing. His shirt sleeves were rolled
up and he'd taken off his tie. He'd eased his shoes off and rested his
head back against the wall, so that sometimes he dozed off to sleep
and woke up with a disconcerting grunt or snort.

General Bohnen was still wearing his fully buttoned jacket and
sitting upright on a hard chair very near to the bed. He had arranged
it so that he was facing his son, from whom his eyes never wandered.

At 3 a.m. Captain Goldman came quietly into the room as he
had done every hour, almost as if to accompany the chiming of the
church clock. Goldman looked as if he'd just climbed out of bed. He
ignored the other men except for a quick glance at Corporal Walker.
He checked Farebrother's pulse and listened to his breathing. Then
he put a hand on the unconscious flyer's forehead to feel if the skin
was cold and clammy: it was, and that wasn't a good sign.

This time when Captain Goldman left the room General
Bohnen followed him into the kitchen. If Goldman was aware of
Bohnen behind him he gave no sign of it until he poured the coffee.
Then he held up a plain white mug and said, "Want some?"

"No, thanks, Captain."

So it was "Captain," thought Goldman—usually a sign that

someone was going to pull rank on him. He sipped from his cup of coffee. Then he opened up the cookie jar hoping to find a doughnut, but the jar was empty.

"You didn't take his blood pressure this time," said Bohnen.

"Just the pulse," said Goldman.

"It's my son in there," said Bohnen desperately. "Am I supposed to stand around watching you drink coffee and let him die?"

"There's nothing more I can do for him, General."

"So I'll get someone over here from Wing. I'll talk to the Medical Services in London . . . maybe the British have specialists . . ."

"I understand how you feel, sir, but your son's chances of recovery would not be increased by that. Moving him would be out of the question. And I really don't believe there's any specialist who would do anything other than what's already been done here."

"And what exactly *has* been done here?" Bohnen found it impossible to keep the hostility out of his voice although he tried hard.

"How much medicine do you understand?"

The doctor's question and the way he asked it confirmed all of General Bohnen's most bitter prejudice. No one, it seemed, was permitted to ask questions, let alone get a proper answer, unless they were a member of this elite. "I'm not a physician, Captain Goldman, but I want an answer just the same."

"I understand how you feel, General."

"Do you have a son, an only son, who's near to death in the next room?"

Goldman shook his head. He picked up an alarm clock and a newspaper folded tightly to reveal a half-finished crossword puzzle.

"I want an answer, Captain."

Goldman looked Bohnen in the eye and spoke mechanically. "My primary incisions into the abdominal cavity showed very bad hemorrhaging. I was working with local anesthesia because the patient was so weak. I injected the peritoneum—the tissue that covers the intestine and holds it in the abdomen. Then I sutured three wounds of the mesentery and five wounds of the intestine, and I trimmed and treated some other less serious damage. Finally I closed the abdominal cavity and worked on the cuts in the abdominal wall." Goldman sipped his coffee and shuddered at the bitterness of it. "I've been through the whole thing in my mind, but I don't see that anything more, or anything different, could have been done for the patient."

"And where are you going now?"

"I'm going along the hall to the night duty room. I'm setting the alarm clock to wake me up well within the hour so I can come back to look at the Captain."

"Are you the only doctor they have here?"

"There are two of us at present, so we're taking twelve-hour duty shifts. There's a field order in—the lights are still on across there in Operations, and that's a sure sign tomorrow's mission will be a big one. I've got a kid down the hall with an ulcer that's not responding to treatment and an abscess case that's keeping the night staff busy."

Both men were angry, each felt he was the victim of a system that did not tolerate outsiders. General Bohnen poured himself a cup of coffee, and interpreting this as a dismissal, Goldman left the room. Bohnen sipped the hot coffee standing by the sink, looking at the shiny white mugs upturned on the drainboard and at the handwritten notices about switching off the fan and the water heater. He didn't hear Walker come into the room and he was startled when the corporal suddenly spoke.

"You were out of line there, General," said Walker. He spoke quietly as men do speak at night.

"What do you mean?"

"Dr. Goldman shouldn't be spoken to that way."

"Why not, Corporal?"

Walker put up a hand to press his aching neck muscles. He was tired, very tired, or he wouldn't have spoken to a general that way. "He's the best, that's why. Doc Goldman graduated with honors from Johns Hopkins. His father is a professor of surgery and consultant surgeon at four or five New York hospitals. Doc turned down a chief surgeon's post and a big salary to get into the war. Last month the Bomber Group surgeons at Narrowbridge had Doc over there to do some tricky surgery they couldn't handle."

General Bohnen wasn't convinced yet. "If he's really that good he should be at one of the big base hospitals."

"He wants to get into the fight! He wants to get into an infantry outfit. Goldman is Jewish. His uncle was a top surgeon in Frankfurt until the Nazis sent him to a concentration camp. Goldman's at war with the Nazis, a personal kind of war. He doesn't need you to tell him to do his best when he's fighting to save the life of some kid who's been out there killing Germans. Goldman would have cut off his own right arm this afternoon if that would have improved your boy's chances."

"The wreck had to be moved," said Bohnen. "There was no alternative."

"I've got kids myself," said Walker. "I pray every night that this lousy war ends before they get drafted."

"It should have been done before I got here," said Bohnen. "Everyone knew it would have to be moved, but they left it to me to give the order." Walker looked at him but showed no sign of sympathy, and this angered Bohnen. "What the hell do you people know about me and my boy? You stand there in judgment, but how can you know what it cost me? If I'd left him out there, you would have called it reckless. Because I cleared the runway you think I've got no feelings. Back home you've got your kids, Corporal. You saw them grow up. Good, I'm happy for you. But I lost my son when he was growing up. I lost him the day I went down to see him off on the train. I bought him an ice cream and told him some jokes to make him laugh and told him to love his new father the way he'd always loved me. I lost him then, Corporal, because his mother took him away and poisoned his mind against me so that I never got him back again. I watched the train move off till it was out of sight and I went back to an empty apartment and got very drunk for the first time in my life. When your child had measles or mumps you could bring him candy and hold his hand. When Jamie was sick I got arid little notes from his mother telling me not to send him presents because it upset him. Did you ever have someone return a toy airplane and a book about Lincoln to you because they were 'militaristic' and not the kind of thing she wants to influence *her* son? Do you know how many times I traveled three thousand miles across the country in order to spend just a few minutes with my son? Do you know what it cost me today? Well, before you answer, Corporal, let me tell you that you can't even guess. So don't lecture me about how to fight the war, and I don't need your advice on fatherhood either."

"You should try and get some sleep, General," said Corporal Walker. "No one can go on forever without sleep."

"There'll be time enough," said Bohnen.

Farebrother had only a few minutes of consciousness, and they came soon after General Bohnen had spoken with Goldman and Walker. He was all alone with his son—Corporal Walker was changing the dressing on an abscess in the room along the hall, and Lieutenant

Morse was in the washroom—and Bohnen was grateful that there was no one else present.

He held his hand as he used to hold it when Jamie was small. "We'll make it, Jamie. You and me. Just like the old days, remember?"

But Farebrother's mind was wandering. He was in the air. "I should have stuck with the element leader—that's a wingman's job."

"Jamie—son—your dad's here."

"Mickey Mouse? Mickey Mouse?" He smiled. "Is that you? Did you shake them off, MM?"

"Everything is fine, Jamie," said Bohnen, putting a hand on his son's forehead. The skin was cold and clammy and the breathing quick and shallow. "Everything's fine."

"MM? MM? Listen to me, MM, you've got to listen."

"I'm listening," said Bohnen.

"The hell with all of them, MM. You go ahead . . . with Vera, I mean. You do what you think is right, MM. Always do what's right. I shouldn't have ever told you anything different."

"What about your dad?" said Bohnen.

"MM? I can't hold formation."

"Jamie."

"I'm trying, MM, but she never was a good ship—you were right about that."

"Jamie, listen to me. It's your father."

"Goodbye, Mickey Mouse, and thanks. No need to worry, I'll glide to the coast. Tell Vicky I'm gliding to the coast." Farebrother settled back comfortably into the pillows and smiled before closing his eyes again. Bohnen looked around and found Lieutenant Morse standing by the bed.

"That ship should have been in a museum, General, but Jamie wouldn't change. He thought she was lucky for him."

"He thought he was talking to you," Bohnen told Morse. "He said to go ahead with Vera—maybe you know what that means. Do what you think is right, he said."

"I'm going to have to go soon, General. I'm on the board and it's going to be a tough one tomorrow. We lost the Colonel yesterday. I'm leading the squadron."

"I know," said Bohnen. He'd given Major Tucker operational command of the Group and sent a teleprinter signal requesting that Tucker be confirmed and promoted accordingly. He deeply resented the way that Tucker's first order had been to make Morse a Squadron Commander and restore him to flying duties with immediate effect. But Bohnen didn't allow this resentment to show as he shook Morse by the hand. "Good luck, Lieutenant."

"Jamie had the best crew chief in the Group, General. If there'd been any sign of trouble on that tire or the landing gear, Tex would have seen it."

"By the time you get back here, Jamie will be waving from the window," said Bohnen.

"I'll be getting along then."

"Goodbye, Mickey Mouse," said the General.

Captain James Farebrother went into a coma about five o'clock that morning and died at nine thirty-three, as Lieutenant Morse was leading his squadron out for take-off.

Epilogue, 1982

Mickey Morse was standing by the farm gate near the squadron dispersal, the gate secured by a rusty padlock. MM rattled the gate, but it remained firmly blocking the way to his past. From here he could see the hut that had once been the 199th Squadron pilots' room. Rube, Earl, and Jamie had been photographed with him sitting on the step. Now the hut was just a roofless skeleton, but there was a small concrete toilet nearby that remained as solid as ever.

A new crop of wheat transformed the airfield, the wind making it ripple like a rolling green ocean. But the ocean parted and dull sunlight shone on the ridged concrete of the runway where Jamie Farebrother's *Kibitzer* had folded up.

Victoria arrived with his overcoat. "Put this on, darling. You know what the doctor said about your getting a chill." They had both aged gracefully in the way that so often happens to couples who have enjoyed a lifetime of mutual love and respect. She'd put on a little weight around the hips, and Mickey had lost much of his hair, but they were recognizably the same people who'd been here long ago.

"I was thinking about Madigan," said Mickey Morse. "He changed all our lives, you know."

"Vince Madigan?" She buttoned up his new overcoat and tidied the woolen scarf around his neck. He liked to be fussed over despite his objections.

"Vera's husband shot Vince, but he should have shot me. They kept all that out of the newspapers, but that's what happened. We both know it."

"We've been all through that, Mickey darling. You promised . . ."

"I think Vera saved my life. I think Vera told her husband Madigan was her boyfriend . . . I think she wanted to save my life."

"Poor Vera. I dreamed about her the other night. I suppose it was being back home in England again after all these years . . . I'd found myself thinking of her."

"That little colonel, with all the Hollywood double-talk. He arrived on the base even before I'd heard about Vera being killed. He told me about the double murder, and Reg Hardcastle's suicide—a *crime passionel* he called it. He ordered me to go on leave."

"And you came to find me in Wales and tell me about Jamie."

"I guessed you were pregnant that night when Tucker did his dance routine. By the following week he'd taken over the Group and been promoted to colonel. It's funny how I never liked Tucker at the beginning. Something seemed to change him when he took over."

"My mother tried to get me to Scotland to have the baby. You would never have found me there."

"You cried when I asked you to marry me."

"You didn't ask me to marry you. You said we ought to get married."

"Same thing, isn't it?"

She hugged him. "Of course it is."

"Everything happened because of Madigan. You met Jamie, I met you, I met Vera. Everything started with that dumb ox Madigan."

"Poor Vince and his Mozart records and that sexy voice he sometimes forgot to put on. He told me he was always unlucky in love."

Mickey Morse snorted. "He told everyone that, it was his regular spiel." He'd half turned to look at the big bus containing other members of the 220th Fighter Group Association tour. It had driven along the perimeter track and was waiting for them. "Old Tarrant is getting out and coming over here. What's he want?"

"Be nice to him, darling. He's writing the reunion up for the Association newsletter. He's taking it very seriously."

"Tarrant was the biggest goldbrick on the base. No one liked him. Some nerve he's got taking over the newsletter."

Harry Tarrant had become a plump red-faced man. He had a ball-point pen and loose-leaf notebook poised as he reached them. It was hard to reconcile this genial figure with the hard-eyed military policeman Morse had so disliked. Tarrant was wearing a short red plaid jacket, slacks, and white shoes. On his head there was a floppy red hat that advertised the security company for which he worked. Tarrant smiled at Mickey. "It's a real pleasure to have you and Mrs. Morse along on this trip."

Morse greeted this compliment with glacial indifference.

"It's been wonderfully well organized," said Victoria.

Tarrant nodded to her. "We try. We try," he said modestly. "I'm getting some notes together for the newsletter next month," he explained while writing "Morse" at the top of the page.

"What have you got so far?" said Morse, turning to see the notes.

"Did you know that Tex Gill, one of the crew chiefs, got to be full colonel before he retired in 1975?"

"Yeah, I knew that."

Tarrant smiled very briefly and then consulted his notebook. "Duke Scroll was hoping to join us, but his wife is sick. He was vice-president of a big airline until he retired last year. He's trying to persuade us to have the next convention in Palm Beach, near where he lives."

"I would have thought he could get cheap airplane tickets," said Mickey Morse.

"I wouldn't know about that," said Tarrant awkwardly. He glanced at Victoria and smiled sympathetically.

"And Tucker?"

"He'll be there tomorrow at the ceremony. He got a star before he retired. Did you hear about that?" Tarrant had stepped into cow dung and now he was wiping his shoe on the lowest bar of the gate.

"We all thought he'd get one before the war ended," said Morse. "He might have done it too, except that he took over the Group instead of getting a staff job at headquarters."

"It's hard to think of Tuckie as a general," said Tarrant. "He aways comes to the reunions, and he's always full of fun. You'll see tomorrow, Mrs. Morse, he's the life and soul of the party." He wrote "Tucker career?" in his book. "Of course, he wasn't always full of fun. It took him a little while to find his feet, didn't it, Mickey?"

"Tucker turned out tops," said Morse. He remembered the day the Germans surrendered. Tucker left his office and came across to find MM in his quarters. He came in all alone, closed the door, and produced a bottle of scotch. He poured two drinks in silence and handed one to MM. Finally Tucker just said, "We made it, MM." The others had all gone by that time—dead, injured, or finished their tour of duty. Tucker and MM finished the bottle together and ended up drunk in a ditch after falling off Tucker's bicycle. "Tucker's a good guy," said MM.

"What happened to the doctor?" said Victoria. "He was nice to me, I remember."

"I guess you mean Captain Goldman," said Tarrant. "His name is on the officers' roster, but the Association was never able to contact him. By a lucky chance, I found out about him yesterday from Mr. Walker—the very dignified-looking guy with the diamond stickpin— he owns four drugstores in Chicago. Do you remember him, MM? And did you see him arriving at the airport in a limo with his own driver? It's hard to believe the guy was just a corporal medic, eh?" He flipped through his notes. "Yes, here we are: Goldman. He was transferred to a surgical team that went onto Omaha Beach on D Day. Goldman was killed when a mortar shell hit the tent they were using as an operating theater." Tarrant beat a tattoo on his notebook with his pen, which also bore an advertisement for his security company. "You'll be at the ceremony tomorrow? At the lunch, Bobby Baxter will formally take over as president of the Association."

"Baxter!" Morse laughed scornfully. "The guy who flew as Tucker's wingman? President? That creep wasn't with the Group more than ten minutes. I was right there when he took to his chute over Munich, or Brunswick, or some damn place. Baxter spent his war in a POW camp. I remember the way Tucker was always getting cards from the guy asking if we'd send him cigarettes and candy. Baxter!"

Tarrant waited patiently. He already knew MM's views on Baxter's suitability for high office. He smiled, but not so broadly as to be disloyal to the new president. "Bobby has been really active in the Association, Mickey. Last year he canceled the second week of his vacation and came all the way back from Hawaii just to be with us in New Orleans. And he's at every meeting."

"Did anyone ever get word of *my* wingman, Rube Wein?"

"I tried everything, Mickey. We put a notice in the Retired Officers' Association publication, and I wrote to Washington and to his old addresses."

"You should have written to Berlin," said Morse. "My guess is that Rube never got as far as a POW cage. Those Krauts got him just the way Rube said they would."

Tarrant shifted uncomfortably. "Well, let's not jump to conclusions, MM. We have some German veterans at the lunch and presentation tomorrow."

"Don't tell me not to make waves, Tarrant. When you were busy booking some poor dogface for having too many beers, those bastards were trying to kill me."

Victoria took his arm and tugged at him to signal that he was being difficult. Tarrant tapped his notebook and said, "And what about you good people? I didn't get my book out to talk about the others. Let's have a little background on you." Tarrant held his Olympus camera up to frame a photo of them against the background of the old dispersal hut. "You're the top ace of the Group, MM. You're more famous than any of us." Tarrant's voice was muffled as he held the camera close to his face. "My eldest was reading an aviation magazine the other day, and I looked over his shoulder and saw your picture. I told him, 'That's a real close buddy of mine,' and he could hardly believe it. Don't scowl, MM, let's have a happy picture."

"Kinzelberg's more famous than I'll ever be," said Morse.

"Ha-ha!" said Tarrant.

"Is that the one who got twenty years?" said Victoria. "The one who was in the newspaper?"

"The judge said he'd milked nearly a million dollars out of that bank," said Morse.

"Now, was Kinzelberg the one who had the crap game?"

"Are you losing your mind, Tarrant? Kinzelberg was the Exec's sergeant clerk . . . tough-looking bastard with a scar on his face. Wouldn't give you the time of day unless he checked it back with records. Boyer was the man you were always after."

"Boyer! Boyer! Boyer!" Tarrant snapped his fingers. "How could I forget that name? Duke Scroll made my life hell about Sergeant Boyer and his crap games. Trouble was, every time I caught that SOB in action, I'd find Colonel Dan there with him, holding the dice."

Morse laughed. "Boyer never joined the Association. I wrote to him a few times and he told me he was the superintendent of an apartment house looking out over Hilo Bay in Hawaii. But I got someone to look him up on vacation and they said it looked like he owned the place. He's made enough dough, I'd reckon."

"Now back to you two," said Tarrant, having closed his camera case carefully. "I'm right in saying you're English, Mrs. Morse? That you two met here, while Mickey was flying missions?"

Victoria nodded.

Encouraged, Tarrant said, "And MM was already a contender for top-scoring ace in the Air Force when you got married?"

"Yes," said Victoria. "I spoiled that, I'm afraid. Mickey proposed and we got permission to marry and a leave of absence. It was all arranged by a colonel named Shelley. But by the time our honeymoon was over, someone had bettered the Rickenbacker score and a pilot in the Pacific was in the news."

"And I see from the records that you are a consultant to Bohnen and Morse Electronics and Leisure, Incorporated." Tarrant looked at Mickey's custom-made overcoat and at Victoria's expensive clothes and said, "Sounds like you had it made right from the start. Now, all this will be written up properly by Fred Fryer, who used to be with the PR office—he's a professional writer. I'm just taking the notes for him. Did you study electronics under the GI Bill?"

"Business management," said MM. "But I never finished. I was too dumb for college."

"Rubbish," said Victoria.

"My wife graduated from Cambridge University. Write that down," said Morse, and Tarrant did so.

"Mickey left college to earn more money to look after me and little Jamie," said Victoria, "so don't believe any nonsense about him being a dropout."

"Just the one child named James. Have I got that right? People get mad if I get the names wrong."

"We wanted more," said Morse. Victoria took his hand and squeezed it affectionately.

"Mickey became the manager of a small company manufacturing motor cruisers. He earned enough to put Jamie through Harvard and then MIT."

"There was a boom in small boats," explained Morse.

"Wasn't there something about your son inventing a camera? I'm a pretty expert photographer myself, so I noticed that name in one of the photo books. That's your son, the handsome man with his wife sitting just behind the driver?"

"Jamie built a neutron radiography camera, a special sort of X-ray machine that can show tissue differences. That was the machine that launched our company."

"So who is Bohnen?" said Tarrant. "The guy who put up the dough?"

"A distant relative," said Morse. "He bankrolled us. All his stock was left to our Jamie after he died, but we keep his name on the shingle. It's a sort of thank-you, and it's been lucky for us."

"It sure sounds like it," said Tarrant. "Say, how does your company handle its security?"

"That's not my department," said Morse.

"Well, let me give you one of these anyway," said Tarrant, passing him a business card that showed Tarrant as "Manager: new business department."

Morse pushed it into his pocket with no more than a glance. "Tell me, Tarrant. Why did you bring us over to England at this time of year? I haven't been really warm since we arrived at the airport. Don't these lousy hotels have any heat?"

"We get a good deal on airplane tickets and hotel rooms when we schedule the reunion out of season, Mickey. A lot of the members wouldn't be able to come unless we kept the cost rock bottom. Poor old Kevin Phelan had to borrow the money for the trip this year. He's told everybody that, so I'm not breaking a confidence."

The driver of the bus touched his horn, and Tarrant looked at his watch. "We'd better get back to the others. We've got quite a schedule." He looked at his notes and read from them as they walked. "Gymnastic display by the local Boy Scouts, an exhibition of model aircraft at the village hall, a visit to one of the most historic college buildings in Cambridge, tea and sandwiches at Steeple Thaxted with a formal speech of welcome by the mayor. Back to the hotel to freshen up, and then dinner at the King's Head in Lower Collingwood." He looked up and smiled proudly.

"Sounds okay," said Mickey Morse. On the wall of a ruined building Victoria saw a freshly painted slogan: "No Nukes! Yanks Go Home!" She kept her arm linked in MM's and pretended she hadn't seen it.

Acknowledgments

The extent to which I have benefited from advice and assistance over the six or more years during which this book was prepared obliges me to record my debt to some of those who helped. I apologize to those whose names, due to lack of space, my scribbled notes, or my fallible memory, are not included; neither have I listed documents or books (published and unpublished) that provided background for a period that is fast fading into history. But this is not a history book, and the events depicted are not always based upon true ones and the characters do not depict real persons either living or dead. Needless to say, any mistakes here are of my own making and not the fault of any of those who showed such kindness in helping my research.

In the U.S.A., I particularly thank (in alphabetical order) Ken Allstaedt (78th Fighter Group), Sheldon Berlow (352nd Fighter Group), Paul Chryst (91st Bomb Group), Robert DeGeorge (navigator, 323rd Bombardment Squadron), Frank G. Donofrio (Memphis Belle Memorial Association), Milton Green (91st Bomb Group), the late Gordon Hunsberger (355th Fighter Group), Willard Korsmeyer (fighter pilot), Robert E. Kuhnert (secretary, 355th Fighter Group Association), William E. McGavern (91st Bomb Group), Joe G. Myers, Jr. (5th Service Squadron), Peter E. Pompetti (pilot, 84th Fighter Squadron), Charles W. Redenbaugh (pilot, 358th Fighter Squadron), Howard E. Sisk (ground mechanic), Aleck Thomas (pilot, 323rd Bombardment Squadron), Jack M. Webb (flight engineer, 374th Bombardment Squadron), Henry D. Wertz (355th Fighter Group), and Major General Stanley T. Wray (commander, 91st Bomb Group). Special thanks also to my friends Colonel Art Jackson and Colonel Lou Malone, pilots who provided very helpful advice and encouragement.

Help came from many veterans' associations and from their journals and newsletters. Editors were unfailingly kind when asked to publish inquiries. In particular, the newsletter of the 355th Fighter Group; the newsletter of the 388th Bombardment Group Association; the newsletter of the 3rd Strategic Air Depot Association; *Flight Patterns*, the publication of the 369th Fighter Squadron Association; and *8th Air Force News*, the journal of the Eighth Air Force Historical Society. A great deal of information came from experts and enthusiasts in England. Malcolm Bates deserves a special thank-you for getting me started, and Wing Commander "Beau" Carr (pioneer RAF pilot and author of *You Are Not Sparrows*) helped to arrange for me to be included in a tour Eighth Air Force veterans made to their bases in England in 1978. Tony Beeton (East Anglian Aviation Society) assisted me considerably during that research trip, as did many others, including Malcolm Osborn (of the Nuthampstead Airfield Research Society and well-known member of "Friends of the Eighth"), David C. Crow (U.K. liaison for the 355th Fighter Group Association), and Vince Hemmings (curator of the 91st Bomb Group tower museum at Bassingbourn). Writers were generous with their help and encouragement, including Roger Freeman (author of *The Mighty Eighth*), Danny Morris (*Aces and Wingmen*), and Ian Hawkins (working on a book about the 100th Bomb Group raid on Münster). The newsletters of "Friends of the Eighth" and the East Anglian Aviation Society were also most informative. Technical help came from the very experienced pilot Tony Gaze in Australia and from Paul Coggan of "Mustang International." Fighter pilot Witold "Lanny" Lanowski generously made tape recordings for me. That unfailing source of twentieth-century history, London's Imperial War Museum, helped me from across the ocean when I needed details of Luftwaffe air activity over England. They also provided access to their aircraft collection at Duxford. Mr. G. Clout of the Department of Printed Books is to be especially thanked. My friend Seán O'Driscoll was also a great source of USAAF facts and figures. I was particularly lucky in having advice from General John M. Bennett (100th Bombardment Group) and Colonel William J. Hovde (355th Fighter Group), both famous participants of the air battles of which I write. They, together with Captain E. M. Porter USN (fighter pilot and test pilot) and John Tiley (historical consultant), most kindly read my manuscript and made valuable suggestions. So did Jonathan Clowes at an earlier stage of the work.

This book was produced on an Olivetti word processor which

was also used for storing much of the notes and research material. In connection with this I would like to thank Mr. David Maroni of Olivetti and all the staff of Bryan S. Ryan, their agents. Professor Maurice Lessof of Guy's Hospital, London, provided advice as he has before for other books, and for this I thank him warmly.

Mr. Anton Felton and his secretary, Jean Stokes, gathered material concerning Britain's wartime regulations, rationing, etc. For this I also thank most warmly the sources they used: the Press Office of the Ministry of Agriculture, Fisheries and Food; Mr. G. Whiteman, assistant librarian at the Central Management Library of the Civil Service Department; and Mr. Richard White at the Department of Energy. For research on Cambridge in wartime, my thanks are due to my friend Charlotte Metcalf and Mr. Michael Farrar, County Archivist of the County of Cambridgeshire. In California, Bill Jordan (W.C.J. Inc.) was a source of much valued advice, and he provided me with telex and other facilities during my researches in the U.S.A. In London, Ray Hawkey helped my book in numerous ways, and so did Ray Barker.

Finally, may I thank my publishers, Brian Perman of Hutchinson and Bob Gottlieb at Knopf, who were so personally involved with the writing of the book. Thanks also to all their staff, particularly those who helped with the editing of the manuscript.

A Note on the Type

The text of this book was set on the Linotype in a type face called Baskerville. The face is a facsimile reproduction of types cast from molds made for John Baskerville (1706–75) from his designs. The punches for the revived Linotype Baskerville were cut under the supervision of the English printer George W. Jones.

John Baskerville's original face was one of the forerunners of the type style known as "modern face" to printers—a "modern" of the period A.D. 1800.

Composed by Maryland Linotype, Inc.,
Baltimore, Maryland.
Printed and bound
by R. R. Donnelly & Sons, Co.,
Harrisonburg, Virginia.

Designed by Virginia Tan.